D1107751

A Trumpet for Jackie

ROBERT OLIPHANT

A Trumpet for Jackie

Prentice-Hall, Inc. / Englewood Cliffs, New Jersey 07632

Library of Congress Cataloging in Publication Data

Oliphant, Robert (date)
A trumpet for Jackie.

I. Title.
PS3565.L455T7 1983 813′.54 83-13907
ISBN 0-13-931881-X

Printed in the United States of America.

10 9 8 7 6 5 4 3 2 1

Editorial/production supervision by Eric Newman
Book design by Linda Huber
Jacket design © 1983 by Judith Kazdym Leeds
Manufacturing buyer: Pat Mahoney

Prentice-Hall International, Inc., *London*
Prentice-Hall of Australia Pty. Limited, *Sydney*
Prentice-Hall Canada Inc., *Toronto*
Prentice-Hall of India Private Limited, *New Delhi*
Prentice-Hall of Japan, Inc., *Tokyo*
Prentice-Hall of Southeast Asia Pte. Ltd., *Singapore*
Whitehall Books Limited, *Wellington, New Zealand*
Editoria Prentice-Hall do Brasil Ltda., *Rio de Janeiro*

ISBN 0-13-931881-X

for Matthew and Jason

A Trumpet for Jackie

September

Sherman Oaks, California: Sunday, September 17, 5:00 P.M.

The front door. Halfway down the steps Jackie Hayes found himself wondering whether or not he had locked it. He stopped, turned to go back.

"You locked it," said Rita, whose clear, young mind kept remorseless track of every detail.

"Are you sure?" Jackie remained where he was. Concerned. Irresolute. The week before he had come home to find the patio door open. A serious lapse. Especially in a neighborhood where iron bars on the windows announced the presence of furs and jewelry inside.

"I'm sure." Rita walked quickly ahead to the Ferrari. "Do you want me to drive?"

"You're not tired, are you?"

"I'm fine."

"Go ahead, then."

They lowered themselves into the Ferrari and Rita deftly eased it out of the driveway and into the maze of hillside streets that wound through their section of Sherman Oaks. She was a good driver. Intent. Humorless. Able to accommodate simultaneously the noises of car stereo, air conditioner, outside traffic. All this with a calm, remote poise to her small features, a poise that proclaimed her capable of moving untouched through any crowd, any set of circumstances.

She was not a small woman. Slim and long-legged, she habitually pushed the car seat far back when she drove. In high, calf-flattering heels she was taller than Jackie. Even more so when she swept her long, dark hair up. Young and strong, round-cheeked, firm of flesh and purpose, she was Jackie's third wife.

Their original bond had been woven out of joy: pleasure trips to Hawaii, to Acapulco. Long and lazy evenings that took them slowly up to a fine, sustained pitch of coupling frenzy. Fine food, fine service, fine clothes. Fine company in which he wore her tall, cool loveliness like a new diamond sparkling all the more when set beside his own stocky frame, square jaw, mild blue eyes, and straight hair. An attractive coupling. A companionable bond despite their difference in age.

The difference in age had worried him at first. After his divorce from Judy, he had been determined not to marry again. But Rita had seemed ideal: a clear sheet of paper upon which to stamp his image, a sheet of paper uncluttered by past entanglements, past bitterness. So there was more involved than sensual indulgence or the pride of possession. To marry Rita was to marry enthusiasm, curiosity, energy—ideal qualities to bond with experience and position. A perfect match. A perfect balance.

Only in the last year had the balance begun to tilt a little. Rita had learned. She had grown. And she had become more and more eager to build a grand palace from the modest materials of his small television production company, Jay Jay Productions. New scripts, new projects, options and proposals—she shuffled them around on her vice president's desk with gusto and remorseless optimism: mappings of a better, quicker route to a glorious goal for the two of them.

A glorious goal, though distant, like a cloud-capped mountain peak, below which two climbers linked together dispute their choice of trail. A dispute measured less by words than by pressure: firm and unending. A friendly pressure. But draining. Especially to a middle-aged climber whose high-priced internist prescribes exercise and weight loss, along with pills and supplementary pills to counteract the effects of the original pills.

Jackie braced himself as Rita made a last-minute, jolting

stop at a red light on Ventura Boulevard. She was restless. More and more inclined to sulk. He looked over at her and smiled reassuringly.

"It'll mean a lot to Vito," he said. "When he called the other day, he made a big thing out of it."

"Don't drink too much." Rita kept her dark eyes focused straight ahead. "You get sleepy when you drink too much—and Bruce is sure to have a bar set up."

"I know."

"Wine with dinner, too."

"I know." Jackie nodded as though to fix the map of the evening in his mind. First Embers West, where Vito Scalza was playing; then Bruce Poirier's giant house in Beverly Hills, where important people in the entertainment industry, smiling and hard-eyed, would jostle one another. For him, Embers West; for Rita, Bruce Poirier's. A fair exchange, one that left each of them feeling slightly aggrieved.

"And remember, we can't stay too long."

"Just one drink," said Jackie. "Just long enough to catch what's happening."

A lot was happening at Embers West. Jackie could sense it even before they sat down. Five musicians. Five instruments. Piano. String bass. Drums. Vibraphone. Vito and his clarinet. Five voices: sometimes sly and witty, sometimes raucous; like old friends cronying together outside a small-town barbershop. Cascades of apparently aimless chatter. Rambling on and on. Self-absorbed. Yet bent toward order and nuance by Vito's clarinet. A thin, intense man with a big head, he shepherded the others through several false endings and breaks to a final sharp button of a conclusion.

"Hey, hey!" said Jackie.

"Yeah!" "Zap!" "Right on!" came from other parts of the room: short, forceful barkings that sparked the applause.

"Watch him milk it," Jackie whispered to Rita as Vito's big head swiveled round the room while applause clattered on for about thirty seconds. Then, just as the sound was beginning to taper off, Vito pointed an imperious finger at the drummer, who promptly executed a brisk solo break, and the five cronies were off in one last wailing reprise of the final chorus. No false endings this time. Just a closing, sustained high note on the clarinet. A note supported by runs, arpeggios, and thumpings underneath; a note held out long, long, very long, until cut off with one short gustatory unison grunt. A grunt not unlike that of a weightlifter as he puts his virtuoso burden down. And a grand way to end a set.

"You like all this, don't you?" There was a smile on Rita's calm, remote face.

"Home territory." Jackie, relaxing more and more, breathed in the smell of stale beer as though savoring the bouquet of one of Bruce Poirier's fine wines. A smell given body by the dim, cavernous coldness of the place; given bite by the acrid haze of cigarettes. It was a smell he had breathed in his early days on the road with Vito in countless bars, clubs, taverns, and ballrooms: a smell of saloons and saloon music. Like a creditor, it forced itself upon him, demanding recognition of old debts and losses.

"What do you think?" Vito had circled the room like an affable commuter train, stopping at several other tables before coming to a halt at theirs.

"Great," said Jackie. "I see you got yourself a drummer who can keep time."

"How about these vests?"

Jackie's mild blue eyes clouded with thought. There was a long, ruminative pause.

"I like your red vests," he said finally. "They make you look friendly."

"You think so?" Vito's voice, oddly high, was incredulous with pleasure.

"People will always come up and talk to you if you're dressed a little off beat," said Jackie. "Red vests give you a good . . ." He paused to search for the right word.

". . . image?" supplied Rita. In the last few months she had begun to function quite expertly as a thesaurus in their conversations.

"Image," agreed Jackie. "A touch of color like that gives you a friendly image."

"Wonderful!" Large head bobbing, Vito bounced off to another table.

"His other clothes don't fit very well," said Rita.

"Maybe. But he sure plays good."

Jackie gave the matter further thought as the waitress, who looked as though her feet had started to hurt, took their order: gin for Jackie, Perrier water for Rita. Despite his age, Vito was playing amazingly well—still in total control of his instrument and of the musicians he had assembled. Much better, in fact, than Jackie had expected when he had agreed to stop by.

He listened with pleasure as Vito, returning to the bandstand, played a long, effortless cadenza that took the group into a soft, moderate tempo version of "Moonglow." It was a warm sound: a big wide ribbon of sound that unrolled like endless velvet. The same sound he had heard from Vito during their days together with the Jeff Styles Orchestra.

It was good to sit and listen to Vito. But it was painful, too. Especially for a trumpet player whose horn lay locked in its case, untouched for years and years. Listening to Vito, Jackie could hear himself joining in: an obbligato here, a harmony part there, even a solo to balance matters. On the other hand, he could also hear the actual croaking that would have come out if he had accepted Vito's invitation to bring his horn and sit in. An inept, pitiful croaking: an embarrassment for Vito, a humiliation for himself. And since Vito was almost ten years older, there was not even the excuse of age available.

Jackie sipped his drink and continued to applaud enthusiastically. But his thoughts were bleak. He had started out as a trumpet player: first with the circus, then with Jeff Styles. And he had been a good trumpet player, good enough to play with the world's greatest jazz orchestra: an orchestra rich in tonal color, rich in individual solo voices—including Jackie's. To hear the Jeff Styles Orchestra was like wandering through a cathedral. To sit in the middle of it was to feel one's voice grown preternaturally strong and vibrant. To remember it was to remember a time in which one's talent had been bright and shining, recognized by all. A talent lost, allowed to slip away through foolishness and indolence.

"We really should be going." Rita's whisper was soft and insistent.

"Can't walk out during the middle of a set," said Jackie. "Vito's feelings would be hurt."

He looked at her with sudden irritation. And under the irritation, anger—vague, formless, untargeted. Anger at the downward slope of his life: his memory, his business fortunes, his arteries, his muscle tone, his force of will and personality. No lip. No wind. No energy. No stamina. No future. Married to youth, he found himself resenting its presence in her, its absence in him. A dark moment that only much later would be recognized as a marker of brighter things to come.

Rita kept silent and sipped her Perrier water. A glaze of self-sacrificing endurance came over her cool, remote features. It was as though she hoped her withdrawal would be sensed up on the bandstand and force the set to a speedy close.

To his dismay, Jackie found himself supporting her implacable force of will. He was ready to go, ready to travel to Beverly Hills, there to mingle with people who dealt with talent as a commodity, not as a painful reminder of age, decline, and loss.

When the set was over he got up quickly. But just as quickly Vito bounced down from the bandstand and came over to them.

"There's a fan of yours here," he said. He nodded toward a table just to the right of the bandstand where a fortyish man in a gray jacket had risen and was looking at Jackie expectantly.

"We have to be running along," said Jackie.

"A dinner engagement," said Rita.

"I wish I'd known that." Vito's face was solemn, tinged slightly with unspoken reproach. "I'd have brought him over last intermission."

"It wouldn't do any harm to say hello." Jackie smiled at Rita as though to suggest that the compromise was benign and reasonable.

"No harm at all," said Rita. "I'll go on ahead and get the car started."

With a sigh Jackie followed Vito over to the table where the man in the gray jacket was waiting. The man was smiling, his alert brown eyes gleaming with satisfaction.

"All the way from Germany," said Vito with pride. "Herr Ludwig Zweifel is president of a jazz club there."

"From Austria," corrected Herr Zweifel as they gravely shook hands. "Your solo recordings are great favorites in Vienna."

"Pretty scratchy by now, I bet." Jackie, his eyes still on the door, did not sit down.

"Digital recreations." Herr Zweifel's soft voice was friendly, unruffled. "I think you'd be quite pleased with what we've done."

"I'm sure I would." Jackie reached into his blue blazer and took out a business card, feeling constrained to make his exit more palatable. "As you can see, I have to rush off. But I'd really like to hear about what you're doing. Why don't you stop by the office sometime and tell me about it?"

"It would be an honor," said Herr Zweifel. He took the card and carefully put it into his billfold.

"Thanks a million for coming." Vito took Jackie's hand and pressed it warmly.

"It was great," said Jackie. "You were great."

"I think I'm playing better than I ever did." Vito's large eyes were bright and excited, as though lit up by a vision of pure, glowing fire. "I love to play, I love to play for people. It's the challenge I like—when they come up and say, 'What can you do with this one?' I love a challenge like that.

"I can do the rest of it," Vito continued, words tumbling out one after another under the pressure of haste. "The orchestrating, the composing, even the conducting—all dressed up in white tie and tails. But there's nothing like playing." He shook his head and looked down at his hands: broad and flat they were, with blunt, stubby fingers. "It just feels better when my hands are working."

"That's right." Jackie smiled at Herr Zweifel.

"Woodworker's hands," said Vito. He held them out for Jackie's inspection. "My father was a cabinetmaker, you know."

"Good hands, a good head, a good heart—what more do you need?" Jackie paused awkwardly, then stepped close to Vito and kissed him on the cheek. "Stay on it, huh?"

"You too." Vito nodded his big outsize head as though confirming the existence of some obscure truth.

Leaving the table, Jackie headed for the door and out to the parking lot, where Rita was waiting in the Ferrari. It was an expensive car. Far too expensive for a trumpet player. But just right for a television producer with a beautiful young wife. And it took them with swift efficiency to Bruce Poirier's expensive house in Beverly Hills, there to dine with important people in expensive clothes, entertained by aspiring talent and a trio of strolling violinists in white tuxedos.

Vito Scalza went back to the bandstand and got his drink. He brought it back to Herr Zweifel's table.

"I'm sorry it didn't work out better," he said.

"It opened the door." Herr Zweifel took out Jackie's card and inspected it. "A great artist."

"You should have heard him play in the old days."

"I did." Herr Zweifel's alert brown eyes were somber, reflective. "But I was at the time far too young to understand the significance of such matters."

"That's always the way it is." Vito took a long pull from his drink and stared thoughtfully at the bandstand. "Is there anything you'd like to hear when we go back?"

"Something lively," said Herr Zweifel.

"They're all lively." Vito's large eyes glistened with good humor. "The only difference is the tempo."

Studio City, California:
Tuesday, September 19, 10:30 A.M.

"Technology." Jackie directed Herr Zweifel's attention toward the large illuminated board at the far side of the studio. "You can't have a complicated quiz show without complicated technology."

"Do you produce many such shows?"

"Only two right now," said Jackie. "But they keep us busy enough—and they keep a lot of people working."

"Does it keep you yourself quite busy?" Herr Zweifel's alert brown eyes surveyed the last-minute preparations being made for the taping of "Word-Right": audience filing docilely in, technical aides traveling well-worn paths.

"Sometimes it runs smoothly—other times I have to put out fires every day."

"It's good of you to show me around."

"I enjoy it." Jackie smiled and led Herr Zweifel out of the studio. "It gives me an excuse to split from the office and see what's going on."

They continued on their informal tour, stopping in at another studio to watch part of a show in progress. As usual, the tour itself was a smooth, well-paced sequence: interesting to the visitor but not too overwhelming in its speed or richness of detail. A polished sequence. Like a sales presentation kept bright and shiny through constant use, a sales presentation that might someday be made to a prospective purchaser of Jay Jay Productions. It was with genuine pleasure that Jackie had taken time out to entertain Herr Zweifel, discussing studio problems and potential opportunities.

Herr Zweifel's visit had also permitted Jackie to postpone the unpleasant task of phoning his brother in Kansas City. Thorvald had called earlier, told him of Clint Lawler's death, and urged him to fly out for the memorial service. Properly so. Clint had always been a good friend and mentor. But Rita had pointed to an important meeting coming up with Bruce Poirier at the network. And she had also pointed to Thorvald's habit of asking for financial help, particularly when supported by the family's collective face-to-face force. Once on the phone, Jackie would have to decide and make his decision explicit. The phone call, the decision, the inevitable conflict that would follow—these were well worth postponing in favor of a modest grand tour.

As was customary, Jackie concluded the tour by driving his visitor back to the offices of Jay Jay Productions: offices that occupied the second floor of a small two-story building on a narrow street lined with walnut trees. A quiet conclusion, especially when matched against the hustle and bustle of the studios two blocks away. An excellent opportunity to catch one's breath and get further acquainted in the privacy of Jackie's office.

It was not a large office. But there was a feeling of permanence to it, almost as though the occupant had whittled his initials here and there. On the near wall were several rows of framed glossy professional photographs portraying performers from the long-running "Judy's Guy" show: a show that Jackie and Judy, his second wife, had produced and starred in together for many years. On the far wall was a smaller group of pictures from Jackie's days as a musician: the Jeff Styles Orchestra; Jackie's first band—with his first wife, Lorrayne, seated dark and prim in front; Jackie's lounge group—with Judy striking a comic pose; various solo instrumentalists—including Clint Lawler; even a few mementos from the Kale Brothers Circus, featuring the Flying Glaubers and the eighteen solemn virtuosos in red regimentals and bearskin shakos of the Kale Brothers Concert and Marching Symphonia. Jackie's office was not a museum, but it had a fair share of antiquities on display.

"Charming!" exclaimed Herr Zweifel as he walked in and caught sight of Jackie's musical gallery. "You must have some unusual stories to tell."

"Everyone has unusual stories to tell." Jackie remained standing by the door. "You should hear Vito when he gets going."

"An amazing man." Herr Zweifel focused intently upon the Jeff Styles pictures in an effort to match Vito past with Vito present. "But *your* career has been much more varied, has it not?"

"Vito stayed on the track," said Jackie. "The right track."

He sat down at his desk, a big plank of oak cluttered with memoranda and financial statements, some of them held down by the trumpet mouthpiece Clint had given him. It was a very good mouthpiece. Custom made. Deep cupped. Just right for controlling the full range of the horn.

"Do you regret leaving the Jeff Styles Orchestra?" Herr Zweifel, now inspecting the circus pictures, put the question absently, almost as though it were a matter of no import.

"That's the way it fell."

"I do not understand."

"A figure of speech. It means I started out as a trumpet player and ended up in the picture business."

"By choice?"

"More by chance, I'd have to say. One thing always leads to another, you know."

"And here you are." Herr Zweifel's eyes were now trained upon Jackie. He nodded approvingly and smiled. "What we call a *universal-genie.*"

"I'm not sure I follow you."

"One of our idioms," said Herr Zweifel. "A universal genius, you might say."

"I don't fit into that category at all."

"Why not?" Herr Zweifel left the picture gallery and came over to Jackie's desk. "Trumpet player, bandleader, television performer, television producer—you have achieved distinction in all these."

"Not that much." Despite Herr Zweifel's friendly manner, Jackie felt uncomfortable, as though he were being prodded somehow. "A lot of people did those things, and did them better—Clint Lawler, for one."

"A great loss." Herr Zweifel pointed to the largest photograph of the short, thick-set black man, his trumpet pointed high in the air as though about to take off in flight. He nodded at Jackie sympathetically.

"The best." Jackie picked up the mouthpiece for a moment, then put it back. "High, low, loud, soft, fast, slow—he wrote the book."

"Many of us feel that your style is much like his."

"I always tried for a singing sound, if that's what you mean. But I never came close to what Clint did."

"A singing sound." Herr Zweifel paused to savor the phrase. "We don't get to hear that kind of music very often these days."

"Styles change."

"Good jazz music never goes out of fashion," Herr Zweifel said. "Are you familiar with our Montreux jazz festival?"

Jackie nodded. He watched Herr Zweifel sit down, not without a feeling that the conversation had been guided step by step to a key point.

"Some of us would like to use members of the Jeff Styles Orchestra next summer," continued Herr Zweifel.

"You'd have trouble getting them together," said Jackie. "A lot of them are gone now."

"We were thinking of a small group—Vito Scalza, yourself, perhaps."

"You mean you'd like me to play the trumpet for you in Switzerland?"

It was Herr Zweifel's turn to nod. He sat back in his chair easily, his eyes sparkling with pleasure at the idea.

"It's a great honor to be asked." Jackie chose his words carefully. "But there must be other trumpet players you could get."

"Not with a lyric style."

"How about Otis Marshak? He's still active, isn't he?"

"A great virtuoso, I grant you. But not a truly singing sound, as you yourself put it."

Jackie looked over at the pictures for a moment. Otis was in only one of them, a picture taken just before Jackie gave notice and left. He had not meant to give notice, merely to complain about the way in which Otis sabotaged his cup mute solos into the microphone by rattling a music stand or coughing at a key moment. Otis had been an irritation after his first week. An irritation not to be endured, in spite of his high-note pyrotechnics. Bad for the section. Bad for the overall ensemble sound. Lorrayne had agreed, had encouraged him to force the issue with Jeff. But Jeff had shrugged the issue away, accepting Jackie's resignation as a matter of course—without protest, without visible signs of regret. So Jackie had walked out of Jeff's hotel room, ashamed and angry—at Otis, at Jeff, at himself for quitting the greatest jazz orchestra in the world.

"Otis would do a very good job for you," he said stiffly.

"Vito Scalza would prefer to have *you* make music with him."

"I'm really all tied up with the business here." Jackie gestured toward the gallery of performers on the near wall as though enlisting their smiles in his behalf.

"Surely you could get away for two weeks. It would be a delightful vacation for you and your lovely wife."

"You don't understand," said Jackie. "I'm really out of shape when it comes to playing."

"Of course." Herr Zweifel paused, then went on. "But a little practice would surely bring most of your skill back."

"It would take more than a little practice, I'm afraid."

"The appearance would be a short one, undemanding, not more than an hour."

Jackie sighed. For a moment he could feel the same pain he had felt listening to Vito play: a pain born of the conflict between what he could hear in his mind and what he knew would come out of his horn.

"Playing the trumpet isn't easy," he said finally, in a soft far away voice. "It's like lifting weights and pinching yourself at the same time. You have to keep at it every day, even when you're in top form. For me to do even a halfway decent job, it would mean a year's practice."

"A full year?"

"A year. Eight months, at least. Eight months of scales and whole tones, six hours a day, day after day."

"I had not realized so much was involved."

"Most people don't," said Jackie. "They think you get out there and sort of make it up as you go along. But all they see is the tip of the iceberg—the performance. What they don't see is the amount of concentration and work behind the performance."

"Is it concentration and work you begrudge?"

"Some do, I suppose," said Jackie. "But I always liked it. It was a good way of setting yourself up for the day—better than drinking."

Herr Zweifel laughed appreciatively. Then he leaned forward and smiled.

"I have the feeling you would like very much to get back to your practicing," he said.

"Believe me, I'd like nothing better." Jackie's eyes clouded slightly as he let his mind play with the idea for a little. "But I'm retired from active duty now."

"Retired from music but not from business, are you not?"

"That's the way it is." Jackie rose and stepped toward the door as a signal that the exchange had gone as far as it could. "Someone has to mind the store."

"There are many storekeepers," said Herr Zweifel. He got up. "But there are few trumpet players of your stature. Could you not perhaps give the matter further thought? It would mean a great deal."

"I'll think about it," said Jackie. "If I change my mind I'll let Vito know."

"That would be splendid." Herr Zweifel smiled and let his eyes take in Jackie's music gallery once more. "You have many admirers in Europe, old friends who would like to see you."

Jackie let the conversation wind slowly down. After Herr Zweifel left, he came back to his oak desk and stared at his telephone for a moment. There was still his Kansas City phone call to make. He got up, walked over to Clint Lawler's picture. Characteristically it was an action picture, one that caught the energy and force of the man. Like Vito, Clint had stayed on the right track, traveling at his own generous speed until the track ran out, still playing his horn in his early seventies. One of the few people in the world who do what they do superbly well—and keep doing it. Someone who should be honored. Honored with a memorial service. Admirers and old friends, as Herr Zweifel had put it. Coming in from far-off places to pay their respects. From Chicago. From New York. Even from as far away as Los Angeles and Studio City, California.

Jackie sat down at his desk. He picked up the trumpet mouthpiece. Hefted it. Put it gently back. Then reached for the telephone.

An impulsive action. One with serious consequences, as he would later come to realize.

Kansas City, Missouri: Wednesday, September 20, 4:00 P.M.

Jackie was careful to lock the door of the rented Datsun. Standing beside it, he suddenly remembered he had forgotten to bring an overcoat with him to Kansas City. The lateness of the flight, the standing in line at the Avis counter—these had swept him up in a haste-driven rush to reach the funeral home where the memorial service for Clint Lawler was to be held. But now, standing under an overcast sky that hinted of rain, Jackie felt the autumn wind sting his cheek, nip at his ears.

Not an unpleasant sting. More of a brisk admonition to go directly about one's business. Which Jackie did: walking down the block as fast as he could, eyes alert for the sight of his brother waiting at the door.

Thorvald was not there. Jackie looked inside for a moment, then came back out. He took up a post immediately to the right of the door and stood there: half watching for Thorvald, half reviewing the plans they had made. Thorvald had been explicit enough; he had urged the importance of Clint's memorial service, making a firm commitment to be there himself, and he had told Jackie that the family would gather for dinner at their mother's house. Everyone would be there: Mother, Thorvald, Hildegard, the nieces and nephews, even Thorvald's oldest boy from the university at Lawrence, Kansas. Everything planned, everything in order.

Except for Thorvald. Jackie watched the last few clusters of people, black and white, disperse and make their way inside. He stood there alone, his mild blue eyes hardening as the awareness that Thorvald was not going to come began to seep in along with the chill in the air. Excuses would be made, he knew. Good ones. And he was used to such excuses. From Thorvald. From Hildegard. From his mother.

They had always been able to snare him with a web of words, a web whose filaments were subsequently rearranged into a new design after he had taken the action promised. When he had dropped out of high school to go on the road and send money home, there had been words of gratitude accompanied by the assurance that Thorvald and Hildegard would pitch in and do their share later on. But later on they had found a need for college education, then for further help—with a new car, a new house, a new roof for the old house. Always supported with good reasons, good excuses.

Jackie shook his head and went inside, wondering whether his anger should be targeted toward Thorvald and the family or toward himself for constantly allowing himself to be pushed. For the first time he realized that he was very tired. Tired of acquiescing. Tired of doing what other people wanted him to do. For a moment, just before he sat down in the back of the room, he felt a strong burst of anger—anger that made him want to rush back to his rented Datsun, drive it to the airport, take the next plane back to Los Angeles, and hole up in a motel room with a good bottle of gin.

Like a balloon released, Jackie's anger floated off at the sight of a big, broad-shouldered black man coming up to the lectern at the front of the room. Somber and commanding, the black man had the mark of a preacher about him. His presence was reassuring. And it had been a long time since Jackie had heard good preaching: passionate, hortatory sermons, full of words and phrases that cracked like a whip out over the congregation to touch even the back rows and rivet their occupants into quivering attention. Fire-and-brimstone talk. Stars-in-the-crown talk. Plain talk for plain people living on the edge of private anger, shame, and terror.

But there was to be no sermon. Instead the pastor announced that there would be two short tributes to the memory of Clint Lawler: the first by Mr. Cy Harris, Clint's longtime friend and personal manager; the second by Dr. Robert Green, a professor of urban studies at a local community college. Following these two tributes there would be a short benediction, after which Clint's friends were invited to an informal gathering at a nearby hotel.

It had been comforting to see the pastor come up. But it was even more comforting to see Cy Harris. Cy had been the booking agent for Jackie's band right from the start. He had been a good agent. A good friend. Good company, too. The latest jokes, the latest stories, a rich fund of anecdotes going back to his early days as a *tummeler* at a Catskills resort—Cy was, like many agents, more entertaining than most of the entertainers he represented. He was a big man—deep-voiced, ebullient in manner, given to wearing dark blue suits, above which his bald head and horn-rimmed glasses gleamed like an affectionate beacon.

Cy's tribute was dignified and brief. The chronological facts of Clint's life. His own forty-year association with Clint. Clint's career. His honors. His state department tour a few years back. His generosity to friends and younger musicians. His integrity as an artist and a human being. By the time Cy finished, a succinct picture of Clint had been sketched and held before them. Fittingly so, Jackie felt. There was greatness in Clint. Goodness, too. Cy was right to take a few minutes and spell it all out.

There seemed to be a parallel rightness in the choice of Dr. Robert Green as the second speaker. Cy was white, Dr. Green was black; Cy was older, Dr. Green was young. Where Cy's remarks were made from notes, almost impromptu, Dr. Green's statement was thoughtfully prepared, if one were to judge from the typed sheets of yellow paper he took from the inner pocket of his tweed jacket. Though no preacher, Dr. Green clearly intended to make a significant statement and speak at length.

He began by celebrating jazz music as a uniquely American art form, then went back to trace its origins in the tribal rhythms and chants of Africa. Earnest and detailed, he then proceeded to discuss minstrel shows . . . the oral-formulaic nature of folk preaching . . . ragtime . . . Scott Joplin . . . Jim Europe . . . King Oliver . . . Freddie Keppard . . . Fletcher Henderson . . . Horace Henderson . . . Horace Silver . . . Oscar Pettiford . . . Oscar Peterson . . . giants all in a pantheon of Afro-American artistic expression.

"And so we come to a giant among giants." Dr. Green, suddenly conscious of the passage of time and the growing restlessness of his listeners, smiled and began to quicken his pace. "A man who was truly *primus inter pares,* a star among stars, a musician's musician, an entertainer's entertainer. In honoring Clint Eastwood, we honor both the man and the tradition.

"Clint Eastwood touched our lives with happiness," Dr. Green continued in a low voice, undisturbed by throat clearings and other audible signs of discomfort.

"Lawler," came a soft whisper from one of the seats in front of him.

"He was an artist," said Dr. Green, raising his voice slightly. "An artist among artists, many of whom were directly influenced by the seminal work of Clint Eastwood."

More throat clearings. Chair shufflings. A few coughs. And finally a loud, clearly audible whisper from the side.

"Lawler," went the whisper, urgently. *"Lawler."*

Immediately responsive, Dr. Green smiled reassuringly and raised his voice even further.

"Clint Eastwood is a symbol of achievement for black people all over the world!" he thundered.

"No, no!" came an agitated voice, loud enough to ride the crest of the other murmurings. "It's Lawler."

"Lawler."

"You've got the name wrong."

Dr. Green stopped smiling. He looked down at his yellow typescript, then looked helplessly over at the pastor, who rose and came up beside him to whisper in his ear. Then the pastor returned to his seat. There was silence while Dr. Green recovered his composure—and his smile.

"And just like Clint Eastwood, Clint Lawler was a truly great American," he said, nodding his head as though to reassure them all of the felicity of the comparison. "A great musician. An inspiration to us all."

Hastily he gathered up his yellow typescript and stepped down. More silence. Then the big, broad-shouldered black pastor came back to the lectern and delivered a short benediction.

It was over.

Jackie remained in his seat for a few minutes. He watched the others file out, wondered what their thoughts were. His own were dark, angry, resentful. Not so much because of the name confusion as because of Dr. Green's use of the occasion as a platform for a lecture reflecting his particular concerns and purposes. Another web of words spun from selfishness and complete disdain for the man they had come to honor. Better to have had readings from Scripture: great, rolling periods from the Bible.

Language as timeless as the ocean itself, absorbing each singular grief into one common universal domain. The room was almost empty. Jackie took a few deep breaths, then got up and went outside.

"Is there a law against buying an overcoat in California?" rumbled a deep voice behind him. It was Cy.

"There should be a law against college professors," said Jackie. He looked truculently at the people milling about on the sidewalk below them, as though blaming the group for what had happened.

"It's what the family wanted."

"Why?"

"They're local people, so they wanted a local boy."

"He didn't do very well," said Jackie, mild blue eyes still hard. "Especially for a closing spot."

"It didn't do any harm." Cy looked around and nodded approvingly. "This is where he started out; these are his people. It was better to do it here than in New York."

"I hope they get *my* name right when the time comes."

"Would it matter?" said Cy. "It wouldn't be the first time someone got mixed up on the lyrics." He looked up at the sky, taking note of a heavier accumulation of clouds than had been there earlier. "Let's go on over to the hotel together."

"I don't know," said Jackie. "I'm supposed to meet my family for dinner."

"Meet them for breakfast." Cy's bald head and horn-rimmed glasses beamed down at Jackie. "Meet them afterwards. There's going to be music—lots of it."

Jackie paused. He could see the gathering take shape in his mind. A room big enough for a piano, for a set of drums. Food. Liquor, perhaps. Old friends of Clint's, black and white, many of them bringing their instruments. Not a wake in the classic sense. But close. And with a couple of choruses of "Didn't He Ramble?" to get things started. Music to blow Dr. Green's words out of everyone's mind.

"You've played someone else's trumpet before," continued Cy. "It would be great to hear you again."

"I'm way out of shape."

"Then listen. Listen and talk. It's been a long time since we've seen each other."

"I'd like to," said Jackie slowly. For a moment he considered going with Cy and phoning Thorvald from the hotel; then decided to stick with a course of action already set. "But the family's expecting me. I simply can't let them down."

"Too bad." Cy shrugged. They started down the steps together. "Anyhow, it's good to see you—even for a couple of minutes."

"I'll try to stop by the next time I'm in New York."

"Don't just try, man." Cy held up a monitory hand. "Do it. Maybe I can get you a split week somewhere."

"I'm too old for that kind of action these days." Jackie smiled and started back toward the rented Datsun. With wry amusement he envisioned the spectacle of fifteen musicians piling into a chartered bus for a trip to upstate New York, closing on Wednesday night, then packing up and driving straight through to open in North Carolina the following evening. A young man's business. For a young man with a good lip and a good digestion.

The car was farther up the street than he had remembered it. For a moment he halted in confusion, trying to get his bearings and make sure he had not taken off in the wrong direction. But the direction was right. And the Datsun was where he had left it. He unlocked the door, got in, sat there considering the best route to take.

A wave of sadness washed over him. Set in motion by Clint's death, perhaps. Or by the exchange with Cy. Or by the sense of isolation that comes from sitting in a strange automobile in strange surroundings. He felt like weeping: wished that he could, wished that tears would flood through the channel opened up by his anger at Thorvald and Dr. Green. But he did not weep. The knack of it was something he had lost long ago.

It began to rain—lightly, but enough to stir him into movement. He started up the motor, turned on the windshield wipers. There was comfort in the noise. Even more comfort in the feeling of the car in motion.

By the time he pulled up in front of his mother's house, Jackie was in reasonably good humor. This was his family. These were his people. People for whom he had always wished nothing but happiness and good, good things.

Beverly Hills, California:
Thursday, September 21, 9:45 A.M.

Miss Claudine did not believe in weights. The conviction was a strong one, based on her experience in other health spas before coming to Firm 'n' Flex. Weight lifting enhanced bust contours, it was true; but at a heavy price: a heavy neck, bulging biceps and forearms, massive knotting of muscle on the back. All supported by spindly legs rendered noticeably grotesque by the contrast.

"It's legs, girls," she barked at her early morning professional women's class. "Your legs are your essence. Long, lovely deep roots that bring the earth's energy up to the rest of you. The only way to keep those juices flowing is to kick, kick, kick."

Obediently the members of the class kicked: kicked high and mightily. It was a good class. Intent. Businesslike. Uncomplaining. Under thirty for the most part. Some in black leotards. Some in shorts. Some in sensibly loose gray sweatsuits. Most of them were important people. Successful in banking, in public relations, in various branches of the entertainment industry. Keeping their bodies in trim like finely tuned imported automobiles designed to be driven fast and far. The kicking was like a final act of polish: hard, stretching, abrasive; but fully justified by the glow and luster it gave them.

"Beautiful!" Miss Claudine clapped her hands in approval, then looked at her watch. "That's it for today. But let me remind you again about our karate class starting next week. I think some of you are ready for a little more challenge."

Rita Hayes smiled. She stood still in place for a moment, breathing in the faint scent of sweat still lingering in the air. Then she started for the showers. Coming to Firm 'n' Flex at eight-thirty in the morning was a perfect way to start the day. Especially the kicking part, which she executed with the consummate skill of a former high school drum majorette from Hattiesburg, Mississippi. Not the leading majorette. That post had gone to a stubby-legged lawyer's daughter. But the best one. Tall for her age. Tall enough to stand out in parade. Tall enough to attract attention: some of it admiring, some of it envious.

She showered and dressed quickly, not even stopping, as she often did, to scrutinize the flatness of her stomach, the firm, flowing taper of her thighs. White skirt. Dark blue blouse. Expensive in cut and material. But not ostentatious. Almost as though she had decided to mute the natural eroticism of her body's message in favor of something more subtle, more ambiguous.

It was only when she started up the Ferrari that Rita's spirits began to sink a little. Jackie's decision to visit Kansas City had been made without his consulting her on the matter. Not desertion. But close. More like a feinting withdrawal: a withdrawal intended to mask a deployment of forces elsewhere. The excursion to Embers West was certainly a case in point. And so was the reluctance to option new properties. Natural signs of discontent, her therapist had termed them. Signs pointing in the wrong direction.

The thought of her meeting with Bruce Poirier sank her spirits even further. Bruce had encouraged her to acquire a number of properties—novels, feature scripts—promising her that he would be able to get network approval for them: approval that would guarantee Jay Jay access to financing. But the approval had not come through. So there the scripts sat in her office: valueless, yet draining their reserves as each option came up for renewal. The meeting, she knew, was intended to explain, to reassure, to give her ammunition for use in dealing with Jackie. Fine words. Fine promises. Yet nothing tangible to take back in triumph.

Rita was used to promises. Six years back she had left

Hattiesburg, Mississippi, giving up a good, steady job as a legal secretary for an uncertain role in a fly-by-night public relations firm in New Orleans. There a visiting assistant director had urged her to try Los Angeles, promising her easy entry to studios and production companies. She had gone, knocked on all the doors. Blown by winds of hope from interview to interview, agency to agency. Baited from time to time with an occasional speaking part, especially when a tall, semi-Amazonian type was called for.

There had been men in Los Angeles. Many of them. Speaking fair words and discoursing knowledgeably about contracts and casting needs. But the words had never taken flesh; after two years of smiling pliability, Rita had grown cautious, curt, distrustful, even combative. And the men had begun to drift elsewhere. So Rita had gone into real estate.

She had done well. Her cool remoteness had served as an effective catalyst in bringing buyers and their illusions together. Prestige homes, emotional homes, fixer-uppers, lease options, wrap-arounds—she had juggled them all like twirling batons from her drum majorette days. In the process she had met many of those whose doors had been closed to her as a tall, semi-Amazonian type. Producers. Directors. Writers. Agents. Accountants. Record people. Film people. Television people. On the basis of these contacts she began to involve herself in the development and marketing of properties colored with much more illusion than the residential properties of real estate. Creative properties. Scripts. Outlines. Proposals. All calling for the art of the telephone: an art sauced with the pure delight of dispensing promises—as opposed to pleading for them.

A natural transition, a good move. But she had kept her real estate license. Happily so, since it was a divorce-occasioned sale that brought her into contact with Jackie, who was very much at loose ends with Judy gone and his daughter, Louise, at school in Santa Barbara. Not content with being a middle-aged man's playmate, she had gradually begun to play a more and more important part in Jay Jay Productions. A small company. Big enough for new ideas. Her ideas. Ideas that soared higher and higher. In marked contrast to the spirits now sinking beneath them.

Rita would have preferred to meet Bruce at the network. But he had suggested a morning meeting at his country club immediately after his early tennis session with the club professional. A logical place. Not too far from her own office. Pleasantly intimate. Located somewhere between the cautious neutrality of a business address and the stronger innuendo of a cocktail lounge.

She parked the Ferrari and walked through the club building to the tennis courts immediately outside. She scanned the eight courts, caught sight of Bruce down at the far left. His game finished, he was coming toward her. But she did not wave; instead she turned to inspect a brown, wiry woman on her near right, a woman who was carefully baking the underside of her chin with the help of two aluminum reflectors. Then, just at the right moment, Rita wheeled round and let Bruce, coming up, have the full force of her sudden smile, at the same time letting her eyes travel his hard young body—only a few years older than hers: a body revealingly displayed in tank top and thigh-hugging tennis shorts.

"A debacle!" said Bruce. He looked back with mock ruefulness at the far court. Without waiting for a reply he took her directly into the lounge, a large room with deep-green leather couches; empty except for two bald-headed men playing liar's dice at the bar. Bruce beckoned for a waitress and ordered iced tea for the two of them: iced tea with fresh mint leaves. All this done with great speed and dispatch.

"You'll like the iced tea," he said, in much the same tone that one would say, "You'll love the Taj Mahal." His large, liquid brown eyes brimmed assurance that the matter was important—to both of them.

Rita started to speak, but Bruce held up a warning hand.

"I know you're upset," he said. "And I want you to understand that I'm upset, too. Believe me, I was as surprised as you were when the committee turned us down. But I've talked to them and they're really much more enthusiastic than the actual correspondence would indicate."

"Are they ready to reconsider?"

"Tomorrow, no. In the long run, yes." Bruce sipped his iced tea with obvious gusto. "What they're looking for is the quality of your in-depth financial commitment."

Rita paused, trying to sort out what Bruce was saying from his flow of language. Not an easy task. Bruce talked fast and impressively, sometimes impenetrably.

"You mean they want us to spend more money?" she said. "Where? And on what?"

"I'm not sure it really matters where or what." Bruce smiled, showing perfectly aligned white teeth. "Talent, script revisions, director and design input—it really doesn't matter, as long as you demonstrate an ongoing capability and commitment."

"We're trying to *make* money, not spend it."

"You have to understand that money today is just another commodity—something you process, like oil or cotton."

"The banks don't think so."

"There are other sources," said Bruce. "New sources, unconventional sources. And I feel I owe it to you to put you in contact with some of those sources." He smiled again. Quietly, suggestively, his large, liquid brown eyes intent upon her.

Rita smiled back. Under her cool, remote exterior she was beginning to come alive with a tingling awareness of what Bruce was talking about. He was talking about family money, she was sure. Money from his mother's family, the Bonnets. Money that had in effect bought him his vice presidency at Universal Broadcasting Network. Money coming from the South and from its prospering economy. Old money. New money. Money from the earth; from strange, far-off places with treasure-trove names. The smell of it clung to him: not like sweat, but like a rich, expensive lotion on his smooth brown skin.

"Los Angeles is not the world." She smiled, pleased with herself for overcoming a sudden urge to touch his muscular right forearm with her lips, perhaps going so far as to give it a small bite.

"Now you're thinking creatively." He lowered his voice and moved closer to her on the deep-green leather couch, allowing his leg to brush for a moment against hers before settling back. "If you're willing to pursue some of these more unconventional resource opportunities, I'd be privileged if you'd let me open a door here and there for you."

"It sounds lovely." Rita paused, ran her tongue just behind her lower lip, barely visible, before going on. "But it's not exactly up to me, you know."

"I understand that."

"Jackie tends to be conservative in things like this."

"I understand that, too." Bruce gave a quick, self-deprecating shrug. "That's why I wanted to talk it over with you first."

"Would you talk to him?"

"If he's interested, I'd love to talk to him." Bruce looked over at the men playing liar's dice by the bar. "Put all my cards on the table and fill him in on exactly where the industry is heading. After that, if he's still interested, I'll set up a meeting with some people I know in New Orleans."

New Orleans! To Rita the name was like a giant bell pealing out glad tidings of a triumphant return. A return to grand houses heretofore glimpsed only from afar. Houses where fine gentlemen and delicate ladies spoke softly. Houses with intricate wrought-iron grillwork. Houses where old servants, wise and loyal, served chocolate in the afternoons.

She smiled at him with affection. Affection tinged with wariness, with speculation as to his motives. She was sure he intended for her to make the New Orleans trip—and with him. But she was not sure how far he intended to go beyond that. Nor was she sure about her own desires.

"I'll talk it over with Jackie when he gets back from Kansas City," she said. She smiled coolly, as though adding a note of threat to their assignation, then rose, towering above him for a second.

"The sooner, the better." Bruce got up, looked easily down at her. "I'll walk you out by way of the courts."

They went outside. Three of the courts were now in use. But clouds had begun to block the sun's rays, so the aluminum reflector woman had put aside her instruments of worship and was standing with several other onlookers. As they walked by, Rita gave her a close, evaluative stare.

The woman had a good body. Cared for. The way a body should be cared for: with exercise, massage, thoughtful application of creams and sunshine, so that each part blended into one harmonious concoction very much resembling an expensive exotic drink.

But a good body deserved a good face. And that was more difficult: to have a face where lines of venom and worry were smoothed away under a timeless soft patina laid down by thoughtful attention and—where needed—surgical art. From her sessions at Firm 'n' Flex Rita knew that a woman in her sixties could still buy a good body, while a good face still remained a much more inaccessible gift.

As they passed directly opposite her, Rita was happy to see the good body turn toward them and reveal a face equally good, equally cared for: a face almost insolent in its assertion of immunity from age, aging, and dissipation.

A lithe, supple young body. A fairly smooth older face. Not bad for a Southern California woman probably in her late fifties. A target to shoot for. Especially for someone who was twenty-six and already going to a health spa every morning.

But as the woman detached herself from the group and came up the steps in front of them, Rita was shocked to see the impression of youth shattered by the woman's small rosebud mouth: a mouth from which a broad, flat red tongue darted uncontrollably in and out, almost like that of a blacksnake probing the air for intimations of food and warmth. It was as though the marks of age, banished from the surface, had managed to burrow their way deep inside, where from time to time they pertinaciously asserted their presence in full view of all.

A twenty-five-year-old body. A forty-five-year-old face. An eighty-year-old tongue. To Rita the combination was too unsettling, too ambiguous—so much so that she averted her eyes, raising them only when the woman addressed Bruce directly.

"Hello, lover," came a deep, throaty voice. "Didn't I see you at Frank May's party last week?" Dart, dart went the ambiguous woman's tongue.

"I'm Bruce Poirier."

"Of course you are. Love those shorts. Are you playing now?" As though supporting her query, the tongue darted probingly out again.

"I'm all through."

"So am I. Finished. Unless I can find that chauffeur of mine."

With springlike step the woman of ambiguous age swung provocatively off to the right. Rita and Bruce continued on to the parking lot. There, in neutral territory, goodbyes rich in promise and excitement were said, and Rita drove off.

A good meeting. Surprisingly so. One that opened up some new doors. Interesting doors. Doors that would lead her in time to stature of her own, power in her own right: necessary cushioning against the time when arm muscles would start to sag and wrinkles form. The trade-offs were certainly clear enough: a good body for wealth and power; then wealth and power for a good body. If desired. Perhaps in years to come the power would be enough, especially for a bartender's daughter from Hattiesburg. Her therapist, Dr. Melissa Stritch, had summed it up with uncompromising candor, "The best thing about having a Ph.D. and a private practice is that you can eat yummies any damn time you feel like it."

Yummies! Chocolates! Cakes and pies! Meringues! Eclairs! Napoleons! Sherbets, ice creams, agreeably thick malted milkshakes! There had been times when Rita, implacable of will, had taken spoonfuls of ice cream one by one, chewing each slightly before spitting the residue out—thus simultaneously enjoying the pleasures of luxury and self-denial.

Self-denial. Even now the cruel discipline of Miss Claudine made her want to wince visibly and cry aloud. But she had endured. She would endure. She would prevail. And she would sign up for the karate classes next week.

Malibu, California:
Friday, September 22, 4:00 P.M.

"Barry's going to run the tape back to the entrance for you." Judy motioned her daughter to a couch directly opposite the television set.

Louise Hayes sat down and watched Barry work the buttons of the video recorder, freezing Judy-on-the-screen in mid-gesture and spinning her into a blurred backward gallop. He seemed to have more mechanical skill than Kevin, her mother's previous companion. Otherwise he was cut from the same attractive cloth as his predecessor: tall, well-muscled, strong of wind and limb, sun-bleached and sun-bronzed from years of earnest surfing.

"Great timing!" Barry pointed admiringly to Judy-on-the-screen as she walked across the stage to begin the interview.

"Too slow," said Judy-in-the-room. She was a trim, tautly strung woman, with vivid red hair and pale green eyes.

"You're fantastic." Barry smiled over at Louise and shook his head as though overwhelmed by the keen perception of his patron.

He was an ideal companion for Judy, constantly labeling in superlatives everything she did. If the label was rejected, he merely shifted the beam of his admiration to shine upon the superior wisdom of his critic. A simple technique, but always effective, always welcome.

Taking her cue from Barry, Louise watched in respectful silence as Judy-on-the-screen bobbed her red-thatched head and popped her pale green eyes in a chain of bantering about her recent dinner theater work. It was a performance Louise had seen many times. Judy-on-the-screen, Judy-in-the-room—they were both parts of the same whole: two pictures superimposed upon one another like a double exposure in which some details correspond and others clash violently.

Louise shifted uneasily on the couch. She was a quiet girl: barely twenty, shy, soft-spoken, given to hiking and gazing at small birds, and with light brown hair that must have emerged as a last-minute compromise between Judy's carrot blaze and Jackie's dark hair. She had expected that Scott Giraud, her fiancé, would be sitting by her side, filling the room with brilliance. With Barry, Judy-on-the-screen, and Judy-in-the-room ranged against her, she felt more than ordinarily small and inconsequential.

The original plan had called for Scott and her to drive down together from Santa Barbara. But Scott had then arranged to read his poems at a UCLA afternoon seminar given by a fellow scholar-poet. So he had left early in the MG, leaving her to follow in the pick-up truck after her climatology class. The change in signals had upset Louise; she had looked forward to making a grand entrance with Scott: introducing him to her mother, and letting matters progress in a warm glow made even warmer by the sunshine streaming in through the picture window of the large Malibu beach house. A good setting for an introduction. But bad timing as far as the entrances were concerned.

The ideal arrangement would have involved bringing Scott and her parents together in the same room: much like a well-crafted episode from their "Judy's Guy" series. In the series reruns on independent stations, they were still linked together. And so were their initials, which signaled to all that Jay Jay Productions was firmly rooted in the heady, early years of television. But the marriage, like the show, had ended—helped along, Louise felt, by her own departure for preparatory school and college. A necessary departure calling for changes in script and casting: young men for her mother, a young woman for her father.

"I hate it when they lip-sync." Judy-in-the-room glared

angrily at the appearance on screen of a young woman singing through long dark hair. She nodded to Barry, who obediently turned the picture off.

"Scott's coming up from Los Angeles," said Louise.

"Why not?" Judy stared out toward the ocean as though calculating the distance. "That's where the action is."

"Fantastic action," said Barry.

"Bruce Poirier over at UBN sent me a pilot." Judy turned her pale green eyes to a white-bound manuscript on top of the piano.

"It's dynamite!" Barry smiled proudly at Louise.

"He said that maybe I should kick it on to your father."

"To produce it?"

"Something like that." Judy began to snap her fingers as though to a tune humming inside of her. "What do you think?"

"I think it's a wonderful idea." Louise went over to the piano and looked at the script for a minute. "You always liked doing the series."

"Do you think I should send it to him?" Judy looked at her anxiously. "I know it needs a lot of work—but it might fly, especially if he could get someone like Walt Kodaly to rewrite it."

"Jay Jay is the logical place, isn't it?" Still standing by the piano, Louise smiled encouragingly at her mother.

"I don't know," said Judy. "I just don't know." Restless, she began to pace the room, moving, like a prisoner doing an exercise stint, in and out of the sunlight that poured in from the large picture window.

Barry went over to the window and gazed out at the ocean, stretching luxuriously. He turned around.

"Let's surf!" he said, finally breaking the silence. "We really need it."

"Scott should be here any minute." Louise looked at her mother nervously, as though fearful that Judy-in-the-room would disappear as suddenly as Judy-on-the-screen had.

"You can come get us." Disposing of the matter, Judy nodded at Barry.

"Love it!" cried Barry. "Love that surf!"

With great whoops Judy and Barry ran off to put on their costumes—shiny black wetsuits, stiff carapaces that made them look like large beetles set loose to scurry through the house. From her post on the deck Louise watched them run down the steps and make their way gingerly through the sandy surface heat of the beach, carrying their small, trim fiberglass boards.

Energy. Restlessness. Tension seeking release. Louise had always seen her mother as a high compression engine in need of coolant—either reassurance or sheer physical movement. For years her father had tended that engine; so had she. Like a well-drilled team of mechanics they had stayed in the pit, in the background: alert to every sign of strain, ready to assist whenever special care was needed. The divorce had not been bitter; it had merely been a slight reallocation of responsibilities.

Louise waved vigorously to signal her continuing attention. Attention, encouragement, appreciation, approval; these seemed to be what she had to offer—and what she offered best. Like her mother, Scott was talented and brilliant. And like her mother, Scott needed tending. It was a need that had grown more and more apparent in the last few months as Scott's career prospered: a career that had gradually crept between them like a small, furry creature whose demands for stroking were insatiable. Originally kind and thoughtful, Scott seemed to have changed a great deal in the last few months.

She was still out on the deck when she heard three rings at the front door: sharp, peremptory, evenly spaced.

"It went very well," said Scott. Standing in the doorway, he tilted his white cowboy hat back and fluffed out his curly black beard. He was of moderate height, lean and wiry, with an olive complexion and snapping dark eyes.

"Wonderful!" said Louise. She gestured toward the large picture window. "They're down at the beach."

"This is very nice." Scott looked appraisingly around the room. "It's much larger than Heidi Kissinger's place in Montecito—just right for us, I'd say."

Louise nodded, forcing herself to smile at the implicit comparison between Heidi's small mansion and her own trailer, a mobile thirty-footer that had been perfectly acceptable to Scott in the spring. Heidi was an English major, one of the coterie that followed Scott around. Like Scott, Heidi was from the east coast. As well, she was pretty: dark-haired, bright-eyed, compact, and with the special assurance that comes from years of horseback riding in prosperous circumstances. In terms of the comparison, Heidi had been, and was, a front-running candidate for Scott's company and affection.

Scott was a promising assistant professor of English, popular with the students and already beginning to make a mark as a poet. His father was also in academic life: a professor of history at a small liberal arts college in Pennsylvania. So it had been natural for Scott to set his sights early and high: winning prizes and fellowships with rapacious skill as stepping stones in a career that pointed ever and ever more upward. Perhaps it was a need for Louise's encouragement and approval skills that led him to seek her out. Perhaps it was the similarity in their background: both growing up in the shadow of a brilliant, self-obsessed parent. In any event, Scott had taken the initiative and moved into her trailer, along with numerous books, records, papers, and visitors coming around at odd hours.

At first she had found the noise and talk attractive. She had joined in, tried her best to be witty and intellectual; she had endured the occasional slights from Scott's growing coterie of admirers. But in the last month the slights had begun to increase: directed at her—and her trailer.

"I know the trailer's getting crowded," said Louise. "But it's easier to take care of than a house—and it's mobile."

"Roots." Scott beamed at her and stroked his beard. "To put down roots is a way of dramatizing commitment."

"How about a garden?"

"Exactly!" Scott held up his right index finger to indicate that an important point had been made. "What we need is a house with plenty of land—fruit trees, perhaps."

"Maybe we'll be able to manage it someday."

"Why not now?" Scott gestured expansively. "Why shouldn't we start our life together in a way that meets our entertainment obligations properly?"

"Obligations?" Puzzled, Louise stared into his eager dark eyes, trying to find some justification there for hordes of hungry students and junior colleagues descending upon them. And she the one to cook and serve.

"That's what academic life is," said Scott. "Deans, chairmen, visiting scholars, visiting poets—a good table is essential to a good career."

"I hadn't thought about it from that point of view."

"It's worth thinking about—and worth talking over with your father, I'd say."

"Don't you think we might be getting in over our heads?"

"Not with the right kind of help." Scott looked at her steadily. "In the long run a house for us now will turn out to be a splendid investment."

"I don't know," said Louise. She tried to imagine herself presenting the idea to her father, justifying the expense in terms of its contribution to Scott's artistic and academic career. Like a jeweled shrine needed to house the Holy Grail. Her father was used to genuflecting before careers: her mother's, Rita's, and now Scott's. As was she, content with living in the shadow—in contrast to Scott, who had somehow been able to kindle his own flame.

They walked out to the deck and stood there watching, absorbed in the endless rhythm of the surfers down below them. Boards pushing slowly out. A point of poise, of calculation. A kneeling down as in prayer. Then bravely erect: balancing, twisting, tilted far off the plane of earthbound law. Swiftly slanting in, sometimes to collapse near the shore with fiber boards exploding skyward, sometimes to skid like sleds across the bordering wet sand. Above, the sun. Below, the kelp, the clam, the crab, the broken glass, the plastic cup, old bottles, tires, shreds of rubber gear. And on the surface, simply motion—motion free from all constraint. A halfway house for those who, though wingless, yearn to fly.

"Did you see the last one?" cried Judy as she and Barry bounded up the wooden stairs that led to the deck.

"Very impressive." Louise nodded enthusiastically. Then she introduced Scott and stepped back to allow matters to proceed.

"That's a great beard," said Judy.

"A fantastic beard." Barry rubbed his own smooth chin as though to assess its possibilities.

"I approve of this beach." Scott's gesture was capacious and dramatic, taking in beach, ocean, small craft, and countless black dots in between.

"Love it." Barry shook his sun-bleached thatch, drops of water spraying. "Love that beach."

"I'd love to change." There was a note of reproof in Judy's clear, bell-like voice, as though the conversation had deviated from its proper concerns. "Why don't you play the tape for him?" She darted down to the far end of the deck and into the house.

"Just push the blue button to run it back," said Barry, who paused to do a few deep knee bends before following Judy's wet trail.

Louise went back into the living room, settled Scott on the couch, fumbled with the video recorder for a while, and finally brought Judy-on-the-screen back to regesture and remouth her earlier performance. When the young lip-sync woman came on and began to sing once more through her long black hair, she turned the machine off.

"What do you think?" she said.

"Excellent—much better quality than the university machines." Scott looked thoughtfully around the room, taking in the piano, the paneling, the profusion of overstuffed furniture, the generous expanse of glass framing the sky and ocean outside. "We could be very happy in a place like this."

Judy and Barry came in, she in white cocktail pajamas, he in white jeans and a flowered Hawaiian shirt.

"What do you think?" asked Judy. She glowered at the giant screen.

"Charming!" Scott smiled easily, shaking his dark head in apparent wonderment. "And it strikes me that the interview form is very much like free verse: structured and open-ended at the same time."

"How about that?" Judy turned her pale green eyes coldly upon him.

"Scott has wonderful rapport with his audience when he gives a poetry reading," said Louise, trying to establish a friendly, common ground.

"In the temple of art we are all communicants." Scott smiled and rose as though called upon to recite, taking up a position near the doorway. "Listener, do you know I care?" he began in a slow, chanting voice. "What's your name? Are you surprised to know I care?"

There was a pause. Louise smiled over at her mother, who had begun to fidget noticeably now that Scott had seized the stage.

"I do care," continued Scott. He looked smugly around the room.

"Can you do this?" cried Judy. She jumped up and began to walk on her hands, her white cocktail pajamas sliding down to bulge at her knees like bedclothes rolled down for the night.

"Isn't she too much?" Barry beamed proudly at Louise, who was beginning to shrink back into the couch.

"Love is always a surprise," said Scott, shaken but still undaunted by the upended white pajamas billowing through the room in front of him.

"Do a flip!" Barry grinned broadly and clapped his hands.

"So is life itself." Losing its chant-like quality, Scott's voice had risen to a puzzled squeak as he stepped back to give Judy room: room for a run that started from the deckside window and closed with a blazing red-hair-over-white-bare-heel flurry of action.

"How about this one?" Now back on her feet, Judy rushed over to the piano and struck a long rolling arpeggio. "Here's my version of Hank Mancini's immortal 'Moon River': *My liver . . .* (plink, plink) / *Makes me feel so sad . . .* (plank) / *Because it's going bad, you see. . . .* (plank, plank, plink)."

"Dynamite!" Barry applauded vigorously. So did Louise, knowing it was called for. And so did Scott, who had come back to the safety of the couch.

"I think you may be right about that pilot," said Judy, breathing deeply, but with evident satisfaction.

"Pizza!" screamed Barry. "Let's have pizza. I'll phone out for lots and lots of health-food pizza."

"Sensational!" Good humor restored, Judy got up from the piano, came over to Barry, gave him a kiss, and turned to bathe the others in her approval. "After that we can watch movies and play cards."

There was a long pause. Scott looked at his watch, a Seiko Louise had given him. Louise looked at Scott. Judy looked fondly at Louise. Barry looked admiringly at Judy.

"It's late," said Scott.

"And it's a long drive up to Santa Barbara," said Louise, trying to impose the strongest sanction possible upon their departure.

"But I think it would be fun if we stayed." Scott smiled urbanely, stroked his beard again, and gave another look around the room, almost as though he were an ambassador bent on accommodating himself to the strange customs of some exotic heathens.

Louise smiled gratefully up at Scott; he benignly down at her. Better to stay, it seemed, than retreat. Better to put one's familiar artillery away in the face of superior firepower. Better to yield a proper deference to forces as wild and elemental as the sea itself. This was her mother's house. And she the queen of this small court. Thus it had been in Louise's childhood. Thus it would always be in a house where reassurance stuffed each crack and kept the winds outside to howl unheard their promises of age, failure, loneliness, ultimate neglect, and loss.

Barry quickly phoned for health-food pizza in large quantities, pizza that soon arrived piping hot, smeared with olives, cheeses, small meats, and creatures from the sea. Judy and Louise had made a generous salad in a large earthen crock.

They ate from paper plates, drank fine wine from Waterford crystal; watched the news, watched Judy do her imitation of the news; played canasta and watched a musical on cable TV; watched Judy do her imitations of Jimmy Durante, Barbara Walters, Harpo Marx, Marjorie Main (with pillows), Liberace (with a candlestick and wig), a golf ball soaring toward the cup, a lighthouse, bacon sizzling in the skillet, numerous repulsive children of uncertain age and sexual taste.

Nor did Scott disdain these gifts, he who had learned to wear intriguing hats while reading from his sheaf of poems.

"You need a new car," said Judy, who had come out to see them off—Scott in the MG, Louise in the pickup truck.

"It runs fine," said Louise. "And it has four-wheel drive."

Her mother was unimpressed.

"Tell your father you need a new car," she said. Then she went back inside.

"And a new house," smiled Scott. "A new house for his princess—and mine."

He kissed her goodbye forcefully, as though reasserting the basic color of their relationship after its brief eclipse. Then he set his white cowboy hat firmly on his head, hopped into the MG, and roared off into the evening.

Louise stood there looking sadly at her truck. It was a good vehicle for a geography major. And it was good for pulling the trailer. But it wasn't nearly as good as the Ferrari that Rita had gotten last year. A house might help to balance matters out. It was a balance she knew her father wanted to maintain.

"It's no fun trying to cut Christmas in half," he had awkwardly admitted to her after the divorce, a situation that she had accepted with good grace. But Barry and Rita had come along to cut even more deeply into her modest portion, leaving her stranded on a small plot with only Scott, eventually, for company.

A new house. A big step. Pliable herself, she recognized the quality in her father. A quality of finding more pleasure in pleasing than in being pleased. A handsome new house would please Scott; pleasing Scott would please her; pleasing her would please her father. So there was triple pleasure from a single action. More than enough to justify the expense.

Los Angeles, California: Tuesday, September 26, 11:00 A.M.

Green light. Jackie started up the Cadillac and moved into the intersection, totally oblivious to the large streak of red hurtling down upon him from the left. It was not until the red van, running the light, sounded its horn that Jackie was jolted into applying the brakes and coming to a full stop. He braced himself for the impact, for the crunch and the twisting of jagged metal, but the van swerved just enough to avoid him and raced on past.

It was all over in less than a second: the red van out of sight, traffic returning to its normal rhythm, Jackie starting up again and proceeding cautiously toward the freeway. All over. Except for a racing pulse. And a widening pool of anger at the pit of his stomach. Anger at the faceless driver of the red van. Anger at the other vehicles that clogged the streets. Anger at himself for failing to guard against the natural hazards of driving in metropolitan traffic.

The anger did not last long. Nor did it find expression, beyond a tightening of the jaw and a stronger clenching of his hands on the wheel. To Jackie, control of anger was as natural as music itself: a useful skill learned early, mastered well, giving shape to whatever formless urges lay beneath. A useful skill, a profitable, ingrained habit. Particularly when dealing with anger in others.

He had grown up with the anger of his father hovering over him. Martin Reilly Hayes had been a drinker. Not a steady, predictable, day-after-day drinker. But a drinker subject to periodic bouts with bottle and friends, bouts sometimes lasting only an evening, sometimes lasting as long as three or four days. Always unscheduled, always unpredictable. Except for an ominous, threatening absence from the dinner table.

On such occasions Jackie would lie awake in his room, long after the younger children had gone to sleep. Lying there he would wait for the sharp, echoing slam of the front door to signal his father's entrance and the onset of direct conflict: dark rumblings overcut with high, edged reproaches. Rumblings that would deepen in force and find support in scrapings of chairs, crashes of glassware, roars and blows, piercing screams. All of it a discordant mass of sound tugging him into action.

White-faced and trembling he would jump out of bed and come downstairs, always intent upon making peace, restoring quiet. Sometimes successful through soft, smiling words, he had, more often than not, learned to muffle his own outrage, accepting slaps, cuffs, large roars, and small sneers as natural elements of his childhood climate. Great, clouded storms always in the offing, even on the fairest day.

Unable to control the climate, he had logically chosen to control himself. Self-control, his Grandmother Hansen had called it, praising it as part of man's estate and pronouncing it with the emphasis on *self*—as though it were an integral item in the household vocabulary. Self-control. Control of anger, passion, tears, and grief. Control like a notched dial on the radio spun to mute each symphonic storm to softer, more manageable background hummings, hummings that could come out to roar and sob only when filtered through a coiled length of silvery pipe—a trumpet. Self-control. From the age of seven he had bundled up in it as though it had been a heavy wool overcoat. A notably useful, serviceable garment fitting like the skin itself.

Keeping alert and driving cautiously, Jackie continued on to the Griffith Park Zoo, where he had arranged to meet Walt Kodaly. A good meeting place. Out in the open, a reasonable concession to Walt's habit of coming there several times each week to sketch the animals—principally lions. On the surface an odd pastime for a retired television writer, but not for a retired writer who had started out as an apprentice clown with the Kale Brothers Circus.

Walt had already been with the circus four years when Jackie joined it in Beaumont, Texas, coming down from Kansas City with his trumpet at the age of sixteen to play marches and shouts with the Kale Brothers Symphonia. A good job, especially during the later part of the Depression. A man's job, with plenty left over each week to send home and plug the void left by his father's departure. And a challenging job: playing and transposing strange, crabbed parts brought from Europe by haughty acrobats and aerialists—like the Flying Glaubers. There Jackie had grown, filled out, learned about music, about liquor and women. Learned almost everything, as Walt put it, except good judgment.

Good judgment. It seemed to Jackie that Walt had been born with it. A sense of timing. A sense of how audiences would react to a piece of business. A vision of how a new act, fumblingly stitched together, would work in its final, polished form. So Walt's advice and potential help were well worth a trip to the zoo before making the heavy financial commitment necessary to produce the series pilot Judy had sent over.

As planned, Walt was waiting for him by the lion compound. He was a short, compact man—dark, almost saturnine, still graceful in his movements, and with high cheekbones like those of an American Indian strain somehow transported to the plains of Hungary in past millenia before a more recent transposition to Aliquippa, Pennsylvania. Sketchbook in hand, he was staring thoughtfully at the largest lion, who was comfortably disposed high up on a big flat rock.

"How's it coming along?" said Jackie.

"Not bad." Walt opened up the sketchbook to display several drawings, newly done. "Myra says I should try abstract painting, but I get a kick out of drawing what's there—or coming close, at least."

"I was thinking you could do with a little action." Jackie nodded at the lion dozing on the flat rock. "Just like our friend with the mane up there."

"He doesn't need it." Walt closed his sketchbook with an air of finality. "Neither do I."

"Judy's very excited about that script they sent her."

"Why shouldn't she be excited? It's the same formula as 'Judy's Guy,' except that she's married to a struggling hotel owner instead of a struggling bandleader."

"Nobody is claiming it's Shakespeare," said Jackie defensively. "But I think there's a good chance it will work, even take off—especially if you come into the picture with us."

"There's always a chance—it's just the odds that vary. And I have the feeling you could lose a bundle trying to get this show off the ground."

"Why?"

"I still keep track of what's going on." Walt started walking toward the polar bear grotto as though seeking new horizons. "It's a different ball game. The audiences are different. The industry is different. You've got cassettes, videodiscs, cable, and the rest of it. And the important people are all new now."

"New and young," said Jackie, thinking back to Bruce Poirier's party. Apart from a few elder statesmen, most of the executive and production people there were alien creatures: "baby moguls," as they were called, business types with degrees from Yale and Princeton in place of a background in burlesque, band booking, radio, and peddling.

"That's the way it should be." Walt nodded sagely, as though stating a sound tribal truth. "There's no point in hanging on until you fall on your face."

"Judy doesn't think so."

"Performers never do. They're always hungry for a bigger piece of the audience. And they don't care who gets cut up in the process."

"And you think I might get cut up doing this script?"

"Look at the facts," said Walt. "With 'Judy's Guy' we were all lucky. You and I ran into each other at the right time. You and Judy were used to working together in front of a live audience. You had Paul Ciardi to advise you about holding on to the rerun rights and a lot of things that turned out to be a lot more important than any of us thought at the time."

"But you have to admit that it was a great series—and a lot of fun, too." Still undaunted, Jackie smiled cheerfully at Walt.

"I don't deny 'Judy's Guy' was a good show—better than most."

"It still is," said Jackie firmly. "Just last week a fellow came up and started talking about buying complete rights for all of the shows."

"Who?"

Jackie paused for a moment, searching for the name of the man Bruce Poirier had introduced him to. A young man. Smooth, with a slight Southern drawl. Knowledgeable. But his name was blurred now. A minor lapse: like the small slips in spelling and arithmetic that had begun to creep upon him more and more, together with lapses in attention and alertness—like the encounter with the red van. Signals of minor importance taken individually, but bothersome in the aggregate. At times disturbing.

"Someone from down South," he said finally. "I didn't pursue it beyond telling him it was out of the question."

"Too bad that show is all tied up in trust." Walt sighed. "This might be a good time to sell it off."

"It's not that tied up." Feeling that his lapse had been covered well, Jackie looked at the polar bears: contradictory creatures with powerful bodies and small, oddly gentle heads. "I'm the sole trustee and I have the power to buy or sell assets until Louise is thirty-five."

"Why don't you do it?"

"It's a family thing—my name's on it along with Judy's, so I just feel better keeping it in the family, even though the royalties don't add up to that much."

"You're probably right," said Walt. "But you're wrong in wanting to take on a risky property like that pilot. I think you ought to cut loose and enjoy life a little more."

"I'm enjoying life." Jackie tried to smile convincingly.

"What happened to that fifth-wheel trailer and pickup truck you bought a couple of years ago?"

"Louise has them up in Santa Barbara—she's living in the trailer while she goes to school."

"Isn't it sort of big for her?"

"She's living in it with her fiancé." Jackie reddened a little. "But now they're talking about buying a house."

"Weren't you and Rita going to take off and tour the country in that trailer?"

"That was the original idea. She was saying she wanted to write."

"It was a great idea," said Walt firmly. "Still is. Traveling around seeing all those little towns we used to work with Kale Brothers. You're certainly at the age when you've earned the right to do some of the things you've always wanted to do—see Europe again, maybe even get a boat and sail around the world."

"If the trailer is such a great idea, why aren't you and Myra doing it?"

"We're thinking about it—we've even looked at a couple." Walt cocked his head and looked thoughtfully at Jackie. "You said Louise was talking about a house, didn't you?"

"A big new house." Jackie sighed. "Big—and expensive."

"Do you think she would be interested in unloading the trailcr?"

"I bet she would." Jackie brightened. "And I know she'd like to see you. Why don't you drive up to Santa Barbara and take a look at it?"

"Maybe I will."

"She's grown," Jackie smiled with pride.

"Everybody grows," said Walt darkly. "With the exception of those who stay on and on in the same rut."

"That's easy for you to say." Jackie frowned, sensitive to the implied criticism. "You and Myra started your family early, so you have only yourselves to worry about now. It's different with me—I've still got a lot of responsibilities."

"What responsibilities?" Walt looked him up and down as though taking stock of what was there. "Other than taking better care of yourself, what do *you* have to worry about?"

"I've got the company, and that means twenty employees who depend upon me to keep the store open—to say nothing of all the work we provide indirectly."

"They could get other jobs if you took off."

"There's my family in Kansas City—nieces and nephews who need my help in getting an education, my mother, my brother and sister. They've always depended on me to help when things went wrong."

"Maybe things would start going right if you eased yourself out."

"I have to stay in." Jackie stiffened. "Even if I could sell the company, there wouldn't be much left after I took care of the indebtedness. And remember, you've got a five percent share still riding on the books."

"Don't worry about my five percent," said Walt. "Worry about taking it easy. How long has it been since you and Rita had a vacation?"

"We went to Hawaii last year."

"Take another one. It might do you some good."

"I'll give it some thought." Jackie smiled and gave Walt's lean hand an affectionate squeeze. "As soon as I get everything running smoothly again."

"You don't have that much time, you know," said Walt. He walked a few steps toward the gate with Jackie and paused. "None of us do."

Time. Jackie pondered the matter as he drove back to his office. It seemed to him that each day, like his peripheral vision, was shrinking in size. A serious concern for a man who had once been able to carve four hours of practice time out of every morning before the Kale Brothers afternoon show.

Morning. Or evening. An hour's work on the trumpet might do a little good. But not this particular evening. He was scheduled to go somewhere with Rita. A dinner, perhaps. Or a play. Or a dinner *and* a play. He wasn't sure. But there seemed to be a feeling of urgency coloring each day, as though his world would fly apart into random fragments if he turned his thoughts away for the smallest instant.

A bleak feeling. A feeling to be controlled, lest it force him to drive too fast—and carelessly. "One must be brave and careful," Clara Glauber had once said, smiling down at him from the trapeze during one of the circus rehearsals back in the days when the two of them had been young together: she as one of the Flying Glaubers, he as one of the circus bandsmen.

Brave and careful. Good advice. Advice worth following—especially the second part.

Burbank, California: Wednesday, September 27, 1:30 P.M.

"Very attractive," said Rita. "But she has chubby legs."

"She's an on-the-button singer." Jackie shifted position and tried to focus his attention upon the rehearsal in progress on the stage below them.

It was a big stage. A large space for the band over at the right. A generous performance area in the middle. A long desk for the host at the left: a desk flanked by chairs in which the show's guests would sit and display themselves to the studio audience and to the squad of television cameras recording the proceedings for transmission to the hundreds of United Broadcasting Network stations that nightly carried "The Steve Warren Wind-Up Show."

A big stage. A big show. Important enough to insist on live performances from its guests. So rehearsals were essential. Even though the singer had been allowed to bring in her own conductor, along with a few key instrumentalists familiar with her music, the challenge was a substantial one. A challenge shaped by the pressure of time and by the unfamiliarity of the setting.

Jackie was beginning to wish he had not introduced Rita into the setting. Ever since breakfast she had been quite restless, clearly anxious about their upcoming conference with Bruce Poirier. Sensing her mood, Jackie had suggested that they come over to UBN early, say hello to whatever old friends were available, and wander around and get a feel for the place. A good idea. But they had ended up at the rehearsal, drawn there on impulse by the commanding sound of music. And the music had somehow made her more tense.

"I wouldn't be surprised if Bruce were in his office right now," said Rita.

"The appointment is for two o'clock." Jackie leaned forward slightly as though to catch the full force of the eight-man brass section, coming in as one to scream an ending to the singer's number: an ending like a large, extravagantly bushy tail whimsically tacked on to a small creature.

"It never hurts to be early." Rita frowned at the singer and the band, then let her features relax into their usual calm, remote symmetry. "And the music is terribly loud."

Jackie smiled understandingly at her, noting with dismay that his left hand was starting to clench. He tried to weigh the merits of the case, balancing his selfish wish to hear the band at work against his generous agreement to come over and talk to Bruce.

"Why don't you go on ahead?" he said finally. "I just want to stick around for a little and see if they play any real jazz." He reached over, patted her hand before she could draw it away.

"Don't be late." Rita stood up, briefcase in hand.

"You can leave the briefcase," said Jackie. "I'll bring it."

"No trouble." Rita stepped out into the aisle, then smiled down at him. "I want to go through some of the paperwork again."

Relieved, Jackie watched her stride down the aisle to the apron, where she picked her way past the cameras to the corridor. Nor did the briefcase hamper the flowing grace of her movement. As always she was a joy to watch.

He settled back to enjoy the singer's second number. She was a slim young woman with short, curly blond hair, vivid coloring, a large mouth. An air of meticulous intensity that reminded him of Lorrayne, his first wife. The same alertness. The same quiet persistence, almost schoolteacherish in its drive for accuracy.

Lorrayne had been good. Not a great singer, like Connie

Haines or Ella. But good enough to sight-sing a part and bend a melody into her own distinctive shape. And smart enough to pick tunes that didn't tax her modest range too much. He had met her at one of King Randolph's late-night sessions: informal battlegrounds for musicians brave enough to match themselves against King's habit of turning the simplest tune into a nightmare of pitfalls and potential embarrassment. Fast company. But Jackie's circus experience in transposing violin and flute parts had helped him keep up with King at the piano. And on a good night, which was when Lorrayne first saw him, he had come close to cutting Clint himself: much like a cocky challenger in a barroom brawl going up against an established knifefighter. Greatly impressed, Lorrayne had been quick to leave her escort and seek him out.

Lorrayne had always been ambitious. She had been the one to fuel his anger when Jeff Styles had hired Otis Marshak. When he had given Jeff his notice, she had brought Cy Harris in to encourage him to form his own band, tailoring arrangements, and style to fit her singing. With the band a success, she had been surprised to find herself in the background when the band was hired for Ben Butler's radio show. More fast company. A fast-paced show. A good show. Good experience: reading lines, developing a sense of character. "The funniest line in the world won't work if it's out of character," Ben always insisted. A good principle. He had learned it, followed it later on in putting "Judy's Guy" together. An interesting progression: from trumpet player to bandleader to radio character. A progression set in motion by Lorrayne's ambitions—for herself and for him.

Character. Consistency in temperament and action. Lorrayne had certainly stayed in character: letting the band break up when he was drafted, as opposed to what Dick Stabile's wife and some of the others had done. Later, when her solo career had begun to slip, she had broken up the marriage, divorcing him when he was still overseas in favor of a wealthy Florida hotel owner. Her choice. Her decision. And why not? She had always been good at making decisions—while he, never a composer, had seemed to do his best improvising on melodies originating elsewhere.

Jackie watched the blond singer wrap up her second number, holding out the last note and gradually softening it so that the illusion of sound lingered on well after the song's end.

Talent. How rare it was. Like the lead trumpet man on the Wind-Up Show. Perfect control, perfect consistency: dominating the entire band through force of personality. Not a great jazz player. But a great talent. And as Colonel Kale used to say, "Talent makes its own rules." Strong rules. Assertive, demanding rules. So that the talent, whatever it was, kept an identity of its own quite separate from that of the person who possessed it. Lorrayne's voice, his trumpet—somehow they always managed to crowd into bed each night with the two of them. Small wonder that Rita resented that part of him; to her it was a monstrous vegetable capable of growth given the least encouragement.

It was almost time for the conference. Jackie urged himself up and headed for Bruce's office. He walked into the waiting room, reassured to see Rita sitting there calm and businesslike in her quiet blue silk dress, briefcase beside her. Almost immediately Bruce Poirier opened the door and smiled them in. Once inside, the three of them sat down, making an informal triangular grouping: Bruce on a small black leather sofa, Jackie directly across from him in a tubular chair, Rita in a far corner equidistant from both.

"It's good news," said Bruce. He looked over at the telephone on his desk and sighed with apparent relief. "I've already talked to the people in New Orleans and they are very, very interested in getting involved."

"That's a great town," said Jackie. "I worked the Monteleone Hotel there a couple of times." Guardedly he nodded and smiled approval.

"It's much more prosperous now." Bruce laughed expansively; his eyes were sparkling with good humor. "Many of us feel it's developing into one of the more important financial centers of the country."

"Glad to hear it."

"Rita tells me you might be interested in raising a little development money." Bruce leaned forward and lowered his voice to a reverential tone appropriate for the discussion of such matters. "And I'd certainly like to help you get started in that direction."

"It's always nice to have more money to throw around," said Jackie. "But it's hard for me to understand why someone in New Orleans would want to get involved with a small operation like ours."

"Visibility." Bruce sat back, letting his white, perfectly aligned teeth gleam as though the reasons behind the proposition were self-evident. "Jay Jay may be small in the industry, but the name is one they see all the time on the 'Judy's Guy' reruns."

"That's nice to hear." Jackie smiled at Rita. "I wish the banks out here felt the same way."

"You can't blame them for being the way they are." Bruce was suddenly sober, sympathetic. "They have to pay for their money just like everybody else."

"And it's different in New Orleans?"

"In a way." Bruce nodded inclusively to the silent corner of their triangle. "As I told Rita, you'll have a much better chance if you explore some of the newer, less conventional sources of working capital. Believe me, it's there in the pipeline, waiting to flow your way."

"I don't want to sound negative," said Jackie, mild blue eyes narrowing a little. "But why don't these unconventional sources go ahead and put their money in conventional places—stocks, bonds, mortgages and bank accounts?"

"A good question." Bruce looked down at Rita as though calling her attention to Jackie's shrewdness. "It's one I raised myself. And the answer boils down to one word—*diversification.*"

"You mean a little here and a little there?"

"Exactly," said Bruce. "There's so much involved, principally from oil and agribusiness, that it makes more sense to spread it over as large a base as possible, particularly on a long-term approach—which is what your line of credit with them would be."

"If they're interested in the long run, why don't they just jump in and buy the whole company?" Jackie glanced at Rita, who shook her head.

"That's what some of the Europeans are doing, of course. But it makes more sense for an American outfit to lend to people who already are established—especially in the picture business."

Jackie paused, trying to slow down the tempo of the discussion. Bruce's answers had come quickly and smoothly, very much as though each question had been anticipated. Good lines. A good script. But somewhat obscure in its motivation. He began to wish that his attorney, Paul Ciardi, had come along to help out.

"Rita tells me this is a family connection of yours," he said finally.

"That's right."

"I can't help wondering why you're willing to go to all this trouble." Jackie smiled pleasantly to soften any possible sting in his words. "It's almost as though you were volunteering to co-sign the loan with us."

Bruce got up and went directly to his desk. There he picked up a blue-bound script from the top of a small stack. Then he turned around and held it aloft.

"Paper," he said. "This place is nothing but a paper factory. Scripts, outlines, proposals—that's what I process. Sometimes I send them over to the story department. Sometimes I evaluate them personally. But my job is to make sure they keep coming our way."

"If there's a shortage, why have you been turning our things down?"

"Those are consensus decisions," said Bruce. He shrugged. "But my primary responsibility is to make sure we have strong material to pick from—and lots of it."

"Rita spent a lot of time putting those things together." Now directly in the middle, Jackie turned toward her and smiled. "You can't blame us for getting a little discouraged."

"Time is one thing. Money is something else." Bruce put the blue-bound script down with an air of finality. "If you had a good line of credit opened up, that would be a very important factor."

"Couldn't you get the same results by opening the door for someone else? Why us?"

"To be frank, I feel a little obligated to you and to Rita. After all, I was the one who encouraged you to explore some of these ideas. Also I have a lot of confidence in you."

"I told you he was on our side," said Rita.

There in the middle, flanked by Rita on the far side and Bruce at his desk, Jackie felt as though a pair of interrogators was beginning to work on him. He smiled at Rita. He smiled at Bruce. He tried to think of another point to raise. Still, his mind was blank.

"It sounds fine," he said. "But I'm not sure we're really ready to expand our little operation. It's a big decision for us."

"I'm not asking for a decision." Bruce sat back on the edge of his desk, one long leg dangling easily. "Give it some thought, talk it over. After that, if you're interested, I can set up an appointment in New Orleans for you with the Bonnet people so that they can get a picture of what you've been doing and what you'd like to do."

"It's all in here," said Rita. She gestured toward the black briefcase, then rose. "I can spell it out for them in fifteen minutes."

"Rita's been involved in most of the newer projects." Jackie got up and smiled proudly. "If there's any selling to be done, she can do it."

"Then she's the logical one to make the trip," said Bruce. "Or both of you," he added hastily.

"We'll give it serious thought," said Jackie. He shook hands with Bruce to enforce the sincerity of his statement. "The way you describe it, it sounds like an unusual opportunity."

"It's a godsend," said Rita, her cool, remote face suddenly enthusiastic and animated as they moved toward the door.

Enthusiasm. Optimism. There was enough of it to float them out of the office and down to the parking lot. It was only when they got into the Ferrari that the glow subsided, leaving an awkward blank space to be filled.

"I thought it went very well," said Rita. Ignition key in hand, she had turned toward Jackie. It was clear that she expected something to be resolved before she started the engine.

"Very well."

"With a little more flexibility, we certainly won't have any trouble handling Louise's wedding."

"That's true." Jackie found himself beginning to tighten—partly because he sensed he was being pushed, partly because he had avoided telling Rita about Louise's plans for a new house.

"You don't sound very happy about it."

"I'm happy." Resolutely Jackie tried to count his blessings. Assuming it was legitimate, Bruce's offer would make it possible to help Louise, his brother, even Judy—if they could get a couple of good writers to work on her script. Logically it should all add up to a feeling of great relief.

"It's just what we've needed all along."

"We've been doing all right." Jackie felt himself tighten even more at her implication that matters had been going badly.

"Now it will be better." Smiling, Rita reached over and gave his hand an affectionate pat. "You'll see."

Ordinarily he would have responded to the promise in Rita's voice: a promise of no further conflict, no further tension. But he was still irritated by the neatness with which every question had been answered, every objection parried. Mild blue eyes avoiding hers, he set his jaw and stared out the window.

"I think I'll feel better if I talk this over with Paul Ciardi," he said finally.

"Suit yourself." Hand withdrawn, Rita started up the Ferrari and drove back to the office. In silence.

As she drove, Jackie tried to read the coldness in her. A coldness born of pain, perhaps. Pain at having her neatly packaged gift put aside. Or perhaps the coldness was born of disappointment. He knew that Rita loved the excitement of power and that she yearned for a more commanding stage than the modest platform offered by Jay Jay Productions. But he also knew she wanted to write—to create, as she liked to put it. For a moment he sketched out a picture of the two of them careening about the country pulling Louise's trailer. A pleasant picture, even as a fancy. Warmed by the thought, he reached over and patted her on the thigh.

"It'll all work out," he said.

"I hope so." Eyes still cold, Rita squealed the Ferrari into a left turn that jolted the truck coming against them to a sudden stop.

Pasadena, California:
Friday, September 29, 2:30 P.M.

Still warm. Still smoggy. Even in Pasadena, a flat, breezeless stretch of land edged with high black rock, like a large Dutch oven slammed down between the ocean and the desert. But with an illusion of coolness shaped by older houses, older office buildings: buildings that whispered of delicate ladies and refined gentlemen coming in to transact their business with poised, unhurried dignity. A good place for an attorney like Paul Ciardi to carry on the probate practice established by his father back in the twenties.

Jackie had met Paul in Germany during the war, when both were stationed in Weisbaden: Jackie organizing shows and playing occasionally for the huge, clotted mass of men waiting to be sent home, Paul handling administrative chores in the Special Services office. Their friendship had ripened after Jackie's coming to Los Angeles in the early fifties. When Jackie married Judy, Paul had been his best man; when the divorce took place, Paul had worked out the details of the trust established to make sure the income from reruns of the "Judy's Guy" show would ultimately go to Louise. A good friendship. An old friend. Like Walt. Like Cy. But tied a little more closely to present concerns.

It struck Jackie as very much in character for an old friend to be housed in a venerable setting like that of the Fidelity Trust Building. A dignified building. Permanent. Contrasting sharply with the offices at UBN, where the corridors were narrow and nameplates slid in and out. Here the corridors were broad enough for compact squads of lawyers to march abreast, heels clicking with purpose on marble floors. And the office doors were each like a deep breath taken before a long, uncluttered, cogent argument. Solid. Brass handled. With frosted glass and large black stenciled lettering. A sober place. A setting calling for Brooks Brothers suits and secretaries in long-sleeved blouses. Not a place for coming to the point straightway.

"One parade a year for the whole country," said Jackie. Standing on the small balcony of Paul's office, he gazed thoughtfully down at Colorado Boulevard. "Back in Missouri every little town used to have four or five a year, not even counting the circus."

Paul Ciardi, seated comfortably behind a black mahogany desk, put his fingertips together and pondered the matter. He was a chunky, fair-complexioned man, reassuring in manner—very much like a favorite uncle with puzzles and magic tricks hidden about his person.

"It's a maximum effort," he said finally. "Every New Year's Day the national capital moves from Washington to Pasadena, along with all the floats, bands, pretty girls, and horse platoons."

"They could use some elephants." Jackie squinted down Colorado Boulevard as though expecting the Kale Brothers parade of extravagance and virtuosity to come into sight.

Colonel Kale had always insisted on a good parade. And he had always ridden in front: florid, large-faced, waving his broad-brimmed white hat at the children and adults lining the main street of whatever small midwestern town they were in. Eau Claire, Beatrice, Wichita, Amarillo, Texarkana, Wausau, Council Bluffs, Mankato, New Ulm—hybrid names for a hybrid people, a people blended from many diverse strains. Germanic, Indian, Romance, Celtic, African. A people mirrored by the circus itself as it pulled together creatures and performers from all over the planet to be unified under one giant tent.

Putting up the tent was as grand a display as the parade. A display of total team effort directed toward making the circus come alive in a single moment. Just as he had led the parade,

Colonel Kale was always the architect of that moment—checking the position of the elephants at the far end, ready to pull the center pole up; making sure the work crews along each side were all in place. Like a sea captain bringing a huge vessel alongside a quay, Colonel Kale was always in charge: totally in command, totally responsible. And the moment was always a breathtaking one. A final look around. Murmurs falling off to complete silence. A sharp blast on the whistle. A large many-voiced groan during which the huge tent suddenly took shape: a cathedral urged up from a flat gray pancake. A grand display to watch; even grander to be a part of.

Jackie's part had called for him to pull a rope with one of the work crews. After three years at it, he pulled well: powerfully, sweatingly, stripped to the waist, glorying in the newly discovered strength of a nineteen-year-old young man whose chest and shoulders have filled out. Not as grand a display as the total effort. But a display worth watching, especially by a girl like Clara. An aerialist, one of the Flying Glaubers, Clara had at first been scornful of Jackie. Understandably so, given the immense gulf between featured acts and musicians in the circus hierarchy, coupled with the natural disdain of a European for provinces beyond the sea, reinforced by her father's expectation that she would in time marry Hans Kuhlmann, leader of the equestrian act. It was not until the circus played Mexico, Missouri, that Clara Glauber began to take notice of the young man playing the clear, high notes in the Kale Brothers Symphonia.

The notice was something Jackie deeply yearned for, yearned for with the faint emptiness inside of a young man who cannot stop thinking—day or night—of a marvelous, far-off vision. To Jackie, Clara was the most beautiful, accomplished creature imaginable: compact, golden-haired, gleaming fair skin hurtling bravely through the air. A winged goddess changing back into human shape only when a return to earth was called for.

But Clara was not a goddess. She was a young woman. A young woman who liked to laugh, sometimes to tease. A young woman who herself treasured dreams and bold imaginings, especially in the company of a strong young man much closer to her in age than her father—or Hans. By Springfield, Illinois, she and Jackie were good friends. By Mason City, Iowa, they were lovers. Suddenly distant in public. Careful to meet in safe, unlikely places.

Wausau, Wisconsin, was their last meeting. Summer heat.

Humid. Flashes of lightning in the distance ushering in a storm. The circus almost completely asleep in the early hours of morning. Except for the animals: especially the big cats, pacing their cages nervously in the animal tent. Except for Jackie and Clara, buried together in a heap of hay on the far side of the tiger cages. Hunger for each other slaked, they had talked in whispers, each edging the other toward dreams of good, good things: marriage, children, home and garden—all located on a fanciful island midway between Kansas City and Frankfurt, Germany. With the coming of the rain—quick, furious, then fading away—they had drifted off to sleep.

Water. A big bucketful. Right in Jackie's face. Along with the bright, angry glare of a bull's-eye lantern held by Colonel Kale. Beside him, Clara's father and Hans Kuhlmann, who was lashing out with a whip and drawing blood. The matter resolved by Colonel Kale: a resolution calling for Jackie's immediate departure for the Wausau railroad station, there to watch the drizzling rain and grieve over the loss of one's *liebchen:* the loss of Clara: blond, sweet smelling, sweet tempered, given to constant touchings and slight caresses, disappearing after the season into Germany.

Later on, in Germany after the war, Clara had sought him out, coming down the aisle to the stage after a concert, standing there quietly like a fair promise of joy recaptured and recapturable. Older, wiser, still brave and careful, she had managed to survive in a shattered land where a pack of American cigarettes could buy an heirloom brooch. But for both of them the promise had been blunted by the fact of marriage: he to Lorrayne, she to a tank commander lost somewhere in the eastern zone.

Asking nothing, giving much—Clara had smiled away his awkwardness, taken his hand, pressed it, wished him well, and walked away. Slowly. Slowly enough to be called back, had he been brave enough to raise his voice, wise enough to see his need for her. A frozen moment. One of many that seemed to be surfacing lately: like chips of ice broken off from a large chunk of time when much had been possible, little achieved.

Jackie sighed. It was clear that there was small chance of seeing Colonel Kale and his troupe march down Colorado Boulevard toward him. He left the balcony and came back into Paul's office.

"Getting restless?" said Paul.

"In a way." Jackie's eyes turned back toward the balcony. "I miss being on the road sometimes."

"You and Rita could do some traveling. Europe, perhaps." Paul eased his chunky frame back into his high leather chair. "One of my clients has a villa in Spain you could use as a home base."

"Rita might like Spain," said Jackie. "She's been talking about writing a novel. But she wouldn't like traveling around all the time."

"How does she like being vice president of Jay Jay Productions?"

"She likes it fine. But she feels we should be moving ahead faster."

"What's holding you back, then?"

"Financing." Jackie, oppressed by the weight of the word, sat down heavily on the sofa in front of Paul's desk. "What we really need is development capital."

"You're not thinking of invading the trust, are you?" Paul leaned forward, intent and cautious.

"Of course not. I've always kept that separate—run it through the bank and let them reinvest the income. Just the way you set it up."

"Good." Relieved, Paul eased back into his chair again.

"I was thinking more about getting a loan," said Jackie. "The way I did when we got 'Judy's Guy' off the ground."

"Things were different then." Paul sighed sympathetically. "Production costs were lower. Interest rates were a lot lower."

"There's a vice president at UBN who's offered to open some doors for us."

"Where?"

"Down South. New Orleans. It's a family connection."

"Do they have a name?"

Jackie paused, searched his mind with irritation for the name Bruce had mentioned. Rita, too. But it was blurred. Crowded out by memories of the circus, possibly.

"I don't remember," he said finally. "We covered a lot in that particular session."

"How much are they willing to loan you?"

"All we need. And well below the current interest rate."

"How do you feel about it?"

"I'm not sure," said Jackie. "Jay Jay isn't doing badly. But things seem to be getting tighter for us."

"Maybe you should cut back a little instead of talking about expanding."

Jackie shook his head. The conversation was beginning

to grow uncomfortable. Paul was raising the same questions he had asked himself earlier.

"I can't," he said. "I just have too many different tables working. So a loan seems the only way out for us."

"It's not a good way," said Paul. "You could end up more in debt than you are now. Do you think this is a good time to gamble?"

"It's a gamble for them, too."

"People who loan that kind of money never gamble. Haven't you ever wondered why the bankers are running everything now?"

"If they want to run Jay Jay, why don't they buy it?"

Paul put his fingertips together again. A thoughtful gesture. He gazed out the window as though a clearer picture might take shape there.

"I don't know," he said. "But I'm pretty sure you're going to end up with someone in New Orleans telling you what to do."

"Good advice is something I can always use." Jackie smiled, pleased that Paul's questions had lost a little of their force. "That's why I came over to see you."

"At this point I can give you only a general rule to go by," said Paul, his fair face serious and reflective. "It's not a good idea to rely exclusively on one customer, is it?"

"No."

"Along the same lines, I don't think you should tie yourself up with one lending source."

"Money's pretty tight in this town."

"Then try someplace else. You still know a lot of people in New York, don't you?"

"A few here and there."

"Before you get too strongly committed to these New Orleans people, I suggest you talk it over with people you actually know." Paul smiled, stretched for a minute. "If they can't help you out, maybe they can give you better reasons for not going ahead than I've been able to drum up on such short notice."

"You never used to be so cautious."

"I don't think I'm any wiser now," said Paul. "But I'm older. And so are you. Too old to take any more big gambles. Too old to stand any big disasters."

Jackie got up. The conversation had not turned out as well as he hoped. He had hoped for reassurance, enthusiasm: words from Paul to tilt his spirits more in Rita's direction. But he had gotten a specific suggestion, at least. An action to take. Possibly a fruitful one.

"I'll check with you after I get back from New York," he said.

"Don't forget to take an overcoat," said Paul, seeing him to the door. "I forgot mine last trip."

"So did I," said Jackie, oddly reassured by the knowledge that a well-trained legal mind could be foggy in small housekeeping details.

The Cadillac was on the second level of the parking complex in back of the Fidelity Trust Building. A low, dull-white structure. An implicit promise of more construction to come, and of demolition of venerable, marble-floored buildings. Jackie started his car and drove to the freeway, headed back to Studio City.

The morning freeway traffic was light, and the driving was pleasant. Jackie stayed in the slower lanes: relaxed, unpressed, idly mapping out what he would tell Rita when he got back to the office. Absorbed, he did not notice the first few hiccups of the Cadillac's motor: hiccups that modulated into gasps, gasps that commanded him to take the nearest exit in hopes of making it to a service station.

Just inside the exit the motor died completely. Jackie coasted on a few yards and came to a safe stop on the shoulder, a broad space of concrete slightly shaded by a block of oleanders set there to soften matters for the inhabitants below. A green, quiet place.

Forgetfulness again. Jackie did not need to look at the gas gauge. A couple of days before he had noticed it was low. But he had put off going to the service station. Now the penance was his to pay: a hot walk in the sun to the nearest phone, followed by a long wait for the auto club truck. He got out of the Cadillac, slammed the door shut in fury.

A green Ford pulled up in back of him. A black man got out. He was dressed in gray bib overalls. Suddenly wary, Jackie tensed. But the black man turned out to be a generous spirit, offering to phone the auto club so that Jackie would be able to stay with the car—and save some time. Jackie wrote down his customer number and gave it to the black man, then watched him drive off.

A couple of other cars, rounding the curve, stopped and the drivers looked at Jackie queryingly. Jackie waved them on, indicating that help was on the way. His anger began to diminish, and he walked over to the oleanders, standing there in the shade and smiling at the small kindnesses shown him.

After several other cars had gone by, a Dodge slowed down

to inspect the situation. Three young men were in the front seat. Jackie smiled and waved them on. But after a minute the three young men reappeared, this time on foot.

"We thought we'd come back and see if you needed anything," said the tallest of the three. In his horn-rimmed glasses and jeans, he seemed very much like one of Louise's fellow students up at Santa Barbara.

"Thanks," said Jackie. "But the auto club is on its way."

"We'd be glad to get some gas for you." The tall young man smiled and came closer.

"They'll be here soon." Jackie smiled back, nodding cheerfully at the tall young man and at the other two: a short, wiry man with close-cropped dark hair and a slightly older, long-faced man in a checked sportcoat. Clean-cut, he thought. There was always something pleasant and reassuring about clean-cut young men.

"Hot, isn't it?" said the tall young man. He looked down the exit and sighed. "I guess we'd better be getting back to our car."

Jackie was starting to reply when the blow came. A short, businesslike chop in the kidneys from behind. Followed by the pinioning of his arms, also done from behind. Still struggling, he watched the tall young man come up, reach inside his jacket, lift out his billfold, riffle through it, take out the money, and throw the billfold down on the pavement.

"How much?" came a voice from one of the two holding Jackie.

"Only twenty." The tall young man looked at Jackie's Cadillac in disgust. "You phony bastard!"

"Next time, old man, you'd better carry some real money," said another voice from behind. There were several more blows, angry ones targeted again toward the lower back and kidneys: blows that pitched Jackie forward on his knees, gasping for breath while the three young men hurried off to where their car was parked.

The whole transaction had not taken more than a minute and a half.

Jackie managed to get back on his feet, then into the car. Waiting for the auto club truck to come, he tried to think of what he might have done, how he might have fought back. A random attack. Unmotivated. Unplanned. A quick sortie against a target of opportunity. A vulnerable target: a vulnerable old man who should have been more cautious. An old man whose only muscle was his money.

He sat there taking short, quick gasps of breath as though his lungs and chest had conspired to block off larger quantities of air. Hands limp, he surrendered himself to the waves of pain washing over him: some dull and constant, others cresting in sudden, irregular surges. Voices speaking a language unintelligible and primitive, but insistent in their claims upon his attention. The body revolting against the dominion of mind, crying out and protesting, "Why did you bring us here to be abused? Why have you neglected us, let us grow flabby and short of breath when we have served you well? Why have you let us decay into a weak, vulnerable blob of useless matter?"

Weakness. Uselessness. The message was unmistakable. More painful than the pain itself in celebrating the vacuousness of his life. Too weak to defend himself. Too weak to keep his small company afloat. Too weak to help his daughter get started in her life. Too weak to help the mother, brother, and sister who had always been able to depend on him. Too weak to please a young wife growing sulky and restless. And too fearful to be anything other than cautious and prudent. A weak, useless, fearful, gasping creature turned in upon itself, barely conscious of the traffic hurtling past him.

"I'm surprised they didn't cut you with a knife or something," said the auto club driver. He was a wiry young man, quick in his movements as he poured a couple of gallons into the tank and got the Cadillac started.

"Does this happen often?"

"All the time." The young man shrugged. "If you leave your car, they strip it in two minutes—if you stay with it, they rob you."

"They sure knew what they were doing." Jackie shook his head ruefully and managed a wan smile.

"You were lucky," said the young man as he got back into his truck.

"I guess I could be worse off." Moving gingerly, Jackie slid into the driver's seat and positioned himself.

The feel of the car responding to his guidance restored his spirits a little, bringing them up from total despair to a level that permitted him to think seriously about risking a trip to New York.

October

New York City: Wednesday, October 11, 1:45 P.M.

To a walker's eye, most of the buildings in downtown Manhattan are the same height: slabs of granite that wall off the pavement and channel traffic along as though in obedience to the laws of hydraulic pressure. The spires, the crenelations—these are visible from the air. But not to a passer-by swept down Fifth Avenue by a stream of movement setting a rapid pace. A pace that blurs the awareness of where one building leaves off and another begins.

Except for Rockefeller Center. A structure set back somewhat from the street. Almost as though the old man himself, suddenly extravagant, had decided to scatter a few extra square yards of concrete among the citizenry as a way of letting portions of the traffic spill off and pause for a moment. No benches, though. Merely a place for stopping on one's way to one's proper business destination. A place for inconsequential talk. And street musicians modestly positioned against an imposing wall.

"Why don't you stay over for a few days?" Cy Harris waved his newly lit cigar toward the street musicians as though commanding them to play. "It wouldn't hurt you to knock on a few more doors."

"Nobody's buying," said Jackie. "They're all nervous about where the industry is going." He stared at the street musicians, wondering what they would sound like when they started to play. There were three of them: banjo, tuba, and tenor saxophone. Young men. Well dressed. The saxophonist in a heavy white crew-neck sweater. His case open in front of them as a receptacle for whatever coins and bills might be forthcoming. Live music, mendicant but sound of wind and limb. Somewhat shaming in its overt confession of uselessness.

"It wouldn't hurt you to unwind a little." Half a head taller, Cy looked down at Jackie and nodded as though the matter had been settled. "We could go hear some music, talk over old times. Cut up a few touches here and there."

"I'll unwind in Acapulco." Jackie smiled easily, tried to keep from stiffening at Cy's calm, agentlike prescription of where he should go and what he should do. "Rita and I are taking some time off next week."

"We could run up to Boston."

"What's in Boston?"

"Otis is fronting a local group in one of the jazz clubs there."

"I thought he was keeping busy in Europe."

"With Clint gone, Otis has a lot of things opening up for him here." Cy took a long, expansive puff on his cigar, then focused his attention upon the musicians across from them.

Just like shooting pool, Jackie thought. One good stroke and the balls break into a playable pattern, each in the right place for its position in the sequence. Clint's death, Clint's bookings unfilled, Otis's availability, Otis's commitment to another agent, the implicit threat of Jackie's appearing in the audience with Cy as an alternative to Otis—the sequence was a clear click, click, click of colored balls heading for the right pockets. All done with intuitive skill, laconically: not like the yards and yards of business-school chatter that Bruce Poirier and other baby moguls were in the habit of unreeling. Perhaps it was a difference in climate: the West Coast sunshine breeding loquaciousness, the East Coast chill commanding people to save their breath. Or perhaps it was because Cy was used to dealing with musicians and their use of language as a pointer toward matters inexpressible, so that a few words spoke volumes in a shared context. A good context. Wary, but basically friendly.

"It would be interesting to hear what Otis is doing now," said Jackie. "But I promised Rita I'd get back as soon as I could."

"That was a good promise," said Cy. "A good promise should always have a built-in escape hatch." He looked down at Jackie from the commanding position of a three-inch edge in height, then moved closer in to press his case. "There's still some money in Boston—bankers, old friends. We could run up tomorrow and wing it for a couple of days."

"My winging-it days are over."

"They're never over." Cy stepped back and gestured toward a young woman coming down the steps. "This town is full of good stuff, all of them dying for a little excitement."

Jackie looked at the young woman. Blond shoulder-length hair. Compact rather than lean. A full figure, almost old-fashioned in its swellings and curves: contours that announced their identity under the discreet coverance of a white jacket and blue skirt. Pink, fair, smooth, rounded: no sharp edges, one could be sure. Not like Rita. Or Judy. Or Lorrayne. Much more like Clara than the others were. He watched the young blond woman walk toward them and then slant her course away to join the sidewalk traffic. For a moment he considered following her: tracking her through the crowd to an office, perhaps, or a coffee shop. Some place where contact could be established, pleasantries exchanged. A brief moment. A brief thought. But enough to make his loins quicken and tingle.

"Young girls need young fellas." Jackie gave a short laugh, then shook his head as though to scold himself for considering Cy's suggestion. "I've got enough complications in my life as it is."

"What's complicated?" Cy gazed toward the three musicians, who were beginning to warm up their instruments in preparation for an organized assault upon the autumn air. "We hustle up to Boston, take a couple of nice ladies to a nice place for dinner, and then we all go hear what kind of story Otis is putting down these days. It's the simplest thing in the world."

"Not for me."

"That's what friends are for." Cy snapped his fingers to indicate that the matter was clearly resolved. "A friend is someone who's able to simplify your complicated life for you."

"One of the reasons my life is so complicated is that other people have been simplifying it year after year on their terms." Jackie's mild blue eyes hardened at the thought, and he looked bleakly at the tuba player, who had been running scales softly.

"I started out when I was twelve years old playing an instrument—a cheap second-hand Holton cornet. And I thought that old piece of junk was the greatest thing in the world."

"Maybe we can find another one for you up in Boston." Cy smiled cheerfully, almost as though Jackie's sulky passion was an encouraging sign.

"It wasn't the horn," said Jackie. "It was what I could do with it. I blew into it; something came out. I pushed a valve down; something happened. I could put something of myself into it—my frustration . . . my anger, maybe. Whatever it was, it was something I could control. That's what an instrument is—something *you* control, something *you* do something with."

"Do you think these guys feel that way?" Cy looked speculatively at the trio.

"I hope so. It's a lot better to play an instrument than be one."

"You're not an instrument. You're an important person—the kind of person thousands of lovely and interesting ladies are dying to meet, especially in Boston."

"Will you lay off the Boston for a minute?" Oddly satisfied, Jackie felt a tide of rage swell up: a series of waves, some close in, some taking shape further out. "There's no reason why you have to work on me the way everybody else does, just as though I'm nothing more than a thing with keys to press—the money key, the approval key, the status key, the power key. Just like I'm a computer. Or a piano." He paused and looked sadly upward for an instant. "Going out of tune, too."

"That's what I've been trying to tell you," said Cy. "There's many a good tune played on an old violin." He caught Jackie's arm and focused their attention upon two women coming in from Fifth Avenue. "Isn't this a great town? Maybe we'd be better off staying here and catching one of the new shows."

Jackie looked at the two women. Like Rita, they were both dark, both thirtyish, both very elegantly turned out: jeweled, coiffured, vividly colored in costume. Hothouse flowers. A far cry from the young blond woman. Or Clara.

"I'm tired of being played on," he said. "Rita's been pressing buttons to make me borrow money and expand the business. Judy's been pressing buttons to make me put something together for her. Louise has been pressing buttons to make me set her up in an expensive new house. And now you're working on me to stay over and do some running around."

Unruffled, Cy watched the two women pass before them and go up the steps.

"You're a great guy, Jackie," he said. "And a great talent. But you need a little pushing every now and then."

"I'd rather do my own pushing," said Jackie in a low voice, very much like that of a small child who persists in stating a hopeless case to a giant all-knowing parent. Even though the street musicians were a little out of tune, it was good to hear their playing wash away the need for conversation.

The three were far from incompetent players. The saxophonist had invested his statement of the melody with a good rhythmic bite, while the tuba and banjo held up their end with reasonable skill. But they were obviously uncomfortable playing outside, spiritlessly weaving their way through "That's A-Plenty" as though the size and grandeur of their surroundings had crushed them even more than the obliviousness of the people passing by.

Cy and Jackie listened without talking until the tune ended. Then Cy went up and dropped a couple of bills into the open tenor saxophone case. After talking to the musicians for a moment, he came back, snapping his fingers to their slightly more enthusiastic version of "Strutting with Some Barbecue."

"They're not the greatest," he said. "But anything's better than amplifiers on the sidewalk."

Jackie nodded. On their way down Fifth Avenue they had encountered three of them: self-contained, battery-powered rigs that supported the efforts of a singing zitherist and two singing guitarists, each of whom filled the air with a compelling volume of sound.

"Everything's electronic now." He looked sadly at the trio: a small, impotent substitute for all the magnificent bands he had played with over the years. "Not too long ago those guys might have been working steady, or at least hanging around Charley's bar hoping to pick up a casual."

"That's right," said Cy. "It's all electronic—amplifiers, stereo, video, cassettes. And you're sitting right in the middle of it because you were pushed at the right time by the right people."

"Like you?"

"Like me, like Lorrayne, like Judy." Cy raised his voice a little to compete with the music. "If it hadn't been for Lorrayne pushing you, you would have stayed on with Jeff until you were too old to make a move on your own. Instead, you were able to step out, put a band together, and make a name for yourself before you were even twenty-one years old."

"Lorrayne always looked out for number one." Jackie

looked out toward the Fifth Avenue as though Lorrayne might be heading toward them: dark, slender, sharp-edged, ready to make her case forcefully and without compromise. She had made her case and gotten her divorce, logically enough, in his absence, when he was still in Weisbaden: after he had met Clara and some of her family by chance at a concert, after he had put Clara on the train for Düsseldorf to search for her husband, after a wrenching battle between his duty toward Lorrayne and his yearning for Clara. Duty had won, as had Lorrayne, whose sense of timing had always been good. Good for her, bad for him.

"Everybody looks out for number one," said Cy firmly. "And that's why you should be grateful to the people who push you down the right road, even though they may be looking out for themselves at the same time. I don't deny I've made my ten percent from you. But I don't think you should deny the good things that came your way—even when you were dragging your feet."

"I've never been a foot dragger." Raising his voice to match the music, Jackie began to flush. "I started working when I was sixteen, and I've never stopped."

"There's a difference between working hard and working smart. And that's where the advice and pushing come in. If it hadn't been for me and Lorrayne, you wouldn't have auditioned for the Ben Butler show, isn't that right?"

"Who's to say whether that was a good move or not?"

"It was a good move and you know it." Sure of his ground, Cy softened his voice. "From trumpet player to bandleader to radio personality—more than enough to set you up when you came back from the Army."

"It wasn't enough to keep a big band going."

"It was enough to keep you working with a small group when everybody else was going broke."

"That was a good group," said Jackie. "There are times when six pieces can swing a lot more than sixteen."

"Good or not, it wouldn't have lasted very long if it hadn't been for Judy. And she was the one who did the pushing for the sketches and the rest of it. Am I right or wrong?"

"You're close." Discomfited, Jackie concentrated on the music for a moment, mentally charting the part he might play and wondering how long it would be before Cy hammered him with the obvious conclusion: that Lorrayne and Judy, driven by intuitive wisdom, had joined forces to prevent his ending up as a middle-aged street musician pitied by few, ignored by many.

It was true that Judy had done the pushing. Not in so

many words, perhaps. But just as effectively, through a constant discontent made manifest by tears, dark moods, sleeplessness, and despair. "Your breathing," she would hiss late at night, giving him a sudden shove. "It's keeping me awake." A problem to be solved—by comfortable words, by soft tales and stories of hard times in Kansas City, wry times on the road, until sleep crept in to nudge shut those pale green eyes and blot out their frightened vision of danger, dread, catastrophe, and loss. Her discontent, his duty. A perfect match. Sulfur and wood, flame and fuel. Enough for a good-sized blaze.

The blaze had begun as a small flicker. He had met Judy during the last years of his postwar big band. During their run at the Palladium in Hollywood, he and his band had been tapped for an off-night booking in Santa Barbara. A command performance it had been, since Mabel Kerr was a powerful person by both birth and marriage: daughter of one potentate, widow of another. Cy had insisted he take the date, even though it meant driving up in the late afternoon immediately after a business session. So he had gone, sending the band ahead in the road bus.

The job had gone well. A giant striped tent set up as a dance pavilion on the velvet green lawn to the right of the swimming pool outside the main house: a granite castle flanked by outbuildings and guest houses. Plenty of people—great and near-great and would-be-great, all cheerfully assenting to the logic of a compulsory hundred-mile drive from Los Angeles up the coast. Courtiers come to wait upon the queen, seek preferment at her hand. A large hand: pudgy, bejeweled, imperiously waving directions to her orchestra to "keep that goddamn music peppy."

They had kept the music peppy: danced the crowd, entertained them, danced them again, and yet again, until the people began to melt away in the summer darkness, some staying over in the guest accommodations, some staying at the Santa Barbara Biltmore Hotel. All of them paired off, all disposed of. Except one: a taut red-haired girl of about twenty-five with pale green eyes weeping bitterly among the statuary. Odd girl out in the conventional maze of recouplings and repairings called for by summer evenings, good food, fine wine, and peppy music.

Judy's tears had demanded comfort; comfort had led to companionableness, lovemaking, marriage; marriage had led to joint concern with her faltering career as an actress: too pretty for a comic soubrette, not pretty enough for a sultry ingenue. Concern had led to traveling with the band, singing novelty songs and doing short skits. The skits had led to a modest venture with a filmed half-hour comedy show: a show following some of Ben Butler's principles—never a line out of character, always a consistent level of quality. And the show had led to busy, productive years: busy enough to shove the discontent into a manageable corner, almost like a small caged beast hibernating for several seasons. Talent. Judy's. Lorrayne's. His own, perhaps. A beast that bites when the performance is over and the applause begins to taper off. Not the kind of pet one wants to keep around the house. As his own mother might well have sensed.

Jackie looked at the three musicians, speculated on the degree to which their thin sound managed to blot out, even for a few moments, whatever pain had walked in with them. Then he looked up at Cy, who had started out as a drummer before he shifted to straight *tummeling.*

"I suppose we all need a little pushing now and then," he said.

"Not me," said Cy. He lit another cigar, inhaled deeply. "I've always worked better for carrots than sticks." He paused, reveled in his cigar briefly before licking away at the implications of his image. "You can stand only so many sticks, but you can never get enough carrots. Good food, good liquor, girls, people who know your name and want a favor—as long as my digestion holds up I'll keep hanging in there."

"Do you ever handle novelists?"

"Not directly. But I can open doors."

"Rita's been talking about writing a novel," Jackie said. "She's good with words."

"It takes more than words," said Cy. "It takes time. And from what you tell me, she's all tied up with the company."

"If I could sell the company, she'd have plenty of time. But I'm not sure what she really wants to do."

"She's probably not sure herself." Cy nodded sagely. "Maybe she needs a little push, a nice surprise dumped in her lap. If you were lucky enough to unload Jay Jay, I bet she'd dig in and write a winner I could do something with."

"Even though you're not a book man?"

"It's all peddling." Cy shrugged, then smiled broadly. "And that's why I love to stay on it. Up here I hold the keys to glory. Down in Florida I'd be just another old dude with a few bucks telling everybody how important he used to be." He gave Jackie's arm an avuncular pat. "Besides, I get a lot of kicks representing talented people."

"Like Otis?"

"I was thinking along those lines." Cy's dark eyes lit up behind his glasses.

"Isn't he all tied up?"

"Arrangements can be changed." Cy grinned. "Now that Clint's gone I could keep Otis busy for the next ten years in this country alone, which is more than that English guy can do for him."

Jackie's brow furrowed as he gave the matter thought. It was good to have something to focus upon, good to have the conversation shift away from painful territory. He had spent most of his life listening to why-don't-we's and why-don't-you's; so he had acquired the knack as a natural habit of response.

"Why don't you talk to the agent first?" he said. "Maybe you can work something out where everybody's happy."

"I've never had much luck with those English people," said Cy. "They're all so smooth you never know where they're coming from."

"If it doesn't work, you can make a pitch to Otis later on, can't you?"

"I've always been more comfortable talking face to face."

"If Otis is here, I bet his agent is, too."

"I suppose so." Cy shifted position, turned his attention to the musicians again.

"Why don't you make a couple of calls and find out what's happening?"

"I'll think about it." Cy stiffened, then relaxed. "You don't have to push me, you know."

"That's what friends are for," said Jackie easily.

Cy laughed, looked at his watch. Unruffled by the small reversal, he headed toward the musicians, Jackie following.

"Not bad," he said to the saxophonist, then crumpled up a bill and pressed it into the young man's hand.

"Stay with it," said Jackie, pausing to sort through his billfold and coming up with a twenty.

"You're Jackie Hayes, aren't you?" asked the tuba player.

"That's right."

"My mother watches your 'Word-Right' show all the time."

"That's good to hear." Jackie paused awkwardly, pleased but oddly irritated by the disappearance of his music from the consciousness of young musicians. Jeff Styles, his own band, even the "Judy's Guy" show—they had all surfaced, ridden the wave for a while, only to sink down to the bottom again: there to wait for dredging up by lovers of the quaint and curious—like Herr Zweifel.

"I guess Boston's out, then," said Cy as they turned to head for Fifth Avenue.

"I think I'd better get back to my own action."

"Too bad you're not playing any more." Cy shook his head. "I could sure keep you working."

"It would take me six months at least to get into any kind of shape at all," said Jackie. "That's what I told the Montreux fellow when he stopped by to make his pitch."

"What Montreux fellow?" Cy stopped, suddenly attentive. "What pitch?"

"Some Austrian named Zweifel wants Vito and me to put something together for their festival next summer."

"That would be great."

"It sure would." Jackie considered the prospect: the practice, the solitary combat with self, followed by performance. Old friends. Old men, almost. Though still capable of lively, compelling sounds. "But I can't leave the store."

"That's too bad." Cy shook his head as though confirming the truth of a profoundly melancholy proposition. "It would be like old times to hear you lay down a story again."

Cy headed back to the agency, Jackie to his hotel. He was in no hurry and walked slowly, taking in the noise and bustle of traffic.

"And where would you be going all by yourself?" It was a woman: neat, almost matronly, dressed in a tweed jacket and skirt, standing in a doorway from which she could single out and address a likely prospect.

"Home," said Jackie. "I'm on my way home."

He quickened his step: blushing at being singled out as a mark, irritated with himself for not coming up with a better answer.

The quickness in his step gave purpose to his thoughts. Cy was probably right about Rita; she needed a push, a nudging by chance or affection. Even though he knew there was little chance of selling Jay Jay, the idea itself gave him pleasure. It was as though he had suddenly seen a perfect gift in a store window. An expensive gift: too expensive, too far away, for immediate purchase. But a gift to think about for later on when circumstances might be more favorable, fortune more benign.

Acapulco, Mexico: Saturday, October 21, 3:00 P.M.

Rita took several deep breaths before walking over to the server's position. Long, measured draughts of air that filled the lungs and stretched the elements inside: nerves, muscles, capillaries, and connecting tissue. A long pull, a quick release. A primary source of leverage, according to Miss Claudine, who constantly asserted the reverberative linkings between will, body, and mind. Calming, slow, methodical: like a wise general marshaling forces into position from which to launch the next attack.

Tennis lessons were not always battles for her. The pro back at the Sherman Oaks club had been skillful in avoiding them. But he was an older man: reassuringly paunchy, shrewd in his reading of the trade. A former tournament player, he was able to stand almost motionless in center court and control the course of play: keeping up a line of cheerful encouraging chatter and letting an attendant chase the shots and points outside his circle of movement.

The Encantada Hotel pro was a younger man: blond, flat-stomached, intense in manner and approach. Still an active competitive player. And with a residual sulkiness at being required to strike a posture midway between dominance and acquiescence. Not an easy balance to strike, especially with clients who are used to the symbols of power and to its reality—winning. So the lesson had quickly moved from a parade of strokes and suggestions to the higher ground of actual battle.

A good battle. For Rita, tennis was a perfect aggressive art: almost martial in its weaponry, like archery or pistol shooting. And with the added virtue of presenting a moving target who was equally armed and able to fire away in return. The hotel pro was skillful. But Rita knew she was giving him a good game: hard, darting, gleefully forceful, sometimes taunting and exultant over a powerful, well-placed shot that stretched him close to the limit. As he was beginning to do to her. Hence her deep breathing. Hence her need to mobilize forces and concentrate her will.

Rita had never played tennis as a girl. Back in Mississippi the game had been reserved for young ladies of good family. If the family was good enough and rich enough, the young ladies were whisked off to private schools in the east, there to learn requisite leisure skills and to replace regional drawls with a uniform, crisp, articulated speech that bounced off the front teeth with a buzz capable of cutting through any discussion. If the family was not sufficiently rich, the young ladies stayed home and attended local schools, learning their tennis at the local country club.

Rita's family had been neither good nor rich. It was too large—indecently so, she felt. Two older brothers, two older sisters, two younger brothers, and a younger sister; and she in the middle, available for teasing and household chores. It was a visible family—partly because of its size, partly because of Billy Ingleton's job as bartender at the Benevolent and Protective Order of the Elks. Everyone knew Billy Ingleton: tall, raw-boned, handy with his fists, ready to take the dogs out hunting, in and out of season. And everyone located the children with reference to Billy as a visible marker, so that Rita was consistently known as "one of Billy's younger girls." From the time they reread the American Legion essays as a basis for taking the prize away from her and giving it to Lawyer Tipton's daughter, Rita had seen her family for what it was: a lumpy, soggy bowl of mush submerging her in one indistinguishable mass of common fecklessness. And her greatest fear was of sinking back into that bowl, surrounded once more by high, smooth surfaces impossible to ascend—except by will, body, and mind all working together. As in tennis, a game that she had learned after coming to California.

Forces mobilized, she arched into her serve, straining to realize the maximum profit from her height. The serve pocked across the net to her opponent, who dutifully and professionally returned the ball in a manner that permitted her to make another well-placed solid stroke. But the next return was not as opportunely positioned. Nor was the one that followed it, as her opponent began to bear down upon her: no longer pliable, no longer deferential, hammering her down in the smilingly brutal way natural to all men, in the same way Lowell Wilkerson had done in her dressing room after she had won the Beautiful Daughter of Dixie contest. There had been no point in screaming. Not with the other contestants snickering nearby: half afraid of his wrath and good-family power, half glad to see her humiliated for leading him on and then turning her back when the crown was hers. A humiliation to be struggled against in silence, endured in silence. And recalled in silence as a reminder not to tease, not to be imprudent.

As the pro's hammering continued, Rita kept her calm, remote poise, even when running from one side of the court to the other. She even managed to smile as the score tipped past the balance she was accustomed to from her paunchy Sherman Oaks teacher. One way of surviving a battle, she had learned, was to deny its existence—a denial possible only if the smile continued to appear and reappear like a friendly spirit summoned from within.

She was still smiling when she drove her last shot into the net. Not a teasing smile, but enough to bring the young blond hammerer to her: enough to remind him as he came closer that she knew the degree to which she had forced him to grunt and clench his teeth. Close enough to touch. Deliciously so, since physical contact, even by accident, could come only from her. Close enough for her to imagine the two of them in congress: an intertwining chiaroscuro of combative flesh driven by opposing polarities—fair for dark, dark for fair.

An exciting picture. A picture she could see taking shape in the eager hazel eyes of the man looking at her. A picture to be scrubbed away with gentle firmness. "Look, admire, sniff the scent of power and desirability that hangs in the heavy humid air between us," her calm, remote, small features announced as a matter of course. "But plans have been made, a direction charted; and I ride out a wind of my own choosing until I choose to choose otherwise."

The tennis courts and pro shop were only about a hundred yards from their bungalow. But Rita elected to take the long way around, passing by the racquetball courts on her way to the lobby where she would check with the main desk for mail. She walked slowly, almost as though giving each passer-by a generous opportunity to recognize her and call her by name.

No one did. The Encantada was a new hotel, too new to have a secure position in the habits of people whose affection for Acapulco centered upon the town itself and upon the older inns and restaurants there. In time the Encantada would command their affection and their custom as a complete resort in itself: a towering Aztec pyramid fifteen miles south of town with its own beach, its own golf course, its own restaurants, and even its own small suburb of town houses and apartments. But at present the hotel drew largely from the east coast and south: competing with Florida as a locale for official conventicles of doctors, dentists, sales organizations, and accountants. Pleasant people. Gregarious. Well-to-do. But not involved with either entertainers or their industry.

It was reassuring to have the desk clerk call her by name, even though the two letters were addressed to Jackie. And it was exhilarating to stand in the lobby and let her eyes travel upward, following the four walls that slanted gently toward one another and met in a point far, far above. A cathedral built by architects with a pagan cast of mind. A place for flowered dresses and soft voices.

"Excuse me," said one of the voices. "But if you're from Hattiesburg, Mississippi, then I think we know each other."

Rita turned around to identify the source of the soft voice, its drawl immediately familiar to her. It came from a young woman of about her own age. A young woman in a flowered dress. And with a voice pitched just this side of a ladylike giggle. To her dismay it was a voice that Rita recognized immediately.

"It's Cora Sue Faust, isn't it?" asked Rita. As she spoke, she took complete inventory of Cora Sue: the short, naturally blonde hair, the delicate features, the clear skin and light blue eyes. The inevitable choice for class secretary and head cheerleader.

"It certainly is," tinkled Cora Sue. "Big as life, if you want to call five-foot-two big." Light blue eyes dancing, she giggled again. "Except that it's Cora Sue Faust Calhoun now. Come on over and say hello to Jerry."

Just as she had used to follow the head drum majorette, Rita matched her step to Cora Sue's in making the short parade across the lobby to one of the conversation groupings by the main entrance. On his feet, Jerry Calhoun was taller than Cora Sue. But not much. It was as though the two of them had been pressed together into a scrapbook immediately after the senior cotillion. A scrapbook that Rita had tried to throw away—with success, she had thought.

"I told you it was one of the Ingleton girls." Cora Sue smiled with triumph as they came up.

"I guess I've always had trouble recognizing folks when they don't have all their clothes on." Jerry chuckled roguishly and shook his oval-shaped head. Like Cora Sue, he was fair, with yellowish straw-colored hair that capped his oval face with a round thatch. Broad-shouldered, he was, even for a football player. But big-bellied now. Ovoid all over.

"It's good to see you," said Rita, firmly resolved not to give her name unless asked. "I've been out of touch for quite a while now."

"Everything's still in place," said Cora Sue. "Just a few more children here and there." She gave another giggle. "Including ours."

"Hellions," chorused Jerry. "So when Cora Sue insisted I bring her to the Tri-State Dental Convention, I just had to fill a few more cavities and make it a celebration."

"Jerry's daddy is still in practice, but he's turning more and more of it over to Jerry." Cora Sue paused for an encompassing look around the Encantada lobby. "This is nice, almost as nice as Hawaii."

"We're just down for a few days," said Rita. "Then it's back to the office."

"Where are you living now?" said Cora Sue.

"In California."

"That's a long way from home," said Jerry. "All the rest of your family stayed put."

"I'm in the entertainment business." In spite of herself, Rita found her voice taking on features of the Calhoun's joint drawl. "I'm vice president of one of those companies that produce television shows. We produce 'Word-Right' and a couple of others."

"That's nice." Cora Sue smiled thinly and took Jerry's hand as though to make sure his position remained fixed.

"That's really something!" said Jerry. "If you ever come back for a visit, I'd sure like to have you talk to the Lions Club. A lot of the fellows have been talking about cable TV and what's going to be happening in the next few years."

"I may be making a trip to New Orleans in a week or so," said Rita. "Maybe I'll be able to take a few extra days for a visit."

"We'd all love to see you." Cora Sue redoubled the forcefulness of her grip on Jerry.

"I'd just love to see everybody." Rita's voice was back to normal now, her self-possession unshakable. "Part of my job is looking for talented young people, and I'll certainly be more than happy to talk with anyone you feel might be interested in knowing a little more about what's involved in getting started." It was a good speech, one that made Cora Sue's eyes light up: a speech that established who Rita was and what Rita might have to offer, a speech filled with implicit promise—as all speeches should be. A speech that left the listener quiet and humble, lest an error in tact cause the promise to be withdrawn on the basis of some vague, unaccountable Olympian whim.

Her excellent closing speech permitted Rita a quick departure from the Calhouns, still searching for her name, she was sure, as she headed for the bungalow suite. "Of course it's Rita," she could imagine Cora Sue saying. "She was the clever one who used to write the stories for old Miss Morgan's English class." Rita had always been good at imagining what people were saying behind her back: envious words, sometimes, but more often words of awe and admiration. "Brilliant." "I'd like to be in her shoes ten years from now." "She's the one, she's the one." It was a chorus whose voices and melody changed according to her fancy: a fancy that kept actual people at a distance while populating the mind with more manageable simulacra.

The habit was one she had finally unveiled to Dr. Melissa Stritch, who had immediately characterized it as wholesome and productive. Fantasy, as Melissa put it, was actually a map drawn by the mind and imposed upon reality—in contrast to dreams, which are drawn by reality and thrust into the mind when its defenses are weakened by sleep. "Build those castles in the air," Melissa would smile. "Big, beautiful castles that we can share and find foundations for." So Rita had nurtured her knack of private colloquy into a full-fledged skill, much as though she could summon up white corpuscles at a moment's notice to surround and absorb the smallest invasion from outside.

The Calhoun invasion was not unfamiliar. There had been other occasions when voices from the past had taken flesh and confronted her. Two years ago her youngest brother had descended upon her asking for help in getting started, a request she had already visualized and toyed with in her mind. As a result she had been able to speak her response from a prepared script: pleading inability at first, followed by the suggestion that her brother invest what funds he had in one of her ventures. Horrified, her brother had quickly gone back to Mississippi, there to tell all that California was a land of dry holes.

But her response to the Calhouns had been different. Rather than putting them to flight with entreaties, she had drawn them to her with promises: promises that signaled a desire on her part to make use of them. In her mind she could hear the voices begin to swell: "Rita Ingleton Hayes is going to tell us about long-range prospects." "Rita Ingleton Hayes spoke to the high school seniors last Tuesday." "Rita Ingleton Hayes displayed a warm, generous interest in our talented young people." Pleasant voices. Voices that urged her to make a long-deferred triumphal trip back to Hattiesburg, Mississippi.

A trip worth talking over with Melissa. Perhaps by telephone that evening.

Jackie had been dozing when she left the bungalow. But he was awake now, sitting in a chair on the small back patio, gazing out over the bay as though expecting to see an important vessel appear on the horizon.

"It looks different," said Jackie.

"What does?" said Rita, a little disappointed at not being able to jump immediately into a description of the tennis match. She had planned to characterize it as something less than a total "debacle," following the elegant patterns of Bruce Poirier's vocabulary.

"The ocean looks different." Jackie's mild blue eyes continued to peer out over the water.

"It's the same ocean."

"You'd never know it."

"Why?"

"I don't know," said Jackie. "It just looks different."

"Different from what?"

"Different from what we used to see in Malibu."

Rita took a deep breath. It was as though Judy and Louise had suddenly slid down a wire from wherever they were to demand attention: applause, perhaps—just like one of the Flying Glaubers Jackie had told her about. A strong wire. Too strong to cut. Like her own: stretching finely out to Mississippi, waiting for her to slide back.

"Maybe it's the atmosphere," she said. "It's more humid here."

"I wonder what it looks like from Spain."

"Why Spain?"

"Paul Ciardi says it's a good place to go."

"What part?"

"On the Mediterranean somewhere."

"Maybe we can go there someday." Rita sat down across from him and smiled at the prospect of putting a greater distance between them and Judy: stretching the wire out so that it became thinner and thinner.

"Would you like that?"

"It's something to look forward to," said Rita. "There wouldn't be any telephones, any people pulling at us."

"It might get boring after a while."

"Not for me," said Rita firmly. "I'd write."

"Write what?"

"A novel. Melissa tells me I could write a real winner of a novel."

"Lots of sex?"

"Lots and lots."

"She's probably right." Jackie nodded encouragingly.

"She's right about many things," said Rita. "Like decisions and how to make them."

"I thought we weren't going to talk about that until we got back."

"We're not talking about it. We're talking about Melissa."

"Do you really think it would do any good if I saw her?"

"It would do us both a lot of good."

"Why not?" said Jackie. "It might be worth a try."

"I'm going to take a shower." Rita got up and came over to her husband: bent down to him, kissed lightly. Lightly. But with a touch of promise.

Just a touch. Just enough to spark a thought: a thought to curl in among the others that lay shapelessly forming and reforming far back behind his mild blue eyes. Just one thought among many. But a thought that would grow. Growing slowly, little by little. But growing large: large enough to be recognized in time, pondered, examined and reexamined, not without surprise and pleasurable wonderment.

A slow growth. But a sure one, coinciding almost exactly with the end of her shower: the steps approaching, faint, hesitant; barely audible over the sound of the spray hitting the slope of her back and washing down in branching rivulets, like the touch of many, many obsequious lovers.

A pause. Not long. Barely long enough to let the presence

between them build, almost visible in the moist tropical air. Followed by recognition. Not a word. Not an invitation. Just a sigh: low, pleasurable. Like running water itself. Water people they were. Smooth like seals or otters. Purified by water: almost chastely so. Servicing one another with soap, with rubbings slowing to caresses at times. Then nuzzlings, mouthings; oblivious of the spray seeking to intrude itself into eyes, ears, breasts, thighs, small crevices, and livened private parts.

Action. Larger movement. Leaving the water behind now: gurgling approval and encouragement. There. There. Right there in the moist, steamy enclosure: he a tree, straining upward; she a strong dark vine, winding around him, plunging down to be sought out, clutching her way toward earth itself—absorbed and absorbing. Almost wholly consummate. Almost. Yet keeping one slight part away from him, him unknowing: him so strong, and still so weak, so grateful for the chance to please—almost. And hers the thought.

Later, lying beside him in bed, Rita noted that the room had grown darker. The shadows were beginning to lengthen outside, like those on a sundial crying the passage of time. Time spreading out in front of them as a smooth green lawn reaches down to the ocean. Day by day. Night by night.

"Spain might be nice," she said, thinking of the novel she would make out of her life, giving each voice its proper shape upon the page.

"Sure would."

"What would you do?"

"Look at the water," said Jackie. "Every day is different when you look at the water."

"Anything else?"

"Play the trumpet."

"Anything else besides that?"

"That would be plenty—as long as you were there with me."

She drew him to her once more, letting her long dark hair wash over him: her affection quickened by his admission of her sufficiency to him. Even in a far-off place.

New York City: Wednesday, October 25, 1:00 P.M.

"Here's to the Boston Pops," said Cy Harris, raising his Old Fashioned to salute the proposition and the consequences that it implied for his guest and for him.

"Super!" The guest sipped his glass of white wine and looked around the room with the approving gaze of an anthropologist permitted to observe the sacred mysteries of a remote mountain tribe.

"Jazz clubs are great, but I've always felt Otis belonged in a concert setting." Cy let himself ease back into his leather chair and let his dark eyes travel down the Aquiline Club's high mahogany bar.

It was an old bar: brass-railed with a large, beveled mirror. A good bar for well-dressed men to stand and mingle at before splitting off into the paired encounters called for by their dining room reservations. A bar without stools is a fluid place: an overt invitation for movement, clusterings, introductions by mutual friends, brief exchanges tilted toward smiles and jollity.

Ordinarily Cy would have been standing at the bar, talking with the other members of the Aquiline Club. But since his guest was English, he felt it more appropriate to have drinks at a corner table where the two of them could get acquainted and take each other's measure without interruption. Though never codified, the rules of the Aquiline were clear: openness at the bar, privacy at the tables. Good rules. Rules that softened the potential abrasiveness of unrestricted informality.

The Aquiline was far from being one of New York's older, more exclusive clubs. It had started as a speakeasy in the twenties, with gambling on the top two floors: floors that now housed workout facilities and game rooms. With the coming of Prohibition, the building's clientele, largely theatrical agents, had pooled their resources, bought the building, and organized a framework designed to ensure their continued access to congenial surroundings. The framework was still the same, and so was the building, although the focus of interest had shifted since the war from theater to more amorphous concerns: music, films, publishing, personal management, and other kinds of peddling. A mixed bag. But fundamentally homogeneous, since the members were continually shifting from one professional locale to another: wearing different hats but keeping the same tastes in food, liquor, and fellowship.

Cy waved to Ralph Alevy, who was standing down at the far end of the bar with a tall, sixtyish man in tow. Not untypically, Ralph had started as a band booker, then moved on to talent agency and literary agency work, ending up as president of a small textbook-publishing company. Ralph waved back and gestured with an imaginary pool cue in clear invitation.

"Do you shoot pool?" said Cy. "We generally have a little action upstairs after lunch."

"We used to play snooker at university," said his guest. "More than was good for us, I'm afraid."

Cy nodded respectfully. Before acting on Jackie's suggestion that he approach Otis's manager, Ian Clarke, he had made a few inquiries about his guest, who was said to be proud to the point of obsession regarding his degree from Fitzwilliam College, Cambridge University. A degree that had stamped its pattern upon his original north country speech: lowering the vowels and shaping the palatal sibilants into a perfectly symmetrical set of sounds, sounds that invested the most ordinary of words—like *super*—with echoes rich in dignity and power.

"Clint was a great pool player." It was an appropriate statement for Cy to make, one that maintained the tonality of their meeting—a meeting intended to persuade Ian Clarke to let

Cy do some actual booking of Otis in engagements Cy had access to. Engagements like the Boston Pops concert next month, which Cy had already presented as a gift and as an indication of what could be accomplished by reasonable men working together.

"I dare say," said Ian absently, his attentions focused upon the tall, sixtyish man at the end of the bar with Ralph Alevy. "But you know, I do believe that's Lord Rycroft down there."

"Friend of yours?"

"Not quite." There seemed to be substantial awe in Ian's voice, even though his smooth, blandly roundish, ruddy face remained composed. "He's a publishing person. Very, very important."

"We get some pretty heavy dudes in here," said Cy, pleased at being able to offer his guest an additional gift. "Would you like to meet him, say hello for a minute before we go in to lunch?"

"I think that would be very nice, indeed," said Ian, eyes still on Lord Rycroft: reverentially so, as though a medieval saint had descended to bless and illuminate the Aquiline Club with the full brilliance of his aureole.

They rose, drinks in hand, and began to work their way down the mahogany bar. A slow progress, since custom demanded greetings and short essays in small talk from those who elected to join the mingling. But at length they reached Lord Rycroft: tall, bright-eyed, sandy-haired, sharp-nosed—good-humored and accessible in the way lords are supposed to be when they find themselves in comfortable surroundings, yet somehow keeping a sense of frosty distance in the most noisy gathering.

"I thought you'd be over," said Ralph Alevy as they came up. "I've never known you to turn down a chance to break a few." He turned to Lord Rycroft. "This one is far from being a master, but he's the best available this afternoon."

"My father told me never to be too available," said Cy. "It tends to run the price down." He smiled easily at Lord Rycroft and stepped back while Ralph began the introduction process.

"I believe we met at Broadcasting House," said Ian to Lord Rycroft. "It was in connection with one of your recording company ventures."

Lord Rycroft nodded assent, and the two began to trade mutual acquaintances back and forth—like schoolboys establishing friendship by exchanging marbles. Cy and Ralph beamed approval for a couple of minutes, after which Cy bent in closer toward Ralph, by way of indicating a natural division in the grouping.

"What are you going to do, start recording those schoolbooks now?"

"Everything's open," said Ralph. "It's all a matter of how you put it together."

"We all need a little action," said Cy.

"Like this afternoon?" Ralph smiled cheerfully. "My boss is more of a shark than he looks."

"I thought you were the boss. You've always looked like a boss-type guy to me, especially lately."

"I still am. But our company is part of Lord Rycroft's communications group now."

"When did all this happen?"

"Last week. He showed up, made an offer, and the family decided it was a good chance to get out."

"How about you?"

"I stay," said Ralph. "His lordship wants to acquire companies, not run them."

"Arab money?"

"I don't think so." Ralph reached into his pocket and pulled out a money clip. "Most of it looks just like this."

Cy looked over at Lord Rycroft and Ian Clarke, trying to assess the balance between them. It had not yet reached the point where Ian was doing most of the talking, so he felt free to stay with Ralph a minute longer.

"What's he looking for? Maybe he'd like to buy a couple of singers."

"No singers," said Ralph. "Just small non-public outfits that will give him a good mix over here. A newspaper here, a radio station there, maybe a television production company or two—I'm trying to help him get a feel for the territory before he hits the West Coast."

"I don't know about this afternoon," said Cy, eyes once more on the two Englishmen. "I may be tied up for a while."

"It's more fun with three."

"I'll see what I can work out."

It was not a plea for help, Cy knew. Merely a request to lighten the load a little: converting a one-on-one match into a fun-loving threesome where good humor enveloped the edges of competitiveness like a generous white shaving foam. Cy realized he had not picked up a pool cue since Clint's death, so strong had been the linking of the game with their friendship. And he realized that it was as a pool player he missed Clint most: the hours spent together calculating angle and English, the surface banter masking deeper affection. To pick up cue and bridge with Clint gone seemed somehow improper at this point. A factor to be weighed against Ralph's request.

With Lord Rycroft's eyes beginning to glaze just slightly, Cy hastened to detach Ian and steer him toward the dining room. There they busied themselves with ordering lunch, Ian looking occasionally around the tables on the off chance of seeing still another aristocratic face in this modest colonial outpost.

It was a good start, Cy felt. There's something about an Englishman that dearly loves a lord, his father had always said in pointing to the original Harris turf. For Isaac "Packy" Harris, growing up in the slums of Bristol, it had not been an attractive land; he had been more than happy to try his fortune as a middleweight boxer overseas. In the States he had held his own, gone the distance with the famous Harry Greb once, put a little by, and bought a dry-cleaning shop in Brooklyn: a logical venture for a fighter who had always dressed nattily. Jewish enough to see the English with detachment, English enough to maintain a distaste for overt sentimentality, Packy had been quite a curiosity in the neighborhood. He had raised his three sons with strictness and with wholesome worldly wisdom, urging them always to look beyond the surface of things to the real state of the person on the other side of the shop counter.

The state of Ian Clarke seemed to be reasonably euphoric, thanks to the encounter with his lordship. So Cy decided to launch his proposition midway through the main course.

"I'm sure Otis will hold up his end just fine," he said, his voice tinged with thoughtfulness, as though reassurance were somehow called for.

"It's an idiom he's comfortable with." Dextrously using knife and fork to mince, shovel, and carry in one fluid motion, Ian barely looked up. "He's done beautifully at Montreux, as you probably know."

"Is he going to do it this summer?"

"They've asked us, but we're holding off the decision until after the beginning of the year."

"I wouldn't be surprised if you had a lot of first-rate offers between now and then," said Cy.

"We've had our share already," smiled Ian.

"It's not just a matter of numbers—it's the big numbers that count."

"Those will come."

"They might come a little more quickly if we worked something out." Cy's voice was slow, his manner deliberate. "I still get a lot of inquiries about Clint, and you wouldn't believe the size of the mailing list I've built up over the years."

"That mailing list would be lovely." Ian sat back, his smooth round face almost cherubic, his eyes still darting around the room. They were large eyes, unusually protruding.

"I was thinking of something a little more ambitious."

"We all are, I'm afraid." Ian sipped his wine and nodded contentedly.

"It's a matter of packaging." Cy bent forward and traced a pattern on the white tablecloth. "I was more than glad to recommend Otis to the Pops people, and I'm sure he'll do just fine. But it's one thing to do a couple of numbers sandwiched in between Strauss waltzes, and another thing to put a complete show together—including supporting acts."

"You're not talking about stepping in to stage things for Otis, are you?"

"Not at all. He's the star, he's the bright red ribbon the people see. But I think you'll agree that the rest of the package is important: a singer here, an opening act there. Two and a half hours of concert time is a big chunk to fill."

"I really don't see what sort of role you're proposing for yourself in these matters." Ian's brow furrowed slightly beneath his very crisp, light brown curls. "Otis plays the trumpet; I handle the place and sequence of his engagements. What else is there?"

"I think I've demonstrated that I can open up a lot of things for Otis here, and you'll have to admit that Clint's concerts always had consistent quality. The logical thing is for me to handle Otis the same way. All you have to do is give me whatever blocks of open time you have and let me fill them for you."

"It is logical," said Ian. "And I have a great respect for logic."

Cy nodded, waited for Ian to pursue the matter further. It had been a good sequence of strokes: the drinks, the encounter with his lordship, the tactful assertion of capability, followed by the proposal itself—the last ball of the run softly easing into the right pocket. He was pleased with himself for following Jackie's suggestion to operate as a collaborator, rather than as a seducer.

He looked around the dining room with affection. With a home in Scarsdale and a wife obsessed with the servant problem, he had come to spend more and more of his time at the Aquiline, almost as though it were a resort in the Catskills and he a permanent fixture: part guest, part livening element. The sight of Ralph Alevy and his lordship across the room reminded him that perhaps he had an obligation to start playing pool again. Perhaps he should have started a couple of weeks ago when Jackie was in town; Jackie had always liked to rack up the balls and dig in—like Clint.

Clint again. Cy smiled at his guest and tried to shake the thought away. And the grief. A grief measured not just by affection, or mutual interest, but by hours and hours spent together in doing something pleasurable. For some men, the bond is forged by fishing; for others, by golf or long afternoons of yarnswapping. Trivial linkings. But strong.

"It rather reminds me of what my old tutor at Cambridge used to say," Ian continued. "The logic is excellent, but it's the premises that need looking into." He pushed his plate back, dabbed at his small mouth with a napkin. "To be perfectly frank, I feel you're assuming much more competition than is actually there."

"Of course there's competition," said Cy. "Otis is a beautiful player, but he's certainly not the only one in the world."

"I'm aware of that."

"There's plenty of competition for concert dates—Dizzy, Miles, Maynard Ferguson."

"Contrariwise." Ian's protruding eyes lit up. "None of them really is in a position to compete with what Otis has to offer."

"They're all great players, aren't they?"

"Granted. But none of them is linked up in the mind of the public with the Jeff Styles era."

"What's so important about that?"

"It's the way people feel about it," said Ian. "It was a great orchestra, and they played lovely music. But it was also a great time. A powerful nation winning a war, rebuilding continents, moving upward in every way. I believe Otis will be perceived as a symbol of that time—here, just as he has been in Europe."

"Do you really think all that's involved?"

"I'm sure of it." Ian looked down at his watch for a second. "And I'm also sure that everything you have to offer will come to us of its own accord."

"You seem to have it all figured out."

"I've given it some thought." The small mouth stretched into a smile. "There's a lot involved, as I'm sure you must understand."

Cy understood. He understood that there was nothing more to say, nothing more in the way of rabbits to lift out of the hat. So he and his guest moved away from the topic to more general matters: other instrumentalists, recording possibilities, new technologies, even singers—like Lorrayne, recently widowed and starting to make appearances down in Florida. Appearances whose domain might be widened if circumstances permitted.

They did not cut the lunch short, but let it drag on for a little longer: through coffee and dessert, after which Cy took Ian downstairs and ordered a cab.

"Quite a surprise, seeing Lord Rycroft here." Ian nodded approvingly at the people passing by them outside the entrance.

"Did the two of you have something interesting to talk about?"

"Mutual friends," said Ian affably. "That's how the empire works, you know."

"It's the same all over." Cy paused, decided to make one last try. "Otis and I have always gotten along well."

"That's good to hear." Ian's manner was less affable now, his eyes unsmiling.

"Why don't you talk it over with him and see how he feels about it?"

"I really don't think that would be wise," said Ian slowly. "And I'm sure we'd all be very upset if you pursued the matter any further than you have done here with me."

"I understand."

They stood there in silence until the cab pulled up, absorbed Ian, and took off toward the Barbizon Plaza. At loose ends, Cy went back to the Aquiline bar and ordered a drink. The bar was quiet, almost empty. So he stared at his reflection in the large, beveled mirror for a while. Not a bad face: well cared for, the hair well groomed. But grimly set for the moment: partly through disappointment, partly through anger at the threat implicit in Ian's last words. There was always some of it in the music business, growing out of the people themselves and their grounding in liquor, vice, drugs, and other forms of barely sanctioned social excess. A threat not to be dismissed.

Agents like Ian Clarke were strong medicine. Softspoken men. But tigers in representing their clients. Like lovers, too. Jealous lovers in the violence of their revenge upon seducers, actual or would-be. A working over by a hired specialist in the form. A broken arm or leg. Even a shattered kneecap. The threat of measures like these was always something to consider—"self-help remedies," the lawyers called them. From what Cy knew of Ian Clarke's record, there would be no reluctance in taking extreme measures, if necessary, to protect a valuable client like Otis.

He sighed, tried to push the anger away, some of it centered on himself. Perhaps it was time to close it all out the way Jackie had talked about doing. Of course, what Jackie wanted was to get back to the trumpet. And he probably would do just that if he could ever find a buyer for his production company. And if that happened Otis Marshak would not be the only trumpet player in the world of Jeff Styles–nostalgia the Englishman had summoned up in such glowing colors. Assuming that's what Jackie wanted. Assuming he would be able to get his sound back. Assuming—most fancifully and optimistically—that a buyer could be found who was looking for a small, closely held television production company.

A buyer like his lordship, perhaps.

Cy stayed in the bar a little longer, turning the notion over in his mind, feeling his spirits rise as matters took palpable shape and sequence—like a well-stroked ball caroming toward its intended placement.

He decided to wait outside the dining room entrance, where he lit a cigar and inspected some of the line caricatures on the wall. Old caricatures they were: Otis Skinner, Walter Hampden, and several whose names were unknown to him. A time past; yet ringing on like old melodies taking new shape.

"Were you still planning on a little action, gentlemen?" He beamed expansively as Ralph Alevy and Lord Rycroft came up.

"Nothing fancy," said Ralph warningly. "Just a friendly game."

"That's the only kind I know," said Cy.

"Lovely," said Lord Rycroft.

Encino, California: Friday, October 27, 10:00 A.M.

"To life!" Dr. Melissa Stritch raised her coffee cup as if in benediction over Jackie and Rita. It was a large cup, gray at the top and gradually shading through a progression of lines and squiggles to a solid brown at the bottom. Lines and squiggles. The room was filled with them: Dr. Stritch's notepad, the Persian carpet in front of her desk, the large abstract paintings flanking the three of them.

Jackie sipped his own coffee and stared at his wife's therapist. He had expected something more subdued, rather than a room filled with violent exotica, not the least of which was Dr. Stritch herself. A short woman. Plumpish. Robed in flowing apricot silk. Small, hot, black eyes: very much like those of Madame Morgana of the Kale Brothers sideshow, an orderly row of tents housing a bizarre assembly of skills and attributes, each supported by impressive credentials listed outside.

The Institute for Creative Interaction, which housed Dr. Stritch, was equally impressive, equally well credentialed. Three Ph.D.s, four MSW's, even a D.D. and an M.A. Oxon.—it was a big operation: its offices and seminar rooms occupying almost a complete floor of a well-appointed Beverly Hills medical building. A more discreet setting than that of the sideshow: more expensive, cleaner, sweeter smelling. But with the same lingering feeling of impermanence, as though the whole operation could be closed down and trucked out on a moment's notice: carpets, desks, squiggly paintings, credentialed name plates. A feeling hardly calculated to reassure.

Jackie knew that he had not come to Dr. Stritch's tent for reassurance. He was there in response to a prodding—Rita's. And he was there to be prodded further: prodded to make a decision about Bruce Poirier's loan. His trip to New York had postponed the decision; the few days in Acapulco has postponed it further. But he recognized the force of logic and circumstances bearing down upon him. Logic, fairness, duty: he could sense their presence in the room, ready to be unleashed upon him like the dogs of the railroad police when he was young. Alert, curious, bad-news dogs they had been: big enough to threaten, small enough to be picked up and placed in an open boxcar, there to prod the occupants into movement.

"Life," murmured Rita. There was a faint smile on her calm, remote face. It was apparent that the ritual was familiar to her.

"It's good coffee, isn't it?" Standing beside her rolltop desk like a priestess, Dr. Stritch trained her hot black eyes directly upon Jackie.

"Sure is." Jackie obediently took another sip.

"Good coffee, good vibrations, good work, good sex—that's what life offers us." Dr. Stritch took a gulping pull from her cup, smacked her lips, put the cup down, and rubbed her hands together as though ready to take up another part of the ritual.

"Life," murmured Rita again. Seated on Jackie's left, she reached over and wrapped her long fingers around Jackie's hand in a monitory squeeze. Jackie nodded but kept his eyes fixed upon Dr. Stritch, who was now contemplating her coffee cup.

"Fear!" Dr. Stritch turned suddenly upon them, biting the word out. "It's fear that cripples us—fear of intimacy, fear of success, fear of love, fear of all the good things waiting for us." Hot black eyes still intent upon Jackie, Dr. Stritch lowered her voice to a slow-paced resonant whisper. "And the biggest fear we have is the fear of admitting to ourselves that we're afraid."

"I used to be afraid." There was a far-off look on Rita's face. "I used to have nightmares about being attacked and raped by big black men in Mardi Gras costumes."

"I didn't know that," said Jackie. He looked at Rita with mild wonderment, trying to imagine what other fearful shapes might have been racing through her mind as she lay sleeping beside him. With Judy, the shapes had taken on voice, commanded attention, returned night after night. But Rita's nights had always seemed peaceful: stillnesses that struck him as a natural extension of the long, dark, flowing hair framing her on the pillow.

"There's a lot about Rita you don't know," said Dr. Stritch. She smiled possessively. "Would you like to know how Rita conquered her fear?"

Jackie nodded.

"First we talked about the fear." Dr. Stritch looked reflectively around the room for a minute. "We put it into words, brought it out into the open, turned that nightmare into a daymare."

"It wasn't easy," said Rita.

"It never is." Dr. Stritch wheeled and pointed a querying finger at Jackie. "Do you know what the *mare* part of the word means?"

Jackie shook his head as though to shake away any lingering association with horses thundering away through the mind's black passageways.

"Tell him," commanded Dr. Stritch.

"Story," said Rita. "It means 'story.' "

"I didn't know that," said Jackie.

"You know it now," said Dr. Stritch flatly. "But it's also important for you to know that there's more to conquering fear than talking about it." She turned to Rita. "Tell him what you did after we brought that fear out into the open—tell him in a loud voice."

"I bought a gun," shouted Rita.

"What else?"

"I started taking karate lessons." Rita underscored the force of her words with a violent gesture.

"You never told me anything about all that." Jackie put his cup down on the low table in front of them.

"Why should she?" purred Dr. Stritch. "Why should a woman have to be afraid of keeping secrets from her husband?"

"I thought married people were supposed to stay level with each other."

"Supposed!" Dr. Stritch's deep breath billowed the folds of her apricot-silk gown. "That's a word we never use at the Institute for Creative Interaction."

Jackie quailed, fearful lest his unwitting use of the obscenity require stern measures: measures like those of his Grandmother Hansen, who had washed his mouth out with soap and threatened him with an enema to cleanse him of foul language.

"We each have to create our own values," said Rita softly, pulling his attention over to her.

"Look at this painting." Dr. Stritch's commanding tone pulled Jackie's eyes away from Rita to the large array of lines and squiggles beside the rolltop desk. "It has value."

"Very interesting," said Jackie.

"To you it's interesting." Dr. Stritch smiled pityingly. "But to me it's beautiful, very beautiful—so much so that I paid the artist five thousand dollars for it."

"Five thousand dollars," murmured Rita. "It's a very valuable painting."

"I adore it." Dr. Stritch contemplated her treasure for a moment, then wheeled round and advanced upon Jackie. "Want to buy it?"

"I don't think so."

"Why not?"

"It's a very big painting—too big for our living room."

"We have room," said Rita. "Why don't you let your true feelings come out?"

"I like paintings of real things." Jackie smiled at Dr. Stritch, softening the potential offense in his words. "Oceans and mountains, mostly."

"Exactly!" Dr. Stritch nodded at Rita as though a very important point had been made. "To me this painting has value, but not to you. Isn't that right?"

Jackie nodded, pleased that they had rounded a corner and were heading away from direct conflict.

Dr. Stritch moved over to a plum-colored chair by the window. She sat down, carefully disposing her apricot-silk gown so that only the tips of her small black shoes were visible.

Rita continued to smile.

Somewhere in the vicinity a woman began to scream: a high wail, wordless, yet sustained and curved by the rhythms of speech. Dr. Stritch got up and went over to a panel of buttons by her rolltop desk; shrugging, she pressed one. Music filled the room. Bossa nova music. Guitar and flute, with an engaging flow, filling up the empty spaces between the sharp cries coming from one of the other offices.

"Do you realize what you've done?"

Jackie stared blankly at Dr. Stritch, wondering if she were

going to call him to account for the pain and anger shrieking in to play against the flute's angular melodic line. He shook his head and tried to concentrate on Dr. Stritch.

"You've just made a decision," said Dr. Stritch. "You decided not to buy my painting. Isn't that right?"

"I guess so."

"And you were able to make that decision because your own personal values were clearly defined in your mind. Isn't that right?"

"Yes."

"That's all there is to it." Dr. Stritch remained standing by the panel of buttons, even though the screaming had ceased. "Once you decide what's important to you, the rest is easy."

"That's his problem," said Rita. "He's never figured out what's really important."

"It's not as easy as buying or not buying a picture," said Jackie. With the screaming over, he felt a little more sure of himself. "It's a matter of balancing one important thing against another."

"Name one." Dr. Stritch came back to her plum-colored chair and sat down again. "Name one thing that's truly important to you."

Jackie did not answer immediately. He looked at Rita, at Dr. Stritch, then back at Rita. It was a two-on-one situation, very much like his conference with Bruce and Rita. But this time there were two women involved, each linked to the other by some deep, purely female bond. "A man can never know," Grandmother Hansen had once told him. "A man can never know what the pain of giving birth is like—that terrible, sweet, sweet, terrible pain. And there's nothing on this earth a son can do to make up for that pain." A sobering thought. An important value.

"Rita," he said finally. "Rita is important."

"I'm not a thing." Rita brushed back her long dark hair. "And I'm certainly not your possession."

"I didn't mean it that way," said Jackie quickly. "What I meant was that I'm happy being with you."

"Are you dependent on her?" Dr. Stritch's hot black eyes were neutral.

A tricky question. Jackie weighed the alternatives and decided that humility would be less offensive than false arrogance.

"I guess you could say I'm dependent upon her," he said. "I certainly miss her when she's not there."

"I knew he'd say that." Rita looked at him with scorn for a second, then sighed. "Sometimes I feel that this relationship is smothering me."

"A good relationship gives each partner a chance to breathe." Dr. Stritch let the image sink in before pointing a finger straight at Jackie.

"Name something else that's important to you."

"I always liked playing the trumpet," said Jackie stoutly.

"How about your work?" Dr. Stritch scowled, black eyebrows knit below an equally black cap of frizzy hair. "Isn't your work important to you?"

"I guess so." Jackie sighed, thinking of the intricate dances that went on each day at Jay Jay Productions: conflicts uncertain in their cause, problems whose solutions led to new problems. "But it gets me down every now and then."

"Why should it get you down?" asked Dr. Stritch accusingly. "You haven't even had your first coronary yet."

"He's in good shape for his age." There was a proprietary tinge to Rita's voice. "Except for the fact that he needs to lose weight."

"I know," said Jackie in a dull voice. The weight was a constant theme sounded by his high-priced internist: less weight, less pills; more weight, more pills. He had given up cigarettes, given up drinking beer to balance out the cigarettes; but still the pounds crept upon him—and stayed. A middle-aged fatted calf—or lamb: like the poor creature that the Arabs in the house next to theirs had slaughtered two weeks ago in a sudden fit of festive frenzy; just as his own arteries would silently one day come to common accord and execute him. A well-deserved fate for a calf that chose to fatten itself, contrary to sound professional advice.

His first coronary. Dr. Stritch made it sound almost noble: a step toward ultimate manhood, like church confirmation.

"Work and sex," said Dr. Stritch. "Why should you be afraid of them?"

"I'm *not.*" Jackie reddened a little, partly at Dr. Stritch's bluntness, partly out of fear that Rita would step forward to catalogue his failures.

"Good." For the first time Dr. Stritch beamed approvingly. "I think you've come a long way since you walked through that door."

"So have I," said Rita. "I think I've finally gotten to the point where I can make a decision on my own."

"Good."

"I've decided to make a trip back home." Rita looked at Jackie and smiled reassuringly. "By myself, leaving the day after tomorrow."

"Don't you want me to come?"

"No. I want to see my family, have some time alone."

"What about Frank May's party?"

"You can go without me."

"I'd feel uncomfortable there without you."

"Dependency." Dr. Stritch shook a warning finger. "Isn't that what we're trying to get away from?" She breathed deeply to underscore her point.

"It certainly is," said Rita. "And besides, the trip will give me a chance to stop over in New Orleans and make a presentation to Bruce's people."

"Wait a minute." Jackie's easy manner hardened briefly. "We haven't decided whether or not we want to go ahead with the loan, have we?"

"That's your decision," said Rita.

"Have you decided?" Dr. Stritch's hot black eyes bore in upon him once more.

"No."

"He needs more help."

"I think I'd better see him again." Dr. Stritch went over to her rolltop desk and pulled out an appointment book. "How about this time next week?"

"Do you think it's a good idea?" Jackie looked anxiously at Rita.

"It's your decision."

"Next week is fine." Jackie sighed, oddly relieved at being able to make a concession.

"How about Frank May's party?" said Rita.

"I'll go to the party."

"Good," said Dr. Stritch. "As I said when we started, life can be good."

Jackie smiled at Rita, nodded acceptance at Dr. Stritch. The three of them seemed to have reached a neutral corner. And next week was a long way off.

As he rose, he noticed that the screaming had begun again.

"You've been wonderful, Melissa," said Rita.

"Oh God!" went the screaming voice, somehow more human in making the transition from animal cries to words, more of an intruder into the room. "Damn . . . damn . . . damn . . ." There was the sound of a slamming door. Not a loud slam, but enough to make Jackie jump in its evocation of slamming doors in his childhood: clearly audible from his upstairs bedroom as a signal of conflict to come—including screams.

"Can you see why I wanted you to come?" Rita rose and looked down at Jackie.

"I think so."

"Do you understand now that I don't care what you decide as long as you're truly able to make the decision for yourself?"

"I thought you wanted me to go ahead with the loan." Jackie got up and looked at Rita with mild wonderment.

"Dependency." Dr. Stritch smiled and shook her finger.

The screaming stopped. From outside there was the slam of another door.

"That's what all this is about." There was impatience in Rita's voice, as though the lesson required repetition after repetition before its import finally settled down upon its target. "It's a simple matter of recognizing that it's your life and your decision."

"Life can be good." Dr. Stritch gestured magnanimously toward the door. "I have the feeling some wonderful things are coming your way."

Just like Madame Morgana. The parallel struck Jackie as they walked down the corridor to the elevator. Dark clouds all the way, but suddenly breaking apart to reveal a rainbow as the client was ready to leave the tent. Madame Morgana had promised him a rainbow once; Clara, too.

They rode the elevator down to the fumes and clatter of a brightly lit subterranean parking area. A noisy place. Deep down. Canted far off from sun, sunlight, rain, and rainbows. Hard benches. Hard faces. But no screams. Only the squeal of tires and echoing clank of solid metal doors.

The clanking made him think of his trailer and pickup, both with Louise now. For a moment he considered phoning her and telling her not to sell the trailer to Walt. It would be good to keep the trailer for a while, even if it just sat there as a reminder that it might still be possible one day to hit the road. A remote possibility. As remote as getting back to the trumpet. But the physical fact of possessing equipment was enough to keep the possibility from disappearing completely.

It might be worth calling Louise about the trailer. Or Walt. Not much of a decision. But a step toward practicing the art.

Beverly Hills, California: Saturday, October 28, 7:30 P.M.

"Too emotional," said Frank May. "A short game before dinner gets way too emotional most of the time."

"I dare say you're right." Lord Rycroft smiled down at the tanned, leathery face of his host: a worn, brown satchel of a face lined and creased by many years of forced good humor.

"If they win, they brag about it while they're eating." May looked glumly at the two tables at the far end of the library. "If they lose, they pick a fight with somebody."

Lord Rycroft gave a small grunt of sympathy; May's brown eyes left the poker players and returned to his guest.

"I can't see why you want to get mixed up with these people," said May.

"It's purely an exploratory trip."

"I know how it is." It was May's turn for sympathy. "If there's anything going on, you have to get on a plane and fly halfway around the world to check it out yourself—even when you don't know anything about it."

"Quite so." Lord Rycroft permitted himself a small sigh. The trip from London to New York had been tiring, the trip from New York to Los Angeles more so; and the strange people in both places had been consistently wearisome, although the pool game with Cy Harris had not been unpleasant.

He looked around the room as though by force of will he might be able to make its occupants fit into a respectable pattern. Originally a library, it was a large, high-ceilinged room in the west wing of May's house: a giant place dating back to the time when both land and resident domestics were easy to come by. With the quiet pride of a self-made man, May had charted its history as though the previous occupants were members of his own family tree: two silent film stars, an oilman, and a banker who had started out as a script writer. Prosperity rooted in scandal: a proper setting for the current president of UBN and his acquaintances.

The guests in the library were a noisy group: some of them playing poker for high stakes, others solacing themselves with strong drink, sad tales, and abrupt businesslike probings of one another. Short men for the most part, with large, hairy ears, shrunken cheeks, and jeweled claws, chattering and desporting themselves like monkeys dressed up, brought in, and loosed in order to make some obscure Darwinian point.

Lord Rycroft had never liked monkeys. In Singapore his colonel's wife had kept one, Binkie by name, whom she would slyly inflict at teatime upon young officers singled out for ragging. Warned of the danger, Lieutenant Rycroft had taken his obligatory bite without flinching. But he had been relieved to see the vile beast and its owner depart for Ceylon the following month, there to wait out the war and the return of their imprisoned master. It being the worst of times, he had not speculated upon the matter, except to hazard that some accurate presentiment might have lurked in Binkie's angry darting eyes.

"Jackie Hayes is a great guy," said May. "But I can't see why you're so interested in meeting him." He turned and gestured toward the large foyer opening out from the library where other guests were milling about, many of them lively, half-naked women in brilliant plumage, their cries given body by the faint throb of drums from the gardens beyond. "We've got a lot of good-looking girls in this town."

"I've always been a great admirer of his."

"Me, too." May's leathery forehead took on a few more creases as he compared imaginary balance sheets in his mind. "He's been able to stay afloat."

"I was thinking more of his older show. It's a great favorite with my wife—and with her mother."

"I was thinking more of his company." May grinned knowingly. "I wouldn't be surprised if someone made him an offer one of these days."

Lord Rycroft smiled at his host's prescience: a prescience based upon simple logic, rather than gossip or tale telling. The growth of Rycroft and Pounder, its recent acquisition policy, his offhand expression of an interest in meeting Jackie—these were components of an easy equation for May to recognize and solve.

"Why not invest in a large outfit?" continued May. "We could make those American funds of yours do a beautiful number."

"I'm sure you could. But we feel we'd be comfortable in a smaller, more intimate relationship."

"I understand, I understand." Warming to the challenge, May wreathed his leathery face in smiles and began to move his well-cared-for hands expressively. "But if it's intimacy you're looking for, we could give you a key decision slot—maybe two."

"Would that be proper?"

"That's the way it works now—a couple of big, big jobs in return for a big, big loan." May looked out toward the foyer again. "That's where we've been getting our teenage vice presidents from lately."

"Is it a good plan?"

"Sometimes." May returned the focus of his attention to the poker players. "It all depends on who you get."

"A gamble?"

May nodded. Drawn by the feeling of intensity in the library, they both took stock of how the play was going. Lord Rycroft noted that several of the monkeys had taken off their coats, rolling up their shirt sleeves to display profusely hairy arms; a few, grim and silent, appeared ready to leap across the table at one or the other of their antagonists.

"It used to be the studio head's brother-in-law," said May. "But now it's the banker's nephew."

"We're not bankers, I'm sorry to say."

"I wish you were."

"Maybe I could put you in touch with someone." Lord Rycroft smiled down at his host in a friendly spirit of joint commiseration; they were both captains of vessels blown by winds set in motion elsewhere.

Originally Lord Rycroft had been destined for a respectable career in banking. But five years in a Japanese prison camp had honed his wits into those of a shrewd trader well able to move from bartering for provender to bartering for manuscripts and subsidiary rights. Under his direction the publishing house of Rycroft and Pounder had prospered. And prosperity compelled growth: expansion into other fields, other markets, other countries. "Where there's muck, there be money," Grandfather Pounder had always said in charting a proper course for the family to follow. So instructed, Lord Rycroft was prepared to do his duty unflinchingly: enduring whatever hazards and discomforts might come his way in the pursuit of growth and long-term advantage. Not quite as respectable a career as banking might have been. But Grandfather Pounder would have approved.

Their moment of fellowship was interrupted by the sound of shattering glass from the far poker table.

"I was afraid they'd get physical," said May. "Let's go talk to somebody."

"Dear me!" Lord Rycroft was surprised by the speed with which May propelled him toward the foyer, though not before he caught sight of a smooth-shaven head, red and glistening with rage, lowered as though to charge.

"Nothing serious," said May. "But they always do a lot of shouting, mostly about who gets to throw who out. They're very status conscious."

"Are all your colleagues like this?"

"Just the old ones." May raised his voice slightly to carry over the shrieking of the half-naked women around them; he looked back at the monkey room with obvious affection. "Street fighters—that's what they are. Very emotional guys. Guys who care."

"Hey, Brooklyn!" The piercing yell came from just behind Lord Rycroft's right ear and was apparently directed at one of the half-naked women festooned over the balustrade at the top of the winding stairs in front of him. Irritated with himself for having flinched, Lord Rycroft moved closer to his host.

"I love those old guys," said May absently. "But it's all I can do to get my wife to let them in the house."

A notable sound of clumpings and thumpings arose from the monkey room. Lord Rycroft turned to see the smooth-shaven head nod approval as a dark, heavy-browed monkey was taken out by two others in shirtsleeves, his arms folded.

"How do they decide who gets thrown out?"

"The one with the smallest office," said May. "Houses don't count."

"Hey, Brooklyn! Are you deaf or something?"

"C'mon up!" came a shrill cry from high above them.

"You come down," commanded the groundling.

Lord Rycroft and May left the conflict of wills unresolved and walked into the east wing. Harkening to the tinkle of a piano, May peered into a large room decked with gilt. A curly-haired young man with what appeared to be a diamond in his nose was attacking a cream-colored grand piano. Milling around him were many extravagantly handsome men and women, mostly young, all tanned and fit.

"Talent." May smiled as a girl in a white satin jumpsuit came up to the piano and positioned herself to sing. "I love to see new talent."

"Lovely," said Lord Rycroft, somewhat distressed to see that the singer seemed unable to hold the attention of her audience.

"Maybe Jackie's in the den," announced May. "He should be here someplace." He led Lord Rycroft to a quieter room lined with Cruikshank prints, mostly fanged caricatures occasioned by the Irish question. In deference to the pictures and their threatening content, the people seemed more decorous, their voices softer.

"Curious." Lord Rycroft inspected one of the prints as May paused to survey the crowd. A terrible, frightening thing: portraying an Irishman beside a gorilla in a way that emphasized the similarity between the two.

"Have you seen Jackie Hayes?" May inserted the question into a discussion of a strange, remote place called the "midland" and its unpredictable tastes.

"Out in the garden," said one of the participants, shrugging as though the question were an interruption to be dismissed in clipped, perfunctory terms. A curious response, especially to a man highly placed. A sign, perhaps, that May's position was more illusory than real.

They retraced their steps and walked out into the garden: a large, several-leveled place with torches and a number of portable heaters designed to neutralize whatever small chill might be in the air. On the lowest level an orchestra was playing some sort of unrecognizable tune: mostly drumming threaded through with the metallic whine of guitars.

"There he is." May pointed to a stocky man in a blue blazer

near the orchestra. "I should have known he'd be near the music."

"Does he still play the trumpet?" Lord Rycroft tried to picture their quarry as Cy Harris had described him: cheeks puffed, one hand fingering the instrument while the other directed the entrances and exits of the musicians in his orchestra.

"That was a long time ago," said May shortly. "Just like everything else." He waved to Jackie Hayes from where they were; Jackie waved back.

A pleasant gesture, thought Lord Rycroft. The gesture of a person who could be approached. A gesture that went with the mild blue eyes and relaxed stance: promising to all that its maker would smile, nod his head in understanding, try to shun combative words and cool impositions. Not a bad sort of chap at first reading.

"Hello, Frank," said Jackie as they came up. "Rita had to go back east, so I'm on my own for a few days."

"My tall friend here just got into town," said May. "He's interested in learning a little about the picture business."

May introduced Lord Rycroft to Jackie Hayes, and as though by common decision they moved away from the orchestra.

"How's Judy doing?" May's leathery face had a far-away look to it: a look suggesting to Lord Rycroft that that topic held more than perfunctory interest.

"Fine," said Jackie, "as long as she keeps busy. She's done a couple of dinner theater things this year."

"That's a good place to take a sounding," said May. "But I'd like to see her in something more ambitious—a full-scale musical, perhaps." He turned to Lord Rycroft. "You never can tell what's going to take off until you see how audiences are going to react."

"That takes something of an investment, doesn't it?"

"Just like Las Vegas." May shook his head. "And there's no accountant that can make those dice get hot for you." He paused and pursed his lips for a moment. "That's why we have so many gamblers in the library."

"A sturdy, serious group, I would say." Lord Rycroft looked back toward the house and tried to imagine what the level of intensity now was.

"I think I'd better check on them." May looked at his watch. "Then I'll come back and see you get some food." He squared his shoulders and walked briskly off.

"He's right about the gambling, you know." Jackie smiled at Lord Rycroft as though to suggest that the picture business should be approached with extreme care.

"I'm sure he is," said Lord Rycroft. "But I suspect one is better off if one stays with a well-known house."

"It's mostly small houses now." Jackie waved around the garden to take in the throng of people: some of them dancing, most of them talking in clusters. "A name on a door and a few key people—like an accordion waiting for air to be pumped in."

"Very much like publishing." Lord Rycroft smiled easily to indicate their common ground. "We provide the framework and our authors flow in and out—sometimes even ending up out here."

"A book gives you something to work with. And like Frank said, a preliminary audience reaction helps a lot."

"That's why we feel it might be a good plan to involve ourselves in more dimensions of the process."

"Sounds to me as though you've thought it through pretty well."

"That was the reaction of Mr. Harris back in New York—in between sinking colored balls here and there."

"If you're talking about Cy Harris, he's good at that."

"He had good things to say about you and your company." With common ground established, Lord Rycroft began to relax. "I was thinking we might have lunch and discuss some alternatives."

"Are you going to be in town long?"

"Just a few days." Lord Rycroft gave a small cough. "To tell the truth, I was thinking about tomorrow."

"I'm pretty busy at the store now." Jackie paused ruminatively. "But with my wife out of town, I could certainly make it tomorrow evening."

"That would do very nicely."

Jackie nodded as though to fix the commitment in his mind. Lord Rycroft smiled: partly in acknowledgement, partly in satisfaction that matters were off to a good start. Although Ralph Alevy had spoken in support of the Harris recommendation, prudence and good policy dictated an informal meeting before proceeding further. Men need to take one another's measure in comfortable surroundings: a party, a club, a golf course, a hunting lodge, a place where introductions can be made and smiles exchanged without forcing. Wine first, commerce later, Grandfather Pounder had always said.

They continued to chat but stayed clear of business matters. Contact established, it was time for small, inconsequential talk. The climate, ordeals of travel and dining out, children, family, pictures of current trends and their direction. Ordinary stuff:

like plain burlap wrapped loop by loop around a new-made graft of twig to tree. A graft to yield fruit later on.

The fruit was about ready to drop, judging from what Cy Harris had said. A businessman bored with his business. A young wife bored with her life. They were both ready for a change: ready to travel, ready to strike out in new directions. As the potential agent of change, Lord Rycroft began to glow inwardly. "One must do well," Grandfather Pounder had said. "But there's a great joy in doing good at the same time one does well." As though in benediction, Lord Rycroft smiled warmly down at Jackie.

And then it was time for dinner. May came back to care for his guest, taking Lord Rycroft up to the buffet and shepherding him through the line. There Lord Rycroft's eyes were treated to a rich expanse of food: salmon in molds, cheeses bristling like hedgehogs with strange-colored excrescences, trees of olives, boats of lettuce, creatures carved from butter and ice, countless other fanciful culinary shapes—all testifying to some obscure, savage totemistic urge. At the end of the table was a conventional roast, portions of which were being sliced by a short, squat Oriental gentleman.

As he approached the roast, Lord Rycroft paused. Not for him the ordinary memories of holiday cheer, where carving was a matter of polite ritual. Instead, memories of Malaysia: tall trees towering over fenced-in shacks, ragged men on parade. There the three recaptured prisoners one by one had bowed their heads as Major Nishegawa, short and squat, took deep breaths and raised his sword aloft to execute them.

"Rare or well done, sir?"

"Rare will do very nicely." Lord Rycroft smiled at the Oriental gentleman; he showed no visible sign of distress as the flashing knife did its work.

"We'll be sitting at one of the more comfortable tables," said May. In great good humor he led Lord Rycroft toward a distant arbor, where several tanned, fit young people, all smiles and gleaming teeth, rose to greet them.

"How did you and Jackie get along?" May nodded approvingly as the wine steward came up to uncork the bottle and fill their glasses.

"Very well."

"He's a great guy."

"Very pleasant, very accommodating." Lord Rycroft smiled around the table as though to include everyone under his umbrella of general endorsement.

"Judy, too," said May in a far-away voice. "She could make it happen."

Lord Rycroft sipped his wine and looked at his host with casual surmise, wondering what triangulations and measurements were taking place in the mind that ruled that wise, old, lined, leathery face. Each thought a pinpoint; but linked up with others in an endless array of connectedness, plausible and potential: paralleled by the sky arching above them, reticulated and decussated by countless little far-off dots of light.

A rational structure. Held in place by force of will. Or even by private obsession. "The madness of the great and powerful has the strength of law for lesser folk," Grandfather Pounder had once said. All the more so when hidden from view, concluded Lord Rycroft, as he continued to study his host. Hidden from view like an eccentric duchess sequestered in a remote country house, there to rule her unknowing tenants from a distance, his host's mind seemed to be busily working out the details of a new speculative venture.

As was his own, now that he had met Jackie Hayes.

Sherman Oaks, California: Monday, October 30, 4:30 P.M.

"I used to love this game," said Jackie. He tried a few more shots, scowling as the cue ball failed to do his bidding properly.

"Games are games." Standing by the doorway, Walt Kodaly took stock of the room: pool table, card table, even a chess board with ivory pieces meticulously arranged. "It takes time to get your skill back."

"Maybe I need glasses." Jackie took a careful sighting and sent the cue ball toward one of the lozenges on the far side of the table. The ball angled off in the direction of one of the pockets but failed to plump in.

"If you don't now, you will soon," said Walt, dark eyes thoughtful.

"I told you Paul Ciardi was coming over, didn't I?"

"You told me."

"I'd rather give you the whole story when he gets here."

"What story?"

"The story of what might happen to your five percent."

"Does it have a happy ending?"

Jackie shook his head, put the pool cue in its stand, gathered up the balls from the pockets, and racked them neatly together on the table. An orderly triangle: waiting to be fragmented into random, spinning trajectories.

"I don't know," he said. "It's complicated."

"Are you in trouble?" With his high cheekbones and dark, serious mien, Walt looked like an American Indian medicine man ready to exorcise whatever evil spirits might be hovering in the room. "I told you once before not to worry about that five percent of mine."

"The company's fine."

"Are you and Rita splitting up?" The medicine man took out his pipe and began the ritual of filling and lighting it.

"Rita and I are fine."

"Then there's no trouble," said Walt firmly. "A good business, a young wife, a good lawyer, a friend who's willing to put down his book and come over on short notice—what more do you want?"

"I don't know." Jackie watched the smoke from Walt's pipe form a small cloud and drift upward. "But I'm seriously considering selling Jay Jay Productions."

"Are you just making noises, or do you have an offer?"

"I've got an offer."

"A good one?"

"Fair." Jackie shrugged and looked around the game room as though ready to put everything in it up for auction.

"Then there's no trouble." Walt's dark, saturnine face gleamed relief and approval. "A young wife, agreeable friends, a business you've been dying to unload—what more do you want?" He made a capacious gesture in clear suggestion that all evil spirits had been disposed of.

"I guess I want to do what's right."

"Right for whom?"

"Everybody. You, Louise, the employees, the family. Like I said before, it's complicated."

Walt sighed. He walked over to the chess board and sat down, staring at the pieces as though contemplating an opening move.

"You're what's complicated," he said finally. He lifted up the white king and placed it in the center of the board.

"No I'm not." Jackie remained where he was, his eyes trained suspiciously on the chessboard. "I've always liked things to be simple and up front."

"They never are unless you make them that way." Walt pointed to the white king. "This is the most important piece in the game, isn't it?"

"Yes."

"And the job of all the other pieces is to protect that piece, right?"

"That's what the rules say."

"It's not just the rules," said Walt. "It's the basic objective in the game—a very simple objective. If you don't keep the king healthy and happy . . ." He pushed the king over with a resounding click.

"I think that game must have been cooked up by a very self-centered person."

"It's common sense." Walt put the king back in place and got up. "But this business is full of people who keep running themselves into the ground against common sense because they feel it's the right thing to do. And most of the time, they're wrong—dead wrong. And dead, too, sooner or later."

"I knew you'd push me to sell out," said Jackie sulkily. "You've been talking retirement for the last five years."

"If you feel people are pushing you, take a good look at what they have riding on whatever piece of real estate is involved." Walt's manner was easy, unoffended. "I have nothing to gain if you pick up on this offer—maybe even a little to lose. And besides, you wouldn't have asked me over if you didn't want me to give you my picture. I was right about Judy's project, wasn't I?"

"I think so."

"I'm right about this too."

"I haven't given you the whole story yet."

"I don't need the whole story," said Walt. "I know you, and I know you've always worried about other people a lot more than yourself."

"There's nothing wrong with that, is there?"

"I think it's wrong for a tired, middle-aged man who's short of breath to spend his time worrying about people who are perfectly able to take care of themselves."

"How about Louise?" Jackie smiled as though the point were unassailable. "You must have done more than talk about the trailer when you were up there. Can you honestly say that she's able to make it on her own right now?"

"You're too much." Walt shook his head as though the evil spirits were too powerful for his medicine-man spells. "You were a lot younger than Louise when you hit the road. So was

I. So were a lot of people we know. What makes you think she couldn't handle things if she had to?"

"It would be better if she finished her education, wouldn't it?"

"That's not the point," said Walt. He started up his pipe again and puffed vigorously. "And it's a good example of how you complicate things for yourself. You bring education into it, because you don't want to admit that Louise is young, healthy, strong, and perfectly capable of going out and getting a job tomorrow."

"I wouldn't want her to do that."

"You're drifting off the point again." Walt raised his voice in irritation. "We're talking about what *you* want to do, and you drift off into talking about what you want *Louise* to do. For someone who complains about being pushed, you sure do a lot of pushing on your own."

"I just want to do what's right," said Jackie in a low voice, almost as though he had been backed against the wall, rather than against the pool table.

"How can you do what's right if you don't look at what's going on?" Relentlessly, Walt continued to press his case. "The fact is that you've worked hard all your life and you've earned the right to do any damn thing you want."

"I keep telling myself that," said Jackie sadly. "But it doesn't seem to be enough."

"Jesus, are you screwed up!" Walt shook his head several times as though to clear his head of intrusive, clogging material. "I wouldn't be surprised if you were all out of gin."

"That's one thing I still have going for me." Pleased at the chance to take direct, satisfying action, Jackie detached himself from the pool table and led the way to the living room. "But I expect my doctor will rule that out one of these days—along with everything else."

"You need someone like that to ride herd on you." Walt sat down on a deep-cushioned sofa and watched Jackie delve into the wet bar's contents and emerge with gin, glasses, ice cubes, and vermouth. "Better to be pushed by a professional than by someone who makes a career out of being on your back."

Jackie brought the drinks over and handed Walt one; then he positioned himself in an armchair directly opposite. As always, a good stiff drink slowed the tempo of their discussion: almost as though the clink of ice cubes and beads of moisture on the glasses had been called in as third parties to distract them from their concerns.

The doorbell chimed. Not unmelodiously. Four notes sounding in sequence to form a major seventh chord. Jackie smiled with satisfaction, got up, went out to the entry hall, and reappeared with Paul Ciardi in tow.

"This is a good way to round out an afternoon." Paul let his chunky frame ease into a chair near the fireplace, putting his briefcase in back of the chair as an unequivocal indication that facts, figures, and judgment could wait until there was a soothing drink in hand. "They're putting up a new building across from us and the noise has made everybody cranky." He nodded appreciatively at the bourbon and water Jackie brought him.

"It's new buildings all over," said Walt. "Yet everyone complains about how bad business is. Where does all this construction money come from?"

"Money is like water." Paul's fair-complexioned face was cheerful, his manner that of a professor delighting in paradox. "No matter where it comes from, it always seeks its level. So some of it is bound to flow this way, even though its source may be thousands of miles off—England, perhaps." He raised his glass to salute the notion and smiled at Jackie.

"What do you think?" Jackie's eyes sought out the briefcase for a moment.

"Just a minute," said Walt. "You said you were going to give me the whole story, and now you're asking Paul to come up with the punch line in the first two minutes."

"Good judgment doesn't come in punch lines." Paul took a long sip of bourbon as though to prepare himself for a long summation. "And I've never known an attorney who could speak his piece in two minutes. After all, as Justice Holmes put it, the law is a seamless web, so any advice I give must perforce involve attention to a number of aspects—legal, financial, and personal."

"Perforce, indeed," said Walt darkly.

"From the legal point of view," Paul continued, "Jackie has an offer from the English firm of Rycroft and Pounder to purchase Jay Jay Productions. They're a legitimate firm and it's a perfectly legitimate offer."

"Great!" Walt's saturnine face was wreathed with good humor as he sat back, obviously relieved.

"From a financial point of view, it's not so great." Paul held up a warning hand. The figures look good, but what they really mean is that they're getting the company in return for taking over the indebtedness—including this big, heavily mortgaged house and the expensive cars."

"It's a good, clean deal," Jackie said defensively.

"You could say that about an amputation—or the guillotine." Paul smiled cheerfully and took a small sip from his drink. "Frankly, I feel that your Lord Rycroft has come over here and picked himself up a quality piece of goods at a bargain price."

"It's a bargain for me, too," said Jackie. "Three weeks ago I would have given anything for a chance to clean out my office and split."

"That's your punch line," said Paul to Walt. "It all adds up to how much Jackie wants to pay his lordship for the privilege of walking away from his own business."

"It sounds to me like you're down on the idea." Walt bent forward, eyes intent on Paul, who had begun to stiffen at what appeared to be substantial third-party resistance.

"It's not a wise move." Paul's manner was less professorial, more judicial. "And I'll tell you why." He looked around the room as though taking inventory of the paintings on the wall—lines and squiggles, for the most part, that Rita had acquired on Dr. Stritch's recommendation.

"There's more than money involved in a move like this," Paul went on. "Right now you're a relatively important person—your company is active, you have people working for you, you have other people who want your attention and favors from you, and the same holds true for Rita."

"Right on the button." Jackie nodded enthusiastically. "And that's exactly what's been getting me down—the people."

"I feel that way myself sometimes," said Paul. "But you have to imagine what it would be like if you closed up shop and became a semi-retired gentleman."

"I'm a semi-retired gentleman," said Walt truculently. "And I think it's great."

"For Jackie, it might very well be a disaster. It's not just that he would have to cut back on his luxurious, tax-deductible style of living. Rather, it's the fact that he wouldn't have the power and importance he's used to. Nor would Rita."

"I don't think Rita would mind," said Jackie. "She's always talking about how she wants to take off and write a sexy bestseller novel."

"I've always had the feeling Rita liked running things at Jay Jay. What makes you so sure she wants out?"

"Underneath it all, I'm positive this is what she really wants. She's always wanted to write. And lately she's been getting more and more tense about the company. I suppose she might be upset a little at first. But in the long run she'll be a lot happier—me, too."

"But you haven't actually discussed this move with her, have you?"

"I've tried to call her in New Orleans. But no luck. Anyhow, she's made it quite clear she wants *me* to decide the big ones from here on in."

"But you haven't discussed this move with her, have you?"

"No, I haven't—but I'm sure she'll go along with any decision I make."

"Maybe." Paul shrugged. "Let's cross that bridge when we know it's safe. In any case, it's clear that you'll have to find something else to do."

"It's not clear to me," said Walt. "You sound like it's essential for Jackie to move from one business to another, replacing old problems with new ones. Why can't he cash out, live modestly on whatever comes in from the 'Judy's Guy' trust, and enjoy himself?"

"A person has to do something constructive." Paul smiled as though the proposition were self-evident.

"There are many ways of being constructive." Walt rose and took up a forensic post by the hallway, widening his arc of vision to include both Paul and Jackie. "Right now I'm on the last book of Gibbon's *Decline and Fall of the Roman Empire,* and I feel that something like that is a lot more constructive than writing formula scripts that will be out of date tomorrow."

"Isn't it better to write your own stuff than read someone else's?" Jackie frowned at Walt's implicit celebration of emptiness.

"Somebody has to read Gibbon," said Walt with fervor. "It's a great work. If nobody reads it, it doesn't exist—just like music that nobody hears."

"Is he making sense?" Jackie turned a puzzled gaze toward Paul.

"From his point of view, it makes perfect sense," said Paul. "But not for you, I'm sure of it. You're going to be ten times worse off if you don't find something interesting to do—something where you have just as much clout and position as you have now."

"But three weeks ago you told me to be very careful about expanding and taking on additional obligations."

"That's right. I told you then that in my judgment you were too old to take on a big gamble. And that's exactly what this proposed sale of Jay Jay represents—a big, big gamble in personal terms. You haven't told me one thing that indicates you've thought about what you're going to do with your life after you hand over the keys of your office to Lord Rycroft's redcoats."

Jackie sighed. He felt himself framed in a conventional courtroom scene: two opposing counselors, each prosecuting irreconcilable points of view. Except that the roles were miscast, since the upholding of duty somehow seemed out of place in a cheerful face like Paul's, while the gospel of leisure lost much of its force when presented by a sober, high-cheek-boned Puritan medicine man. Worst of all was the casting of himself as judge: he who had been damned just last week by other judges for his inability to make decisions.

It was time to freshen the drinks: lightly so for Paul and Walt, but a heavy belt of undiluted gin for himself.

"I've given it plenty of thought," he said finally. "And the truth is that I'd like to spend more time playing the trumpet." He looked at the two of them almost pleadingly. "It would certainly mean a lot if I could play and get a halfway-decent sound."

"You gave that up years ago," said Walt.

"What are you planning to do—go out and play weddings?" Paul's tone of voice was equally scornful.

"At this point, that's probably all I could handle," said Jackie. "But after six months or so of solid practice I might be able to stand up and make a pretty good showing."

"A show's no good without an audience." Walt shook his head. "Who are you planning to play for?"

"Montreux," said Jackie. "One of their people stopped by and said they'd like me to appear."

"What about afterwards?" Paul leaned forward and spoke quietly.

"There doesn't have to be any afterwards." Jackie took a deep pull from his glass. "I just want a chance to put some of it back together."

There was a pause: long enough to let the note of hopelessness in his voice fade away, during which Paul studied the squiggle-and-line paintings with feigned interest while Walt got his pipe going again.

"Why not?" said Walt suddenly. "Everyone always said you were one hell of a trumpet player. Go ahead, man. Do it."

"Where would you do all this? Here?" Paul gestured around the room. "If you sell the company, there's a lot else that goes with it."

"Rita feels she'd like it in Spain."

"I told you one of my clients has a villa there, didn't I?"

"That's one of the things that started me thinking."

"Great!" said Walt. "When does this Montreux thing kick off?"

"Early July."

"We'll make the trip sometime in spring, try to locate my old man's village in Hungary, and stop in to see how you're doing."

"It won't be a particularly big show—just an appearance with Vito and some of the others."

"That's plenty," said Paul. "But I think you're forgetting someone we haven't talked about yet."

"You mean Louise, don't you?" Jackie's eyes were clouded with concern. "She's still in school, and there's her marriage to think of." He gazed out of the window, taking note of how the shadows were beginning to lengthen.

"That's exactly what I've been trying to get across," said Paul. "It's a seamless web. Everything is all linked together—the company, your family, your responsibilities, your lifestyle. You hold them together, and they hold you together. And since it's a web you've woven over the years, you simply can't tear yourself free without tearing yourself apart in the process."

"It takes a spider to weave a web." Walt was still firm. "And Louise is no spider. If you gave that girl half a chance, she'd be happy to be completely on her own."

"I wouldn't feel right turning her loose, withdrawing the support she's used to." Jackie shook his head. "And Judy would raise the roof."

"You may be right about Judy," said Walt. "But remember, I talked to Louise last week. And I'm positive she'd encourage you just the way I'm encouraging you." He came back to the sofa and sat down as though his side of the case had been completely stated.

"I don't know." Paul paused, his usually cheerful face set and serious. "I must admit I can somehow just see you in Spain, practicing every day and looking out over the Mediterranean at night. But it's still a sudden, impulsive move."

"I know," said Jackie. "It's a big decision."

"You've always been good at those." Walt smiled reassuringly.

"Not lately."

"There's nothing wrong with taking plenty of time to think things through." Paul rose and picked up his briefcase. "If you do that, you'll be able to accept the consequences—good or bad."

"Good," said Walt. He got up and squared his shoulders. "I see nothing but good—sunshine and roses."

"That's what Madame Morgana used to say."

"I know. And she was right. As far as I'm concerned, there's a lot more sunshine here than there was in Aliquippa—and we've got rosebushes all over the place."

"Give it some more thought," said Paul. "If you decide to go ahead, I'll work the rest of it out for you."

"At this point I don't know what I'm going to decide." Jackie saw them to the door and watched them walk down the steps together.

"It's a simple decision." Walt turned, intent on striking a final blow. "A one-word decision—yes."

Jackie watched the two drive off: Walt in a Chevrolet, Paul in a Buick. He came back to the living room. A silent place. Like the house. He wondered what Rita was doing, wondered perhaps if she might not be at this moment looking at a telephone: wanting to call, yet firm in her resolve to let the decision be his and his alone. A generous resolve, especially from a strong-willed person: a person grown hard and tense in the picture business, a person who wanted to write, to create, yet needed a push to get moving—as had he.

He sipped his drink, still uncertain, still fearful. Yet calmed and reassured by the realization that others, though disagreeing in particulars, stood united in shared concern for his welfare. Pleasant thoughts. Enough to populate the darkening room with vaguely encouraging shapes. Small shapes, like Clint's mouthpiece, which he had picked up and slipped into his pocket that morning.

November

Santa Barbara, California: Wednesday, November 1, 10:15 A.M.

"I didn't realize you expected me to come to your poetry reading," said Louise. She brushed her light brown hair back as though to smooth any potential abrasiveness away. "You didn't even ask me last time."

"I knew you had a report to do." Scott smiled and stroked his black beard. "But now you're relatively free, so I assumed you'd want to be there."

"I do." Louise looked desperately around his office, trying to find support in the faces of Ezra Pound and T. S. Eliot but flinching under their stern, serious gaze—a gaze almost pitiless in its focus upon far-off unknowable concerns. "I love to hear you read."

"That's good to hear." Scott nodded as though her statement could bear substantial dissection and analysis.

"If it really means a lot to you, I'll phone Dad and tell him I'll be down tomorrow—Mother, too."

"The seminar's coming over tomorrow."

"That's why I felt today would be better." Louise began

to breathe a little more easily, feeling that she had scored an important, logical point.

"It's better, but it's far from perfect."

"He wouldn't have asked me to come down if he didn't think it was important."

"Everything is important," said Scott. "And everything is unimportant—it's all a matter of how you perceive reality."

"That's very profound." Louise smiled encouragingly, wondering if she would ever light upon a phrase as effective as Barry's "You're fantastic!" It was the thought that mattered, she concluded.

"It's not bad." Scott reached for a note pad and scribbled for a minute.

"Maybe he's been able to work something out about the house."

"He didn't say that, did he?"

"No." Louise found her voice dropping.

"Apparently it's more important for you to drive down there than for him to drive up here." Scott stroked his beard again. "Or to put it another way, the drive is more unimportant where you're concerned than it is where he is concerned." His eyes sparkled with pleasure at the neatness of his phrasing.

"I don't see why you have to make things so difficult."

"They're not difficult at all. Your father makes a phone call, and you drop everything to make a long drive down to Los Angeles—what could be more simple than that?"

"What's wrong with it?" said Louise. "I don't mind the drive that much."

"I know you don't," said Scott. "And that's what bothers me most."

"Why?"

"It should be obvious that the drive symbolizes something to you."

Louise bowed her head, waiting for the blow.

"It symbolizes a yearning to return to childhood," Scott continued. "Surely it's no accident that you're taking the coast route, going back to the sea, as it were. And it's also no accident that you're stopping to see your mother, thereby symbolically linking your parents together."

"I don't see it that way at all," said Louise, resisting an urge to once more say, "That's profound."

"Of course you don't." Scott looked up at the picture of T. S. Eliot with reverence. "As Old Possum would say, the whole trip is a perfect objective correlative for your desire to remain in a state of childhood dependency."

"But that's what I am." Louise raised her voice a little in an attempt to ground the discussion in palpable fact. "My father is still paying for my tuition and everything else."

"I'm talking about emotional dependency," said Scott airily. "Sooner or later you'll have to break away."

"You mean get a job?"

"That would help a great deal, but the important thing is to see the problem for what it really is."

"I've already promised them both I'd come down this afternoon," said Louise, wondering how much longer Scott was going to lecture her.

"Maturity consists in knowing which promises to break and which to keep." Scott paused and waited for her approving response. None forthcoming, he turned away from her to scribble on his note pad.

"I really should be going," said Louise.

"It's your decision." Back still turned, Scott was gazing out of the window.

Louise waited for an awkward moment and looked once more into the faces of T. S. Eliot and Ezra Pound. She wondered if Ezra Pound had stroked his beard the same way Scott stroked his: a gesture of complete assurance and command. Great men. Great abilities. Steady fires burning on and on, consuming all the smaller twigs in the vicinity. A proper price to pay for genius to do its work. But painful. Too much so for some, perhaps.

"There's one thing more," she said, trying to smile as though the matter were of no consequence. "I'll need the keys to the MG."

"Why?" Scott wheeled around and glared at her.

"I'd like to drive it," stammered Louise. She held up the keys to the pickup as indication that the exchange would be a fair one.

"Why?"

"It's a long drive, and I think the MG will be more comfortable than the truck."

"It's not that far," said Scott. "And I need the MG tonight for the poetry reading."

"But you said it was a long drive," said Louise. She stared resentfully at T. S. Eliot, feeling that Old Possum was somehow the source of her difficulty.

"I said the drive was a symbol," Scott said patiently. "So

it doesn't matter whether you take the MG or the truck. And since I need the MG, I think it would make sense if you took the truck."

"Why?"

"You're beginning to sound like a small child, Louise," said Scott, his patience now gone. "If you're going to run home to Daddy, I think you should get started before the traffic gets heavy."

A low blow. But not a damaging one. Even though they were relatively infrequent, Louise was usually able to see them take shape, charting their coordinates with reference to previous points in a conversation. In this case, it had been the long-drive business: a point raised by Scott, used by her in rebuttal. Two points. Enough to construct a line traveling in a predictably angry direction. Enough to give her a modest feeling of power and sufficiency. Enough to divert her anger away from Scott and toward the setting that seemed to turn them against each other.

The university setting. Far from wholesome, she felt. Young professors anxiously courting their superiors and the students. Students anxious for approval. All in a warm climate of illusory achievement: degrees, credentials, awards, recommendations. A climate of promise. But not a climate of tangible, productive work. A climate with too much sunshine, perhaps: one that enervated its residents, leaving them ill prepared to endure blizzards, frost, hail, sleet, and rain.

Bad weather. Louise wondered if she could face it. Talking with Walt Kodaly, she had used brave words about leaving school and finding a job. A big step. Maybe a crucial one to restore the balance in her relationship with Scott. As his career had grown, he had changed. So a change on her part might even matters out, bringing something of her own into the commerce between them. It would not be a career, of course—Scott could hardly tolerate another demanding furry creature in their bed. It would only be a job. But the prospect, though fearful, was not unpleasing to her.

She drove the truck toward Malibu, looked with new eyes at the drilling platforms in the ocean, wondered what it would be like to work on one of them: flown in by helicopter in rough weather, wearing a protective helmet, sweating beside rough-talking men, smelling the sour scent of dark sluggish ooze pumped from pools far below. It was hard to picture herself in such a setting. Or Scott. Or T. S. Eliot. She looked at her hands on the steering wheel. Soft things. Stubby, rather than graceful. Like her father's.

"Dynamite." Barry's voice seemed to have a note of relief when he appeared at the door. "We were afraid you might have changed your mind."

"Is that Louise?" Clear and bell-like, Judy's voice sang out from the living room. "Is Scott with her?"

Louise followed Barry down the stairs. Judy was sitting on the sofa, heavy horn-rimmed glasses on, glasses that made her pale green eyes more than ordinarily large and searching.

"Scott is giving a poetry reading." Louise bent down, kissed her mother, found a nearby chair, and composed herself.

"I'm reading a new play." Judy held up a script.

"It's terrific," smiled Barry, looking directly at Louise as though to enlist her support of the proposition.

"It's a musical." Judy shook her red-thatched head. "My agent sent it over yesterday."

"Do you like it?"

"I don't know." Judy got up and began to pace restlessly. "I'm not sure it's right for me."

"What's it about?"

"Shirley Temple."

"Shirley Temple as an ambassador to one of those crazy-weird places in Africa," added Barry.

"That sounds interesting," said Louise. "Where are you going to do it?"

"Right here." Judy shook her head. "Right here where everyone can see me bomb." She went to the window and stared at the ocean for a moment, taking stock of the whitecaps as though they represented a potentially hostile audience.

"You'll bomb them right out of their seats." Barry made the assertion with as much force as he could. "Isn't that right, Louise?"

"You'll be fantastic." Louise tried her best to echo Barry's enthusiasm.

"Maybe." Judy continued to stare at the ocean.

There was a pause. A calming one, Louise felt. And somehow rewarding, as though she had brought it into the room with her.

"Are they playing volleyball down there?" said Barry finally.

Judy stepped closer to the window and slanted her gaze off to the left.

"They're batting the ball back and forth," she said. "But it doesn't look like much of a game yet. Do you want to give that body of yours some action?"

"Action!" Barry smiled happily and sprang up. "I love it." Spirits restored, he rushed out the door, clattering his way down the flight of steps that led to the beach.

"Let's go down and watch him," said Louise, feeling that the physical movement might soothe her mother further.

"Why not?" Judy shrugged and came away from the window.

They took off their shoes and followed Barry, detouring a little so as to travel a path on the wet sand left by the receding tide. Watching her feet sink down and make a clear impression, Louise felt that there was something satisfying about the slowness of their progress, as though the fact of movement were more important than its direction or speed.

"I haven't done any live performing since your dad and I started out," said Judy. The bell of her voice was oddly low—almost a sullen dirge.

"How about your dinner theater work?"

"They don't count. They're all standard pieces—and the audiences don't expect that much."

"It sounds to me like there's more of a chance for a hit with this show."

"There's a chance. But I'm the one who has to take it."

"But it's not really your show, is it? How about the writer, the producer, all the other people involved?"

"You don't understand." Judy stopped to pick up a pebble and threw it into the water with sudden vehemence. "I'm the one who has to go out there and make it happen. So I'm the one they'll make fun of if it doesn't work."

"It *will* work," said Louise. "I'm sure it will."

"I just don't know, I just don't know." Judy sighed, her pale green eyes turned thoughtfully on her daughter. "Why don't you stay for dinner?"

"I told you I was coming down to see Dad." Louise began to feel tight inside. First Scott, now her mother—each pulling at her, each trying to move her into a neatly defined space where she could be fenced in and put to use.

"You can see him any time—probably the weekend would be better for him anyway."

"He asked me to come down."

"I asked the producer to come over and explain things a little more," said Judy, still intent on her uncertainty. "I'd feel more comfortable if you were here."

"I wouldn't have anything to say." Louise gave a slight laugh. "I don't know anything about the theater."

"You won't have to say anything—just being there is enough."

"It'll be fine. I'm sure of it."

"You think so?"

"Positive."

They walked on to where a volleyball net had been staked out on the sand. The game was in progress: three on each side, Barry close in by the net, all of them whooping and leaping in a fine frenzy of physical joy. For Louise, the frieze of movement threw the bodies of the young men into sharper focus: very much as though a shrewd cameraman had chosen to blot out their faces and highlight the play of muscles, the individual taper of each back, the powerful, churning symmetry of thighs and legs. Powerful male torsos lightly whorled with hair: some black, some sandy, some brown.

"Barry's a nice boy," said Judy. "They all are."

"Good." Louise did not dissent, even though the incongruity made her feel uneasy. A strong man's body. A young boy's face: bland, unmarked by pain and failure, especially around the mouth and jaw. Like Scott, perhaps, whose dark beard effectively obscured any reading of his physiognomy.

"I wish your father were involved in all this." Judy bent down and touched her toes a few times. "He understands how these things work." She stopped and gazed back in the direction they had come from.

"Have you talked to him?"

"It's not the talking," said Judy. "It's the being there." She turned her pale green eyes on Barry and the other players for a moment. "Sometimes I wish we were all together in a big, big house."

"How big?"

"As big as the old Kerr estate up where you are." Judy pointed up the coastline. "A place like that would have room for all of us—you, Scott, Barry, your father, Rita, even some of your father's Kansas City people."

"That's pretty big."

"As big as a castle." Judy smiled at her daughter. "We could all have some great times in a place like that."

"It would cost a fortune to run."

"It would be worth it just to keep us all together." Judy sighed, took a couple of deep breaths, and touched her toes a few more times. When she finished, she looked up the coastline again, then at Louise. "I feel like running," she announced. "How about you?"

"I should be on my way," said Louise.

"You could use it." Judy looked sharply at her daughter. "I think you've been gaining weight lately."

"I know." Louise stared for a moment at her mother's body, marveling at its taut efficiency. "But I should get going before the traffic gets too heavy."

"I suppose so." Judy took a few more deep breaths, then stretched herself to make sure everything was in working order. "Try to bring Scott next time, will you?"

"I'll try."

Louise watched her mother angle out toward the packed, wet sand and start jogging up the coastline. After her mother had covered a couple of hundred yards, Louise waved goodbye to Barry and retraced her steps to the beach house.

Taking an opposite course, she drove down the coast highway, turning off at Malibu Canyon Road and heading for the Ventura Freeway. The road was a winding one, tunneling through the rock in spots and rising through degrees to slip its way past the mountains ranged there as a barrier between the moisture of the coast and the dryness of the valleys beyond. Big bare rocks they were, commanding in their placement. In Europe some of them would have been fortified, possibly by enterprising barons wishing to tax the traffic passing below.

Her mother's castle, she was sure, would be a fortified place: strong, secure, inviolate. Perfectly sufficient to itself and those within. And with her mother in the highest chamber: a perfect stage from which to command her audience: a place where doubt and fear could be securely locked away in stout dungeons far below. A place where loyal servitors, amusing and amused, would form a little world coherent in itself. A place where her mother's public and private roles, those of jester and suppliant, would merge into one changeless, satisfying shape—that of queen.

It was with regret that Louise reminded herself of the customary limitation of one queen to each castle. A proper limitation, one which held that any combination, even the most temporary pairing, permitted only one ruler. Rulers and ruled. They seemed to recognize each other, seek each other out: just as Scott had sought her, and she him.

"A tube." Jackie pointed to the several sections of his disassembled instrument. "When you get down to it, a trumpet is nothing more than a long tube." He nodded, pleased with the simplicity of the notion.

"Do you like working with your hands?" Sitting on a bench

in the far corner of Jackie's backyard workshop, Louise stared at the various crooks and valves that Jackie had spread out on the bench in front of him.

She was glad she had thought to seek her father out in his puttering shed. Getting no answer at the front door, she had fought back a sudden urge to drive back to Santa Barbara, then circled the house, taking a chance that she would find her father by the pool or in the workshop where he kept his tools and music paraphernalia. It was a small building, originally an artist's atelier, perhaps; and its capacities were strained to the limit in shelving Jackie's collection of orchestrations and scores. But it was a congenial place, well lit by overhead panes of glass, and with a modest workbench on the side facing the pool. More congenial than the house, which bore Rita's stamp.

"Sometimes," Jackie said in answer to Louise's question. He looked at his short, stubby hands for a minute, then put them to work swabbing out a valve casing. "I guess I've always been better working with my hands than working with people." He finished swabbing, assembled the instrument once more, picked up a medicine dropper, and put a few beads of oil on each of the three valves.

"Are you going to play it?"

"No." Jackie worked the valves a little, then fitted the instrument back into its plush-lined case, where it lay cradled like a large gleaming piece finding its proper place in a jigsaw puzzle. "When you've got one sound in your head and you hear another coming out, it's bad news." He snapped the case shut and turned and smiled at her. "Besides I've got a lot of other things cooking now."

"People things?"

"That's right."

"It might be better if people cooked for themselves." Louise's light brown eyes were distant, tinged with sulkiness, as she envisioned her kitchen activity in preparation for Scott's seminar. Good food, good wine, good talk—those were his requirements. The food and wine from her, the talk from him and his guests—including Heidi Kissinger.

"Someone has to do the cooking," said Jackie. "Otherwise it wouldn't get done." He nodded affably and picked up the trumpet case and put it gently in a nearby corner.

"Why does it have to be you?" said Louise pointedly.

"It's my job, I guess." Jackie smiled at her as though the answer were self-evident. "I was brought up to be a steady guy and take care of my obligations to people."

"What people?"

"Lots of people—the people who work at Jay Jay, my wife, my friends, my family back home, you and Scott. As Grandmother Hansen used to say, a man is measured by his responsibilities."

"I'm old enough to be responsible for myself."

"You still have your education to finish. After that you can start out on your own."

"I'd rather do it now." In her mind Louise began to draw a picture in which she and Scott would occupy equal space: both working, both contributing, both sharing in the business of living—including the cooking.

"What about school?"

"It's starting to get me down."

"Trouble with your courses?"

"No." Louise shook her head and brushed back a strand of light brown hair. "But it seems sort of pointless running around with people who all pretend they're going to be anthropologists someday—or state senators."

"Scott likes it, doesn't he?"

"He gets paid for it. It's his job. And I'm certain I'd be a lot happier if I had a job, too."

Jackie paused, went over to a shelf of orchestrations, and began to stack them a little more neatly. When he finished he sat down directly across from Louise.

"Walt Kodaly told me you were making sounds in that direction," he said. "That's one of the reasons I asked you to drive down."

"I'd been thinking about it before I talked to him," said Louise. "It's not impulsive, like wanting a new car—or a new house."

"That's what it all comes down to," said Jackie. "Money."

"Are you in trouble?" Louise looked out the window toward the house as though calling her post-adolescent stepmother to account.

"Not really. In fact, I have a chance to sell the company."

"Sounds good."

"It's not that good." Jackie looked thoughtfully at her. "There's a lot of indebtedness involved, so we won't really end up with that much. And that means it's going to be Thin City for a while."

"So my pulling out of school would help, then, wouldn't it?"

"It would help in cutting down expenses," said Jackie. "Though I wouldn't blame you if you wanted to keep going."

"I meant what I said." Louise tried to conceal the nervousness that had suddenly crept inside her—like that of a small child whose grandiose dare has unexpectedly been taken seriously. "But what are you and Rita going to do?"

"Spain." Jackie pointed to the trumpet case in the corner. "Rita wants to write, and I can certainly use the time to get my chops in shape."

"How does Rita feel about it?"

"I haven't told her yet."

"She might not like it, you know."

"I think she will." Jackie's voice was firm, confident. "I know she's used to all the action here. And I wouldn't be surprised if she gave me a bad time at first. But I also know she wants me to take charge a little more. Once she gets used to the idea, she'll be fine."

"How about you? Assuming Rita really wants to let the business go, is this what you want for yourself?"

"I think so. It looks good to me." Jackie shrugged. "But I'm not really sure if it's the right thing or not. Maybe all this talk about playing the trumpet is just a way of ducking what I really should be doing."

"That's possible," said Louise, feeling very wise and profound. "But you won't know unless you try."

"I suppose so."

"So don't worry about me." Most of her nervousness gone, Louise rose and came over to her father, maternal in her gesture and manner. "I'd like nothing more than to see you cut loose."

"Great!" said Jackie. He got up and rubbed his hands together with an air of accomplishment. "Where would you like to go for dinner?"

"Why don't we eat here?"

"The housekeeper is off today."

"I can cook."

"Do you want to?"

"Very much—especially for you," said Louise. She looked toward the house again, suddenly confident of her capacity to enter an alien realm and deal with its unknown quantities.

North Hollywood, California: Wednesday, November 1, 10:00 P.M.

"Not bad." Standing at the Embers West bar, Jackie nudged Vito slightly as the young man with frizzy blond hair held out a long note on the clarinet while the vibraphonist clanked out a rapid series of chords underneath.

"He's great!" Vito bobbed his large head to underscore the point. "I've seen him come in cold and hit a high G that's in perfect tune."

"You do that all the time."

"He'll be able to do it all the time if he stays on it." The song over, Vito applauded enthusiastically, looking around the room with a proprietary smile. Despite Vito's urging, the rest of the audience was relatively lukewarm; it was apparent that they had come to hear Vito play, not a protégé.

"That's what it takes."

"It helps." Vito turned his large eyes on Jackie, not without a touch of accusation. "But the desire is what keeps you going. You ought to know that."

"I know it." Jackie's voice was low. "But I don't know where it comes from." He gave a small laugh and shook his head. "If I did, I'd get my doctor to write me out a prescription."

"It's there, it's there. All you have to do is give yourself half a chance."

"I've been thinking about it."

"Think some more," said Vito. "Then give that German cat a phone call and tell him you're definitely going to make it."

"Herr Zweifel?"

"Yeah." Vito snapped his fingers as though to make the name stick. "I never can keep track of those weird foreign names."

"I don't know." Jackie focused for a minute on the music: a light, delicate version of "Stealing Apples." "I've been shuffling the pieces around but they don't seem to fit yet."

"They fit," Vito said firmly. "You've been looking at dollars and cents so long you can't see it—that's what the trouble is."

"It still doesn't seem like the right thing to do."

"What's wrong about getting your chops back in shape and making some good music?" Vito looked at him incredulously. "From what you told me, you're in a position to do it, and it's certainly something you want to do. So tell me one reason why you shouldn't do it."

"It's too much like running out." Jackie thought back to the bleakness left by his father's disappearance. "Too much like these clowns who talk about retiring, buying a boat, and sailing around the world."

"But you're not buying a boat." Vito pointed up to the bandstand. "You're coming aboard to help keep the damn thing afloat. Music is something you make together, and it sure as hell takes good people to make good music."

"You could get someone else if you had to."

"Not someone as good, not somebody with your stuff. You know that."

"Somebody almost as good, then."

"Almost is never good enough. You know that too."

Jackie sighed. First Walt, then Louise, now Vito. Different people. Different points of view. Different arguments. And Vito seemed to be the cleverest: almost as though he had taken Paul's responsibility pitch and transposed it to a new, compelling key, a key with a completely unexpected resolution—like the bridge of "All the Things You Are" shifting from E into A flat.

"I'm not sure I'm up to it."

"It's the one thing you *are* up to. And if you want my opinion, that's probably what you're afraid of."

"Maybe you're right," said Jackie thoughtfully. "Rita's therapist says we're all afraid of success."

"What instrument does she play?"

"Nothing, as far as I know."

"Then she doesn't know as much about it as you do."

"She makes sense sometimes."

"Not this time," Vito said. "Success has nothing to do with it. What you're afraid of is being absorbed—absorbed to the point where all you can think of is getting a better sound to lay on top of all those little notes dancing in your head. You used to practice six hours a day, right?"

"That's right," said Jackie, thinking back to hours spent blowing whole tones, blowing scales, transposing, memorizing, transforming, inverting, turning a common vocabulary of tricks and melodies into a private idiom.

"Six hours sounds like a lot, but it's nothing compared with all the thinking that went on—thinking nothing but music, music, music the other twenty hours of the day."

"Eighteen," said Jackie automatically. "Six from twenty-four is eighteen."

"Exactly." Vito shook his large, outsize head pityingly. "Like I said before, you've been working with those damn numbers too long."

Numbers. Jackie sighed, leaned back against the bar, and studied his drink. Vito seemed so sure of himself, so unassailable—almost as though over the years he had built up a completely self-contained world. A private world. Proof against bad luck, loss of popularity as public taste ebbed and flowed. Proof against ill health, sickness, even death itself. Proof against the noble laws of arithmetic and sound reasoning. For Vito, everything seemed to add up the way he wanted it to.

Jackie had always liked arithmetic; he had taken pride in his ability to scrutinize the apples and oranges, pecks and bushels, of the problems in elementary school: staring at the most dismal of facts straight on until he was able to fit them into a thrifty pattern. "We have to face facts—they're not going to run away," Grandmother Hansen had always said, making the point with grim relevance when it was clear that the head of the Hayes family was not going to return and deal with the material facts he had left behind: coal bills, house payment, food bills—barely diminished by an occasional bag of groceries from the Pendergast machine's generous bounty. With his mother in tears and his grandmother grimly implacable in her logic, Jackie had been the obvious candidate for facing the arithmetic.

He had been able to work the problem out: face the arithmetic and face the music at the same time. The two had seemed to fit together: balanced sides of the same equation. A talk with his trumpet teacher, Professor Varga. The offer of a job with Kale Brothers—and at a weekly wage four times as much as anything a sixteen-year-old boy could hope to make, even at a full-time job. It had all added up: the figures neatly assembled on a ruled sheet of yellow paper passed around the kitchen table. A good solution. Greeted coldly, he had noted. But finally accepted, on the condition that he return home when enough money had been saved and put away.

There had never been enough money. And so, reluctant to appear at the door empty-handed, he had stood shivering in the Wausau railway station and worked the equation out again, taking his horn, his bleak prospects, and his grief at losing Clara up the tracks to the high point of the grade, where freight trains had to slow their speed. Good arithmetic. Free passage to wherever the next train might be headed, there to disembark and try to recoup his losses.

Hopping freights. Sometimes hazardous, what with high speed and sudden turns capable of jolting the unwary loose to fall beneath a bright slash of wheels, along with attacks from the railroad police: big, husky, well-fed men with clubs, guns, dogs, and the law in their pocket. But hazards worth facing. And faced by many—drifters, homeless men, gentlemen of the road, bindle-stiffs.

At the top of the grade, a red glow. Not beside the tracks, but faintly visible in a nearby hollow. A coal fire in a rusty oil drum: ringed round with men, gaunt and thinly clad. A place for caution, balanced against the sound of hymns being sung. A place, perhaps, for a tenor part, lightly riding above the melody and winning modest welcome. Good arithmetic again.

Around the fire, low talk. Sad, beaten voices with most of the anger whipped out of them. One angry man, on his way to the American Legion headquarters in Indianapolis. And a fearful man, telling stories of gangs of wild boys, the oldest no more than twelve, coming down from the hills and bushwhacking solitary wanderers. Another equation to solve: whether to stay with the group or travel on alone.

A freight train grunting its way up the grade. Grunting heavily, moving slowly: slowly enough for a running man to match the pace set, hurl case and goods into an open doorway, jump up and in. Good arithmetic. Good gauging of distance and speed. Good choice, taking the chance alone.

A good freight car. Straw at both ends: straw and excelsior used for packing. Dry. Warm enough. Protected from drizzle and nighttime chill. A time for sleeping, humming softly to the complex Latin rhythm of the wheels beneath: throbbing a dance for dancers without legs. A time for sleeping, not for dreams.

Traveling on. Past small towns, past fences, telegraph poles, past domain of cloud and rain. Speeding through a land of clear sky, lit by a full moon yielding ample light to look around and see a soft dark blur standing out against the slats not far away.

Creeping up. Fearful, yet driven to explore and probe: to come upon the body of a fellow creature face down, motionless, still warm, shoeless. Beside the body, a large club, sticky at one end.

Creeping back. Giving way to nausea, retching mixed with tears of fellow feeling for a forked creature shorn of breath, dignity, name, and shoes. Grief giving way to fear: fear of suspicion, fear of husky men with dogs and guns, fear of blame, fear of guilt already half admitted.

Action. A crawling back to the face-down body. A tugging at the shoeless feet. A slow progress, tugger and tugged, to the doorway, followed by a shove that sends the face-down man tumbling out, arms and legs enlivened by momentum, bouncing down the embankment like a consummately relaxed clown. A clown, perhaps a tenor, or a handsome blue-eyed man, or a coldly staring countenance of reproach. In any event, not a face to look at.

More action. The club. The one remaining trace of actors and play, assault and catastrophe. A club about the size of a baseball bat, sticky at one end. A club to seize, to heft, then fling out with force so that it arched far, far away. Leaving emptiness: in the freight car, and inside as well. Good arithmetic. Good subtraction.

"The numbers have to come out right," Jackie said finally. He put his drink back on the bar and looked around the room, mild blue eyes narrowed as though balancing the customers against the cost of the musicians. "If they don't, you can't pay the rent, and nobody wins."

"Does that mean you're a loser if you're not a big winner?"

"Come off it, man." Jackie gave a short laugh and smiled knowingly at Vito. "Last time I was in here you were going on and on about how much you loved a challenge." He pointed up to the bandstand. "And right now you're just dying to get back there, pick up your axe, and cut that little guy into pieces."

"There's a big difference between doing your best and putting everything on a dollars-and-cents basis."

"What other measurement is there?" said Jackie. "How do you know whether it's good or not if you can't draw a bottom line somewhere?"

"You know." Vito's large eyes blazed a little. "And that's enough to keep you going."

"You're not trying to tell me you're working here for nothing, are you?"

"I might as well be," said Vito. "My wife and I have enough stashed away to live on, more than enough. Like I told you before, I'm playing here because it's not real if you don't get out and play for people."

"Maybe later on I'll be far enough ahead of the game to get back to the real stuff. Believe me, I'd do it in a minute if someone came up with a better offer for Jay Jay."

"Numbers again." Vito shook his big head sadly. "For someone who plays the way you do, you've got the soul of a bookkeeper, always looking for a good bottom-line figure to tell you who you are. What are you going to do with all that loot, leave it to the church?"

"I'd like to be able to pass something along."

"Why? Did anyone pass anything along to you?"

"No."

"Did it do you any harm to make it on your own?"

"I wish I'd been able to get a better education."

"If you had, you would probably be teaching high school somewhere right now—trying to get a bunch of no-talent kids into shape for the big football game. Instead you were lucky enough to get into fast company right away at a time when everything was cooking." Vito paused and pointed to the young clarinetist. "Look at that kid—he's got good stuff, and the best gig he can get is playing back-up tenor saxophone for a couple of hillbilly guitar players who dude themselves up in weird costumes and sing out of tune. But even though it's all funny hats now, he stays on it. You were lucky enough to get the best musical education possible—and get paid for it. And you still have the guts to come in here wearing almost a thousand dollars' worth of clothes and whine about the bad cards you got on the first deal."

"I guess I shouldn't complain." Jackie reddened a little and began to wish Vito would go back to the bandstand.

"Why don't you think about passing something along besides money—money that will probably do a lot of harm to the people who get their hands on it?"

"What else is there?"

Vito took a deep breath and reached for his tall drink again. It was obvious to Jackie that he was uncomfortable, almost as though he had been pushed to the wall and forced to yield up the contents of a hidden pocket.

"You know how it is when you're playing jazz," Vito said slowly. "Most of the time it just comes out—you hear the changes, one thing leads to another, and then it's over." He took a long pull from his drink and stared down at the floor between them. "Still, there are times when I sort of stand back and notice things I'm doing."

"Like what?"

"A lick here, a run there, maybe an interval jump or a way of phrasing—little things that I've picked up over the years."

"Where from?"

"Other players, mostly. Buster Bailey, Russell Procope, Fazola, Benny—little things that they did which somehow hit my ear and stuck there. Not just clarinet players, either." He looked up and smiled at Jackie. "I've even noticed a couple of your tricks sticking out at a weak moment."

"I'd always thought I was the one who did the learning where you were concerned."

"It works both ways," said Vito sagely. "But you're right about the general drift—the older guys lay down something, and the younger guys pick it up. So a little of it gets passed along year after year."

"Like teaching?"

"No." Vito shook his head emphatically. "It's much more chancey. I'd say it was more of an example—not an example you copy completely, you understand. Just an example that leaves a little bit of itself floating in your head along with everything else." He lowered his voice as though to reveal a private madness. "I wouldn't be surprised if a couple of those bits have been floating from one head into another for a thousand years or more—going back to the first wooden whistle some strange, bearded cat whittled out and started blowing on. Take my old man, for example."

"He wasn't a music player, was he?"

"No. He worked with wood, though. And he had a way of seating drawers he picked up in the old country. Very smooth, very smooth. And who knows where he got it, to say nothing of where it started."

"Jesus!" Jackie lowered his voice to match Vito's, stared into Vito's large eyes with awe. "You have it all worked out, don't you?"

"I've had plenty of time," said Vito, relaxed and pleased that his secret could stand the test of open discourse. "About ten years ago I was laid up in the hospital for six months—all I could do was run scales in my head and think."

"I never realized you were a heavy-thinker type."

"I can't help it. Sometimes my head gets spinning and spinning so much I can't stand it. The only time it stops is when I let the music take over." He looked around the room and waved to a couple of tables. "And that's what I'm going to do now, since it seems to me we've beaten it to death pretty well."

"I'd say you've done most of the beating," said Jackie. "Every time I get up you knock me down with one of your crazy ideas."

"I've given you my best shot." Vito started for the bandstand, paused, and turned around to face Jackie once more. "So are you going to get in touch with this Zweiback dude or am I?"

"Zweifel." Jackie smiled and took a deep breath. "His name is Zweifel."

"Don't change keys on me. Are you going to call him or not?"

"I'll call him," said Jackie. "And I'll call you after I've talked to him."

"Great!" Vito beamed happily, then wheeled and strutted up to the bandstand. At his approach the young clarinetist started to step down, but Vito put up a warning hand. "Stay on it," he said. "Why don't we play some duets?"

A duet. To Jackie the notion was attractive. He and Rita: making their own music in Spain, cutting free from the demands of family, discontented employees, business problems, social obligations. A seamless web, Paul Ciardi had called it. A web woven by spiders to trap flies with. Suddenly he knew he was going to break out.

When Vito and the young clarinetist began to play, Jackie remained at the bar, smiling and nodding his head in time to the music.

New Orleans, Louisiana: Thursday, November 2, 11:00 A.M.

Chicory. Rita looked down at the white cup in front of her with irritation: irritation at herself rather than at the Monteleone Hotel waitress who had just set it down. She had ordered the chicory automatically, lapsing back into an old New Orleans habit in the same way that she had lapsed back into putting sugar on her tomatoes at the family dinner in Hattiesburg. Serious lapses. Serious enough to take up with Melissa in their assertion of the power of the past: a disease lying dormant until circumstances and lack of control urge the symptoms forth, like measles breaking out long after the period of exposure.

Her control had for the most part been quite good. Especially in Hattiesburg, where she had been careful to dress severely and speak in complete, exotically worded sentences—putting a cool Olympian distance between her and her listeners. The Lions Club, Rotary, the high school, the local television station—the listeners had all been attentive and respectful. It was as though her private voices had suddenly gone public. Gratifyingly so.

She had dropped her guard a little in her contact with her family. But that was understandable. They had seemed genuinely glad to see her, even though she had stayed at a local hotel. And it had been oddly pleasurable to sit in the living room and listen to her father and brothers drone on about hunting, fishing, drinking, and local politics. So she had smiled without effort, taken her shoes off, said "y'all" when the spirit moved her, and even speculated a little on what it would be like to come back for good to a place where her past and present selves could be fitted together so neatly: as neatly as the twin halves of the croissant on the plate before her.

New Orleans so far was not much of a triumph for her. Even though her trip had been noted in *Variety,* there were no messages for her, no suppliants waiting in the Monteleone's lobby. The night before, she had phoned Melissa, primarily to make sure that Jackie had not canceled his appointment. Reassured, she had promised Melissa to keep in touch and let her know of any changes in schedule or plans. And the plans appeared to be moving along quite satisfactorily: like floats and marchers lined up off Canal Street, quietly positioning themselves for a noisy, garish display at a later-appointed triumphal time.

A quiet hour for her. Rita slowly nibbled on one half of her croissant, then pushed it away, reminding herself that her short immersion in Hattiesburg had probably added almost two pounds. A brisk walk was clearly called for.

It was a good day for walking. Mild. But a tang in the air: a slight promise of rain in a few days. Enough to put a spring in the step as she strode down Royal Street toward the cathedral. Along the way she took stock of what she saw: the shops, the slow, browsing pace of people headed toward her, the faint aura of prosperity that seemed to have settled over the French Quarter like a soft autumn mist. A cleansing mist, like a preparation designed to bring out the luster in old wood. The quarter was much cleaner than she had remembered it, much more docile: suggesting that a committee of thoughtful Southern gentlemen had taken a trip to Disneyland and come back with an explicitly defined restoration plan.

The cathedral was still the same. And so was the equestrian statue of Andrew Jackson in the square facing it. A powerful statue: larger than life, and with a sense of sweating urgency to it. Urgency more appropriate then than now, when battles were fought more discreetly and gentlemen no longer called for their pistols whenever they felt affronted. She sat down on a bench and watched a group of tourists parade gravely past her on their way to view the river and its traffic. A young man, unshaven and muttering, came up and sat down beside her.

"You seem like a young woman of good family," said the young man suddenly.

"What's that?" Though taken by surprise, Rita was able to bark back an authoritative response, coupled with a cold, contemptuous look.

"I dunno." He shook his head and stared down at the pavement in front of them. "I could sure use a cigarette."

"I don't have any cigarettes."

The young man closed his eyes, let his head loll back for a moment, breathed heavily a few times, then bent his head forward again.

"I sure feel bad," he said.

Rita stared straight ahead.

"Maybe a quarter would help," said the young man finally. He looked bleary-eyed at the pigeons massing near them, then gave a low, rasping cough. "Just a quarter, for Chrissake."

It was time to go. Rita rose in one fluid movement and started across the square to Royal Street. Not running. And certainly not fearful. But raging inside at the Southern gentlemen who apparently had decided that it would be more authentic if they equipped their Disneyland with real squalor and real derelicts.

She had wanted to hit him: angered by his pleading insouciance, his youth, his snuffling and whining. It was more than a token blow that she had envisioned: a well-placed kick in the groin, perhaps; or higher up. A salvo of kicks would have been called for: rapier thrusts as sharp and as deadly as those exchanged, taper lit, by hot-tempered bucks in days past when the cathedral's garden had served as a dueling ground.

Her dark eyes were still cold and furious when Bruce walked into the lobby.

"Anything wrong?" Bruce looked quizzically at her. "No problems from Jackie's end, are there?"

"Everything's fine," said Rita, somehow reassured and restored to good humor by Bruce's ability to sense any changes in her mood.

"Excellent!" Bruce led her out to a long black limousine. A uniformed chauffeur opened the rear door for them.

"Where do we come on the agenda?"

"First." Bruce turned toward her and lowered his voice slightly. "But they'll have to deal with a few progress reports at the outset, so we'll be able to relax for a few minutes in the reception room and share insights."

"Splendid." Rita smiled: partly at Bruce, partly in gratification at being able to subdue her habitual Jay Jay response of "Great." A hopeful, positive sign.

It took only a few minutes for the chauffeur to pull up in front of a small two-story stone building rather incongruously set between two sparkling white towers. Incongruous. But not uncomfortable. An impression of aristocratic poise, not unlike that of a wealthy sportswoman who prides herself on her ability to wear overalls and swear with stableboy eloquence. An important building.

"I'll need you for lunch," said Bruce to the chauffeur.

"But Mr. Charley Bob told me I was to drive him up river later on this morning." The chauffeur's voice was soft, lilting, redolent of bayou country.

"I'll take care of Charley Bob. You just stand ready with this car. Hear?"

Rita felt her senses come alive as the chauffeur drove off. There was a feeling of combativeness in the air and in Bruce, who seemed for a moment to have lapsed back to an earlier, more deeply rooted manner of expression. A tenseness centered on the limousine, but growing out of something more serious. Something worth watching for.

"Charley Bob is one of the cousins who stayed home," said Bruce.

They walked into the ground floor of the Bonnet Bank. But where Rita had expected to see tellers and marble floors there was instead only a large, carpeted lobby filled with overstuffed chairs and sofas. Down at the far end, a couple of elevators. Near them, a large desk, almost obscuring the small, wizened man behind it.

Bruce led her to a chair, then retraced his steps and spoke briefly to the small, wizened man. He came back, sat down across from her, opened up his document case, and spent a minute checking its contents to make sure all was in order. Reassured, he clicked the case shut.

"They may ask you some questions," he said.

"What kind of questions?"

"Nothing specific, nothing to worry about. You'll be fine as long as your replies are not blatantly obfuscatory."

Rita smiled, sighed with inward pleasure: feeling herself to be stroked, catlike, by fine language and discreet surroundings.

She felt as though she were embarking on a great argosy, a splendid voyage: pointed toward a future richer by far and more exciting than anything she had ever known. Almost purring, she broadened the arc of her approval to include a short, chubby young man hurrying toward them.

"Brucie!" said the chubby young man. "I need that car."

"Sorry, Charley Bob." Bruce stiffened immediately, clearly irritated at being addressed so familiarly. "Mrs. Hayes and I have a luncheon engagement. A business engagement," he added pointedly.

"I think this family has a problem." The chubby young man glared at Bruce for a second, made a clucking sound with his mouth, and rushed off.

"Charley Bob is the problem." Bruce looked darkly around the room. "His eyes have always been a whole lot bigger than his muscle."

Rita remained silent. Whatever the struggle for power was, it seemed that Bruce had the upper hand. She resisted an impulse to suggest that they take a cab by way of compromise. Power, she had learned, existed primarily in its visible exercise—like Bruce's peremptory ordering of iced tea for her in their first conference on this matter.

A bent old man in a short jacket came up, standing wordlessly by as they got to their feet. He led them to one of the elevators and put it in motion: a slow, barely perceptible movement that took them in time to the second floor. There the carpets were quite thick, cushioning the sound of their progress down the hall to the large, brass-handled doors at the far end.

"Here's Brucie, Grandmère," said a red-faced man. His voice struck Rita as unnecessarily loud: like a great booming church bell intended as a summons to judgment for the frail old woman seated at the center of the broad mahogany table. An old woman with pale white skin and very red hair.

"I know who it is," said the old woman. She darted a venomous look at the red-faced man, who quailed slightly before the sting of her intense green eyes. To Rita, there was something familiar about the old woman's face: as though she were looking at a caricature of someone known, someone recognizable.

Rita stood in front of the table while Bruce circled it and bent down to give Grandmère a kiss. Not a perfunctory kiss, but a full one: on the lips, almost passionate in its force. Then he retraced his steps and returned to Rita, introducing her to the directors of the Bonnet Bank: Grandmère Bonnet, Uncle Myron, and Uncle Homer. The red-faced man turned out to be Uncle

Myron, Charley Bob's father, while Uncle Homer seemed to be cut more from Bruce's cloth: lean, quiet, dressed with cool elegance.

"You've done a good job, Bruce," said Uncle Homer. "We've already taken the vote."

"But not a unanimous vote." Red-faced and scowling, Uncle Myron looked directly at Bruce. "It's not the money I mind, it's the roundabout way we're taking."

"Out of order," rasped Grandmère. "Out of order and shut up." To emphasize the point, she picked up a silver-trimmed gavel and thumped it once on the table. "You'd be a lot better off if you watched those shows—good humor never hurt anybody's digestion."

"I don't think we need any more discussion," said Uncle Homer quickly. He got up, went over to Grandmère and whispered something in her ear.

"No discussion, no more cussing, there's an end to all our fussing." Grandmère rolled her eyes and smiled roguishly at Rita. Again, grotesquely accurate in her caricature of someone known, someone familiar.

"Are you sure you don't want us to make a presentation?" Bruce tapped his document case.

"We're making the presentation," grumbled Uncle Myron. "A presentation of a line of credit long enough to hang out all the washing of this fair parish."

"It might be a good idea if you wait downstairs for a bit," said Uncle Homer. "If the lawyers have any questions, we may want you to come up."

"We girls here don't say 'you may,' " rasped Grandmère. "We say 'you-all may.' " Defiantly she looked them all in the face, one by one. Then she broke into a great gust of throaty laughter: laughter in which Bruce and Uncle Homer joined pleasurably, Uncle Myron reluctantly.

Just like a comedy show, thought Rita. A comedy show done before a live audience. A comedy show starring a small, taut, red-haired woman.

After the old man in the red jacket took them back down to the lobby, Rita continued to ponder the matter.

"It went very well," said Bruce. "They always insist on some kind of personal contact, even when it's the attorneys who work everything out."

"I hope you don't mind my saying it was more than a little overwhelming."

"It always is." Bruce flashed his perfectly aligned teeth

for a minute. "I think it took Frank May six months to get over it."

"You'll have to admit it's different from Bank of America."

"The decor is different." Bruce waved around the lobby. "But the money comes in the same denominations, and it changes hands in the same way. A little eccentricity here and there merely makes it more interesting."

"Your grandmother is certainly a remarkable woman."

"It runs in the family." Visibly relaxed, Bruce looked directly at her, a faint smile hovering on his lips as though to suggest that other surprises lay in store.

"She reminds me a little of Judy."

"Who?"

"Judy Hayes. Remember how she worked in 'Judy's Guy'—the red hair, the rhymes?"

"I suppose you could say there's a resemblance," Bruce said slowly. "But it's certainly something that's never occurred to me." He looked down at his watch. "I don't think we'll have to wait around much longer—and then we're off to Owen Brennan's for lunch."

"Splendid." Rita sat back, her pleasure undiminished by the sight of Charley Bob approaching them.

"Brucie, I really need that car."

"Are you asking my permission, Charley Bob?"

"I'm asking you to be reasonable."

"Are you asking my permission?"

Charley Bob glared at his cousin, set his jaw, took a deep breath to contain his rage and frustration.

"Yes," he said.

"On the surface it seems like a reasonable request," Bruce said easily. "You need the car for a long trip up river, while I merely want it for a short drive right here in the city—a drive that I could very well manage in a taxicab."

"That's right." Charley Bob began to brighten.

"As I said, on the surface it seems like a reasonable request. But we're neglecting one very significant factor."

"What's that?" asked Charley Bob suspiciously.

"Mrs. Hayes and I are lunching together, and that simple fact makes my short trip ten times more important than your long trip. If you had been able to pass algebra, you would have been able to figure all this out for yourself."

It was beautiful, Rita thought—a little cruel, perhaps—but a delicate, ruthless display, like that of a swordsman showing off his skill in making the most out of an inferior opponent. A display intended for her.

"They want to see you upstairs, Mr. Bruce," said the old man in the short jacket, his voice as soft as his approach had been. "Alone."

More tenseness. The clear, pellucid waters suddenly muddied by the stirring of a creature far below the surface. Bruce wavered as the old man bowed and gestured toward the elevator.

"I'll be fine." Rita smiled encouragement at Bruce.

"Why don't you go right on and take that car," said Bruce to Charley Bob.

"It wouldn't be proper." Charley Bob winked at Rita. "I'd just as soon stay here and entertain Mrs. Hayes while you're doing your *devoir* upstairs."

"Don't believe a word he says." Bruce hurled the words over his shoulder as he went off. "We just keep Charley Bob around to tell stories."

Rita watched Bruce disappear into the elevator before she turned her dark eyes back to Charley Bob. Pudgy and with a soft round face, Charley Bob was not much to look at. But behind that smooth exterior lay something worth digging for.

"Your cousin is a very, very important man out west, Mr. Bonnet." She smiled brightly at Charley Bob, watched the round face redden.

"He's not that important." Charley Bob glowered around the lobby for a moment. "This here is what's important."

"I'm sure that's true," said Rita cautiously. "But we certainly think the world of Bruce." Just the right note, she felt: a slipping back into Southern turns of speech, but still under control.

"He's an errand boy, that's all. Nothing but a high-paid errand boy for Grandmère."

"Well, he's sure been good to us at Jay Jay."

"You wouldn't say that if you knew what all this is really about."

"I'm not sure I follow your meaning, sir."

"It doesn't matter," said Charley Bob sulkily.

"I suppose not." Rita gave him a faintly patronizing look. "These business negotiations are pretty hard for you to understand, perhaps. I gather from what was said that you don't have much of a head for figures."

"You're the one who doesn't understand."

"I think you're just making sounds at me, Mr. Bonnet.

Why don't you tell me one of those famous stories of yours?"

"I'd like to, but I have to be going now." Round face red to the point of bursting, Charley Bob looked toward the front door.

"You're not going to run away and leave me here unprotected, are you?" Deliberately, Rita turned her calm, remote face away from his. "But I suppose you feel that protection is Bruce's job, don't you?"

"You're not getting any favors from Bruce, Mrs. Hayes." Charley Bob's voice was cold and hostile. "If you had any sense at all, you'd see what he's after."

"And what might that be, Charley Bob?" Rita continued to keep her face averted, her tone goading.

"Those shows with the red-haired girl in them—'Judy's Guy.' That's what Grandmère wants. And that's what Grandmère is going to get, one way or the other."

"You're quite wrong." Dark eyes narrowing, Rita turned back to face Charley Bob once more. "Those shows have absolutely nothing to do with Jay Jay Productions—they're all tied up in a separate trust. And Mr. Hayes will never, never turn loose of them. It's a sentimental matter."

"He'll turn loose of them when he gets far enough in debt to us." Charley Bob smiled at her with smug satisfaction on his round face. "Grandmère is just as sentimental as he is—and she has damn near all the money in the world."

"Why on earth would that dear old lady be so set on acquiring a couple of hundred old TV comedy shows?" Suddenly empty inside, Rita began to merge picture and caricature together: Judy and Mrs. Bonnet.

"She loves those shows, watches them all the time." Charley Bob shook his head in awe. "And she means to make everybody watch them. Cable TV, satellite transmission, cassettes, video discs—she's going to spread them all over the world."

"I still don't understand why."

"It's not just the money. You ought to know by now that money doesn't mean anything to people who have it."

"Just a commodity," said Rita dully, thinking back to Bruce's original presentation. "But why not do something else with it?"

"It's a simple matter of poor digestion."

"Poor digestion?" Uneasy in the presence of madness, Rita looked hopefully toward the elevator.

"Grandmère has a weak stomach," sighed Charley Bob. "And since watching those shows has helped her digestion, she wants the whole world to watch them so that the digestion of the whole wide world will be materially improved."

"That's incredible."

"It's crazy." Charley Bob was close to tears. "But it's what she wants to do, and when she says frog they all jump—even Daddy. And Brucie is the one who jumps the highest."

Rita watched Charley Bob hurry off toward the desk by the front entrance, pleased with herself for probing until the creature took shape. Not at all the large, scaly, toothed saurian she had expected. Just a small frog: a frog set in motion by sudden currents in a mad old woman's mind. Small. But dangerous.

The principal danger involved her husband. Already undecided about the Bonnet credit offer, Jackie would assuredly pull out completely if he knew what the master plan was. And her wifely *devoir* was obvious: phone him immediately, warn him, keep her guard up as far as Bruce was concerned; and return to a small role in a failing business.

A wifely duty. She had heard the phrase often enough in Hattiesburg, which was where it belonged. In moving out and up, she had replaced it with its proper corollary—husbandly duty. And in that department Jackie had clearly become weaker and weaker during the last year. The inability to decide. The retreat into fantasies about Spain and trumpet playing. The implicit pleading for affection, almost identical to that of the ragged young man in Jackson Square, almost as deserving of coldly silent kicks and blows. And from the top of the balance sheet glared the greatest of his derelictions—a capacity for generating boredom day after day, week after week, year after year.

Boredom. Stultification. Parched earth. Only a failing, middle-aged plant to tend year by year: trying to liven his juices with hers, jog his fraying memory, tempt his dulled sexual palate. A plant whose brittle tendrils were wound round her legs, binding her to the ground when she dreamed of flying. To tell Jackie would bind her permanently. At a time when the Bonnet offer gave her the chance of breaking free and soaring off on her own.

Freedom. Freedom to experiment with new production concepts. Freedom to option new properties. The pleasure of working with new authors, new directors, new performers, new technical people. All made possible by the whim of a crazy old woman sitting behind a mahogany desk in New Orleans. A whim that she could ride aloft, like a sailplane catching an updraft, riding it straight up to new, commanding heights: a ride alive with the danger of miscalculating, of losing control and plummeting downward. A danger to fear. But a ride she wanted desperately to take.

Fear. Something to talk over with Melissa, who was scheduled to phone her after Jackie's therapy session tomorrow. In her mind Rita could hear the voices start again: "It's perfect." "She's brilliant." "Total control of every stage in the process." "Superb timing." "Always able to make the right decision." It would be lovely, she decided, to phone Melissa as soon as possible, so that insights could be shared in depth, and congratulations exchanged in flowing, graceful, unhurried words.

Rita was smiling pleasantly when Bruce came out of the elevator and hurried up to her.

"Where's Charley Bob?"

"He had to leave." Rita laughed, touched his arm for a moment. "Maybe he was afraid you would change your mind about the car."

"Good." Still wary, Bruce looked at her closely.

"It's been a good morning." Rita took his hand and gave it a squeeze.

"Everything taken care of." Eyes sparkling, he looked at her proudly. "Everything, that is, except the celebrating."

"This is the town for it," said Rita.

"Of course." Bruce took a deep breath and exhaled with satisfaction. "If you could stay over for a few days, we could celebrate in style."

"Let's have lunch and talk about it." Rita smiled at him, her eyes on a level with his. "But I'd like to go back to the hotel for a minute or so if you don't mind."

Encino, California:
Friday, November 3, 9:45 A.M.

Sensory therapy. Dr. Melissa Stritch invoked the phrase to herself as though it were a soothing, talismanic mandala. Sight, sound, smell, taste, touch: to her these were avenues for bypassing a client's defenses and traveling deep into private territory. A faint scent of lavender in the room. A cup of coffee as a gift redolent of home and affection. Rich textures throughout; paintings, too. Her own costume: a flowing rose velvet gown with *V*-shaped blue slashes. To encounter Dr. Stritch on her home ground was like stepping into a strange, luxuriant tropical jungle: a jungle where basic passions could break their fetters and bare their teeth. A place where much could be said, and even more expressed.

Dr. Stritch's costume had not been chosen at random. She had studied Lüscher, Koffka, Kepes, and others in search of sensory signals that would at once challenge and reassure. And her doctoral thesis had been a project designed to test the meliorative effects of resident-designed costumes on institutional morale.

A brilliant project. She had gone over to a New Jersey mental hospital with rolls and swatches of vividly colored fabrics, cut them up into workable shapes, distributed them among the members of her control group, and sat back with her notebook to assess the results. Beautiful results. Beautiful costumes: garish cloaks, sashes, scarves, turbans, chevrons and epaulettes, slouch hats with waving plumes. And she had watched with joy as the residents, each uniquely decked out, paraded themselves up and down the corridors of the locked ward: smiling, self-assured, cheerful, and alert.

A brilliant project. But not a successful one. The joy and beauty had quickly fallen prey to the gnawing of small worms: complaints from members of the staff grown uncomfortable and jealous in their plain white coats; complaints from visiting relatives uneasy in the company of vivid silks and satins. So her grant had not been renewed. And the judgment of her superiors had not been enthusiastic, with the result that she had been forced to move into the private therapy sector: a sector where theoretical brilliance was much less important than processing clients at a profitable rate.

In private practice, the setting of fees was a delicate art, especially when the relationship between time spent and value received was difficult to establish, as in the question of exactly how much Mrs. Lyndon should be charged for recent professional services rendered.

An interesting problem. Not much actual time involved: only three telephone calls, making a total of only sixteen minutes spent in securing Colonel Lyndon's release. But the value of those telephone calls appeared to be substantial: a value measurable in terms of Colonel Lyndon's career, the reputation of the United States Marine Corps, overall public confidence in the capabilities of our armed forces, and general social stability. A value that demanded sustained and detailed computation.

She pulled a large note pad out and picked up a 314 Eagle pencil more suitable for sketching than for fee setting. At the top of the pad she wrote down her target figure in large script—$2,000.00. After a pause she put down her first subfigure: a conference fee of $300.00, reflecting Mrs. Lyndon's desperate phone call from outside the security office at Sears, where the colonel had been caught trying to walk out unobserved with a large hunting knife stuffed inside his green bush jacket.

Resisting an impulse to draw a picture of the knife, she set down a professional research fee of $450.00, reflecting her study of Dr. Alma Milhouse's paper, "The Therapist as Fixer: A Positive Role in a Negative Society." After this, a professional consultation fee of $800.00, reflecting her phone call to a particularly hysterical client's husband who happened to be highly placed in the city attorney's office. Then a substantive conference fee of $675.00 to cover the return call to poor Mrs. Lyndon: a soft, soothing call announcing that all had been settled and that the colonel would be released within half an hour.

Total fee for professional services: $2,275.00. Less special client 10 percent discount, $227.50. Net balance: $2,047.50. A good figure, agreeably overshooting the target a bit—better. She underlined the net balance and drew a good-sized Bowie knife pointing toward it. Then she rose, smoothed the folds of her flowing rose-velvet gown, walked out to the billing office of the Institute for Creative Interaction, and gave her computation to one of the accountants.

She peeked round the corner into the waiting room and noted with pleasure that Mr. Hayes had arrived well in advance of his scheduled appointment. A good sign. Particularly in view of Rita's fear that her husband might back out: back out of the appointment, back out of making his decision, back out of a commitment to progress and personal growth, back out of life itself. Repressing any indication of her pleasure, Dr. Stritch billowed down upon him.

"I see you're early," she said grimly. "Do you want to get started now?"

"It's all right with me if it's convenient for you." Jackie smiled up at her, then rose, a stocky figure in an expensive blue silk suit: dark hair, mild blue eyes.

"It's your decision."

"Let's do it, Dr. Stritch."

"Melissa," corrected Dr. Stritch. "With a nondirective approach, first names are called for." She pointed toward the corridor, trying to make the authority of her gesture as inconspicuous as possible.

"Maybe I should do that with my internist."

"That's your decision, Jackie."

First names. Dr. Stritch loved being on a first-name basis with highly placed clients, especially those in the entertainment field. Names that she and her professional colleagues passed around like rare, precious jewels in their commerce with one another—just to utter them was somehow to possess their warm, iridescent glow. And with the intimacy of first names came the intimacy of personal contact: phone calls that extended her life into realms never dreamt of in the Bronx—like her conversations with Rita.

"A lot of things have been falling into place for me,"

Jackie said as he followed her plump, velveted form down the corridor and into the spacious office.

"Not yet." Dr. Stritch shook her head, held up a warning hand. In silence she made Jackie sit down. And in silence she walked over to the panel by her desk and pressed a button. At her touch, loud recorded music assaulted the room.

"Macho, macho, macho man," chanted the record.

"Macho, macho, macho man," repeated Dr. Stritch. She bobbed and swayed to the rhythm for a moment, all the while keeping her hot black eyes trained on Jackie. Intimacy established, she reduced the volume and sat down across from him, letting the absence of speech define their relationship further.

"Do you like this song?" she finally said.

"It's commercial." Jackie smiled a little, nodding agreeably.

"I mean in terms of your own personal values." Dr. Stritch looked over at her large line-and-squiggle painting as if to signal that frankness was called for.

"It doesn't do much for me."

"Why not?"

"The chord changes aren't very interesting."

"That's not much of a response," said Dr. Stritch, still fixing him with her hot black eyes.

"That's the way I see it." Jackie shrugged, looked away from her as though the room ordered his attention for a moment.

"I think this song upsets you."

"That's the way you see it, I guess."

"Macho, macho, macho man," said Dr. Stritch in a soft, insinuating voice. She rose, went over to the panel, and turned the sound completely off. Silence again, followed by a quizzical glance at Jackie. "Do you think of yourself as a macho man?"

"Beats the hell out of me." Jackie smiled awkwardly. "I'm not sure exactly what it means."

"Strong." Dr. Stritch drew the nasal consonant out and shook her jowls with relish. "It means 'strong.' "

"Like a weightlifter?"

"Not like a weightlifter." Dr. Stritch shook the question away. "Strong in human terms, strong like John Fitzgerald Kennedy was strong. Strong in being able to make decisions, important decisions. Are you strong like that?"

Leaving Jackie ample time in which to frame his reply, Dr. Stritch turned away from him and stared pensively out the window, thinking with affection of John Fitzgerald Kennedy and his years—years of vigor, years of promise, years of growth and opportunity, years in which she had broken out from behind the counter of her parents' neighborhood grocery in the Bronx, disdaining her mother's assertion that "girls don't need to go to school—girls need to marry nice boys," disdaining her father's insistence that her small savings play a part in financing the legal education of her semi-literate brother—currently employed as a bill collector in Milwaukee. Years in which she had worked in an art-supplies store and gone to city college at night, years that even now smiled warmly and beckoned to her.

The Kennedy years had seen the accelerating course of her career's trajectory: a plump, self-sufficient capsule finding its proper place in the heavens. Step by step, degree by degree, Melissa Stritch had climbed upward toward distant stars and moons: true always to President Kennedy's dream and hers, lacking only the opportunity to hold that strong hand, stroke that majestic brow, massage that overburdened back, even interpose herself as willing surrogate between that noble head and the assault on it from sullen, vengeful foes. A sadness to be borne, a vision to be cherished.

Putting her vision of President Kennedy aside, Dr. Stritch focused her attention once more on Jackie and nodded understandingly at him.

"It's always hard to make decisions," said Jackie finally. "Especially big ones."

"Daz weisst der Asel," said Dr. Stritch. "We all know that without being told. But what we want to know is what progress you yourself are making?"

"I think I've made some real progress."

"That's easy to say. Can you back it up?"

"What do you mean, 'back it up'?"

"Can you honestly tell me that you're ready to make the important decisions in your life for yourself, by yourself?"

"Yes."

"Even business decisions?"

"Yes."

"What kinds of business decisions?"

Dr. Stritch smiled benignly as Jackie, clearly uncomfortable, began to squirm a little. The conference was going well, moving to the point where a commitment would be made in overt language: language that would subsequently force action to stand behind it.

"Could I take my coat off?" said Jackie. "It's a little warm in here."

"Put it over there." Dr. Stritch indicated a chair on his

left, the chair in which Rita had placed herself a week ago. Nor did the draping of Jackie's expensive blue silk coat over the chair diminish the sense of Rita's presence in the room.

"That's a nice-looking suit you have on," she said. "Did Rita pick it out for you?"

"As a matter of fact she did." Jackie chuckled at the memory. "She likes me to wear high-class threads."

"But do you like it?"

"I guess so." Jackie walked over to one of the smaller line-and-squiggle paintings and inspected it briefly. "Except that it's a little more formal than the stuff I usually wear."

"Why are you wearing it, then?" Dr. Stritch purred softly at him: a fitting prelude for the dominance point she proposed to develop.

"Business," said Jackie, mild blue eyes averted from her.

"Business?" Always flexible in her approach, Dr. Stritch dropped her concern with dominance in favor of a concern with whatever might actually be going on: a concern manifestly proper in view of Rita's absence. "And how is business?"

"Not bad."

"Not bad!" Dr. Stritch rocketed herself up and took a threatening position by the panel of buttons. "Is that the best you can say about your work? What about the future?"

"The future looks good," said Jackie. "Real good for me and Rita."

"How can it look good if you aren't strong enough to make a big decision by yourself?"

"It looks good because I've actually made my decision." Jackie smiled easily, snapping his fingers as though to indicate that an important matter had been disposed of.

"What decision?"

Jackie sighed, came back to his chair and sat down. He loosened his tie, looking for all the world like a prisoner prepared to withstand a prolonged interrogation.

"I'd rather not say what the decision was," he said. "It's a business thing."

"I see." Dr. Stritch came back to her chair and eased her bulk down into it. There was silence during which she sat quietly: poised, receptive—like a large grouper in an aquarium waiting for the next morsel.

"But I certainly want to say that our session last week helped a lot," said Jackie, breaking the silence.

More silence: Jackie smiling at Dr. Stritch, Dr. Stritch smiling at Jackie. Silence that lingered for a while.

"How did it help?"

"It's hard for me to say exactly." Jackie got up and went over to the largest line-and-squiggle painting. "Take this painting, for example. I don't like it, but that's no reason why you shouldn't like it."

"Very good."

"And I really have to put you way up for standing behind your opinion and laying out the money to buy this thing."

"Very good, again."

"So if you like something a lot, the next step is to lay it on the line and do something. Right?"

"Right." Dr. Stritch made an encouraging grimace, coupled with an *O*-shaped hand gesture designed to indicate a direct hit. "Right on target."

"Well." Jackie shook his head as though still overcome by the magnitude of his resolve. "That's what I did."

"A business decision?" Dr. Stritch darted a suspicious glance at the blue silk suitcoat.

"The big plunge." Jackie smiled happily, obviously pleased with Dr. Stritch, with her approach, and with himself.

"I don't understand how what you like fits in with this decision you keep talking about."

"It fits in, but I'd rather not say exactly how."

"That's what you said before," said Dr. Stritch coldly.

"I know." Jackie tried to make himself comfortable, obviously determined not to allow Dr. Stritch total access to the contents of his mind.

"I see," she said. She got slowly to her feet and propelled her plump, velveted frame over to the largest painting. Her back to it, she looked smilingly down at Jackie.

"We've talked about this a little. Could you describe it for me?"

"From memory?"

"No." Dr. Stritch moved away from the painting and over to her rolltop desk. "Just tell me what you see."

"It's a big thing," said Jackie. "About six feet wide and five feet high, I'd say."

"What else?"

"It has lines in the middle—straight lines—with different-sized squiggles in the sides and corners."

Dr. Stritch sat down at her desk and scribbled furiously on her note pad for a minute. When she finished, she held the result up for Jackie's inspection.

"Is that what the painting looks like?"

"Not exactly."

"But I put down exactly what you told me—the general proportion, together with various strokes—lines and squiggles, as you call them."

"I guess I didn't tell you enough," said Jackie ruefully.

"Do you realize that our relationship is one in which you can—and should—feel free to tell me anything? Anything and everything. Your fears, your nightmares, your sexual preferences, your sexual inadequacies." Dr. Stritch looked straight at Jackie with her hot black eyes. "This room is a temple, and what takes place here is sacred. So there's no point in going on if you aren't willing to trust me."

"I suppose you're right."

"Try me and see." Dr. Stritch resumed her seat.

"Basically, I'm just a trumpet player," said Jackie slowly. "That's what I learned to do when I was a kid, and that's what I do best."

Dr. Stritch smiled sympathetically. She had encountered low self-esteem in her clients before: in physicians who wanted to be firemen, dentists who wanted to be stand-up comedians.

"You're more than just a trumpet player," she said. "You're a very, very special person."

"That's right." Jackie, his voice disturbingly forceful, rose and began to pace the room. "I'm actually one hell of a trumpet player—at least I used to be."

"We mustn't live in the past. It's worse than nightmares."

"Exactly. So what I really need is to dig in and practice." Jackie paused, looked reflectively out the window. "Did you know that Rafael Mendez used to practice seven hours a day in the basement of the Chelsea Hotel in Chicago?"

"I don't see what Mr. Mendez has to do with all this. Why should he be important to you?" Dr. Stritch went over to her desk to get her note pad.

"You don't know who Rafael Mendez is?" Jackie frowned at her. "In his prime Rafael was probably the best classical trumpet player in the whole damn world."

The fury in Jackie's voice jolted Dr. Stritch, struck her like a blast from the instrument itself. Drawing back, she inadvertently brushed against the music button.

"Macho, macho, macho man," went the voices. "Macho, macho man . . ."

"Turn that junk off!" shouted Jackie. "Only bad people listen to bad music."

"I respect your values." Though fuming inwardly, Dr.

Stritch forced herself to smile; she turned the music off. "Playing the trumpet, playing golf, gardening and other hobbies—all the good things in life can be yours now, particularly since your wife is willing to help in handling your business."

"She'd rather be a writer," Jackie said firmly.

"Of course she would. And that's why she feels you don't appreciate the sacrifices she's made."

"But I do." Jackie beamed as though delivering a beautiful gift to the temple. "I wouldn't be signing the papers if I didn't feel it would make her happy."

"Papers? What papers? I thought we were talking about your trumpet playing."

"That's right." He snapped his fingers with gusto. "I'm closing out the whole show this afternoon. By five o'clock Jay Jay will be someone else's headache and Rita and I will be off to Spain. Sounds great, doesn't it?"

"It sounds adolescent." Dr. Stritch tried to contain her rage. "What about your responsibilities?" She pointed to the telephone on her rolltop desk. "Don't you think you should phone your wife right now and discuss this with her?"

"She told me the decision was something I had to make on my own. So did you."

"We were talking about a different decision—not this one." With great effort Dr. Stritch kept her voice from rising in pitch.

"What's the difference? It's my life and my decision—isn't that what you said?"

"I was talking about reality decisions, not running off in pursuit of some adolescent fantasy."

"Who says it's a fantasy?" said Jackie in a hurt voice. "I think it makes a lot of sense." He strode over to the large painting as though to underscore his point. "Aren't you the one who said we have to create our own values?"

"Not when they're the wrong values. And not when you refuse to be open and aboveboard with your partner."

"I want to surprise her." Jackie's eyes were distant, his face smiling. "If it's all right for Rita to have secrets, why can't it work the other way?"

"You're just playing with words here, and you know it." Breathing heavily, Dr. Stritch walked over to the door and opened it. "And you don't fool me—not one bit. After all, what you do thunders more loudly than what you say." She stared implacably at him. "Do you know who said that?"

Jackie shook his head.

"It wasn't Rafael Mendocino, or whatever his name is.

It was Ralph Waldo Emerson." Dr. Stritch bit the information out in a coldly patronizing tone.

Without responding immediately, Jackie straightened his necktie and put on his blue silk coat. He started for the door, stopped and smiled at her.

"I've never been very good at saying things," he said. "Except for doing lines that someone else wrote. But I want to thank you for all the help—especially last time." He took out a small, heavy metal object and hefted it—like a lucky piece.

"That's what you need," said Dr. Stritch stiffly. "Help—lots of it. Maybe even 'round-the-clock care."

"I think you're trying to put me down." Jackie looked straight at her, his mild blue eyes puzzled. "Like that crack about Emerson, as though I'm not supposed to know anything because I dropped out of tenth grade."

"My considered professional opinion is that you will bitterly regret this foolish decision to act out your adolescent fantasies."

"Keep swinging." Jackie smiled cheerfully and sauntered out.

Cocky, thought Dr. Stritch. She watched him go down the corridor, shoulders squared, pace brisk: almost as though marching to a tempo set by a brass band located inside his head. Cockiness. The quality was odious enough in young men: young men who used to come into the grocery store and make leering remarks about melons, cantaloupe, meat and potatoes; but cockiness in an older man was abominable, especially when buttressed by a childish delight in childish things.

She went back to her desk and tried to compose herself by drawing a picture of dear Jack Kennedy. The boyish shock of hair, the manly jaw, the firm mouth, the lines and crinkles, planes and shadings: they all flowed easily from her hand to the paper. It was a face she had drawn a thousand times and would draw again: keeping his presence alive in her temple like a constantly rekindled votive flame.

The picture finished, she reached into a side drawer and pulled out a business card: exquisitely engraved, with a name and telephone number written on the back. Not unexpectedly, her phone call took a minute or so to complete; so she began to draw again—not dear Jack Kennedy this time, but objects: rapiers, broadswords, Bowie knives, even a pair of six shooters.

Sensory therapy: working as always to soothe mind and spirit. By the time her New Orleans call was completed, Dr. Stritch was perfectly composed. And when she spoke, her words were soft, unhurried: like a stout line, quietly paid out, foot by foot, into a deep, dark, beautifully capacious woodland pool.

A cold pool, Dr. Stritch told herself after giving Rita the news. No anger flaming forth. No words of stunned disbelief. Only a long pause, followed by a curt request for more details. Then another pause, this time followed by a slow, measured restatement of the message—almost as though Rita were taking care to stamp every bit of Jackie's betrayal into her mind, there to fester and grow great.

As she put the phone down, Dr. Stritch found herself wondering exactly what Rita would do. Nor did the irony of the matter escape her: a decision insisted upon last week, a decision made this week—but not the decision expected. Dr. Stritch tried to calibrate Rita's rage, using her own irritation as a point of reference and balancing the magnitude of Jackie's crime against Rita's offensive capacities. An explosive calculation. Explosive enough to drive her back to her 314 Eagle pencil and another sketch of President Kennedy.

Sherman Oaks, California:
Friday, November 3, 9:30 P.M.

To Jackie, California had always been an implausible place. Congenial but misshapen, as though Kansas and Missouri had been upended and stretched out on a north-south axis. Inconsistent, too. An artificially green truck garden sucking its water from hundreds of miles away, rather than submitting its oranges and lettuce to the alternating whims of sun, wind, and rain. Snow in the mountains now and then, but never in the valleys. Warm days mottling the year like unpredictable slashes of color on one of Dr. Stritch's flowing gowns. After twenty-five years in the state, Jackie still found it strange, almost indecent, to take a drink out to his patio on an autumn evening and sit there watching the red and blue points of light wink their way overhead to Los Angeles International Airport.

The airport. He had expected to be there right now waiting for Rita to appear: tall, cool, unruffled, her dark hair like a shout carrying over the throng of disembarking passengers. The decision, the sale, the villa in Spain, the large, uncluttered block of time for writing and practicing: these were gifts ideal for the brisk tempo and cheer of an airport concourse. A place for goings and comings—and beginnings.

He had tried to phone Rita from Paul Ciardi's office. But without success. And just as well, since the call had been on impulse: an impulse set in motion by Dr. Stritch's unaccountably harsh judgment regarding his action. A strange lady. Inconsistent. Almost implausible—like the state and its climate.

Dr. Stritch had suddenly gone back to the old rulebook at the end of their session in her sacred temple. To his ear, she had sounded like a preacher in her sudden invocation of responsibility, of right and wrong. Familiar themes. Themes he had grown up with: stated simply by Grandmother Hansen, stated with rich, embroidered eloquence by preachers in their temples. Preachers whose voices sang like violins, throbbed like dark, threatening drums. Preachers who improvised upon their themes like marvelously versatile jazz musicians: building chorus after chorus until the listener's mind surrendered completely to a sense of flight and movement. Preachers who always preached from the same rulebook, drew from the same repertoire. Preachers far outpacing Dr. Stritch in their virtuosity and passion.

Of all the preachers Jackie's grandmother had taken him to hear, the Reverend Sam Justus had been the most impressive: a white-maned, intense, fire-breathing rock of a man who descended like a great dragon upon Kansas City twice each year, setting up his giant tented temple on the north side of the fairgrounds. It was to that temple Jackie had gone on a hot, humid June evening: holding on to his grandmother's hand as they filed in with hundreds of others. A large group: variously drawn from Baptists, Lutherans, Presbyterians, Pentecostals, with even an Episcopalian here and there. Working people. Hard-handed. Some bent, lame, sick, and mournful. All drawn by the hope that Reverend Sam would breath new fire upon them, would burn their fear and shame into small cinders to be blown aloft by voices raised in brave, exultant song.

Before the spectacle, the setting of the stage. Preliminary hymns. Short exhortations from lesser spirits: preparing the way with gospel and announcement, ensuring that the benches and folding chairs would be filled with people suitably admonished, hushed and ready.

"Hot!" Reverend Sam had bounded in upon them, shaking his white mane as though to shake the affliction away. "But hot or cold, wet or dry, it's God's world we live in day by day, every day. Isn't that right, my friends?"

Soft, affirmative mumbles peppering the tent. A nod and a grunt from Grandmother Hansen: tall, fair, composed, almost oblivious to the small boy beside her craning and straining to see over the bulky man in front of them.

"God made this world." A large, ham-sized hand had shot up, cupping itself as though to hold an imaginary globe. "He made it and everything upon it, over it, and under it—just as he made you, me, and every man, woman, and child that ever was and ever will be. He made it as a place to work and as a place to play—as a playing field for the great game of life. And He was careful to tell us what the rules of the game are."

From Grandmother Hansen came another approving grunt, followed by a squeezing of the small boy's hand to ensure attention, to warn against squirming.

"You all know those rules." The hand had begun to point, stabbing around the tent as though to single out the guilty. "They're written down in a timeless rulebook." The hand had darted into a pocket and extracted a small Bible to be waved aloft. "Those rules have always told us what's fair and what's foul. They've always told us how to tell when an honest run is scored and when a batter is truly out. They've always told us whether we're really winning or whether we're losing, losing, losing—in this world and in the next. And as every single one of you knows—man, woman, and child—those rules are not easy to live by. They're hard rules. Very hard."

A sigh here and there. But mostly quiet in the tent: the people still, the silence broken only by the sporadic movement of heart-shaped rattan fans passed out at the door as a visible sign of grace and welcome.

"Just rules, fair rules. But hard rules. Rules made by a hard, just God—a God who is perfectly able to throw a transgressing player out of the game at any time. But that hard God is also a kind and merciful God—a God who wants us to win and keep on winning as long as the breath stays in us. God is not just an umpire who takes pleasure in calling us out. He's also a coach who's rooting for us to win and who gives our basic strategy—a strategy that will always work for us, no matter how hard the rules and times may be."

Amens of agreement from all over the tent. Even from the small boy, well aware of what hard times were and what they meant as each day clocked by. Hard times like a cold gray cloud: never lifting, muffling hope and movement. The stockyards half empty. The men laid off from packing plants and factories. Farmers turning out with shotguns to fight eviction. Hard times desperate for hope. For a chance to win and keep on winning.

"And how do you win a ballgame?" The question had been softly put, the bright eyes under the white mane searching out the farthest reaches of the tent. "You win through doing your duty inning after inning, day after day—no matter how bad the scoreboard looks to you, no matter what the fans in the bleachers are shouting at you, no matter how weak your team seems to be."

A glance toward Grandmother Hansen from the small boy. A glance seeking reassurance regarding the fortunes of their team at home: all of them crowded into a small frame house where low voices could be heard downstairs late at night. Voices that whined, bickered, growled, and roared: voices whose freight of pain, anger, and despair was audible even when the words had been blurred by pillows and bedclothes.

"And there are so many things you have to do." Still sympathetic, the deep, resonant voice had grown firmer. "Fielding!" The ham-sized hand had stretched out to snatch an invisible ball. "Throwing the ball straight and true." A muscular right arm had tensed and whipped out with explosive force. "Camping under a fly ball!" The white-maned head had been cocked back, gazing heavenward while the body beneath it circled the platform.

"So many, many things to do and keep track of." The bright eyes had looked pityingly around the tent. "It's no wonder that we all make errors—serious errors that go down on the scoresheet in indelible red ink to be added up on judgment day. Errors that hurt us at the same time they hurt the chances of our team."

A glance down at the dirt floor from the boy. A shame-filled awareness of errors made, errors that stood out all the more when made by the only brunette in a family of blond, flaxen-haired people: a brunette sometimes called the "black one," sometimes glared at silently as an alien presence yet to prove itself deserving.

"But did you ever know a team that won a ball game simply by avoiding errors? Did you ever know a team that won without people on it who were willing to step up to the plate and hit?

"And that's the loneliest part of the game, isn't it? The loneliest part—and the hardest. Many times the devil himself seems to put an extra hop on the pitch coming our way—or a curve that stays straight and then breaks at the last moment.

"And isn't that why our merciful coach has given us a

mighty and potent aid as the final element in his strategy to help us win the great game of life—for ourselves and for our team?"

From throughout the tent, a satisfied sigh as a cramping blue coat was shed and white shirtsleeves were rolled up, followed by Reverend Sam's bending down to pick up and hold aloft a large baseball bat: holding it parallel to the ground so that each eye could make out the black lettering on it—J-E-S-U-S.

"And isn't this mighty and potent aid a wonderful equalizer against the devil's trickery? Can any of you deny that it doesn't give us a wonderful, wonderful way of making up for all those errors we're bound to make during the game?"

From the wings a small, brilliantly white baseball had come hurtling out to be caught by Reverend Sam.

"There you go, Pride!" The ball tossed up and driven with masterful force into the tent's far wall: smacking into it with a sharp report. "There you go, Lust. . . . You, too, Gluttony." Two more baseballs tossed out and hit by Reverend Sam to different parts of the giant tent. "There goes Sloth . . . Pow! . . . Greed and Envy . . . Zip! Zap! Zap! . . . Anger and Despair, there they go." More balls thrown out, tossed up, attacked with force, driven out over the heads of the gasping people in the tent.

"And isn't it a wonderful, wonderful game when you dig in and take your swing? It's a game where we can learn the rules, it's a game that's often filled with hard times and hard luck, but it's a game where our coach has done his best to help us win. And when you get right down to it and face the facts, it most certainly is the only game in town. Am I right?"

"Right!" came back as a tentwide shout, even from the small boy.

"And the Lord's team is the only team in town. Am I right?"

"Right!"

"And you're all here as an act of Christian witness to put your names down as members of that team's roster. Am I right, right, right?"

"Right, right, right!"

At this point a great shaking of tambourines, followed by the entrance of a short, stocky, dark-haired man.

"And right now as you bear witness to the fine young people passing among you, our minister of music, Dr. LeRoy Staggers, will give praise and thanks to the Lord with his silver-tongued trumpet, playing an offertory anthem we all know and love— 'The Holy City.' "

A trumpet. A sound familiar to the small boy from parades and Salvation Army bands downtown. But not a sound like that produced by Dr. LeRoy Staggers. Alone, unaccompanied, rich, soaring, capable of sentiment-laden vibrato or virtuoso triple tonguing—his sound seemed to streak the darkest corners of the tent with light: kindly, dominating, challenging, demanding. A fit presence to hover over them while young men and women in baseball uniforms passed tambourines down each row, collecting tangible wagers on the outcome of Reverend Sam's great game.

After the trumpet, singing punctuated by prayer and by people coming forward to confess their errors and renew their commitment to the rulebook. All washed by the silvery sound of Dr. Staggers's trumpet: leading the hymns, softening to accompany Reverend Sam's spoken words, even flourishing a short cadenza to signal a change in mood or procedure.

Careful querying then from Grandmother Hansen. Was the meaning clear? Was the relationship between team and family apparent? Was the importance of trying to do one's duty a notion striking home with the impact of a strongly driven ball? Was not the service moving and beautiful?

To the queries, thoughtful answers: answers which indicated that Reverend Sam's great bat had hammered home all intended, answers enthusiastic in their assertion of power and beauty—"especially the trumpet part."

A trumpet. A thin white jet of sound strong enough to reach the highest building, put out the worst of fires—without or within.

Good preaching always left a mark, like a bruise noticed long after its occasion. And the bruises from Dr. Stritch were still noticeable, especially the effects of her cudgelings about responsibility and adolescent fantasies. Perhaps he was in fact running away from taking his proper turn at bat. Perhaps he had broken an obscure rule in the rulebook, all the more powerful for never having been stated explicitly.

Dark thoughts. Dark as the air around him.

Jackie took his drink back into the house. It was dark there, too. A few lights were on downstairs, but nothing at all beyond the first half of the stairway leading up to the master suite.

Still thoughtful, Jackie went slowly up the stairs and turned the knob of the bedroom door. As always the knob turned easily. But the door seemed oddly hard to push open—as though something behind it were blocking his entrance, giving gradual way with a slight scraping sound as he opened it.

Once in, he looked down at the obstacle: trying to make it out in the dimness of the room, barely recognizing the twisted mass of dented, yellow pipe as the remains of his Selmer trumpet.

Jackie was still puzzling over the matter when Rita rushed upon him.

It was a silent attack. No screams. No imprecations. All that took place was a single, sharp blow to the neck, just above the left collarbone. Had Rita's hands been toughened by a few more months of work at Firm 'n' Flex, the blow would have been a cruelly disabling one. But it was well placed enough and powerful enough to jolt Jackie off balance and send him reeling toward the escritoire nearby, there to take an astonishingly high kick launched at the sternum by the right leg of a former drum majorette still in superb physical condition.

With an instinctive response derived from watching countless barroom brawls, Jackie charged his assailant: a charge that swept the two of them across the room and up against the far wall. There, still puzzling the matter, he held her pinned for a moment, noticing for the first time that Rita was naked.

Thus distracted, Jackie was easy prey to a sharp knee coming up from below to take him in the groin. A blow that thrust him back, gasping in pain. A blow followed by two more kicks: one burying itself in his stomach, the other glancing off his right hip.

Another kick. But wide of its mark, fortunately. And here Jackie was even able to grab the weapon and hold on, sensing correctly that this narrow, arched, toed thing was the major weapon in Rita's arsenal—apart from her superior wind and excellent muscle tone.

Still in pain, he forced himself to hold on and apply what pressure he could to her instep, twisting at the same time so that she was forced to turn her body in the same direction. Despite the dim light he was now able to see her better: dark hair fanning out toward him, long, strong legs swelling upward from the feet to firm, purposeful thighs and buttocks.

Until that moment Jackie had never realized what a magnificently hairy creature his wife was. Long, thick, dark wires that lashed the air in front of him, as much a part of back and spine as of the small head from which they grew. And further down below, more hair curling round, in, out, and up like the fur of some writhing woodland thing: feral, prowling by night, lithe and squirming: a thing with life and passion altogether separate from the cool, remote face that sat above and uttered speech at breakfast. . . .

Further speculation was driven from him when Rita whipped abruptly to the right and twisted free.

"Bastard!" she howled, advancing upon him and releasing another deadly salvo of kicks. "Dirty, flabby old Yankee bastard!"

Still at the far wall, Jackie looked toward the door, planning to break for it as soon as he could catch his breath. But Rita moved intently in upon him, crouched in a dark coil ready to spring. Instead of kicks now, chops and blows. Even a number of scratches from her long, capable fingers: scratches that struck Jackie as oddly reassuring in their womanly flavor. Reassuring—almost sexually magnetic.

Driven against the wall, Jackie felt a sharp pain in the upper part of his thigh: a gouging caused by the pressure of the wall against a small, heavy metal object in his pocket. Automatically, he reached down and pulled out Clint's mouthpiece, clenching it in his right hand as though determined to preserve the last working part of his instrument.

The heavy metal mouthpiece was still inside his fist when he hit Rita, giving the blow a forcefulness fairly close to that of a half-roll of dimes in the fist of an experienced bartender. But even without the mouthpiece, it was still a good blow: a solid right hook driven by a chest and shoulder still strong and heavy from years of deep breathing and energetic brass playing. A good blow: enough to draw blood, trickling down from the left side of Rita's small mouth, enough to jolt her back, enough to permit Jackie a break for the door and a race down the stairs, losing his footing midway and sliding to the bottom in a series of bone-wrenching bumps, step by step.

He did not stop to check his wounds, but sprinted to his Cadillac, got in, locked the door, sat there gasping and wondering if his long-threatened coronary occlusion was about to make its appearance. He waited a few minutes for the murderer to reach up from behind the front seat and choke the life out of him. By the fourth minute he was breathing more easily; by the fifth minute he was pulling out of the driveway and heading down the street, the road opening up in the glare of the headlights like a white tunnel carved through arching foliage. A low, limping progress. But safe.

Safety. It was linked to movement, he felt. So he drove

and drove, winding over the mountains to Westwood, then out to Santa Monica and back again, staying always on the freeways: freeways still throbbing with traffic, ribbons of moving light in which he formed a small contributory glow, ribbons tying the great dark mass of the night up into an orderly package, speaking of a world whose rules were thoughtfully drawn up as guidance for large and small, high and low, all purposefully moving forward at varying rates of speed.

Purpose. As he drove, Jackie tried to put himself in Rita's mind and chart the route traveled: like that of a truck slowly accelerating down a hill to a point where braking gears give way under the pressure of a momentum built up in stages.

There had been anger all along: cold and constant discontent with their modest state, anger brought to higher pitch by his reluctance to act upon the Poirier offer. Anger relentless in its pressure. Seeking allies and support: a reasoned case from Poirier, a deep and personal probing from Dr. Stritch in her Madame Morgana costume. Support buttressed with Rita's own assertion of sacrifices made and goals forgone.

So many assertions. He had tried to accommodate them all: taking the talk about decisions and novel-writing at face value rather than recognizing the talk for what it was: a flow of words intended to sweep him in a desired direction. He had mistakenly acted upon what had been said, oblivious to what was intended.

A serious error on his part. In his well-meaning literal-mindedness, he had forced the responsibility for his choice upon her: making the grotesque thing her child, her creation, as much as his—joining humiliation to anger as fuel for her rage.

Her rage would subside in time; control would return to her cool, remote features. And there would be more talk: neutral, dispassionate, merging their opposing madnesses into a rational compromise—a compromise to be amended later on as he grew weaker, she stronger. Thus it had always been with Judy, with Lorrayne, with his family in Kansas City—grandmother, mother, brother, sister. More talk, more errors.

Her rage. His error. The logic of the mating suggested his own complicity in her attack as a balance to her complicity in his decision. A complicity born from a surface willingness to please coupled with a dark, barely conscious urge to dwell in his own private world. A culpable complicity: more culpable than hers, certainly, almost as though each time he slipped into bed beside her he brought with him a dark presence that seeped its way beneath her firm warm flesh and stayed there—breeding serpents.

Still driving, Jackie shook his head at the mazed linking of action and motivation. A linking too knotted to disentangle: as intricately woven together in the mind as in the world outside—madness, music, sweat, betrayal, ritual slaughter, lust and love, drunkenness, absorption in work or play, growth, self-immolation, decay—all turning inward and outward, doubling back upon themselves as well. Not just good things, as Dr. Stritch had smilingly asserted. Bad things, too. The whole ball game jumbled up and played in a dimly lit tent: a dark garment rent with flashes of sunshine.

A serious error. A serious matter. Something to sleep on—alone. One decision at a time seemed to be as much as he could handle. But Jackie was quite sure he would not seek Rita out. Nor would he court her favor. A resolution to hold in mind: like the memory of his mangled Selmer trumpet.

Santa Barbara, California: Friday, November 10, 5:00 P.M.

"I thought you had a paper to do for your climatology class." Scott stared coldly at Louise for a moment before smiling expansively at his small group of admirers. "But I suppose we can always use another numbers person."

"I decided to let the numbers go for a while." Louise's tone was airy, assured: a cheerful breeze set in motion by her good fortune at Road Runner headquarters. "I feel lucky enough to place a bet for us if you have any suggestions." She let her eyes drift away from the group to take in the large green oval stretching out before them.

The oval was speckled with smaller designs: circles, octagons, irregular mazes, long and narrow rectangles—each making up one of the courses negotiated during the gymkhana that afternoon. Here and there tents had been set up. Round red-and-white-striped tents, medieval in flavor. Tiny castles that blended with the horses to enforce the impression of a large number of chess pieces set awry on an outdoor board. A pleasant sight: more decorous than a football game, earthier than a fashion show.

Louise had not intended to go to the gymkhana. The original plan had been for Scott to go by himself, while she went down to Road Runner headquarters and placed an ad offering the trailer for sale. But her trip had taken a number of unexpected turns—fortunate ones. So it was late in the afternoon when she finished: late enough to mesh perfectly with the timing of later events at the gymkhana.

"It's gone very well," said Scott. "Almost like a piece of the East Coast imported to civilize our crude western recreations." He nodded with approval at the people: many of them in riding costume, others in sober tweeds. Not a cowboy hat in sight—even on him, since he had wisely chosen to wear his black-billed Greek seaman's cap.

"My trip went well too." Louise smiled at him, excitement in her light brown eyes.

It was with some distress that she noted Scott's reluctance to splinter off from his group of students and closet himself with her for a minute to hear the story she was bursting to tell. A good story, she felt. An unexpectedly happy ending. Certainly a much better ending than selling the trailer, which had seemed the only alternative available to keep them going while she looked for a job paying more than the minimum wage. A story to tell in private, not to a group of apple-cheeked girls in black hats and jodhpurs.

"Bravo!" Scott broke away from her and waved his Greek seaman's cap to attract the attention of a compact dark-haired girl carrying a silver cup and headed in their general direction. "I knew Heidi would carry the field before her."

Wishing that she had won a cup of her own to display before Scott when the time was right, Louise nodded equably as Heidi Kissinger advanced upon them. Hers had not been an easy victory. But she had persevered: first mustering up courage enough to see the editorial director of Road Runner Publications, and then going on step by step to move the conversation from maps and numbers to a specific discussion of word processing techniques. Maps, weather and climate data, computer print-outs, demographics: they had all seemed to fit in with an enterprise devoted to reaching recreational-vehicle owners. And she had been able to put them together into a coherent picture for the gray-haired lady with rimless eyeglasses: a picture with a place in it for herself—as editorial assistant. Not a handsome salary. But a handsome start. And as handsome a prize to bring home as anyone could wish.

"That's a lovely trophy," she said to Heidi.

"I wish it were filled with something cool and refreshing," said Heidi, her voice hovering just on the edge of a plaintive whine.

"A rescue party!" Scott beamed and pointed to a refreshment stand on the far side of the oval. "I hereby appoint myself Stanley in search of Livingston, Gawain in search of the Green Knight, Dante in search of Beatrice." With a couple of the younger students in tow, he rushed off.

"We all just love Scott," murmured Heidi, her eyes following his seaman's cap as it described an arc paralleling that of the oval. "Brilliance and thoughtfulness—it's a truly mellow combination."

"Very mellow." Louise smiled at Heidi. Since Scott had held a number of seminars in the trailer, she had become a little more familiar with the way Heidi and the other students expressed themselves: a cryptic, almost private manner of speech in which small peaks of rational meaning thrust themselves up occasionally—often with startling effect.

"Very creative, too, don't you think?"

"Very much so," said Louise.

"But then you're used to being around creative people, aren't you?" Heidi smiled to indicate her admiration.

"I guess so, if you can put show business in the same category as avant-garde poetry." Ever since Scott had called her to account for blurring the two, Louise had been cautious in making generalizations.

"I didn't realize your father played the trumpet until Daddy said something about it when he was out here last month."

"It's always meant a lot to him," said Louise.

"But he doesn't make records anymore, does he?"

"No."

"That's a shame."

"Styles change." Louise shrugged. "Audiences change."

"Sad." Heidi's voice was absent, detached, her dark eyes charting Scott's progress around the oval. "But it's nice to have a hobby when you're older."

"It's not just a hobby," said Louise defensively. "He's a great artist."

"Loyalty is a wonderful quality—something I'm sure Scott treasures in you a great deal." Heidi looked at her directly, then down at her silver cup, as though taking comfort in its hard, glossy, tangible surface.

"I'm very proud of my father right now."

"Why now?"

"Because he's finally going to do what he likes to do and can do—play the trumpet."

"I think that's truly mellow," said Heidi with great force. "And you wouldn't believe how much Mother and I have tried to get Daddy interested in things like that."

"I don't think it's quite the same." Louise looked at Heidi cautiously, not sure whether to take her statement as a serious one or not. Either way a strong response was called for. "There's a lot of work involved—hours of practice every day, month after month. A completely different way of life from what he's been used to."

"I think I understand where you're coming from." Heidi smiled cheerily. "It's like retiring and settling down to concentrate very, very hard on your golf game."

"Not quite—unless you're talking about someone who has been a former world's champion."

"We're all world champions," said Heidi. She looked down at her silver cup again. "Especially to those who love us dearly."

"That's very profound." As she made the statement, Louise realized that she wasn't quite sure whether she meant it or not. It was a response Heidi herself might have made—half ironic, half serious; dark enough to wound a little, bland enough to avoid giving direct offense. Almost as though Barry had taken to saying "Fantastic!" with the biting tone of a complete cynic, while at the same time accompanying the word with a sweet, understanding smile. A strange quirk, almost endemic among certain groups of academic people—English majors in particular.

Heidi shrugged as though to indicate that Louise's approbation was a mere bauble compared with the other jewels that came her way.

"Any cliché is profound," she said. "Especially if you live with it long enough."

"I suppose so." Louise realized that she was becoming uncomfortable, largely because her knack of making encouraging remarks was useless in dealing with the Heidi Kissingers of this world—people who had grown up expecting approbation as a natural right. People quite different from Scott, from her mother. People undriven by ordinary hungers. People who controlled their circumstances as they controlled their horses—with slight, imperceptible pressures and expectations.

Louise turned her attention to a girl taking her horse over a series of jumps. Like most of the other riders, the girl was young, blank-faced: perched on the steaming brown creature as though there for a purely ornamental purpose. But the jumps, though not high, were close together; and it was apparent that the girl was in complete control of her animal: urging it into the air at precisely the right point, slowing its pace after each descent so that the next leap would be perfectly timed. When the girl finished her course, Louise joined in the slight ripple of discreet, restrained applause, wondering at the same time what series of jumps Heidi Kissinger planned to take her through when Scott came back.

She felt out of place, invisible: a little like the dark-faced men in brown jackets who roamed the oval scooping up the droppings. A proper duty. Necessary to keep the turf in shape for weekly polo matches held there. But not a duty to be acknowledged, or even perceived. A necessary but unapplauded element of the proceedings—like herself.

Scott and the others came back with paper cups of punch. As might have been expected, Heidi was served first.

"Very mellow," she said, taking a small sip. She looked at her watch and smiled generously at the group.

"You're riding again, aren't you?" asked one of the other girls.

"There's plenty of time." Heidi smiled easily at Scott. "And I want to hear a little more about Louise's father and his trumpet."

"Just like Gauguin." Scott glared at Louise for a moment, then gestured in the general direction of the ocean. "If you can imagine Gauguin running off to Tahiti and painting with disappearing ink." He basked in the small, warming wave of laughter for a moment before looking sharply at Louise again.

"I think it's magnificently mellow." Heidi tossed her glossy dark curls in mock anger, then handed her victory cup to Louise as though bestowing a gift upon an orphan. "And I think Louise should have a prize or something for encouraging him." Free of the cup, she held up her hands to signal an important announcement. "And now, dear people, I must depart and do my duty."

Louise watched Scott walk Heidi around to where the grooms were readying her horse, struck with mild wonder at how strong the impulse had been to throw the heavy silvered thing at the two of them. By the time Scott came back, her anger had subsided; but there was enough left to push her forward to meet him in an uncluttered private spot, there to make her feelings known.

"That business about the disappearing ink was pretty strong," she said to him. "How would you feel if my father made belittling remarks about your poetry?"

"If they were clever remarks, I'd lead the applause myself." Scott looked straight back at her and shook his head in disgust. "And I would submit in addition that you made a serious error when you introduced the topic."

"What kind of error?"

"It was an error in judgment to let those people know that our circumstances are . . . different."

"It's my father's circumstances that have changed, not ours." Louise stared at him suspiciously. "Are you thinking of moving out or something like that?"

"Not at all. I am totally committed to this relationship." Scott moved closer to her, let his dark eyes burn into hers for a moment. "And I expect the same from you."

"I'm sorry I was so sensitive," said Louise, breathing a little easier now that the void beneath her seemed to have closed up.

"I'm to blame." Scott stroked his beard and made a capacious gesture that took in their whole setting: oval, riders, judges, barriers, courses, spectators, even the dark-faced men in brown jackets. "I'm to blame for not letting you know how all this fits together."

"All what?" Louise followed his gesture, puzzled by his assertion of overall pattern and order.

"The whole social fabric, the university, our relationship, my career." Scott led her away from the oval as though to find a better vantage point. "I've never taken time out to give you the why and wherefore of things, have I?"

"I never expected you to." Reassured, Louise found herself taking his hand, as though to let some of her confidence flow from her into him.

"I don't really like all this." Scott stopped their progress on a grassy knoll, turned, and made another capacious gesture. "Girls like Heidi and the others are all spoiled, selfish little things with far too much money to throw around. But they're my students, and the students in a place like this can make or break a beginning instructor."

"I thought it was the senior professors who decided about tenure and things like that."

"Decisions are always based upon someone else's decision. The students gossip among themselves, then gossip with their professors; the professors gossip among themselves, then gossip with the various deans and chairmen. If you don't have a strong current of gossip flowing with you, you're usually out in the first year."

"You've made it past the first year. Can't you let down a little now?"

"It never ends," said Scott in a dull voice. "They're always looking you over, looking for some kind of weakness that will justify letting you go. If you work hard, they fire you because you have no imagination. If you're brilliant, they fire you because you lack humility. One way or another, they can always ease you out."

"They can't ease everybody out, can they?"

"No."

"Then how do they decide who's going to go and who's going to stay?"

"Trust," said Scott shortly. "They want to be able to trust you—like a servant who won't run off with the family silver when the chance comes along. They want to be comfortable with your background, with your pronunciation, with the way you entertain, with the way you look at literature. It's like being pledged to join a fraternity—except that the rushing period can take twenty years."

"It sounds dreadful!"

"It is—even though you get used to smiling all the time, disagreeing in a way that lets them know you're really on their side in the long run. You have to put yourself forward and be modest at the same time, be progressive and yet show respect for Milton, Chaucer, and the rest of the junk nobody reads or wants to read—junk that's there because it's considered part of the furniture. And above all, you have to be witty—always ready with a bright, spontaneous remark to ease the tension, to smooth things out."

"I think I understand," said Louise. "It's as though you're on stage all the time." A wave of sympathy swept over her and washed her irritation away.

"That's close." Scott smiled at her. "And that's why I feel so comfortable when I'm with you."

"I'm glad. And I'm glad to have had some good luck down at Road Runner."

"How much luck?" Scott stopped smiling and looked at her closely.

"Much more than I expected."

"You didn't sell it right then and there, did you?"

"Better than that." Louise smiled proudly. "I worked it

out so we'll be able to keep the trailer." She paused dramatically, then offered her shining trophy up for his admiring inspection. "They offered me a job in the editorial department."

Scott looked at her stonily and let her hand drop away from his.

"You agreed to sell the trailer," he said, spacing each word out as though for the benefit of a small child. "We talked it over and you agreed to sell the trailer."

"But it's a good job." Louise continued to smile brightly. "I'll be bringing home as much as Dad used to send me."

"That's not the point."

"If that's not the point, what is?"

"The point is that you agreed to do something and now you're trying to back out of it."

"But why sell the trailer when I'll be bringing my share in to pay the bills?"

"It's a matter of trust, of commitment."

"I'm dropping out of school, getting a good job—how much more commitment do you want?"

"I want you to sell the trailer."

"But the recreational-vehicle market is down now—especially for used rigs. Can't you understand that I'd be selling it for less than it's really worth?"

"I understand that you agreed to sell the trailer so that we could have a little more to work with and move into a place where civilized people could visit us without feeling that they were submerged in a lower-middle-class submarine."

"It was good enough when you moved in last spring." Louise looked at him angrily, as though an attack upon the trailer were worse than an attack upon her own integrity.

"Things were different then."

"The only difference is that you got a raise this fall and I got a job, so I'd say we were much better off."

"Not quite." Scott sighed as though the exchange were becoming tedious. "I'm better off, and you're worse off."

"What's wrong with that?"

"It's not fair," said Scott patiently. "It's simply not fair for me to contribute more than you do."

"But I was contributing more than you were last spring and summer—a lot more."

"So you *do* agree that things were different then."

"Have it your own way." Louise was almost sobbing at this point.

"Not quite," said Scott. "My way involved selling the

trailer, so that we could start out as partners on an equal basis. My way is an open, honest way in which agreements are made and honored." Eyes cold and unmoved, he stared unwinkingly at her. "I don't think I've had my way at all."

"I thought you'd be happy about the whole thing." Louise turned away from him, trying to keep the tears from flooding forth.

"I'm sure you're sincere. I'm sure that's exactly what you thought." Scott lowered his voice, as though overcome by a great sadness. "And that's the worst part—that you simply have no conception of what is truly important to me, no conception at all of what my values are."

"Try to understand."

"I understand, Louise—far more than you realize." He took Heidi's cup and left.

Louise watched Scott walk down the knoll to the oval, an area whose resemblance to a gaming board was even more pronounced when viewed from up above. And she one of the pieces: moved from square to square until cornered beyond hope of rescue and pushed off the board. From where she was she could see the riders, the spectators, even Scott in the center of his group—clearly marked by his distinctive Greek seaman's cap.

Conflict. They had fought before: small battles over symbolic issues: encounters that lifted the tension, let warmth and passion in after a few days of monosyllabic coldness. Highs and lows, love and anger, warmth and coldness—both polarities were needed to keep the current flowing. And she had sensed his need to scratch and claw occasionally: a wholesome need in a creature forced to keep purring in the presence of students, colleagues, superiors, and deans. There had even been times when she had felt closest to him when they were lashing out at each other: as though both were acting from a script calling for a happy ending—in bed.

But this conflict was different. There was a grim logic to it, a simple reminder that she no longer had anything to contribute to his career. And since his career was the important consideration, it was time for her to step aside or be pushed. Scott had sought her out when his position was weak; with his position improved, it was time for him to move on to someone who could offer him more. The move would have come sooner or later, Louise realized: like the termination of a redundant employee on a trumped-up charge.

Grief over losing Scott, jealousy over Heidi Kissinger and her poised control of the matter: Louise was surprised that her tears did not last longer, rack her body with heartfelt sobs. And she was shocked by the insistence with which her mind presented and re-presented a new, fresh, relatively trivial concern—her editorial job at Road Runner Publications.

Appalled at her own callousness, she found herself hoping Scott would spend the night with Heidi, so that she would be able to get a full night's sleep in preparation for her first day at work.

Jávea, Spain:
Tuesday, November 28, 4:30 P.M.

"My body is Spanish but my mind is the mind of a Scotswoman," said Señora Uhrquart with quiet pride. Her dark eyes flashed truculently, and she looked around the office of the small travel agency with visible disdain.

"I guess it gets pretty cold there." Jackie nodded pleasantly and smiled at the travel posters as though underscoring his point. The travel posters were warm, appealing: crying the attractions of Majorca, Costa del Sol, and Costa Blanca.

"Even in the summer." Señora Uhrquart finished changing his travelers' checks into pesetas and made out a record of the transaction in neat, squarish script. She was a short, precise woman in her early thirties: strong-faced and with a full figure hovering on the edge of plumpness.

"Is that your busy time on the Costa Blanca?"

"June, July, August—everyone comes down on holiday then. Right now it's mostly pensioners." Señora Uhrquart looked out the window as though to chastise the road for its lack of traffic, then turned her dark eyes back upon Jackie with curiosity.

"It looks like a nice place for people who want to take it easy," said Jackie.

"Tranquilidad." Señora Uhrquart shook her short, close-cropped black curls disapprovingly. "Everyone takes it easy here—too easy." She looked at her watch. "In Glasgow, the taxi would have been here ten minutes ago."

"I'm in no hurry." Jackie shrugged Señora Uhrquart's combative words away. "This is the first chance I've had to catch my breath since I left California."

With just a trace of travel anxiety remaining, he looked over at his luggage in the corner of the room. It was all there: two suitcases, a large garment bag, and his new Selmer trumpet. And he was with it. Both of them ending up in the same pocket after caroming from one airport terminal to another: Los Angeles to Kansas City, Kansas City to Miami, Miami to Madrid, Madrid to Valencia. A journey progressively more unsettling as it approached its target, culminating in a fifty-kilometer jolting nightmare of a taxi ride from the Valencia airport.

It was not a journey he had planned to take. If anything, it had come as a result of one improvisation after another. After Rita's attack, he had tried to resolve their discord several times. There had been a meeting at Dr. Stritch's office. There had been a couple of lunches. And there had been a carefully neutral conference in Pasadena with Paul Ciardi. He had tried again and again to justify his well-intentioned mistake, enlisting the support of sound arithmetic in support of their Spanish venture. But Rita had been obdurate, implacable in her insistence that he back out of the sale. Equally obdurate, he had refused, finding himself suddenly fearful of her. There had been no more blows, no harsh and wounding words: only a cold hatred in her eyes and a clear promise of litigation in the offing.

Paul had urged him to hit the road—fast. But Spain had seemed out of the question at first, since the original dream had been built from joint elements: his practicing coupled with Rita's writing. So he had taken flight for Kansas City.

Kansas City had not worked out. His brother had been cool, almost openly resentful of his inability to continue help long taken for granted. And his mother had been critical: shaking her white head over his irresponsibility in running off to pursue a frivolous goal. Once honored for his aid, he was now an object to be judged, to be cudgeled for past errors and flaws of character. Even his father's departure had somehow been entered on his side of the ledger as a black mark. "The black one," they had called him when he was little: an alien one in a tall, flaxen-haired tribe, one whose acceptance was always contingent upon the payment of ransom. With no more ransom to pay, no more gifts to give, he had left after a few days, feeling like a Santa Claus whose empty pack has been greeted with cold contempt and harsh words.

A feeling of shame. But also, oddly enough, a feeling of great relief: as though a burden had been put down, never to be taken up again.

From Kansas City he had gone back to California, taking his trumpet up to a cabin in the redwoods just outside Porterville. A secluded place. But not secluded enough, according to Paul Ciardi, who had come out the following weekend and counseled immediate flight to Spain. So Jackie had packed up his trumpet once more and set off in his original, planned direction, like a fugitive headed for a vacation resort, bringing with him a baggage of fear and loneliness in place of conventional expectations.

"Is that all the luggage you have?" Señora Uhrquart's dark eyes were thoughtful. "Our understanding was that you were going to stay for quite a while."

"That's right." Jackie smiled easily at her. "I've leased the villa up through July. Is there any problem?"

"No," she said, looking suspiciously at some papers on her desk. "It's quite in order—but it's a big place for one person."

"I'll be doing a lot of work." Jackie gestured toward his trumpet case as though the object would substitute for further explanation. "And the solitude will help a lot."

"Are you a writer?" It was clear that Señora Uhrquart was in a mood to exchange confidences.

"I'm a musician."

"There's not much of that here—not compared to Glasgow." Señora Uhrquart shook her dark curls vigorously. "Only a little band that plays in the square sometimes. In Glasgow they had pipers and dancers every Sunday."

"Did you like it there?"

"I liked everything." She sighed. "Everything except my husband's mother."

"That's too bad."

"It was dreadful. 'Mama, Mama, Mama'—that was all he could say." She scowled at him as though holding him personally responsible for Mr. Uhrquart's disloyalty. "So I had to leave him and come back here."

"I'm sorry it didn't work out." Jackie's mild blue eyes were sympathetic. "But you certainly learned English well."

"Accounting, too." She looked around the travel agency's cramped quarters with disgust. "I ought to be in a more responsible position."

"How about banking?"

"They're all Falangistas." Señora Uhrquart sat back and lit a cigarette. "Don Pepe talks to Don Jaime and they both talk to Don Pedro so that everything stays in the family. A woman doesn't have a chance."

"Maybe things will get better."

"Maybe." She took a pull on her cigarette and looked steadily at him. "I'm hoping to get a job with a construction company when things get better."

"Good luck." Jackie paused and searched for the appropriate phrase. "*Buena suerte.*"

"You'll need that," she said. "There are few who speak English here—outside of the British themselves."

Jackie nodded. The most unsettling part of the trip had been the step-by-step immersion in another language: a language assaulting ear and eye as a constant reminder that he was on his own. The people friendly enough. But intent upon their own concerns. As he his. And Señora Uhrquart hers.

She seemed to be a forceful woman. Able. Very competent at her job with the *Viajes Intour* travel agency and its ancillary enterprises of changing money and acting as rental agent. But overqualified, as the business school jargon of the States put it. Abilities and aspirations outstripping the opportunities available. Almost like a jazz musician playing in a burlesque house or strip joint, as Jackie had done during his first year in New York. A frustrating time.

Frustration. He could sense it in her. Frustration in her job. Frustration in her marriage to a man who had failed to forsake all others. A serious failure. Culpable. An ingrained disloyalty, taking as its primary concern something other than a mate's hopes and fears. A betrayal as strong in thought as in actual deed—like playing the trumpet.

He looked once more at his trumpet case, trying to balance it against the pack of burdens he had taken on and carried over the years. It was a balance strongly tilted toward the trumpet, he had to admit: a balance measured more in affection than in action, much as though he had continued to keep a mistress in his mind while giving her up as far as appearances went. A mistress with whom his commerce continued in spite of good intentions, fair promises, reasonable compromises, and apparent surrenders. Rita's assault upon his Selmer trumpet had been a proper gesture: a gesture striking out at the distorted balance of power between them.

Power. There was never enough of it to go around. Its presence in one person was measured by the relative powerlessness of another. Señora Uhrquart's mother-in-law desired power over her son and Señora Uhrquart; Señora Uhrquart desired power over her husband and mother-in-law. Don Pepe and Don Jaime desired power over people who on their part fervently desired the same power over Don Pepe and Don Jaime. It seemed as though the primary characteristic of the species was its bossiness: an insatiable urge in each person to tell another person or persons what to do—sometimes with logic, sometimes with tears, sometimes with threats, sometimes with subtle pressures barely noticeable in their application.

The trumpet had always been his strength: permitting a surface surrender to pressure while keeping his precious private treasures locked safely away. He was an alien in spirit even more than in appearance, as his family must have sensed—though never putting the awareness into words. Rita, too. Suddenly contrite, he smiled humbly at Señora Uhrquart.

"Do you have any advice on how I should handle things while I'm here?" he said.

"You'll need a housekeeper," she said. "If you like, I can arrange for someone to come in."

"How about meals?"

"Since you're by yourself, I would suggest taking your evening meal out most of the time—the restaurants here are fairly inexpensive, and there are several within walking distance of your villa."

"What about transportation?"

"The *autobus* goes into town from the beach area every hour, but I would suggest you buy a vehicle of your own—you can sell it when you leave." She was beginning to glow with pleasure. "The British are always bringing them in and out."

"That sounds fine." Jackie took a deep breath and nodded as though matters of great moment had been settled between them. "I'm beginning to feel at home already."

"I think you'll like it here," said Señora Uhrquart thoughtfully. "It's quiet—if that's what you want. And the people are a good sort, as long as you don't expect anything done in a hurry."

"Not like Glasgow, then."

"Not at all." She permitted herself a smile. "In Scotland everyone walks quickly."

"Is it the people?" said Jackie. "Or is it the weather?"

"I'm not sure." She looked at her watch with obvious impatience at the slowness of the taxi. "I suppose people keep moving more in a cold climate—but they're basically energetic, just like the Catalans here are more energetic than the Andalusians down south." She shook her head in despair over the disappointing differences between tribes.

The taxi came clattering up. Señora Uhrquart gave him a set of keys and went out to give the driver directions. They put the luggage into the trunk: suitcases first, garment bag on top. But Jackie kept the trumpet case with him in the back seat.

"I'm sure it will be safe in the trunk," said Señora Uhrquart.

"I like to keep my eye on it." Jackie smiled self-consciously, quite aware that his action was one of resistance to her will.

"As you wish." She looked at him with a touch of coldness in her dark eyes. *Buena suerte."*

The driver gunned the motor and they drove off, exploding down the small street as though on an emergency call.

A brave driver. But not careful. Perhaps the drivers in Germany were different: more like Clara in their balancing of chance against capability. Jackie had been careful, dutiful all along. But he had not been brave enough to leave Lorrayne for Clara when the chance came his way. So Lorrayne had left him. Carefulness. Carelessness. Both roads seemed to end at the same destination.

December to July

Burbank, California: Monday, December 18, 2:30 P.M.

"In a couple of weeks this place will be beautiful," said Frank May. His leathery face was wreathed in smiles as he led Rita down a fiberboard-lined passage to Bruce's new office in the UBN story department. "And as you can see, it's out of the main traffic pattern."

"That's always a plus." Rita tried to put just the right note of enthusiasm in her voice as she picked her steps with care through the debris: loose scripts, boxes of papers, frayed color posters of old shows, placards with wholesome admonitions intended to spur the readers and unpaid interns to diligent labor.

It had been something of a shock to find a new name in the nameplate outside of Bruce's old office, along with a new secretary at the reception desk inside. And it had been a greater shock when the secretary had looked blankly at her in response to her mention of Bruce's name. But the blankness had led to a phone call, and the phone call had led to a cheery greeting from May: a greeting culminating in the offer of guidance and company in seeking out the resting place of the most recently transferred vice president in a hierarchy where gradual humiliation permitted all parties concerned to avoid the awkwardness of outright discharge. A shock, but one that could be masked by smiles and fair words.

"Heat! Heart! Hardware!" May read the words aloud with gusto: words emblazoned in large red letters on a placard right outside Bruce's door. "That says it all, doesn't it?"

"Very succinct." Rita matched May's admiring smile with one of her own. "It certainly helps to have things stated simply."

"It's essential!" May turned his shrewd old eyes upon her and smiled knowingly. "When it gets too complicated, we get confused—and so does the audience. Doesn't that make sense?"

"Very good sense," said Rita, hoping that May would not ask her to interpret the slogan further.

"Heat is the most important—conflict, danger, excitement, and all the rest of it. And every story has to have heart—someone to sympathize with and care about. But I'm a great believer in hardware, myself."

"Special effects?"

"Special effects, hospitals, horses, computers, space stuff—anything that looks good to the audience." May smiled a happy, leathery smile. "And pretty girls, too—they fall into the hardware category."

"Very neat." Rita's smile was more forced as she followed May into Bruce's office. May's lectures, she knew, carried more than surface information; they were always indirect assertions of power, subtle reminders of where people stood and should stand. There seemed to be a new forcefulness in the president of UBN: as though a kindly practitioner somewhere had given the old man a revitalizing, energizing transfusion of fresh new blood—or money.

May's transfusion had not brought much benefit to Bruce, it was clear: even though Bruce welcomed them with bounce and numerous flashings of his white, perfectly aligned teeth. The new office was smaller than his old one, the secretary older and more harried; and May's visit was obviously a perfunctory one, designed to maintain the illusion that Bruce's move was a step up rather than a push down a slide that would lead ultimately to complete anonymity. A slide for Bruce to match her own.

Rita sat down beside a large carton of filmscripts and watched the two men banter illusions and necessary pretenses back and forth. Her own pretenses were becoming more difficult to keep up as the news of Jackie's defection permeated the industry. He had left the country too quickly for any kind of legal redress, so she had been forced to settle for a modest allowance patronizingly disbursed by Paul Ciardi: an allowance enough for a rented townhouse in Pacific Palisades, but not much more. The Ferrari, the Cadillac, the house in Sherman Oaks: these company assets had gone into the hopper with everything else, leaving only a small sifting to be shared in even smaller portions, while maintaining the illusion that their marriage was still sound, their business picture still bright.

The loss of material luxury galled Rita far less than the loss of power and its perquisites. Phone calls returned a day late, if at all. Invitations dwindling down to a pitiful weekend when an extra girl was called for. Even Melissa had withdrawn her concern, pleading a tight schedule and celebrating the virtues of one of her less expensive colleagues. It was as though Jackie's departure had thrown up a cloud of dust, making her invisible and inaudible to people who had been glad to seek her out before. A pattern making Bruce's loyalty all the more welcome—and surprising: like a handsome prince continuing to woo a princess who had just been turned into a beggar maid.

It gave her pleasure to fit Bruce's apparent exception into the pattern. A handsome prince in an unhandsome office is obviously on his way to becoming a beggar gentleman: fit company for a beggar maid. His slide must have begun about the same time as hers: though he had kept it from her, just as she had kept from him her knowledge of Grandmère Bonnet's mad urge to possess the "Judy's Guy" shows. Nor did she resent his lack of candor, since she had always found deviousness easier to deal with than plain talk. Bruce's weakness, his pretentiousness, his fundamental dishonesty: these were qualities she could treasure, give herself to in bed without reservation, always retaining for herself a slight feeling of superiority.

After Frank May left, Rita rose and came over to Bruce: standing behind his chair and bending down so that her long dark hair washed over him while she kissed him long and hard.

"You'll be able to get a lot done here," she said cheerfully.

"It's a challenge." Bruce smiled and shot her a knowing glance. "And I always love a challenge."

"I know," purred Rita, thinking back to their last encounter: an encounter during which they had both been able to translate their buried rage and frustration into mutual ecstasy. "And you're the champion as far as I'm concerned."

"I may have to defend my title in New Orleans pretty soon."

"That's where you won it, isn't it?" Rita smiled at him affectionately. "I can't blame you if you feel like going back to the scene of one of your greatest triumphs—one of many."

"There'll be more," said Bruce, visibly relaxing as her words massaged away most of the tension left by May's visit. "But it's clear to me that a plethora of opportunities lies inherently nascent in some of these newer media interface relationships."

Rita squirmed with delight, crossing and uncrossing her long, lovely legs. More than his youth, more than his firm-muscled body, it was Bruce's language that delighted her and moved her: like a shower of sweet rain on a desert yearning for more moisture than Jackie's bleak "Let's check the action."

"Sounds exciting," she said.

"It'll be fun." Bruce sat back and regarded her intently. "But I'll miss some of the theater in this town."

"Anything special?"

"Judy Walsh's show is in rehearsal now," said Bruce. "And I've always been an admirer of hers."

"You're not the only one." Rita smiled at him, thinking for the moment of their common, albeit unshared, knowledge of Grandmère's obsession.

"What do you mean by that?" Bruce darted a sudden, suspicious glance at her.

"I mean that I've always admired Judy, too." Rita's manner was casual, masking completely her delicious feeling of enjoyment.

"Are you on good terms with her?"

It was Rita's turn for suspicious glancing in an attempt to infer the direction of Bruce's thought.

"We've always gotten along well," she said slowly. "It wasn't too long ago that she was talking about doing a show with us."

"It might be fun if we all had lunch together." Bruce's perfectly aligned white teeth gleamed, his spirits visibly improved. "Do you think you could arrange it?"

"I think so." Still puzzled, Rita focused her eyes upon the carton of filmscripts beside her, trying to devise a way to bring Bruce's thinking into the open: a way as effective as the one she had used in getting Charley Bob to reveal Grandmère's plan for putting pressure upon Jackie. "This isn't an errand for Frank May, is it?"

"Does it matter?" Unoffended, Bruce smiled cheerfully at her.

"When?"

"Sometime soon—next week, maybe."

"I'll work something out," said Rita. "But we'll have to fit into her rehearsal schedule."

"I'm flexible." Bruce got up, came over, and took her hand. "And I know you are, too." He gave her a kiss: parental, almost patronizing. "If all the parameters stay in line, I may have some rather astounding news for you in a couple of months."

Rita did not pursue the matter, since it was clear that Bruce was far less vulnerable to interrogation than his cousin in New Orleans had been. But after she left Bruce's domain of heat-heart-hardware, she found the puzzle nagging at her in its demand for a solution in which all the pieces fitted neatly together—even Charley Bob.

The most important piece was the "Judy's Guy" series: a piece locked safely up in trust with the key in Jackie's hands—not Judy's. But Louise was also a piece, since the trust had been designed for her ultimate benefit. And as Louise's mother, Judy had the authority to petition the court to review any actions or lack of action on the part of the trustee. Complicated stuff. Yet Rita had dealt with trusts and trustees in her real estate days, and her experience quickly led her to the conclusion that Bruce intended to persuade Judy that some sort of legal action would be appropriate: persuasion sweetened with guaranteed support for a new series, possibly. Not a bad approach. An approach almost anyone could use—even Charley Bob.

Rita conjured up a picture of Charley Bob in her mind for a moment. It was a picture of a pudgy young man with an unwholesome, whitish face—like an upriver fish: a young man impotently raging under the dominant position of his cousin Bruce, a young man who would be overjoyed at a chance to give his crazy Grandmère a precious gift and replace Bruce in her affections: in meeting his goals. It was a picture that belonged at the center of her puzzle.

There was room for her in the picture: room for her as Charley Bob's guide and collaborator. The position would be one of strength: far more so than had been the case with Bruce, who had kept his purposes veiled from her. For a moment she considered approaching Judy and returning to Bruce, gift in hand; but she knew that Bruce would from then on couple gratitude with mistrust and find a way to pay her back. The logic of events clearly compelled a move to Charley Bob—clumsy and boorish, but much more of a rising star.

A lovely picture. Rita could hear the voices in her mind

chorusing in admiration. And the first step in putting colors to it required a friendly visit to Judy's rehearsal.

"Watch this number," said Barry, gracefully easing himself into a seat beside Rita in the back of the Gemini Theater. "It's dynamite."

Rita nodded and obediently focused her attention upon Judy, a trim, compact figure dominating the stage by virtue of her large gestures and vivid coloring. It was a number in which Judy, newly arrived as ambassador to a tropical country, celebrated the values of democracy by teaching four warring tribal chieftains to sing barbershop harmony together. A simple-minded song, a simple-minded performance, but greeted with murmurs of enthusiasm from all the spectators—singers, dancers, technical and production people, agents, and hangers-on.

"Excellent!" Rita smiled at Barry. Early in her association with show folk, she had learned that enthusiasm must always be sustained—even at the price of insincerity.

"It's a fantastic show." Barry shook his sun-bleached surfer's thatch in awe; he rose, stretched the lingering effects of cramping inactivity away, beckoned to Rita, and led her down a flight of stairs to Judy's dressing room.

"I just had to come over and see for myself." Rita stood in the doorway beaming at Judy with as much incredulous admiration as she could stamp on her small features. "It certainly looks as though everyone's right."

"I hope so," said Judy glumly. Shoes off, she was stretched back on a small green sofa. "Sometimes I think I'm too old for the dancing and all the rest of it." Her pale green eyes were blank with exhaustion, mirroring the arid despair of a Picasso print on the wall opposite: a group of sad, emaciated dancers angularly posed against a rocky background.

"You're terrific, baby." Barry grinned broadly and bounded off.

"It's really great," said Rita. "And you're the one with the magic."

"We'll see." Judy sighed. "I wish Jackie were here." She looked at Rita and shook her head. "He sure picked a bad news time to leave town."

"We're still moving along." Rita sat down across from Judy with a confident smile intended to overwhelm the impression created by the emaciated Picasso dancers. "You'd be surprised how many projects keep coming our way."

"Even with Jay Jay sold to the English?" Judy glowered

as though the action had been an attack upon the concept of a united Ireland.

"We have to be careful, but we can still play a key intermediary role here and there."

"Do you really think this show is going to work?" Still anxious, Judy put the exchange back on its proper course—her talent and its prospects.

"It's fantastic!" Rita shook her head in the same admiring way Barry had done. "No wonder they're talking about a high-budget feature film for you."

"Who?"

"It's just in the planning stage, so there's still a chance it might collapse."

"That's always the way it is." Judy looked past Rita and fixed her pale green eyes upon the sad, emaciated dancers.

"But it's going to be a totally integrated effort if it comes off—promotion, property tie-ins, everything."

"How does the agency feel about it?"

"They haven't been approached yet." Rita smiled easily. "But they will be, assuming you're interested in doing a major film at this point in your career."

"I'm always interested," said Judy with force.

"How about the promotion end of it?"

"All that comes with the territory." The pale green eyes were guarded.

"There's been some talk of tying in the 'Judy's Guy' shows with all of this."

"That's Jackie's department." Alert and intent, Judy looked at Rita. "How does he feel about it?"

"That's where we have something of a problem," said Rita carefully. "Possibly even a legal problem."

"Those shows are in a trust, you know." Judy shrugged and shook her carrot-red hair. "Jackie has complete control of what happens with those things. What I might want has nothing to do with it."

"But the trust was set up on the basis of an agreement between you, wasn't it?"

"Paul Ciardi talked me into signing my name on a piece of paper, if that's what you mean."

"That's exactly what I mean," said Rita. "Did you know that on the basis of your agreement you can go back to court anytime you're not satisfied?"

"I don't like legal things." Judy sighed. "I have enough trouble sleeping as it is."

"Sometimes the legal problems come with the territory, don't they?"

"It's worth thinking about, I guess." Judy wiggled her toes into her shoes so that each shoe was half on, half off. "There's nothing I'd like more than a hit feature film."

"It's oil money," said Rita, pressing the point. "They have it to spend, and they're ready to spend it—especially on you."

"And you really think this show is going to be a hit?"

"I'm positive."

"What did you think of the barbershop quartet number?"

Rita paused, trying to cover her irritation at Judy's steering of the discussion back to present concerns: concerns focused upon a simple-minded song, a simple-minded concept.

"Do you want my honest opinion?"

"You know I can't stand insincere people," said Judy firmly.

"I thought it was adorable." Rita's dark eyes glowed with feigned enthusiasm. "Simply adorable—and filled with heart, real heart."

"Good." Judy completed the process of putting her shoes on and stood up. "That's exactly what Frank May said about it." She shook her head in awe. "I have the feeling this show is actually going to fly."

"I'm sure it will."

"And according to Frank, that will be enough to get a new series off the ground."

"Wonderful." Rita's cool, remote features masked a growing feeling of panic. "A new series would be wonderful for you."

"Wonderful—and busy, busy, busy." Judy began to touch her toes, bending down very far and grunting earnestly. "Too busy for a feature, I'd say."

"But you can't really be sure this show will do well." Rita tried to keep her voice from sounding even the slightest note of desperation. "A lot of Los Angeles openings have run into bad luck lately."

"I know." Toe touching finished, Judy began to limber up further by stretching sideways. "And yet I feel lucky, very lucky—just as though it's all starting to come together."

"You didn't sound quite that confident when I came in here." Rita got up and looked at Judy accusingly.

"I was tired," grinned Judy. "But talking to you somehow made me feel better about that barbershop quartet number—that and everything else."

"I'm glad."

"Thanks for the lift." Judy stopped her workout, came over, and kissed the cool, remote cheek that Rita obediently made available. "And keep that project on the back burner, will you?"

"I shall." She watched Judy sprint off to blaze her way through another solo number, waiting until she was out of sight before murmuring softly, "Slip a disc!"

Discouraged, almost at the point of tears, Rita went upstairs to where Judy's circle of enthusiasts was still sitting. Their whispers seemed to accompany her out: whispers almost overpowering the voices she carried in her mind, voices chanting a chorus of varied praise and admiration. Even as the whispers died away, her voices remained quite low, barely audible, on the verge of complete extinction, so that some kind of protective, supportive action was called for as she strode up the aisle.

"Brilliant," said Rita softly to herself. "Dynamic . . . clever . . ." Starting as small shapes in her mouth, the words gradually became more overt in their articulation, soothing her spirits greatly as they rose in force. "Creative . . . innovative . . . witty . . . highly intelligent."

"Fantastic!" Barry held the door open for her and nodded agreeably. "Everything is definitely fantastic."

Jávea, Spain: Saturday, January 21, 9:00 A.M.

"Trio Los Panchos." Taking pleasure in their familiarity, Jackie spoke the words and pointed to the poster above the *Mar Azul* cigarette machine.

The gray-haired lady behind the bar turned to inspect the poster. It portrayed three middle-aged gentlemen in business suits, one holding a guitar at a forty-five-degree angle. At the bottom was an announcement of their coming appearance in Denia, a small city ten miles up the coast.

"Si." The gray-haired lady smiled. *"Muy bonita."*

"Son muy famosos." Jackie gestured expansively in an attempt to provide his weak Spanish with visual support. *"En Estados Unidos hace muchos años con sus discos."*

"Si." The gray-haired lady nodded agreement, showing little surprise at the international reputation of the three singers. She measured out half a cup of Spanish *café solo,* hot and black, and added boiling water to it so that the result approximated an American cup of coffee—*café Americano.*

It was good coffee: freshly ground and made in a large

gleaming machine directly in front of where Jackie was standing. Jackie took a sip and scrutinized the poster again, wondering if *Trio Los Panchos* still sang in the same high three-part-harmony style. Like Vito Scalza, they seemed to have stayed on the track, even though it now took them to small provincial cities instead of the large audiences of years past.

Jackie took his coffee outside to a glassed-in porch and sat down at a small wooden table. The *Mar Azul* looked out across the esplanade and beach to a bay, flanked on one side by a newly constructed, government-run *parador* not much different from a California Holiday Inn. On the other side was a large villa, boarded up during the off season, as were most of the villas that dotted the two-mile strip of coastline running south. The beach itself was deserted, except for a barefooted young man resolutely traversing the wet, packed sand by the water's edge in obedience to some self-prescribed ritual.

Ritual. It had not taken long for Jackie to fall into one. A half hour of long, sustained tones immediately after getting up, followed by a mile's walk from his seaside villa to the *Mar Azul* for a cup of coffee. After that, a stop to check for mail at *Viajes Intour,* generally coupled with a few words of wholesome advice from Señora Uhrquart. Then it was back to the villa for serious work: three two-hour practice sessions, punctuated by lunch and short walks. By late afternoon it was time for a *copa* at the *Mar Azul* and a little noodling around with the horn: playing actual melodies and experimenting with various tricks. A nine o'clock dinner, sometimes calling for a drive into Jávea proper, followed by bed: solitary, quiet, occasionally sleepless. Jackie's daily pattern was one that carved time up into handy blocks fit for use in rebuilding the skill he had once possessed. A ritual well suited for a dedicated monk.

Jackie took another sip of his *café Americano* and gazed out over the Mediterranean. It always gave him pleasure to see ships on the horizon, making their way to and from Majorca: as though insisting by their presence that the water was placed there for use, not just as a blank blue-green space stretching endlessly and vacantly out—like the Pacific Ocean. Of late he had begun to spend more and more time staring at the sea, envisioning himself as somehow sinking to its bottom: there to exist in quiet peace, barely moving in the play of currents around him, while up above on the surface great waves heaved and rain fell.

Living on the bottom. Unstriving. Filling up the holes in each day with matters of small consequence. Content to get by in a manner calculated to meet minimum needs and not much more: like the street musicians back in New York, or like a grizzled dishwasher drifting from place to place. A tramp at heart, he had always looked with mild amazement upon the course of his career: much as though the railroad police had hauled him from out of the straw, scrubbed him up, and forced him into a fancy costume. One costume had led to another, each legislating its own repertoire of tricks and grimaces, while underneath the easygoing tramp had winced only slightly under the blows that kept him moving.

It takes a stout blow to get a tramp moving. And one blow after another to send him in the direction desired. Blows from sticks: sometimes delicate switches barely felt; sometimes great, knotted cudgels. But always enough to agitate the waters and send a poor creature up to grope along the surface, paddling desperately to keep from sinking down again. According to Cy Harris, carrots were enough. But Jackie knew that sticks had always been needed to drive him: sticks wielded by firm, purposeful hands.

He finished his coffee but continued to gaze at the sea: conscious of his quiescence, wondering how long his own sense of purpose would keep his ritualized schedule from surrendering to the attractions of an easy life in an easy land. Perhaps it had been a mistake to close the door on Rita, whose prodding might well have stemmed from a wise, womanly knowledge that this was what he needed and what he had sought her out for.

Trying to goad himself into action, Jackie pushed his chair back from the table and got up, taking his coffee cup and saucer back to the bar inside the *Mar Azul.* He stared once more at the *Trio Los Panchos* poster in an effort to infer what sticks or carrots were keeping them on course: a course now in shallow waters when matched against their glorious voyages in the great days of Latin music and Latin bands—Machito, Noro and Esy Morales, Miguelito Valdez. The faces of the three middle-aged men were serious, intent, inscrutable, lost in their own concerns. Properly so.

He walked over to *Viajes Intour* to ask for his mail. There was none. He chided himself for his feeling of disappointment: a feeling not unlike that of an employee who quits and then expects to be entreated to return, as had been the case when he had waited in his hotel room for a healing phone call from Jeff Styles. There had been no phone call then; there were no letters now. Properly so.

Paul Ciardi had written a couple of weeks back to inform

him that all was running smoothly: the company running well under its new ownership, Rita apparently content with their interim arrangement and actively engaged in peddling various properties—real estate and theatrical. And there had been a letter from Louise three days ago telling him that all was going well with her job at Road Runner Publications. Good letters. Good news. But bothersome in suggesting that the world he had left was somehow managing to function in his absence as effectively as when he was at the center of it.

He left *Viajes Intour* and started his walk along the seacoast road that led to his villa. A pleasant walk. Quiet. Broken here and there by a passing car and once by the clattering of the local *autobus:* a vehicle that ran hourly from Jávea proper and back. Even a greeting occasionally from people working in their gardens: some of them British pensioners, some from Germany, France, Switzerland, and other prospering countries in Europe. A pleasant place. Comfortable. Even for the Spanish, who seemed to take loving care with their beautiful children. A good place for dark ones like himself.

As pleasant as his walk was, it did not dispel his feeling of uneasiness. He was still in a strange land whose language was difficult for him—with the exception of overtly recognizable borrowings like *el camping* and *el takeaway.* He occupied his villa as a paying guest dependent upon pieces of paper sent him by uncertain mail, set in motion by friendly hands. And if friendly hands could reach this far, unfriendly hands might well have the same power: power to harass and punish, exact just retribution like that dealt out by syndicate people to uncooperative musicians. A power measured as much by vindictiveness as by rational self-interest. A power perfectly capable of mangling a Selmer trumpet—or trumpet player.

Jackie quickened his pace, almost jogging in an attempt to drive his sudden fear away through concentration upon his muscles and breathing. A wise course: one that put the spinning mind to rest by bringing wind and limb into play—like music itself, as Vito had put it. In better spirits, he rounded the curve leading to the villa, pleased at the way his body was carrying him forward. A flattening stomach, hardening muscles: the results of his month's work were already apparent—and gratifying.

He stopped short when he saw a black Cadillac parked directly in front of his villa. For a moment he considered turning around and running back to *Viajes Intour,* his fear given tangible justification by the presence of an American automobile in an isolated section of the *Costa Blanca.* But he forced himself to walk forward and take a look at the man standing beside the Cadillac: a man in a brown leather jacket wearing horn-rimmed glasses, more European in appearance than American. It was not until the man waved at him that Jackie realized his visitor was Herr Zweifel.

"Our friend, Vito Scalza, gave me your address." Herr Zweifel's alert brown eyes glistened behind the lenses of his glasses with obvious satisfaction at his success in matching the contents of a piece of paper against actual concrete, stone, and tile. "I hope my visit is not an inconvenience to you."

"It's good to see you." Jackie smiled cordially and shook hands. "And it's a treat to see something on these roads beside a Ford Fiesta."

"I love this machine." Herr Zweifel gave the hood an affectionate, possessive pat. "It's better than the Mercedes for a long drive—less expensive, too."

"A drive from Vienna?"

"Not today." Herr Zweifel gave the hood another pat. "We came down last week to our villa in Altea, so I decided to drive up and see how you were progressing."

"I'm coming along fine," said Jackie.

"Good."

They went inside, Herr Zweifel inspecting the contents of the villa carefully: living room, three bedrooms, kitchen, dining room, and tiled patio facing the sea.

"It's large," said Jackie. "Much larger than I thought it would be when my lawyer set it up for me."

"Very lovely." Out on the patio, Herr Zweifel peered up and down the coastline in a quick assessment of the neighboring villas. "Quite expensive, I would guess."

"Not bad." Jackie gave an awkward smile. Herr Zweifel's evident prosperity was disconcerting, especially in view of what Jackie remembered from his army service in Weisbaden: respectable people bartering their possessions for cigarettes and chocolate bars; ragged children, buildings in rubble, an air of pinched poverty and defeat. It was good to know that the Germans had recovered. But it might have been more appropriate if the recovery had stopped short of buying Cadillacs and foreign real estate.

"Costa del Sol is more fashionable—and warmer," said Herr Zweifel. "But this is more convenient." He pointed north with an emphatic gesture. "From Barcelona it's practically an *Autobahn,* so my family and I can make the drive from Vienna in less than two days."

"Do you come down often?"

"As much as we can. It's a pleasant change." Herr Zweifel turned his alert brown eyes back to Jackie. "But why should you come here? Spain is very much like your own California, is it not?"

"Fewer phone calls," said Jackie. "It's a good place to work."

"At your weightlifting, as you once described it." Herr Zweifel nodded solemnly to underscore the seriousness of the matter.

"I enjoy it."

"Hard work is always a blessing." Herr Zweifel smiled ruefully. "I have tried to convince my daughter of that simple truth, but she finds it difficult to accept."

"Perhaps we've all made it too easy for our children." Jackie gazed out at the sea for a moment, tracking a tanker as it inched its way along the horizon.

"A natural urge." Herr Zweifel followed Jackie's gaze. "My mother worked hard to make it easier for me, so it was inevitable for me to do likewise."

"Those were hard times," said Jackie flatly.

"Very hard, especially for a widow with nothing to rely on except her own hands and back." Herr Zweifel shook his head. "My mother worked for five years sweeping out the main concourse of the railroad station and sewed costumes at night for the Vienna Opera. I was in my second year as a student at the *gymnasium* before I knew what a washing machine looked like."

"Things are better now. You wouldn't want your daughter to go through all that, would you?"

"No. But I want her to understand that it is her grandmother and the others who worked long hours and did without so that she can wear nice clothes, go to the disco, and talk with her intelligent friends about the theater and modern jazz. The girl is not arrogant. But it grieves me that she does not respect her grandmother's accomplishments more."

"These things take time," said Jackie, feeling more at ease after Herr Zweifel had unburdened himself a little. "Just like playing the trumpet."

"And you are pleased with your work thus far?"

"Like I said, it's coming along." Jackie grinned at his visitor. "Would you feel more comfortable if I played you a progress report?"

"It's not necessary." Herr Zweifel held up a hand to stay Jackie's exit. "I know your recordings, and I know that your integrity as an artist would not permit you to appear unprepared."

"I've never thought of it in those terms." Jackie gave a little laugh. "But I've always liked playing for people—especially those who know something about my kind of music."

"I'm honored."

Jackie went inside and came back with his trumpet, blowing into it and working the valves.

"It sounds bigger inside," he said. "But sometimes I like to bring it out here and make like a fog horn for the ships passing by out there. With an offshore wind I like to think some of it actually travels that far."

He put the instrument to his lips, took a breath, and blew a note: holding it out for well over seventy seconds, using a trick Clint Lawler had taught him for replenishing his air supply. The note came out clear and true, slowly building to a crescendo and just as slowly fading away, the sound under perfect control all the way. When he finished, he put the trumpet down and nodded cheerfully at Herr Zweifel.

"Magnificent," said Herr Zweifel after a long pause. "I would never have believed that a single note could carry so much meaning."

"Anybody can play fast, but there's not many that can play long and keep it from bending out of shape, especially near the end. Would you like to hear some jazz?"

Herr Zweifel nodded.

"It's not easy to keep from playing junk when you're doing it all by yourself," said Jackie. "But I've cooked up some little games I play by myself. Is there anything you'd like to hear?"

"I always liked 'Stella by Starlight.' "

"Great!" Jackie nodded enthusiastically. But instead of playing, he stared out to sea for a couple of minutes, continuing to nod his head in obedience to a tempo threading its way through his mind.

At length he put the trumpet to his lips and began to play, starting with a simple statement of the melody in which the phrasing had angular, unexpected turns. Then he proceeded to embellish it in the next chorus, still retaining a few discernible linkings with the original. After that, a third chorus, then a fourth, a fifth, a sixth, a seventh, and an eighth, each different from the others, yet linked by one architectural conception. At the close, he played a series of cadenzas out of tempo, ending up with the same note he had originally played for Herr Zweifel.

"Good heavens!" said Herr Zweifel. "I've never heard anyone play like that."

"You don't get much chance." Jackie took a couple of

breaths, let his arms dangle loosely as though to let his concentration flow naturally away. "On a record it's in and out in a hurry, and most players can put down a good story for a couple of choruses. But it takes a heavyweight to keep it cooking in the same key for any length of time. Sooner or later you're in danger of running out of ideas and repeating yourself."

"Where do you get your ideas from?"

"Hard to say." Jackie looked down at his horn as though expecting it to sound the answer for him. "But I think concentration has a lot to do with it. I remember Coleman Hawkins one night at King Randolph's—he had just been sitting around and listening for a couple of weeks, and then he came up with his horn and played eight choruses in a row, each one better than the one before. That was when everybody else put their horns back in the case and gave up—even Lester Young."

"Those must have been exciting times for you."

"It's always exciting when you're young." Jackie shrugged. "But I'm glad I had the chance to hear some good people and hold my own now and then."

"I think we're very fortunate to have you appearing at Montreux."

"I'll do my best," said Jackie. "And I'm pretty sure I'll be able to stay out of Vito's way when he gets going—the others, too."

"It seems a shame to submerge your talent in a group—however excellent the group might be."

"It's the best way, and it's a lot of fun to bounce things back and forth."

"Of course," said Herr Zweifel hastily. "But I was thinking of an additional appearance—a solo appearance, backed by a group of your own choosing."

Jackie shook his head.

"That's a different ball game," he said. "I'd have a lot of expectations to live up to—not merely the way I play, but the numbers I've been associated with. There would be arrangements to consider, rehearsal, pacing—a solo thing is like putting on your own little show."

"You've done it before, haven't you?"

"With my own band, yes. But you're talking about putting something together on short notice. I'll be doing just fine to get out there and not fall all over myself."

"It would mean a great deal."

"I don't see why." Jackie looked steadily into Herr Zweifel's alert brown eyes. "It seems to me we've come a long way since you walked into my office. Why not leave well enough alone?"

"I didn't mean to press you—merely to raise the possibility."

"I'll give it some thought." Jackie grinned. "That's what I said before, right?"

"I believe so." Herr Zweifel took a deep breath of Mediterranean air, looked down at the trumpet in Jackie's hands, and shook his head in admiration. "It's been a privilege."

"Me, too," said Jackie. "You're the first person I've actually played for since I started all this."

"Are you happy to be back with your music?"

Jackie paused, held the trumpet up to the light, worked the valves a few more times.

"Right now it feels good," he said. "Real good."

He watched Herr Zweifel drive off in his black Cadillac, headed for Altea, there to do further battle with his intelligent, unappreciative daughter. And he thought for a moment of Louise, feeling oddly grateful to her for setting him free. Better parents grateful to children than the other way round, possibly. A comforting thought: to think of Louise swimming by herself on into the future when the time came for him to sink back down to the bottom.

Denia, Spain:
Thursday, February 23, 11:00 A.M.

"They look like bullet holes to me." Cy Harris walked down the parapet a few steps to get a better view of the wall angling off in front of them.

"Why not?" said Jackie. "A castle's bound to get shot at somewhere along the line."

"From inside?"

"From all sides."

"These came from inside." With the judicious air of a tall, balding owl, Cy disposed of the matter.

"But it's open to attack from below." Jackie pointed to the expanse of ground sloping down the wall where they were. "And that's where the shooting would be coming from, wouldn't it?"

"Some of it, maybe. But it wouldn't make much sense to pepper a blank wall with holes."

Jackie nodded. There was no point in arguing a case with Cy, who was inclined to take the smallest fact and chew it into minute, digestible pieces.

Cy had wanted to see a castle, so they had driven the ten miles over to Denia, where a large hilltop mass of stone and rubble still glowered truculently at the harbor and town below. There were other castles in the vicinity—even a complete walled town carved out of a mountain, less than fifty miles away. But the castle at Denia was closest.

It was also one of the biggest castles available for inspection. Wall after wall, level after level, parapet after parapet, tower after tower. Lots and lots of stone: all of it sweated up the hill under someone's whip. Greeks, Romans, Goths, Franks, Moors, Catalans. They had all made their way up the hill: using rubble left by previous occupants to build their fortresses, and leaving their own work in rubble for use by subsequent builders. Now employees of the government were digging through the rubble for objects worthy of display: a few beautifully tapered Greek columns, some scowling Roman heads, a coin or two, pottery and brooches, even an inscription announcing the services of an enterprising late Latin medical practitioner. Lots and lots of rubble. But enough of the castle left to justify a couple of old men at the gate selling tickets and souvenirs.

"Do you know what I think?" Still chewing on his observation, Cy pointed at the wall as though taking aim with a revolver. "I think they lined somebody up on that ledge and shot them—probably with a machine gun."

"Why there? Why not down inside where they have more room?"

"Better visibility here." Cy pointed down the hill to the houses and streets staggering their way gradually down to the shoreline. "They marched those poor guys out and lined them up where the whole town could see what they were doing."

"Who?"

"I dunno." Cy shrugged, apparently reconciled to the limitations of his detective work. "But I bet they made a big production out of it."

"That's show business," said Jackie. He shook his head sadly, mild blue eyes speculative and remote.

He tried to flesh Cy's sketch out in fuller detail. The men would have been marched there and held in place until word was spread through the town below. Gradually a crowd would have assembled: perhaps sullen, perhaps screaming threats at the executioners. Then there might have been a proclamation designed to make explicit whatever cautionary purpose lay behind the public display of power and determination. After that, silence, followed by a short volley or longer burst of machine-gun fire. All this rounded off with the disposition of the bodies: shoving them over the wall, probably, so that they rolled down the embankment to be claimed later, just as the body of the faceless man had tumbled out of the freight car and rolled over and over again before coming to a final resting place. Executions, bullfights, murder for greed or vindictiveness—they all had a show-business quality to them. First the premise, then the action, and finally the closing punch line or heavy piece of slapstick, capped with a blackout.

"Civil War?" Cy squinted through his glasses at the town as though trying to infer what its military importance might have been.

"I suppose so."

"Which side?"

"Both sides," said Jackie, pleased with the way his mind seemed to be working: less fuzzy, less rambling. "It always takes two sides for a battle—the winners and the losers."

"I mean who did it to whom."

"They took turns." Jackie pointed to the citadel crowning the castle's highest point: some of it restored, most of it a mass of formless rock. "One side builds it up, the other side tears it down and builds a new one—then they wait for a while and start in all over again."

"Long-range planning." Cy looked at the citadel and shook his head. "What these people need is long-range planning so that everything fits together and doesn't come apart every fifty years."

"They're good people, especially on a day-to-day basis." Jackie turned and waved toward the town below. "They're not afraid to close up shop for a break in the afternoon, and they're always having a fiesta for one reason or another—bands, fireworks, speeches, parades, and costumes. Who are you to fly in here and tell them what they need?"

"It happens to be the one thing I'm good at," said Cy easily. "If I can put it together for you, I certainly ought to be able to put it together for them."

Jackie sighed. It was clear that Cy was about to resume the attack, trotting out reason after reason why Jackie should accept Herr Zweifel's offer of a solo performance spot in July. Reason after reason, punch after punch: going the distance in the same way his father must have gone after Harry Greb and other opponents. A friendly attack, but wearisome.

Cy had stopped by with a clear purpose in mind. Like Herr Zweifel, he wanted Jackie to take the plunge with a solo appearance in Montreux: sharing the stage with other players, but showcasing his own material and talent. As a logical prelude, Cy had suggested a break-in performance with a pick-up band at one of the opera festivals—Waterford, Ireland, possibly. Good reasoning. A good purpose: forcing its way into their conversation like an Ozark chigger, there to burn and itch until dealt with to Cy's satisfaction.

Jackie sighed and shook his head as he had done earlier.

"We've been through that," he said. "I don't see why you have to keep pushing me to get out there and fall on my face."

"You'll be sensational." Cy beamed down at him. "And it will sure set things up for some heavy action later on."

"It's all I can do to get my chops in shape—being a leader is more than I want to think about now. Besides, I can't understand why Zweifel wants to change the signals."

"I've been thinking about that." Cy extracted one of his cigars, took a moment or two to get it going. "A change in signals generally means a new ball game, which means that they're probably having trouble in getting a commitment from Otis Marshak and that English manager of his."

"What does that make me—the second team?" Jackie looked coldly at Cy, offended by the implication that Otis was a more desirable commodity.

"It gives you a better chance to stand up and lay down a complete story, and it gives me a better chance to book you any place you want to go."

"I don't know where I want to go and I can't see what all the rush is—unless there's something you haven't told me."

"This business is filled with possibilities," said Cy. "And I have to admit I've been thinking there's an off chance for a really big score if things work out right."

"There are no big scores around for jazz players any more—you know that."

"Otis Marshak and his manager don't think so—they've approached the Jeff Styles estate with a proposal for Otis to front a band using the Jeff Styles name and the Jeff Styles orchestrations."

"That's a slick idea. But anybody can play those tunes, and a good arranger could recreate the orchestrations from the records. Why do they have to get permission from the estate?"

"It's a legal thing—just like your 'Judy's Guy' shows. If you have the whole package, you have a very, very valuable property, especially if it's pushed in the right way—look at the way they've kept the Glenn Miller band going, for example."

"Why would anyone want my 'Judy's Guy' package?"

"Chemistry," said Cy. "For somebody, it could be the essential item in next year's line—or the year after that. Have you ever had an offer?"

"Yes, but I turned it down."

"Did they come back with something sweeter?"

"No."

"That's odd."

"What's odd about it? Anybody ought to know I'd want to keep it in the family."

"It's not what *you* want—it's what *they* want." Cy looked out toward the sea wall and took a reflective puff on his cigar. "Maybe they felt that another approach would work better with a sentimental guy like you."

"There's nothing they could come up with that would make me turn loose of those shows," said Jackie firmly. "They're in trust and that's where they stay."

"There are ways." Cy smiled and patted him on the shoulder. "Maybe they figured you'd be less sentimental if you owed them a lot of money. Didn't you ever wonder why those New Orleans people were so eager to pour all that loot into a small outfit—and at a time when everybody else was cold?"

"Those were different people."

"Different faces, maybe—but I'm willing to bet it was the same people pulling the strings."

"Is there something you know that I don't?"

"I don't know any more about it than you do." Cy blew a creditable smoke ring and smiled again. "But I'm a lot better at putting things together in a long-range way, which is why you ought to trust me a little more when it comes to heavy action."

Jackie sighed and looked down at the town as though searching for a quiet refuge. The Poirier loan offer had never felt right. Neither he nor Paul Ciardi had been able to smell out its purpose. Since it had been Rita's project, Rita might have had some suspicions of the long-range planning behind the offer: suspicions she had kept from him for purposes of her own. Purposes, long-range planning. His sale of Jay Jay had thwarted Rita somehow, demolished a structure built with artful care. Small wonder that Rita's rage had conquered her usual restraint: not unlike his own feelings when he had tried to get Otis fired and ended up walking the bricks himself. Purpose, action, effect: bad enough when following their intended pattern; ten times worse when blown off course by unpredictable winds. A life without purpose in a Mediterranean village—the notion gave him comfort.

"That's all over and done with," he said to Cy. "I'm happy enough taking each day as it comes."

"Exactly—and that's why I'm glad to see you forget about the past and start thinking of the future."

"It seems to me there's more future for Otis with the Jeff Styles material—he was with the band longer than I was, and he's stayed active all along."

"Good thinking!" Cy grinned broadly and clapped his hands like a burlesque comic intent upon quickening the tempo of a sketch. "That's exactly the way I figured it at first. But then I sat down and made a list of the special things you have going for you.

"One." He held up his right index finger as though testing for the presence of a favorable breeze. "You already have a track record as a bandleader and as a guy who likes to keep people happy—while the only thing Otis has ever done is cause trouble.

"Two. You were always more of an all-around player than Otis—a little singing here, a little melody stuff there. When it comes to getting other good solo players and keeping the overall Jeff Styles sound, you'll do a much better job than Otis will.

"Three—and this is the big payoff. You have a lot of visibility going for you from your radio stuff and from the "Judy's Guy" show, where you played a bandleader. So you'll pull a lot of people in just on your own. Otis Marshak and the Jeff Styles Orchestra—that's good thinking. But Jackie Hayes and the Jeff Styles Orchestra—that's dynamite, big-numbers thinking. Like I said, it's only a possibility—and so was going to the moon until someone thought about it and made it happen."

"It's a great idea—I don't deny it," Jackie said. "But what I've been trying to get across to you is that I don't feel like being an astronaut anymore. Let somebody else have the glory—and the headaches. I'll be satisfied to get back in shape and play clubs like Vito. That's enough for me."

"Who's talking about glory?"

"You are—with all this high visibility, name-in-lights stuff. Everyone else may want to be a celebrity and be important, but I don't. If I did, I'd still be back in Studio City with Rita." Sure of his ground, he smiled at Cy.

Cy smiled back, unruffled by Jackie's departure from the normal pattern of client response: almost as though he had another list of appropriate rebuttals tucked away somewhere.

"I'm talking about a chance to do something more valuable and worthwhile than keeping a couple of game shows afloat. Right now there's a whole generation that's never heard Jeff's music—great music. Don't you think that music is worth bringing to the public?"

"I suppose so."

"And there are a lot of good players—friends of yours—who would give anything to play those charts again and make a little bread. Do you want me to come up with a list of names?"

"No." Jackie looked once more at the bullet-pocked execution wall. It felt as though Cy had backed him into a corner, holding his heavy artillery in reserve.

"And think of the younger players you'd be giving a chance. To have that band active again would be an inspiration to everyone. You'd be doing one of the most worthwhile things you'd ever done in your life. And why? Because it would mean a great deal to a lot of good people. Take for example that Italian guy who stepped in to turn Chrysler around."

"Lee Iacocca?" said Jackie, surprised to find the name surfacing so quickly.

"That's the one. Can you honestly say he took on all those headaches for the money?"

"No—he had more than enough from his days with Ford, I guess."

"Exactly. And wouldn't you say he's risking his reputation in taking on a problem that maybe nobody can solve?"

"In a way."

"And if he brings it off, if he turns that giant, bad-news dinosaur of a company around, who's going to benefit more—Lee what's-his-name or the thousands and thousands of families with a paycheck coming in every two weeks?"

"I hope they're grateful to him."

"Grateful! They'll probably forget his name as quickly as I did. As far as he's concerned, I bet the glory doesn't mean a thing compared with a chance to do something really worthwhile at a time when he's probably the only one who can do it—just like you, my shy beachcomber friend."

Jackie looked back at Cy, who was puffing vigorously on his cigar in an attempt to get it going again after his small tirade. It was difficult to disentangle the threads and deal with them one by one: separating flattery from fact, speculation from reasonable possibility. He felt as though Reverend Sam's powerful Jesus-bat had somehow been wielded against him: hammering him down blow by blow, argument by argument, example by example, question by question—like a police interrogator working a suspect over with remorseless skill. An interrogator not to be argued with, not to be diverted—except by soft words.

"Let's take another look at the town," he said. "Maybe get a drink or something."

"Why not?" Cy smiled cheerfully. "I've given you my best pitch, and I certainly don't expect an answer right off."

"I'll think about it."

"Think hard, real hard." Cy clapped him on the back as though setting their walk in motion. "And think *hit*—big, big extra-base hit. I guarantee you that's how it's going to play if everything else falls right."

London, England: Wednesday, March 8, 2:30 P.M.

"Tolkien." Ian Clarke waved a white, well-manicured hand toward the four musicians on the other side of the glass partition. "Those lads are pure Tolkien." His protruding eyes focused unsmilingly upon the two scraggly-haired songwriters seated at the far end of the recording booth.

There was a pause, filled only with a soft crackle of sound from the monitor speaker above them. Finally one of the songwriters spoke.

"Like hobbits?" he said.

"Very much so." Ian nodded curt approval, managing at the same time to suggest that the response had been far too late in coming. "A roast-beef feeling underneath all that violence—that's the furrow I want you to plough in your writing. Do you follow?"

"It's quite clear to me, sir," said the second songwriter.

"We'll have to see about that, won't we?" Ian smiled thinly, looking at each of them as though to suggest that they would have to battle each other for his favor. Two songwriters, each working separately on vacuous material for a vacuous group: the technique seemed to be eminently serviceable.

The door opened and Sid Price came in. He was a large, muscular thirty-year-old with red hair and bushy eyebrows. Soft-spoken. But with hard, impenetrable gray eyes: not unlike those of an experienced dealer in one of the gambling clubs.

"Might I speak with you privately, sir?" asked Sid.

Ian looked at his assistant with irritation. Then he looked down at the two scraggly-haired young men.

"I'll be back directly," he said. "For the moment you might as well turn up the sound and harken to where we are."

"Tolkien," said the first songwriter: voice unctuous, eyes blank.

"There's a good fellow."

Ian went to the door so that he reached it before Sid. When Sid came up Ian stepped back and let his assistant go through the door first. An intricate little dance: the order of precedence changed from that of previous years, when rank went first in a swirl of capes and diadems. A dance with mannerisms of speech calling for "rich" instead of "wealthy," followed by "well off" after the lower middle class—always keen on the scent—had sniffed out the newly defined vulgarity of "rich."

A difficult dance to learn. A dance best mastered in public schools like Harrow and Winchester: where the blander arts of sycophancy could be acquired gradually through cumulative years of cunning adolescent ritual, along with a distinctive pronunciation—part wheeze, part nasal whine, part covertly hostile grunt. But a dance that could be picked up by a clever lad after a year or two at university.

Ian Clarke had gone to Cambridge on scholarship, traveling down from the begrimed mining country of Durham to read history at Fitzwilliam. He had been able to stay only two terms, but that had been long enough to acquire manner and address sufficient for a post with one of the midland newspapers. There he had shrewdly elected to string his bow primarily with articles about American jazz and jazzmen: articles that puffed some, deflated others, and in general advanced his stock as a critic with a keen, if slightly protruding, eye for talent. With the advent of the Beatles and the Stones, he had moved into talent representation and record production, acquiring a rather mixed and profitable bag of clients—including Otis Marshak. Not the most brilliant of careers, but certainly one replete with its fair share of perks.

Once outside the door, Ian brushed back his light brown

curls as though to put himself in trim array for dealing with Sid.

"I take it this is a matter of some moment," he said.

"I think so." Sid's ruddy face was sober, his manner that of one on the brink of dreadful speech—as Ian's tutor always liked to describe the bearing of a bearer of evil tidings. "I've just been on the phone with our New York office."

"And?"

"They tell me that the Jeff Styles estate is deferring its decision on our proposal until July."

"I find that very tiresome," said Ian. "Were they able to find out anything? The estate people seemed quite receptive when I talked with them."

"They were—and up until two weeks ago everything seemed nicely tied up."

"What's the difficulty, then? Is it the money?"

"I don't think so." Sid moved closer in and lowered his voice. "There's been another proposal."

"That's absurd." Ian's small mouth pouted slightly. "Otis is ideal—it's a matter of common knowledge. I'm inclined to suspect that this is just an excuse for being greedy."

"Perhaps so." Sid nodded deferentially and paused a moment. "But apparently a strong case has been made for putting the orchestra under the leadership of Jackie Hayes."

"The television chap? Cracking jokes like a music hall performer?"

Sid nodded again, smiled slightly: as though he would be more than willing to endure whatever whips and scorpions might be deemed appropriate.

"I can't believe the heirs would accept that kind of desecration. Who's the guiding spirit behind all this?"

"A New York agency—Cy Harris."

Ian looked down at the floor, pursed his lips thoughtfully. It was clearly time to refocus the discussion, since Cy Harris was an agency of repute and consequence.

"I think we need to talk about this," he said, looking up and down the corridor as though the place had suddenly grown unduly cramped.

He led Sid down the corridor and into the lobby of the recording company. A large lobby. Filled with people, young for the most part. Young people dressed in garish costumes: berets, overalls, serapes, plumed hats, and other appropriations from the past and from the *demi-monde.* The girls were mostly quite young: pretty in an unformed way: each with the vacant look of an adolescent precociously schooled in a full range of sexual play and perversion: each presenting the appearance of a delicate, many-orificed ceramic piece waiting to be picked up, appraised and carried off.

Ian walked through the lobby at a brisk pace, meeting each impudent stare with his own knowing gaze, feeling very much like an Ottoman functionary in a Stamboul slave auction. The feeling was not new to him, though it had been stronger in days past when his agent's role had required him to judge aspiring flesh quickly and accurately, sensing the potential contents of each vase and calculating to a nicety the various wrigglings, couplings, mouthings, and moans in store for his clientele. As they worked their way through the crowd, his small mouth curved in a half-smile as if to say, "Very lovely, but not today, thank you."

His own personal taste had always been for talent: true talent, talent hovering just this side of genius. To lie with a fine singer, knowing that the slender throat he caressed could soar into high, echoing song at any time. To walk into a room with a superb dancer, knowing that the limbs moving sedately by his side could if desired leap over a neighboring couch in an explosive burst of skill. To feel the hands of a brilliant pianist stroking his light brown curls. These were all pleasures to cherish as much in recollection as in experience: pleasures far more subtle and civilized than the small brute lusts of rock stars and cabinet ministers. And it was with this same passion for talent that Ian had nourished Otis Marshak's career. A selfish passion, perhaps. But genuine—and implacable.

Like any passion it could lead to violence: a coarse assault set in motion by a phone call or a hint to someone specializing in the form. The blows, the threats, the symbolic damage to property, the maiming called for in extreme cases—these never came directly from Ian. But they took their force and direction from his passion: a passion coated with characteristic English respect for bland language and fair address. English hypocrisy, some called it. Still, it had sustained the Empire for many years; and it was for Ian Clarke an ingrained habit of mind—and action.

His face set, he led Sid to a nearby pub, standing by the bar for a minute until he was able to locate a properly secluded booth. There he ordered drinks: Dubonnet for himself, ale for Sid. It was not until the drinks had been brought to their table and paid for that Ian fixed his protruding eyes upon his assistant as though to search out some kind of a solution in the impenetrable gray eyes staring back at him.

"Where do we stand?" he said, small mouth tightly drawn.

"They like our proposal and they feel that the financial arrangements are fair, but they want to put off a final decision until some time in July."

"Why July?"

"Apparently Mr. Hayes is going to appear at the Montreux festival."

"Why should that make a difference?" Ian sipped his drink and made a grimace. "Is he going to act as *compère* and introduce the artists?"

"He's going to play."

"But he hasn't played in years."

"Our people in New York tell me he's been practicing."

"Has anybody actually heard him?"

"No. That's why they're going to make the decision after his performance at the festival."

"What's he going to do there—play a couple of choruses with some of his old hangers-on?"

"I gather the original plan called for something like that," said Sid. "But as matters now stand Mr. Hayes is going to do a forty-minute spot, backed by a rhythm section."

"That's exactly what Otis did last year." Ian took out a cigarette, concentrated on keeping his hands from shaking with rage as he lit it. "I have the feeling there's more to this than meets the eye."

"I'm not sure I follow you, sir."

"Item." Ian leaned forward. "Mr. Harris approached me several months ago with an offer to represent Otis—an offer which I was completely justified in refusing. Item. Mr. Harris then searches around for a shoddy musical substitute. Item. Mr. Harris arranges for his shoddy musical substitute to pass for genuine talent on the basis of a supposedly future appearance at Montreux. Item. On the basis of this deception Mr. Harris approaches the Jeff Styles estate with his proposal in hopes that it will be immediately accepted—after which, I strongly suspect, his intention was to reapproach me with his original offer."

Scowling, Ian sat back and took a few angry puffs on the cigarette in his small mouth. "There's a perfect example of American business ethics at work—shoddy work and big lies."

"Begging your pardon, sir, but do we know for certain that Mr. Hayes is a shoddy trumpet player?"

"He always was," Ian replied firmly. "And it was never more apparent than when Otis joined Jeff Styles—which is why Jeff fired Hayes after less than a week."

"May I speak frankly?" Sid looked down at the table, careful to keep his voice soft and deferential.

"If you can suggest a way out of this madness, I can assure you that my gratitude will take a tangible and permanent form."

"I see two possibilities—a pleasant one and an unpleasant one. The pleasant one is that Mr. Hayes's deficiencies will be apparent to all when he performs in July, with the result that the Jeff Styles estate will accept our proposal forthwith."

"I don't call that particularly pleasant—it means a four-month delay for us."

"The second possibility is more of the worst-case variety, if you'll permit me to say so."

"Get to the point, please," said Ian coldly.

"What if Mr. Hayes performs well?"

"I've already explained to you that that's impossible—he's a personality, not an artist."

"What if he performs adequately?"

"I'll concede that." Ian looked over toward the bar, taking stock of the people standing there: some in colorful costume, some in plain business dress. "And I take it your next point will be that an adequate performance might be interpreted as brilliant—particularly if Mr. Harris is able to bribe his usual quota of American critics."

"I must admit my reasoning was tending in that direction, sir."

"Blast!" Ian looked glumly at his Dubonnet, trying to ferret out a weakness in his assistant's case. He could find none. Then he looked at his watch, wondering how his scraggly-haired songwriters were doing in their competition for his favor. A good technique, to match two talents against one another: a technique that always made any inadequacies embarrassingly apparent.

"I hope you don't mind my bringing all this to your attention, sir." Sid's gray, impenetrable eyes were carefully turned toward the bar.

"Loyalty is a precious thing, Sidney—and so is promptness." Ian gazed toward the bar again. "I'm sorry if I spoke sharply to you."

"I understand, sir—it's a serious matter, after all."

"Serious enough, in my view, to justify a little flexibility in our thinking about a Montreux appearance for Otis."

"I thought we had definitely turned that down, sir."

"Then we'll have to turn it up," said Ian. "I'll get on the phone with them right now, cut our price in half if it's necessary, and arrange for Otis to appear on the same day as Hayes."

"A battle of the trumpets. It has the sound of genius to it, if you don't mind my saying so."

"I don't mind at all." Ian's small mouth formed a cherubic smile. "There are times, Sidney, when I amaze even myself." In good humor, suddenly charitable, he looked over at Sid's half-finished drink. "I think I'll beatle off now and get this particular vessel under sail—but feel perfectly free to stay here and finish your pint."

"That's very kind of you."

"I'm always kind—generous, too, as long as matters proceed pleasantly." Ian rose and looked sharply down at Sid. "And as you know, I have always detested unpleasantness in any form—even when called for by the logic of a situation."

Sid Price watched his employer leave. Then he let his ruddy face relax, sighing at the prospect of a few easy moments alone. Not that he disliked his job with Mr. Clarke. It was a good job: refined, low key, calling for good clothes and good manners. And for a lad from Oldham, just outside of Manchester, it was a great joy to sit behind an expensive desk and be called "sir" by university graduates seeking Mr. Clarke's ear.

A joy and an education in itself: picking up refined turns of speech from Mr. Clarke, guarding against provincialisms like "give it me" and "buke" as a pronunciation for "book." A gradual education it had been: starting as doorman at a Liverpool gambling club, followed by a turn as bodyguard and general knockabout for a local rock group. A process that had led him to a job he and Mum were proud of. A respectable job. Better than bashing people. Better pay. Better clothes.

Sid finished his glass of ale and gave some thought to ordering another. A thought to put by for the moment, especially for a thirty-year-old man who has to keep himself quite fit: fit for bashing people in the event it's called for. In the case of Mr. Clarke, the calls were quite rare: the last one being a slender young drummer boy who had indulged in a bit too much of the old slap and tickle in the wrong quarters, with the result that Sid had been obliged to get one of his mates and bash the drummer boy.

Bashing. The logic of the situation, as Mr. Clarke put it, might call for that kind of thing. According to New York, Mr. Hayes would be appearing with a small group in Ireland before going on to Montreux. So it might be a good plan to travel there and hear the quality of his trumpet playing. Sid's ruddy face was thoughtful as he charted the alternatives: weak playing, adequate playing, brilliant playing. For a battle of the trumpets, the first two were tolerable; but the third was simply out of the question. If Mr. Hayes played brilliantly in Ireland, the battle of the trumpets in Montreux might be a disaster—for Otis, for Mr. Clarke, and for him. To avoid such a disaster, some bashing might be needed, even though—like his mentor—Sid had grown more and more to detest overt unpleasantness.

Unpleasantness. It seemed to come along now and then, though never brought out into the open and called by name. That was how the refined people did it—or had it done: always on the basis of long, labored weavings hither and yon until you took their meaning like a trout striking a lure. That was why Sid still kept himself fit—for bashing. Though it was much more enjoyable to sit behind an expensive desk and be called "sir" by young men who had gone to university.

Jávea, Spain:
Friday, April 20, 10:30 A.M.

"Taiwan." Myra Kodaly pointed to the small red stencil on the bottom of the basket. "It doesn't seem right to come to a Spanish market and buy a wicker basket from halfway around the world."

"Everything's closer now," said Jackie. He gestured around the large piece of ground, taking in the booths and groups of shoppers filing by. "I bet half of the people here are from someplace else. France, Belgium, Sweden, Germany, England—they all come down here and pick up on the sunshine."

"It still doesn't seem right." Myra put the basket back and looked at her watch. She was a small, fair woman with a broad forehead—of Croatian extraction, settled in her ways and in her marriage.

"We could walk over to the square and wait for Walt, unless there's more you want to see here."

"I've seen enough." Myra gave a little laugh. "It seems that all we've done on this trip is see things—museums, cathedrals, palaces, bridges, aqueducts. That man has run me to a frazzle."

They started to move out of the open-air market, heading toward the entrance: a narrow funnel clotted with people jostling their way in. Jackie took Myra's hand and shouldered a way through for them.

"It's no place for being shy," he said, as they reached the street and stopped to draw breath.

"Walt says the Germans are the worst." Myra stared appraisingly at a flaxen-haired couple on the other side of the street. "But they all drive like they're crazy."

"I guess so." Jackie felt himself tighten slightly, as though Myra's criticism had been leveled at his choice of retreat.

"I'll be glad to get home."

"How about Walt?"

"I don't think it's as overwhelming for him," said Myra. "He reads up on everything first, so he has a feeling for where things are and what they mean—but to me it's just standing in one line after another with a lot of strange people jabbering in strange languages."

"They're pretty friendly sometimes."

"Who has the time?" Myra sighed. "When you're moving around, the only friends you make are the clerks at the registration desk." She looked at him sharply. "Everyone needs to put down roots somewhere."

"You did your share of moving around, didn't you?"

"That was different—Walt and I were younger then, and we were trying to find the right spot. But we found it twenty years ago and we've stayed there ever since."

"I guess I'm still looking," said Jackie.

"Maybe you're not looking in the right places." Myra smiled at him and put her small hand on his arm. "A good marriage would make a big difference."

"I haven't had much luck in that department." Jackie smiled back at her. "When you're a three-time loser, it's easier to resist that gambling urge."

"You've just had some bad cards, that's all."

"It's not the cards—it's the combination." Jackie's eyes were thoughtful. "I don't think I'm up to handling that kind of responsibility anymore."

"Responsibility works both ways," said Myra firmly. "A good woman would carry her weight and take care of you."

"I take care of myself pretty well as it is—at least the cleaning, washing, and meals seem to work out all right."

"There's more to it than that—everybody wakes up in the

middle of the night, and when you do it's good to have someone there beside you."

Jackie nodded, wondering what his days and nights would be like after his appearance at Montreux. Like an athlete, he was in training for a big event: practicing, preparing, focusing his mind and body so that everything converged upon one small target. Beyond the target, there seemed only a large, vacant space—empty like the sky above them: waiting to be filled with movement. He wondered if Rita felt equally empty, equally alone.

He shaded his eye for a moment, trying to make out the occupants of the tables on the sidewalk in front of the café across the square. At one of the tables was a short, compact man wearing a white Panama hat and reading a book.

"I think that's Walt," he said.

"I bet he doesn't notice us until we're standing over him," said Myra. "Once he picks up a book everything else gets blotted out."

They skirted a group of school children marshaled along by two black-clad nuns and went across the square, passing by a stone octagonal bandstand flanked by two small fountains.

"Where's the car?" said Jackie as they came up.

"About three blocks away." Walt put his book down and scowled. "There seems to be a lot of traffic here." He looked over at one of the streets flowing into the square: a street from which a local policeman, dressed in white, was routing automobiles and trucks off to the right.

"I don't think it's a fiesta." Jackie gazed around the square in an attempt to assess matters. "But they're always roping traffic off for one special occasion or another."

Jackie and Myra sat down. A small man in shirtsleeves walked slowly up to the table and took their order.

"It's a good thing you got here," said Myra. "This place is beginning to fill up."

Jackie looked over at the table next to them. It had just been occupied by two men: one large and fleshy, the other with a long face topped by straight blond hair. At the table beyond them was a group of young men in work clothes.

"What did you see?" he said to Walt.

"Those towers up on the hill beyond your villa."

"Interesting?"

"Getting there was the most interesting part—I bet I know more about these back roads now than you do."

"I spend all my time at the villa," said Jackie easily. "I have to if I'm not going to fall on my face in July."

"It wouldn't do you any harm to see some of this country." Walt's voice was slightly accusatory. "Have you been to Barcelona?"

Jackie shook his head.

"Granada? Madrid?"

Jackie shook his head again.

"It seems to me you could spare a couple of days here and there to widen your perspective on things."

"I think he's a homebody at heart." Myra's broad, fair face was smiling, as though in pleasure at seeing a basic truth confirmed.

The small man in shirtsleeves came back with their drinks. Jackie took out three hundred-peseta notes and watched the small man fish out a number of coins, placing them on a postcard-sized tray.

"You have to admit this is a great place for good, cheap booze," he said cheerfully, as though the topic might offer a diversion from the friendly proddings directed at him. "A lot of the English pensioners get smashed every night."

"Here's to the decline of the British Empire." Walt raised his glass, a half smile on his dark, saturnine face.

"They're good people," said Jackie. "Friendlier than most, I'd say."

"I don't deny it. But they collapsed—just like the Romans and the Spaniards." Walt shrugged and sighed. "Just like we're doing."

"I don't know that we're on the skids—we're a lot better off than when you and I were growing up."

"Have you tried to get a hotel room with a pack of cigarettes lately?" Walt looked at Myra for support. "Twenty years ago we could have managed the whole trip on five dollars a day—and lived like kings."

"That's progress."

"Not for us. We're coasting while the others are speeding—the Arabs, the Japanese, the Germans, and the rest of the Europeans."

"It was one Mercedes after another coming down from Barcelona," said Myra. "All going eighty miles an hour."

Jackie sipped his drink and thought back for a moment to Herr Zweifel and his Cadillac, blandly celebrated as a good, moderate-priced car. That part of the encounter had rankled: perhaps because of its unexpectedness, perhaps because of his own feelings of age when matched against the vigor and force of a younger man—like the one who had given him the kidney chop on the way back from Paul Ciardi's. If money and power were the old man's muscle, Walt's resentment was quite understandable: much as though a retired general were to have his pension and medals torn away, his victories labeled as defeats, his generosities castigated as betrayals. And all this when failing health and strength prohibited answering the trumpets afresh.

"It looks like we're going to have some music," he said. He pointed to a group of men in red jackets filing up to the octagonal bandstand. There were about fifteen of them.

"Just like Colonel Kale," said Walt. "Small, but heavy on brass."

"That's what it takes in the open air." Jackie fingered Clint's mouthpiece in his pocket as though it were a lucky charm responsible for introducing an agreeable distraction into their discussion.

"Ungebrauchbar," grunted the large fleshy man at the table next to them.

"Das Elite Korps?" laughed the younger, long-faced blond man. He looked directly over at Jackie and winked as though to suggest that mutual amusement was in store.

Jackie did not wink back. Nor did he smile. It was certainly true that the musicians were something less than an elite group. The red jackets were wrinkled, ill fitting in some cases. And a number of the instruments had an aged, dented look: especially the tuba, which was far too small to provide a deep bass grounding for the others. But the group had an air of enthusiasm, and the young men at the table beyond were obviously proud of their friends on the bandstand. Good or bad, the upcoming concert deserved encouragement.

The first selection was a military march: first strain, second strain, trio—all repeated several times as though retraveling of a familiar route might make matters progressively easier. A sound strategy. And by the selection's end the band had reached a reasonable level of volume: though far under the chest-shaking power of the Kale Brothers Symphonia when it led the elephants and wagons down the street.

The bandmaster, an old gentleman with fierce white whiskers, turned to acknowledge the applause. There was not much of it, except from the schoolchildren and from actual residents of the small town. From the visitors only a slight perfunctory rattle: almost as though the concert represented nothing more than a quaint inconvenience. Something to be endured, like a horse-drawn cart on a back road. But not something to be taken seriously when matched against the grand parades of Britain, France, Belgium, and Germany.

The selections that followed were worse: a fast but faltering *paso doble* and a couple of concert pieces calling for solos by various instruments. A noble attempt at variety. But one that made the overall sound thinner and thinner, much like that of a group of climbers puffing and wheezing in their attempt to scale heights beyond their capacity. Jackie continued to applaud, scowling at Walt and Myra in an attempt to enlist their support.

"These guys are dreadful." Walt shook his head in sober judgment.

"You can't have the Hollywood Bowl every place you go," said Jackie. "They're local folks and they're giving it their best shot—what more do you want?"

"This is not good music," said the large fleshy man, staring directly at Jackie. "Why then do you clap with the hands so loud?"

Jackie did not respond. But anger welled up inside: anger at his own decline, anger at flaxen-haired people and their arrogant assumption of superiority to lesser breeds. He fingered the mouthpiece in his pocket and briefly considered letting his anger take the form of a right hook to the German's patronizing face.

He got up without a word and walked through the square to the octagonal bandstand where the musicians, slightly dispirited, were talking over the choice of their next number.

"Soy musico," he said softly to the bandmaster. He pulled out Clint's mouthpiece and held it up as a visible credential.

The bandmaster looked at the mouthpiece and stared closely at Jackie. Then he beckoned to one of his musicians. The young man came forward with his trumpet tucked under his arm.

"*Quiere tocar*?" said the bandmaster. He pointed to the trumpet.

"Si." Jackie bowed to indicate his appreciation. *"Quiere tocar solo."*

"*Solo*?" The bandmaster stroked his fierce white whiskers and gestured around the square. "*Solamente usted*?"

"Una cosa de aprecio." Jackie smiled: partly to underscore his meaning, partly in pleasure at how the words seemed to be flowing out. *"Por ustedes, por la gente aqui, por Jávea, por Españea—solamente yo."*

"Muy bien." The bandmaster nodded to the young man, who handed Jackie his trumpet. Jackie fitted his mouthpiece to it, worked the valves a little; then he pointed to the snare drum

and looked at the bandmaster questioningly. The bandmaster nodded and signaled the drummer to begin a roll, during which Jackie stepped down from the bandstand and took up a position about ten feet in front of it.

At the conclusion of the roll, rounded off with a clash of cymbals, Jackie held up the instrument for the inspection of all. Almost like a matador, he bowed stiffly: first to the bandmaster, then to each side of the square, making a point of gesturing to a few people gathered on the various balconies. For one of the girls on the balcony, a long gaze: held there until she stopped giggling and composed herself to listen. The square was now quite silent, almost as though dominated by force of will, almost as though aware that the solitary trumpet player was going to present a piece of consequence—like *"Zigeunerweisen."*

For the violin *"Zigeunerweisen"* is a traditional exhibition piece, drawing upon the instrument's natural affinity for Gypsy theatrics. But for the trumpet it is as close to impossible as can be imagined: a piece requiring the virtuosity of a Rafael Mendez rather than the free and easy fluency of a jazz player. Jackie had attacked it years before during his days with Jeff Styles, and its dark flavor had drawn him to it again and again during his practice sessions at the villa. A good piece: good for the wind, good for the chops, good for the memory in its demand that each note fall into place the same way every time, good for the spirit in the feeling of accomplishment after taking it up to tempo.

Jackie took a couple of deep breaths, then let his hands go limp for a minute. Then he launched into the opening section, commanding attention with its call-like quality: executed with great volume gradually softening to clear, pure, evenly spaced tones worthy of Dr. LeRoy Staggers himself. After that, the rapid passages: fast, impassioned, soaring up and down like hungry eagles. Frosting on the cake, as Clint used to say in reminding Jackie that a trumpet player should always sing before he starts pulling out the heavy artillery.

Sweetness, texture, spice, and frosting: Jackie shaped his gift so that it filled the square and echoed through the neighboring streets. He finished the last cadenza and let the trumpet drop quickly to his side. There was a moment of stunned silence, then a clatter of applause: applause that built and built to a thunderous level.

Acknowledging the applause, Jackie bowed around the square again, smiled at the balconies, nodded approvingly at the bandsmen and bandmaster as though to express appreciation for their part in a collaborative effort. Then he walked back to the bandstand and shook hands with the old bandmaster.

"Amigos," he said softly. *"Quiere tocar 'Valencia'?"*

A good choice, Jackie was sure: particularly for a town only fifty meters away—a town that thinks of itself as Catalan and insists on saying *plein* in place of *lleno* when filling the tank at gasoline stations. Also a good choice for a trumpet player who has played for a hundred or so Spanish dancers in American nightclubs and theaters.

After the bandsmen had their music in place, Jackie set the tempo: snapping his fingers for almost twenty seconds to pull them all together before starting off. A good number. A good tempo. And a good performance by musicians sprung to life and pushed to new heights: as is always the case when they know that their work is heard by another member of the guild. A performance earning broad and sustained applause.

"Alleman?" The bandmaster looked at Jackie closely, as though trying to weigh the relative significance of dark hair against blue eyes.

Jackie shook his head.

"Français?"

"Americano," said Jackie. *"Estados Unidos."*

The old bandmaster stroked his whiskers for a moment. Then he brightened and beamed around the small bandstand.

"Numero ocho," he said, waving aside Jackie's offer to return the trumpet to its owner. With the music in place, he walked down in front of the bandstand and gestured for a drum roll, after which he faced the square and raised his voice. *"Por el Americano, una cançion Americana."*

More applause as the bandmaster returned to the bandstand. Then a fierce look at the musicians and an authoritative downbeat, exploding them all off into the opening bars of Sousa's "Stars and Stripes Forever." A good choice—even for the tuba player, who blew his way magnificently through the requisite runs. When they hit the last strain, Jackie put the trumpet to his lips and tried his hand at the piccolo part, soaring above the others just as he had back with the Kale Brothers Symphonia.

At the end of the march, a step back so that the bandmaster could acknowledge the applause. Then a ceremonious return of the trumpet to the young man, accompanied by handshakes for each member of the group. A descent from the bandstand. A few bows. A smile for the girl in the balcony. Just like a matador—an aging matador still able to catch a small red flower thrown his way. After that, back across the square toward Walt and Myra, walking at a slow, unhurried pace.

"Muy bien," said one of the young men in workclothes, dark eyes flashing with admiration as Jackie squeezed by.

"Fantastico!" said another.

"Gracias." Jackie smiled and went on to rejoin Walt and Myra.

"That was excellent," said the large fleshy man.

"Wunderbar." The long-faced blond young man smiled and raised his glass.

"Thank you," said Jackie.

"Is it not so that you are a professional musician?" The large fleshy man's eyes were appraising, his manner thoughtful.

Jackie paused. He looked at Walt and Myra, then at the table of young men in workclothes.

"Just another amateur," he said to the large fleshy man. "What's the word for high school—*gymnasium*?"

The large fleshy man nodded.

"I used to play the trumpet in our *gymnasium* orchestra—second trumpet." He looked over at the young men in workclothes, shrugged and raised his voice a little. *"Casi todos los Americanos son musicos."* Then he smiled cheerfully at the two Germans. "It's a great hobby, but a tough way to make a living."

"I'm not sure I understand," said the large fleshy man. "But thank you very much."

"Just like old times," said Walt.

"Not quite." Jackie sat down and let himself go limp for a moment. "But close—a lot closer than I thought it would be."

"Hooray for our side," said Myra.

Santa Barbara, California: Tuesday, May 16, 3:00 P.M.

"Around the world?" Louise turned away from the map and stared at the editorial director in amazement.

"Why not?" Mrs. Salvez picked up a white booklet from her desk. "The response from our Road Agent clubs has been quite good—I'm sure we'll be able to put a first-rate caravan together."

"What if one of the campers breaks down?"

"They'll take tools and spare parts."

"What about the languages?"

"We'll arrange for native guides and interpreters—just like we did when they caravaned through South America."

"What if someone gets sick?"

"They have doctors in China—Russia, too."

"The roads." Louise turned her attention back to the large map on the wall: a map dotted with red pins representing chapters of the Road Agent clubs sponsored by Road Runner Publications. "Heaven knows what the roads will be like."

"That's where you come in." Mrs. Salvez got up from her

desk and came over to Louise, a sheaf of papers in her hand. "Here's a breakdown of our questionnaire results and a listing of the major sightseeing possibilities in China, Russia, and Poland. What we want is the optimum route in terms of roads and weather conditions, along with reasonably spaced stopover points."

"That's a big order," said Louise, already picturing herself poring over masses of geographical data.

"It's a big project—our biggest so far." Mrs. Salvez's hazel eyes sparkled behind her rimless glasses as though the caravan were already assembled: fifty Road Agent couples in colorful costumes, ready to fly for Japan, there to purchase fifty mini-campers for transportation to China and travel across it, veering north to Russia and on to Poland, Czechoslovakia, Austria, Germany, The Netherlands, Belgium, and France—where the mini-campers would be resold at a modest profit and the Road Agents would fly home to complete their caravaning of the globe.

"This place is always coming up with one surprise after another." Louise gestured toward the doorway, beyond which lay rows of desks and word processing machines, their activities meshing like an intricate set of gears to produce travel guides, maintenance manuals, and magazines for the recreational-vehicle market.

"We have to," said Mrs. Salvez. "Most of our members are at an age where they feel they've earned the right to a little adventure, so we have to keep stepping if we want to stay ahead of them."

"When do you want all this pulled together?" Louise stared at the sheaf of papers in the gray-haired lady's hand.

"We'd like a short progress report each week and the final breakdown in five weeks." The gray-haired lady smiled encouragingly. "It would be full time—no more typing or copy editing. And if you have to put in a little extra, we'll make it up to you on your vacation."

"I hadn't even thought about a vacation."

"When you work for Road Runner, it's considered disloyal not to take one." The encouraging laugh was like a tiny silver bell summoning a group to dinner. "And we have arrangements with a number of travel agencies for staff discounts on cruises and air fares."

"That's something to think about," said Louise, trying to imagine herself closing up her trailer and taking off for parts unknown—Spain, perhaps.

She had moved to a trailer park on the Los Angeles side

of Santa Barbara: partly to be closer to work, partly to get farther away from Scott and the university. It had been a good move. And a good separation. No scenes, no reproaches. Only a stiffly formal division of belongings as Scott moved his books and papers from the trailer to roomier quarters in Heidi Kissinger's house. After that, no further contact as his caravan moved on up to its proper height and hers chugged along on a nine-to-five–level series of working days. The distance between them had helped to mute whatever grief and regrets lingered on—surfacing principally at night during the early weeks, but subsiding more and more as her new routine absorbed her.

His phone call two days ago had come as a shock. A double shock: first in the sound of his resonant voice and the echoes it immediately set vibrating in her; second in her own ready willingness to have a drink with him at the Santa Barbara Biltmore when she finished work today. In talking with him, she had been unable to recall only one cutting remark out of all the hundreds she had rehearsed: cold, beautifully phrased observations regarding the skewed nature of their relationship, deft barbs designed to pierce his awareness like little slivers of light unassailable in their logic, unanswerable in their truth. It was as though he had come upon her from behind with his open confession of weakness and need, pinioning her and holding her with that magic voice until her sense of injury drained away—along with her strength and firm resolve.

Louise took the sheaf of papers to her cubicle and began to go through them, feeling that the project so glowingly outlined was already beginning to come apart in her hands as she separated the various reports into piles for subsequent attack. A grand scheme. But totally dependent upon step-by-step planning and research. And even then, the possibility that something could go wrong: a storm, heavy rains, delays at the factory, a shift in political climate, a change in the economy, an error in judgment regarding an unpredicted problem. A grand scheme not unlike her own move toward independence: noble in its intention, tedious and doubtful in its daily progress.

Gradually the papers began to take on a little more order as she went through each pile again, absorbed in making notes of possibilities to explore: in map libraries, climatological reports, and other sources. So absorbed, she spent the rest of the afternoon, not even stopping to think of her Biltmore appointment until the movement and hurly-burly of quitting time swept her out of the office to her car.

The Santa Barbara Biltmore. Neutral ground. Fairly distant from the university. A large lobby. Carpets. Comfortable chairs. Carved wood, dark and lustrous. Chandeliers. A quiet place, especially late in the afternoon. Not a place for the raising of voices: for recriminations or tearful surrender. A safe place for a potentially awkward encounter after almost six months of separation.

"I can't stay long," Louise said as she came up to where Scott was standing, his arms folded, looking out the large window as though expecting an inspiration to materialize out on the large green lawn.

"I understand." He smiled warmly, strong white teeth gleaming in the contrasting frame provided by his curly black beard. The beard was newly and neatly trimmed; so was Scott, judging from the quiet blue suit he had worn. As though some sort of change had occurred—recently.

"This is pleasant." Louise nodded toward the lawn.

"High ceilings." Scott waved around the room. "There's something restful and dignified about high ceilings."

"That was one of the problems with the trailer, wasn't it?" She stared at him and smiled to take the sting out of her words: words that had seemed to shape themselves, hewn by whatever sense of loss still remained.

"I miss that trailer sometimes," said Scott. "It was a lot quieter than where I am now."

"It's hard to imagine you without a lot of people around."

"I'm in a new phase, working very hard on an important project."

"So am I."

"That's wonderful. There's something engrossing and fulfilling about taking on an enterprise of scope, especially when it makes a contribution to public awareness."

They sat down: Louise on a sofa, Scott in a straight-backed chair beside her. It was obvious that Scott wanted to talk about his project more than he wanted to hear about hers. A slight irritation to her. But somehow reassuring in its evocation of a familiar pattern: like an arabesque design in the carpet in front of her, self-contained yet echoed by other lines and curves.

"What are you working on?"

"A major effort." Scott beamed enthusiastically. "I've been approached to do a series for public television."

"I thought you were committed to your poetry."

"I'm committed to poetry—good poetry. And I feel that

this is a superb opportunity to broaden public awareness of what's taking place today. The series will be composed of interviews with contemporary poets who are established in their art and in academic life."

"That sounds like a big production." Louise began to relax, knowing that she was on ground familiar to her since childhood: studios, cameras, directors, technical people.

"We're going to call it 'The Poet-Professors,' " said Scott. "What do you think of the title?"

"Brilliant!" said Louise, feeling that the term was more appropriate than "profound"—or "fantastic."

"A lot of important people are very excited about it."

Louise smiled encouragingly. It was clear that they were going to stay in calm waters: warm, relaxing, yet disappointing to someone who had braced herself for the needle-sharp spray of conflict. Conflict was what she had rehearsed for: reproaches, upbraidings, implicit sexual comparisons and assaults underlying surface disagreements over lifestyle—sparks struck between them that might rekindle a flame however weak and faltering. To find Scott changing direction was unsettling, as though her small, tidy life was about to be invaded by a strange, insinuating creature.

She looked uneasily around the lobby. It was forbiddingly calm. A few old men dressed in bright colors, one of them dozing slightly. A decorous group of ladies whispering at the far end. And a younger man poised just inside the doorway: inspecting her, as she him.

"Here comes one of the people I was telling you about," said Scott. He got up and went over to the younger man: a man dressed in a gray jacket and slightly lighter gray slacks. The two stood there talking for a moment, looking very much like part of a tableau posed by a fashion photographer. Then they came over to her, the young man smiling a white, perfectly aligned smile. Scott introduced him as Bruce Poirier.

"I saw your mother's show last month," said Bruce. "It was splendid." He nodded approvingly, as though allowing the mantle of his warm judgment to envelope the three of them.

"She's worked very hard on it." Louise tried to make her manner cordial, masking as much as possible her frustration. It was clear that the conversation would never drift over to a discussion of her Road Runner job.

"Bruce came up for the day," said Scott. "When I told him what you were doing, he insisted on meeting you."

"It's a little early for our table." Bruce gestured toward

the Biltmore dining room. "Would you like to go into the bar or would you rather stay here?"

"This is fine," said Louise. It was as though a deck of cards had been shoved at her, accompanied by an order to pick one. She scolded herself for not taking into account Scott's knack of changing signals at the last moment. The plan had called for a quiet drink—not dinner with a stranger. Or dinner at all.

"I think it's important to hear what Bruce has to say." Scott sat down beside her, reached over and patted her hand.

"I don't think I need any help." Louise pulled her hand away and stared at Bruce. "It seems to me I've been managing very well the last few months."

"She certainly has," said Scott. "I have to admit I'm very, very proud of her."

"And well you should be." Bruce gave another one of his approving nods. "There aren't many who could drop out of school and build a life for themselves."

"I didn't drop out," said Louise. "I withdrew."

"Exactly." Bruce sat back and crossed his beautifully troused legs to display an ankle and lower calf covered by neat, wrinkle-free gray. "And that's all the more reason why it's not fair for you to be penalized by your own initiative and industry."

"I didn't know I had been penalized by anything."

"Did you know that your father would be legally responsible for your support and education if you weren't working?"

"No."

"How much do you know about the trust your father and mother set up for you?"

"Not very much," said Louise. "And I can't see why you should be concerned—it's a family matter."

"The whole thing came up by chance one day when we were working on the grant proposal for the poet-professor series." Scott stroked his beard thoughtfully. "As a producer, Bruce knows a lot about how these matters work—and I was shocked at what he told me."

"I don't see what's so shocking about a trust established for my benefit." Louise looked at Scott coldly. "My parents worked on the 'Judy's Guy' show together, and they wanted the rights to stay in the family. What's wrong with that?"

"Have you ever looked at the document itself?" said Bruce.

"No."

"Do you know what the responsibilities of the trustee are?"

"No."

"Do you know what the powers of the trustee are?"

"No."

"Do you know that the 'Judy's Guy' rights can be sold or reassigned by the trustee?"

"All that is my father's department." Louise was beginning to feel that she was being backed step by step toward the edge of a steep slope.

"Do you know that the trustee has the responsibility of providing for your welfare—even to the extent of invading the principal of the trust if need be?"

"I don't even know what you're talking about when you use words like that. All I know is that the idea is to keep the rights to that show in the family."

"Not quite," said Bruce. "The idea of a trust is that it should be managed with the interests of the beneficiaries in mind. This can involve selling assets, reinvesting the proceeds, disbursing funds to you. Your father as trustee has a great deal of leeway."

"What's wrong with that?"

"It can mean the loss of a great deal of money—*your* money."

"All that grief." Scott shook his head, his dark eyes moist with sympathy. "All that conflict—all totally unnecessary."

"I'm still not sure I understand."

"Suppose you owned several acres of land in Beverly Hills." Bruce gestured out the window as though to take her on an imaginary trip to realms of luxury and comfort. "That land would be worth a lot of money right now, wouldn't it?"

"Yes."

"Even if it were being used only for parking lots?"

"I guess so."

"If you needed that money, you'd want to sell that land, wouldn't you?"

"Yes."

"And if you wanted to sell that land, you'd be pretty upset if someone tried to stop the sale, wouldn't you?"

"I suppose so."

"That's exactly the position you're in." Bruce gave her a dazzling smile of approval at her grasp of his analogy. "Those rights—your rights—are actually worth much more than the little they bring in."

"How can you be so sure?" Louise looked at him suspiciously. "Those shows are pretty old, you know."

"I'm sure. That's one of the reasons I'm here."

"After the matter came up, Bruce made some inquiries."

Scott looked very solemn, very businesslike. "And he managed to locate a number of investors, each of whom would pay a handsome price for the full rights to all the 'Judy's Guy' shows."

"Naturally I'd expect a reasonable commission." Bruce shrugged as though the element of personal gain were something to be expected—in others and in himself. "But I think you'll be pleasantly surprised at what you end up with."

Louise paused. She looked at Scott, who was nodding happily at the gift he had brought her. Money. It had been the money problem that had wrecked their relationship, like a sudden squall sweeping in without warning to swamp their small craft. And she wondered how many relationships and marriages at the university could survive outside the safe breakwaters maintained by the families of those involved. Money had driven the two of them apart; money could bring them back together.

"Why are you talking to me?" she said. "Why don't you take it up with my father?"

"That's a very good question." Bruce smiled over at Scott, as though paying tribute to her insight. "Your father's still out of the country, isn't he?"

"Yes."

"It would be simpler if you initiated the petition." He stared closely at her, eyes narrowed. "And besides, it's basically your decision, isn't it?"

"I suppose so." Louise brushed back her light brown hair and took a deep breath. "But it doesn't seem right somehow."

"Why?" Scott looked at her incredulously. "It's money that you can use—money that's rightfully yours."

"I didn't work for it, so it seems to me I ought to go along with what my father worked out."

"Even though it means dropping out of school?" said Bruce.

"I told you before, I didn't drop out. I withdrew."

"I think there's something more involved." Scott smiled gently at her. "Louise has always lived in the shadow of other people—her mother, her father, even me in a way. So she's always felt she doesn't deserve things—even when they're rightfully hers."

"That makes sense." Bruce bent toward her. "Why do you feel it's right for you to be pounding a typewriter eight hours a day while your father's enjoying himself in Spain and your mother is holding court down in Los Angeles?"

"I've never thought about it," said Louise.

"Maybe you should." Scott shook his head pityingly.

"Maybe you should think about your father's obligations to you."

"What obligations?" It was Louise's turn to look incredulous. "I'd say I owe him more than he owes me."

"Did you ask to be born?" Scott stroked his black beard and looked very wise. "If you had children of your own, wouldn't you accept the responsibilities involved?"

Louise looked down at the floor, letting her eye take in the various arabesque qualities of the Biltmore carpet. Handsome ones: reds, yellows, greens. All woven together in patterns that flowed in and out of one another so that only the individual eye could decide whether it was looking at a part or a self-contained whole. The parents' parents, the children's children—it was all a matter of perspective. Lines stretching back into the past or forward into the future. Lines of cause and effect, of intent mixed with randomness: good traits, madness, fears and angers, strengths and amiable ways—all passed through the blood from one generation to another. Dizzying to contemplate. Impossible to judge—except for the immediate facts in one's own field of vision.

Louise looked up and scrutinized the two handsome men hemming her in. Like courtiers—or miscreant knights, perhaps. She tried to draw a map in her mind of the route they had taken: Scott coming south from the university, Bruce coming north from Los Angeles. A simple sequence: Scott's project, Bruce's involvement, the mention of her name, the investigation of the trust, the exploration of potential buyers, the meeting with her in the lobby of the Biltmore. Perfectly logical, perfectly direct.

Her Road Runner project surfaced for a moment, reminding her that alternative routes were always possible in a given topography, some leading to the same target by a more circuitous path. One could start with the buyers, for example, move from them to Bruce, who could then approach Scott with an invitation to submit a project, after which the mention of her name would lead naturally to a meeting. A reasonable sequence. Perfectly logical. Just as logical as the first sequence. But more devious.

She looked closely into their faces: Scott's cheerful and self-absorbed, Bruce's guarded. Never skilled at reading people, she shook her head and sighed.

"I don't know about obligations and the rest of it," she said. "But I'm basically happy with things the way they are." Louise could feel herself beginning to stiffen.

"Happiness is a matter of perspective." Scott spoke sharply, dropping back into his old patronizing pattern. "I can't see how you can be happy in a dead-end job."

"It pays the bills, and it pays taxes to support you and the rest of those poet-professors with their adolescent hangers-on—like Heidi Kissinger."

"I think we're getting away from the main issue," said Bruce smoothly.

"No, we're not," said Louise, trying to keep her voice from rising. "The issue is a simple matter of whether I should be content with the life I've made for myself by myself or whether I should get involved with lawyers in an attempt to squeeze a free ride somehow at the expense of my father, who has been giving free rides to people as long as I can remember—to me, to his family in Kansas City, to my mother, to his first wife, to his third wife, to his employees." She paused to draw breath. "I don't see why he shouldn't do what he wants to do without having people give him trouble, trouble, trouble—especially me."

"I know it's a difficult decision." Bruce smiled and looked toward the dining room. "And I feel that you should take at least a week in thinking the matter through."

"That won't be necessary." Louise got up and looked down at them. "I've already made a number of decisions. First, I'm not going to have dinner with you; second, I'm not going to go along with whatever scheme you have in mind; third, I'm going back to do some work that needs doing; fourth . . ." She paused to catch her breath again and collect her thoughts. ". . . fourth, I'm going to be there in the audience when my father gives it his best shot."

"That's the language of a peasant." Scott shook his head. "I wouldn't like to think that Heidi Kissinger has been right about you all along."

"Maybe so. But I can tell you one thing—the Poet and the Peasant Overture is over, *kaput, fini.*" She pointed a quivering finger at Bruce. "And so is your Poet-Professor scam, if I'm not mistaken."

It was a good speech. Good enough to turn her on her heel and march her out the door, head held high. The words floating effortlessly out on a sustained melody of anger: chosen by the tune more than by the sense.

It would make a good story to tell her father when she saw him in Switzerland—courtesy of the Road Runner discount rate.

Waterford, Ireland: Friday, June 30, 3:00 P.M.

Time. An hour and a half of it. A large blank wall waiting to be filled up with something to sustain the attention of almost a thousand people gathered for an open-air concert. A big crowd: drawn from the cosmopolitan mix of Europeans in Waterford for the opera festival. But a small band. Drums, string bass, piano, trombone, clarinet, and Jackie's trumpet. And a small occasion, more on the order of a sideshow when matched against Mozart and Benjamin Britten. But a major challenge for Jackie: to impose order upon a hastily assembled, briefly rehearsed group of London musicians and to present the results in a program designed and paced to please the crowd being seated.

"Super!" said the bass player, a heavyset young man with large hands. He pointed to a group of young women taking their seats in the third row. "I'm getting turned on already."

"I hope they understand English." Jackie smiled at the women: partly to establish rapport, partly to draw from them a feeling for the right note to strike in playing to the audience.

From his position down beside the bandstand, he let his

eyes roam thoughtfully over the semi-circles of folding chairs stretching out in front of him. Hard chairs. Hard enough to demand squirming and changing of position if the pace faltered. The people seemed a various group: some old, some young, some with small children, some dark, some fair—all there as individual fractions waiting to be summed up on the basis of a shared common denominator.

"It's grand to play on top of the beat for a change." The bass player fluttered his fingers as though to make sure they were in working order. "In a rock recording session they lay down an electronic pulse and there's where you have to be—like a bloody metronome."

"That's where the action is," said Jackie. "The rock 'n' rollers own the store now." He looked speculatively at the bass player. A good sound, good endurance. A good ear for laying down interesting lines. Easily the best of the lot he had auditioned in London a few days earlier.

It had been a busy four days. Less than they had planned on when Cy had made the booking as a way of breaking in and getting the feel of an open-air European audience. A change in the festival's scheduling had compelled them to come in earlier, getting rooms at different hotels instead of together. But the pressure had been exhilarating; he had won their confidence quickly, jumping in to salvage the rhythm by playing right on the beat when it appeared to be wavering. And the last rehearsal had been mostly musical jokes and yarns functioning to build a genial spirit: pleasant, friendly, slightly ironic in its distance from both music and audience.

A good start. But slightly irrelevant in terms of the Montreux change of program: a change that called for him to share the same block of time with Otis Marshak, a change that gave him an empty feeling every time he thought of it.

"Do you see any familiar faces?" The bass player gestured toward the audience.

"Yes and no," said Jackie. "Everybody in Ireland looks familiar to me—I don't think there are more than twelve different faces in the whole country, and I've worked with at least five of them back in the States, not counting my own. But I haven't seen anyone I really know."

"There's a British face for you." The bass player pointed to a red-haired, ruddy-complexioned man with bushy eyebrows who was walking down the aisle to their left.

"How can you tell? Ireland has its share of redheads."

"Anthropology," said the bass player. "I've always been

partial to anthropology—and besides, I think I've seen him in London around some of the clubs."

Jackie nodded affably in the direction of the red-haired man from London. A booker, possibly, judging from the seriousness of his manner. Although the concert had not been widely advertised, it was good to know that it was attracting professional interest.

Concerts were never easy. They were too long for a sequence of short numbers, like the separate cuts on one side of a long-playing record; yet they were too short for good-humored trading back and forth. Saloon jazz was more comfortable. "Musical wallpaper," Clint had called it: sounds there as background to the serious business of drinking and chasing women, sounds whose design and color could take on self-sufficient, intricate shapes without attracting attention.

A jazz concert was very much like cutting out pieces of musical wallpaper and putting them in impressive, sometimes overly ornate frames, the results arranged in sequence with appropriate comments like pictures in an art gallery. "Atmosphere," Jeff Styles had said to him once. "You have to bring the right atmosphere up on stage with you." For Jeff the atmosphere had been one of exuberant affection and graciousness, constantly reiterating his basic theme: "It's party time." For Jackie the atmosphere was just a shade less exuberant: more of a boy-next-door quality, a quality of friendly surprise at what was going on, coupled with gratitude to the neighbors for stopping by, listening, finding pleasure, and applauding. A good atmosphere for a radio show like Ben Butler's—or for "Judy's Guy." But not overpowering enough to dominate a long, frighteningly empty block of time.

Jackie nodded to the bass player and to the other musicians. The five men filed onto the platform and settled themselves with their instruments. Then one of the festival's hosts, a tweedy man with a pepper-and-salt beard, walked briskly up to the microphone and made a few preliminary remarks: welcoming the audience, placing the concert in the musical context of an opera festival, soothing the audience into relative quiet, carving out a small space for the seating of late arrivals, and ending with a glowing introduction of the afternoon's attraction—Jackie Hayes.

It was only a short distance from where Jackie was standing to the microphone in the middle of the platform. But he took his time: standing motionless for a moment while the host walked toward him, then moving toward the host and shaking his hand warmly, almost as though it were an encounter between two old friends forced to cut their conversation short in favor of a more pressing social engagement.

A social engagement. A party of sorts. Serious musical business with a friendly twinkle. An opening moderate-tempo version of "I Can't Give You Anything But Love." A little informal chatter, some of which singled out specific groups in the audience—like the young women in the third row. Then a song: each word and syllable bit out clearly, even when playing against the audience's expectations of where they would fall. A good way to start a party: almost like calling the guests by name in its implicit recognition of the musical memories they had brought with them.

Memory. To Jackie, jazz music was basically the art of tapping the listener's memory. A familiar melody, stated and then improvised upon. A quotation from another melody superimposed upon the chord pattern of the original: like a speaker affably digressing from one subject to another. A half-valve distortion of a familiar shape, replacing the tune with the accents of speech itself—just as King Oliver and Rex Stewart had loved to do. Familiarity balanced with surprise: a boy next door doing magic tricks with household melodic objects; but not above doing a handstand or gymnastic feat to keep matters lively. A constant appeal to the listener's expectations: recognizing them as grounds for common sentiment, common jokes, common knowledge of patterns in a language composed only of verbs. It was as though each listener came to the concert with a group of favorite poems, dormant but ready to flood forth when tapped. And Jackie's effectiveness lay in the skill with which he put to use this curious literature: some old and venerable, some trivial and current.

About thirty minutes through the performance there was a sharp, insistent sound from off to the left. A police siren answering an emergency. A shrill sequence of alternating fifths: *dee*-dah, *dee*-dah, *dee*-dah. Ordinarily a distraction. But for Jackie a sound to echo and incorporate into the chorus he was playing at the moment, so that he immediately made the siren's alternating fifths something to play with, something to build upon: stretching the pattern out until the audience was ecstatic with good humor, admiration, appreciation—not unmixed with awe.

After that, the audience was in his hand completely. The remaining time went by in a rapid haze: each number blurring into the next like elements in a perfectly unified glob of sound. Sound floating on top of waves of applause. Sound threading through an hour and a half of time: filling it up with bright colors and artful needlepoint. Almost making time itself disappear for listener and performer.

Jackie acknowledged the applause, took his bows, and gestured to each of the musicians to come forth and be honored individually. Then he stepped down from the platform and walked back to where his trumpet case was. As he put his horn back into the case, he could feel his mind start to spin again, thinking of the challenge posed by his joint appearance with Otis Marshak. No atmosphere there. No boy-next-door friendliness. Only a straight battle between two styles, two kinds of inventiveness, two virtuosities, two different approaches to the same instrument. It would have been better to have his own spot and earn his own applause, rather than walk out onto uncharted, potentially embarrassing ground.

By the time the rented limousine dropped him off at his hotel, the exhilaration of the performance had flattened, leaving only a vague restlessness joined to a tense sort of exhaustion: a feeling that he had been drained of purpose and vital juices. There was a message at the desk asking him to meet one of the Montreux people at the bar in half an hour, so he went up to his room, doused his head in cold water, stretched out on the small bed, and dozed for a few minutes.

The nap helped. Only half asleep, he had felt his arms and back relax, his eyes ease back into their sockets. After twenty minutes his spirits began to brighten, and he found himself looking forward to a good, relaxing drink.

He walked into the bar, looking for the representative from Montreux. But the only occupants were the barmaid and two patrons: a small old man with a pipe and a burly dark man in a tweed jacket.

"I'll have an anise," said Jackie, absently following the same pattern he had in Jávea.

"Would that be a special mixed drink, sir?" The barmaid had a puzzled expression on her oval face. An oval face framed by long dark hair. A rather tall girl, very much like Rita: enough so to start him speculating again on where Rita was at this moment and what she was doing.

"Anise is a foreign drink," said the burly dark man. "They have no call to put you behind the plank if you don't know what a liqueur is."

"It doesn't matter." Jackie smiled easily at the barmaid. "I'll be happy with a straight shot of whiskey."

"It matters a great deal," grumbled the burly dark man. "It's a great shaming thing when a bar's not well kept."

"I'd say it's kept well enough for the likes of you," snapped the barmaid.

"A saucy tongue like that belongs on the street, not in a respectable place." The burly dark man glared angrily at her.

"It's a very nice place," said Jackie, feeling obliged to smooth things over. He smiled over at the small old man, who grunted and turned away.

"And what would you know about it?" The man turned fierce eyes on Jackie. "To my way of thinking you're only a Yank, and you've no call to do anything except keep your opinions to yourself."

A clear challenge. Especially to someone whose time on the road has brought with it recognition of how such matters develop and proceed. Two general alternatives: retreat or submit to an accelerating tempo of insults. And a third: risky in its surprise element, but often effective.

"You look very strong to me." Jackie smiled and moved in close to his adversary, speaking softly and rapidly. "And I bet you're good with your fists, too—just as good as I am, maybe better. So whether we tangle here or outside, it's going to be quite a show, and this young lady is going to call the police, and we'll both end up in jail and in big, embarrassing trouble. It really doesn't make any difference to me. But I have what I think is a much better idea. . . . Why don't *I* buy *you* a drink?" Continuing to smile, he nodded and kept his eyes fixed on the burly man's face.

The man shook his head as though to shake out of his mind the incongruous combination of aggressive close-in stance with soft, friendly words.

"A drink?"

"Why not?" Jackie gestured toward the bottles ranged behind the bar. "That's what it's there for, and that's what we're here for, am I right?"

"Right you are." The burly man nodded curtly and drained his small glass. "I'll have one of these and stand treat for another."

"That's a fair start for a fair day," said Jackie, stepping back a little and reaching for his own glass.

"And how do you like these parts?"

"A great deal—but I'd like to see Cork if time permits."

"Why Cork? It's a dismal place."

"Not the city." Jackie smiled at the barmaid. "The county—I had a great-grandfather come from Kinsale and I've always wondered what it looked like."

"It's a tiny stop in the road by the sea." The barmaid

poured the two whiskeys, leaving the bottle on the bar ready for the next round.

Warmed by the glow of the whiskey and the pleasant inconsequential caress of small talk, Jackie relaxed more and more, nodding as the burly dark man lectured him on the common market and the sins of the British—or Sasseneach. When the red-haired man with bushy eyebrows came in from the street entrance, Jackie nodded amiably at the new arrival, barely pausing to notice the sullen manner of the other newcomer—a tall, raw-boned young man with close-cut curly blond hair. It was the red-haired man from London, he realized.

"You had no business running away from the accident," the red-haired man said.

"What accident?" Jackie stared directly into the red-haired man's impenetrable gray eyes. "I haven't even seen an accident, much less run away from one."

"There's a dented MG outside that says you have." The red-haired man pointed toward the street entrance in clear invitation.

"And I say I haven't," said Jackie, grown suddenly wary by the talk of going outside. He tensed, kept his eyes on the red-haired man's hands: ready to react if they made a threatening move.

To his surprise the move came from the back: a pinioning of his arms by the tall blond, who had come up behind him during the exchange. Only after that did he see the redhead's hands clench into massive, freckled fists, with the right one cocked to deliver a professionally targeted straight-on blow to the face.

Time. A half-second for the whole attack. But long enough to regret eight months of work building up an embouchure about to be demolished by a hired thug in a small bar in a wet, cold country.

Time. Suddenly slowing down: long enough for Jackie to note a glaze descending upon the gray eyes in front of him. A glaze. And a slight slackening of the ruddy face. Both accompanied by the sound of breaking glass: a glass whiskey bottle broken over the head of the red-haired man by the barmaid.

As suddenly his arms were free, and Jackie turned around to see his captor captive, choking in the firm grip of the burly dark man. A good chance to move in, land a series of stout blows to the young blond's midsection, then wrest him free and carry him to the wall: there to hammer until his height sank down like a declining temperature gauge. In fair exchange, the burly dark man took a few rounds with the groggy red-haired man:

pushing him to the opposite wall by the end of the bar to collapse there under the delighted gaze of the barmaid.

"We'll need a fresh bottle of whiskey now," said the burly dark man.

"Aye." The barmaid put the bottle out on the bar.

"And you'll be having one yourself with us, will you not?"

"Don't mind if I do." The barmaid poured herself a tumblerfull.

"Bad cess to them Sasseneach." The man raised his glass and smiled broadly around.

"Amen to that," said Jackie.

"First today." Dark eyes shining, the barmaid lifted her glass ceremoniously, nodding down at the limp form of the red-haired man.

Montreux, Switzerland:
Saturday, July 15, 3:45 P.M.

Louise was glad she had brought a sweater. There was a promise of chill in the air later on when the shadows began to lengthen: a chill whose features could be seen on the ridges and peaks of the mountains rimming the concert ground. Seated in her chair midway up the slope, she had an unbroken line of vision down to the stage. It was a large stage, almost theatrical in size, with wings and with a giant shell behind it to cup the sound and throw it forcefully toward the thousands of people around her.

"It's a big place," said Cy. Clearly restless, he stood up for a minute. "And a bigger crowd than they had yesterday."

"Yesterday went very well." Louise looked down at the stage as though filling it once more with her father and the eight other Jeff Styles veterans who had appeared. "Everybody seemed to like it."

"This one is going to be even better." Cy turned and resumed his survey, brightening as a younger man came down the aisle toward them.

The younger man waved and quickened his pace, gesturing to the three women with him as though a target of some importance had been located. When the four of them came up, Cy introduced them as Herr Zweifel and his family: wife, mother, and daughter.

"The head sound technician is here," said Herr Zweifel. "Would you like to speak with him?"

"Might be a good idea." Taking long, urgent steps, Cy led Herr Zweifel back up the slope, leaving Louise alone to smile awkwardly at the Zweifel family, wondering whether it would be appropriate to attempt a conversation.

"Busy, busy." Herr Zweifel's mother broke the silence. "My son has always been a busy one." She was a small, trim woman with short blonde hair and clear blue eyes. "Five years ago he organized a reunion for his uncle's regiment—tracked nearly all of them down, too." She looked around the packed audience as though stamping the proceedings with her official approval.

"It always amazes me when thousands of people suddenly show up in the same place at the same time." Louise smiled at Herr Zweifel's mother, pleased that the ice had been broken—and in English.

"Good planning." There was a twinkle in the clear blue eyes. "Planning is for the businessman what practice is for the artist, as I'm sure your father would agree."

"Have you listened to his music before?"

"When Ludwig was small, right after the war, I took him to a concert in one of the theaters." She gestured at the expanse stretching down below them: a slow, graceful gesture, like that of a ballerina. "First a small performance for a small boy, then many years later an appearance at a great festival. And in between a dream."

Louise smiled awkwardly, not sure of how she should respond to the grandness of the sentiment. It reminded her a little of Scott: everything falling into neat patterns, pasted and held there with words whose adhesive force always seemed to weaken later on. To think of her father's playing as somehow fleshing out Herr Zweifel's long-cherished obsession made her uneasy.

"All set," said Cy, coming down to them with Herr Zweifel in tow.

The Zweifels walked farther on to take their seats. Louise and Cy sat down, Cy still restless. Down below the stage took life as the rhythm section appeared and took positions. At one of the wings she could see her father, nervously working the valves of his trumpet; at the other was Otis Marshak: a taller, husky man with a broad Slavic face and thinning straw-colored hair. The whole a tableau: quietly waiting for action to begin.

Her father walked on stage first, playing for about fifteen minutes by himself with the support of the rhythm section. Not much time, what with the obligatory medley of old hits and a personable song. But it went well: honest, direct, respectable, even if understated a bit. A solid foundation to build upon.

After Jackie took his applause and walked back to the wings, Otis came quickly out. A curt nod to the rhythm section and he was off: playing fast-tempo material for the most part, emphasizing intricate runs and high notes. Impossibly high notes: closer to squeals than anything else. Not as much variety as Jackie's stint. But flash—much more flash.

Then the two of them came on together, joining forces to attack one tune together for almost fifteen minutes. A good tune: "There Will Never Be Another You." Interesting chord changes taken at breakneck speed. First a statement of the melody together: then individual choruses—five in a row, then eight-bar phrases traded back and forth, then four-bar phrases, then both together going their separate ways—each trying to outdo the other in inventiveness and sheer physical power. For Jackie at the outset, a strategy of boy-next-door tricks: quotations, angular playings against the beat. But in time a movement into Otis's domain: high notes, even a squeal or two, leaps from one octave to another, runs and arpeggios to demonstrate complete mastery of the instrument and the rhythmic pulse sweeping them along.

At the end of the tune, a sudden break in the rhythm, followed by individual cadenzas played against a series of sustained chords. Old-time stuff, but still good: cadenzas traded back and forth, ending in one by Otis with a high, high note—sustained for an impossible length of time. An impossible note to challenge—or match. But Jackie attacked his last cadenza with an air of confidence: rippling from run to run, coming closer and closer to the challenge set to him. Almost there, almost ready to attempt a final matching shriek, Jackie paused and let silence point the way like a great blazing sign. Then he relaxed and hit a low, low note: a note way down in the low trombone range: a B-flat: slightly crackling and vulgar; but loud, even, sustained and true. A note for all to marvel at—even Otis, standing there with a warm smile on his broad Slavic face.

To close with, a fifteen-minute group of tunes composed by Jeff Styles. A good-humored group. Laced with affection: for the music, for the lost leader, for each other as the time chunked its way along. Two trumpets in action together: sometimes trading back and forth, sometimes playing in harmony, sometimes playing contrapuntally, sometimes sharing melody and embellishment. Delicate, affectionate music, underpinned with humor and quiet strength. Music ending to great applause and a joint exit—to Otis's side of the stage.

"That was worth going downtown to see," said Cy, visibly relaxed now that the musical duel was over. "I'm glad I made sure we got a good tape cut."

"I never knew he could play like that." Louise followed him down the slope to the stage.

"Fast company—anyone does better in fast company." Cy hurried ahead to where her father and Otis were standing. "You guys were too much."

"Not bad for a couple of tired old bastards," said Otis gruffly. "My lip feels like chopped meat."

"Me, too." Jackie shook his head. "What's happening next?"

"This is it," said Cy. "Except for a little dinner later on at the hotel with Vito and some of the other people."

"Is there room for a Polack trumpet player with big feet?" Jackie gave Otis an affectionate shove. "With all this over, it has to be party time, as Jeff used to say."

"On the button," said Otis, nodding down from his immense height at all of them—including Louise.

It was time for a singer to perform: a heavy black woman with a voice like rich, grainy velvet. So they quietly moved on.

Party time. Not a big affair. Just a small room on the second floor of the hotel. But large enough to justify some music: accordion, violin, and string bass. As Jackie approached the room he could hear them playing Kreisler's "Liebesfreud." Pleasant music. Lively and yet soothing, especially after the burning intensity of the afternoon.

Jackie paused a moment before walking in to put himself onstage again. A bath, a nap, a change of clothes—these had helped to revive him; but he was still tired. A tiredness that made him appreciate what Otis had been going through year after year. High-priced work. Rewarding in its way. But hard, very hard. Work meriting respect—like the man himself.

He opened the door and walked in, pausing to survey the people waiting for him. Otis was there on his left, sitting at a large table with Vito and several other Jeff Styles veterans. Directly in front, at a smaller table flanking the accordion, were Louise and Cy. On his right were Herr Zweifel and his family:

the daughter whose limitations they had discussed, his wife, and a trim blond woman who was probably Herr Zweifel's hard-working, disaster-surviving mother.

A pleasant-looking woman. Wearing her age like a costume from the opera she had sewn for: a cumbersome costume like his own in a few added pounds and stiffer lines, but not unduly heavy—certainly not heavy enough to mask the supple spirit within.

He smiled directly at her, waved to Otis and the others, and started toward Louise's table: almost reaching it before he stopped and looked over at the Zweifel table again. A thoughtful and searching look. Followed by movement—slowly at first, then more rapidly as his memory began to remove some of the lines from Frau Zweifel's face.

"Hello, Clara," he said, coming up to her and taking her by the hand. "You're looking well."

"Life has not been unkind to me," she said. Fair face agleam, she smiled first at Jackie, then at her son. "How has it been with you?"

"I can't complain." Jackie looked around the small room and nodded. "One thing seems to lead to another as long as you keep moving."

"This is true." Clara's clear blue eyes looked directly at him. "From that strange little town in Wisconsin to where we are right now—it is all one line."

"Starting further back than that." Jackie gazed toward the door as though expecting someone else to enter: Rita, perhaps. Returning to Clara, he smiled broadly. "Going further on, too."

"This is also true."

Still holding her hand, he sat down beside her as waiters in red coats came into the room, carrying trays of food.

ROBERT OLIPHANT is a professor of linguistics at California State University at Northridge. He is the author of *A Piano for Mrs. Cimino* (Prentice-Hall, 1980), which was a *Reader's Digest* condensed book selection and the basis for an award-winning TV drama starring Bette Davis. Mr. Oliphant is a former professional jazz musician and composer of songs and operas.